Friedrich Schiller, William Herbert Carruth

Schiller's Wilhelm Tell

With introduction and notes

Friedrich Schiller, William Herbert Carruth

Schiller's Wilhelm Tell
With introduction and notes

ISBN/EAN: 9783743373037

Manufactured in Europe, USA, Canada, Australia, Japa

Cover: Foto ©Andreas Hilbeck / pixelio.de

Manufactured and distributed by brebook publishing software (www.brebook.com)

Friedrich Schiller, William Herbert Carruth

Schiller's Wilhelm Tell

FRIEDRICH SCHILLER.

SCHILLER'S
WILHELM TELL

WITH

INTRODUCTION AND NOTES

BY

W. H. CARRUTH, Ph.D.

Professor of the German Language and Literature in the
University of Kansas

„Es ist ein Feind, vor dem wir alle zittern,
Und eine Freiheit macht uns alle frei."

New York
THE MACMILLAN COMPANY
London: Macmillan & Co., Ltd.
1898

Press of Carl H. Heintzemann
Boston, Mass.

To

F. S. C.

TEACHER, ADVISER, FRIEND.

PREFACE.

WILHELM TELL has been widely accepted as the best classic play for young students. It finds its place in high schools or in the first year of college courses. The present edition has been prepared with the desire to meet the needs of such students, yet it will serve more advanced students, who need not follow the Notes in detail.

The purpose of the Introduction is to furnish outside material not generally accessible, for the understanding and appreciation of this noble piece of literature; not to do the student's or the teacher's work for him. For this reason suggestions are made, especially in the Subjects for Themes, of studies which the student may undertake for himself.

The Text is that of Oesterley in Goedeke's Historisch-kritische Ausgabe of Schiller's Works, the orthography modernized so far as this would not alter the form and sound of Schiller's language. The Editor has used freely the commentaries of Düntzer, Bellermann, Meyer, Gaudig, Breul, Buchheim, Deering and others. He acknowledges gratefully the careful criticism of Professor W. T. Hewett, of Cornell University, and the helpful suggestions and assistance in proof-reading of Mrs. Frances Schlegel Carruth.

UNIVERSITY OF KANSAS,
October, 1897.

v

CONTENTS.

		PAGE
PREFACE	. . . .	v
INTRODUCTION.		
Sketch of Schiller's Life	. . . . . .	vii
Composition of " Wilhelm Tell "	. . .	xx
Criticisms and Comments	. . . . . .	xxvi
Style and Meter	. . . .	xxxv
History and Legend	. . . . . .	xxxvii
Portions of Tschudi used in " Tell "	. . . .	xlii
The Political Situation	. . . . . .	liv
Specimens of Schiller's Notes	. . . . .	liv
Chronology	. . . .	lvi
List of Persons	. . . .	lix
TEXT	. . . .	5
NOTES	. . . .	173
BIBLIOGRAPHICAL NOTES	. . . . . .	227
SUBJECTS FOR THEMES AND INVESTIGATION	. .	235
IMPORTANT VARIANTS	. . . .	237
INDEX	. . . .	239

ILLUSTRATIONS.

Portrait of Schiller. Frontispiece.

Map. Preceding Introduction.

The Urirotstock from the Axenstein. Act I, scene 1.

The Rütli. Act II, scene 2.

The Statue of Tell at Altorf. Act III, scene 3.

The Axenstrasse, with the Bristenstock above Flüelen. Act IV, sc. 1.

The Tell Chapel at Küssnacht. Act IV, scene 3.

The Reuss with the Teufelsbrücke. Act V, scene 2.

The Schiller Stone. Act V, last scene.

INTRODUCTION.

SKETCH OF SCHILLER'S LIFE.

When Friedrich Schiller was born, November 10th, 1759, at Marbach in Württemberg, Klopstock was thirty-five years old, Lessing was thirty, and Goethe ten. Württemberg was at peace, but the East of Germany was midway in the Seven Years' War.

When Schiller published his first drama, *Die Räuber*, in 1781, Herder and Wieland were the dominant living authors in Germany; the latter's *Oberon* had appeared ten years before. It was the year of Lessing's death, and of the publication of Kant's *Kritik der reinen Vernunft.* Klopstock's literary career was practically finished, and his popularity eclipsed by that of the young writers of the Sturm und Drang period. Goethe had published *Götz von Berlichingen, Clavigo, Werther, Stella,* and some poems, and was already turning away from his early vehemence and irregularity to a more subdued taste. The dominant foreign influence in Germany was that of English writers, especially of Shakespeare, Sterne, MacPherson, Goldsmith and Richardson. Hardly second to this was that of Rousseau and Diderot.

It was the year of the surrender of Cornwallis. Hesse, Württemberg and other German states had leased their subjects to fight for England in this war. The Jews still resided shut in separate quarters in many German cities and were subjected to humiliating constraints and taxes. A year later the last execution for witchcraft took place in German Switzerland.

Though not born in penury, Schiller in his youth knew nothing of luxury. His father, who had begun his career as a barber-surgeon, became later regimental surgeon in the ducal service of Württemberg, and was a lieutenant of infantry at the time of the poet's birth. Later he rose to the rank of captain. His mother was a plain, good woman, but from neither parent did Schiller receive directly any inspiration or aid in his literary ambition. He was early very devout, and for a time it was regarded as settled that he should become a preacher; but soon after his confirmation, — the studies for which had given rise to his first dramatic attempt, a tragedy called *The Christians*, — the Duke invited Captain Schiller to send his boy to the newly established academy at Ludwigsburg. The invitation was not to be ignored, and so, at the Duke's persuasive suggestion, young Schiller began to study for the law, but after three years changed his choice to medicine. The discipline of the school was strict, and along with some excellent features had enough wretched ones to foster the spirit of revolt against law and order inspired by the reading of *Götz von Berlichingen* and *Sturm und Drang*. Among the subjects on which the students were required to write essays for the Duke's inspection were : "Which among you is the meanest ?" and "A description of yourself and of your attitude toward your Prince." While writing under such constraint the homage expected, Schiller wrote to a friend : "O Karl, we have in our hearts a very different world from the real one."

In this atmosphere Schiller composed *Die Räuber*, a play which manifests the climax of the extreme tendencies of the Sturm und Drang period.

Karl Moor, disinherited through the machinations of his wicked brother Franz, tries to get even with the world by becoming captain of a band of robbers. After some experience in this line he returns to his home in time to release from a dungeon his father, who has been imprisoned by the wicked brother, and to rescue Amalia, who has remained faithful to him despite all the threats and persuasions of the wicked Franz. Franz, thwarted, takes his own life to escape vengeance, and Karl, held by his vow to his fellow-robbers, and prevented from resuming a settled life and marrying Amalia, stabs her and delivers himself to a poor peasant in order that the latter may secure the reward set upon his head.

It is a crude, strong piece, full of denunciations of established views and institutions. It is no wonder that the French Assembly conferred its diploma of citizenship upon the author. A German prince said of it: "If I were God, and could have foreseen that Schiller would write *Die Räuber*, I should never have created the world." Schiller himself some years later touched the most serious weakness of the drama when he confessed that he had attempted to portray human beings two years before he had ever really known one.

Although Schiller had to borrow money to pay for printing *Die Räuber*, in 1781, it sold reasonably well and on presentation upon the stage it became widely popular. After graduation, in 1780, Schiller had received an appointment as army surgeon. He left his post, without leave, to attend the first representation of his play in Mannheim, in January, 1782, and soon repeated this indiscretion.

Complaint having meanwhile been made of the offensive
tone of a certain passage in *Die Räuber*, and the poet
having further incurred the Duke's displeasure by certain
poems, Schiller was now rebuked for leaving his post, con-
fined for two weeks in the guardhouse, and forbidden
henceforth to publish anything not pertaining to his pro-
fession. This was intolerable to the ambitious and sensitive
youth, and in September he secretly left Stuttgart in company with a faithful friend, Streicher. Before this a number
of Schiller's earlier lyrics, especially those addressed to
"Laura," were published in a volume entitled *Anthologie
auf das Jahr* 1782.

To Mannheim, Darmstadt, Frankfurt and certain small
villages Schiller wandered in the course of the next two
months. He had taken with him a new drama, *Fiesko*,
and altered it at the request of the manager of the Mannheim theater, only to be told finally that it would not do
for the stage. In despair he sold the manuscript to a
publisher for ten louis d'or. *Fiesko* was well received by
the public, was played with success in Hamburg, Berlin
and Vienna, and then, in the summer of 1783, manager
Dalberg concluded that Schiller was valuable enough to be
engaged as a regular writer for the Mannheim theater,
though the salary was not enough to support him and to
enable him to pay his debts. A much-pruned version of
Fiesko was played in Mannheim but was not particularly
successful. It fared better with the next play, *Luise Millerin*,
published under the title *Kabale und Liebe*, in 1784. During these months of wandering, disguise and fear of arrest,
Schiller had been distracted also by a passion for Charlotte
von Wolzogen, daughter of a lady who befriended him in

his concealment. This passion was not returned, and he tried to cultivate another for Margarethe Schwan, daughter of his publisher.

Fiesko had been brought to Schiller's attention by a remark of Rousseau, that this Genoese hero was the only man of the modern world worthy of Plutarch.

Fiesko, a nobleman of the city, heads a conspiracy against Andreas Doria, Duke of Genoa, but is considerably in doubt as to the purity of his own motives. In fact Andreas is a very tolerable tyrant, and the only excuse for the rebellion is that the heir to the throne, Giannettino, promises to be a very bad ruler. To throw the Dorias off their guard Fiesko pays court to Julia, the sister of Giannettino, and becoming infatuated with her incurs the risk of alienating his faithful wife. To convince the latter that he had not been unfaithful he leads Julia into a humiliating situation. As the conspirators are gathering for the outbreak, Giannettino is killed on the street. Fiesko's wife, following him in male attire to watch over him, dons Giannettino's cloak and being thus mistaken for him is killed by her husband. Fiesko, in turn, is pushed from a gang-plank into the water by Verrina, an uncompromising republican, who suspects in him a tyrant worse than the Dorias. Fiesko drowns, and Verrina, whose daughter had been seduced by Giannettino, exclaims: "I go to Andreas Doria," indicating his opinion that a moderate monarchy was preferable to a reckless, blind democracy.

As may be seen, there is no well-woven, symmetrical plot, but several slightly connected episodes. The tragic outcome is not the inevitable result of the situation.

Kabale und Liebe is a picture of petty intrigue and corruption at a German court, and that of the Duke of Württemberg doubtless furnished many of the elements.

Ferdinand, son of President Walter of the ducal court, loves Luise, daughter of a musician, but is destined by his

father to marry the prince's mistress. As Ferdinand refuses
to give up Luise, Walter has her parents arrested, and then
obtains from Luise, by threats of treating them harshly, a
compromising letter which is shown to Ferdinand. Madd-
ened by this, and hopeless of escape from his father's toils,
the young man drinks a poisoned lemonade with Luise, who
dies after explaining the letter. Ferdinand curses his father
and dies.

The home life of the Miller family, and the picture of
Wurm, the knavish courtier, the tool of President Walter,
show a decided growth in Schiller's ability to observe and
paint details.

In the fall of 1784 Schiller broke the engagement with
the Mannheim theater, feeling unable to produce by con-
tract. He established a journal, *Die Rhenische Thalia*, the
first number of which, containing the first act of *Don
Karlos*, did not appear till March of the following year.
Meantime he had formed two acquaintances which deeply
influenced his life. One was with Charlotte von Kalb, the
unloved wife of an army officer, whose talents and appreciation brought her into a close association with the young
poet, who was two years her senior. The relation was very
intimate, and while helpful in some respects, became ulti-
mately a serious embarrassment to Schiller. The second
acquaintance was with the Duke of Weimar, before whom
he read a portion of his new drama, *Don Karlos*, and was
rewarded with the title of Councillor (Rath).

Though his popularity in Mannheim was great, the poet
was harassed by debts. He therefore accepted the offer of
an asylum with some enthusiastic admirers at Leipzig, who,
led by their appreciation of his genius, had entered into
correspondence with him. Chief of these was Körner,

father of the poet Theodor Körner, who remained through life one of Schiller's most helpful and valued friends. Taking leave of his devoted Streicher, who had been with him much of the time since the escape from Stuttgart, and of Frau von Kalb, Schiller reached Leipzig in April, 1785, whence he followed Körner to Dresden in the fall.

The residence of nearly two years at Dresden is a transition period in Schiller's intellectual development. The intercourse with Körner incited the poet to serious studies in both history and philosophy. As outcome of the latter study, Schiller published *Philosophische Briefe*, which shows the molding influence of Kant. The study of Kant's *Æsthetics* led later (1793–95), under the further inspiration of Professor Reinhold in Jena, to Schiller's brief treatises, *Über Anmut und Würde*, *Vom Erhabenen*, *Briefe über die ästhetische Erziehung des Menschen*, and *Über naive und sentimentale Dichtung*. The historical studies were necessitated for the completion of *Don Karlos*, which appeared partly in the *Thalia*, and complete in book form in August, 1787. This drama was the first written by Schiller in iambic pentameter verse, and has some of the beauties of his later and greater dramas — dignity and sustained power. Technically and theatrically it is no advance over the previous works. The plot is confused, the catastrophe is hardly inevitable, and the reader is in doubt as to who is really the hero. Schiller himself admitted that he changed his purpose in this respect after the drama was half finished.

Don Karlos, Infant of Spain, is enamored of his youthful stepmother. King Philip suspects the pair, and Countess Eboli, a lady in waiting, after being rebuffed by Karlos, causes compromising letters from Karlos to the queen to reach the king. In his distress the king seeks a comforter

and adviser and finds him in the Marquis Posa, who has
recently returned from the Netherlands, a friend of Karlos.
Posa urges the king to political liberality and wins his complete confidence. At the same time he comes to an understanding with the queen to send Karlos to the Netherlands
where he might usurp his father's rule and introduce Posa's
liberal reforms. But when the king, aided by Alva, is about
to close the toils about Karlos and the queen, Posa writes a
letter which he intends shall fall into the king's hands and
make it appear that it is he, not Karlos, who is intriguing
with the queen. The evening before the departure of Karlos for the Netherlands he is arrested by order of Posa, who
fears that he might in his rashness interfere with his own
plan, but the prince is almost immediately set free by order
of the king, who has read Posa's letter. As Posa is taking
leave of Karlos, who is still in prison, he is shot by an
officer of the guard. Karlos goes at midnight to take leave
of the queen, but is surprised in her apartments by Alva and
the king, and delivered to the Inquisition.

Though this drama was based more upon a novel by
Saint-Real than upon history, the studies for it led Schiller
into the history of the time and he published in 1788, after
going to Weimar, his incomplete *Geschichte des Abfalls der
vereinigten Niederlande.* This, in turn, afforded a plausible
ground for his appointment as professor of history at Jena
in the following year. During the Dresden period the
fragmentary tales, *Der Geisterseher* and *Der Verbrecher
aus verlorener Ehre,* also the poem *An die Freude,* were
written.

At Weimar Schiller again fell under the spell of Frau von
Kalb, but this was soon broken by Charlotte von Lengefeld,
to whom he was married in 1790. He was cordially received by Wieland and Herder, and was soon engaged in
journalistic coöperation with them. With Goethe, who re-

turned from Italy in 1788, he did not become intimate until 1794, when coöperation on the journal *Die Horen* brought them together and they became mutually beneficent friends. In 1788 a more intimate acquaintance with Greek literature began, influenced especially by Voss's translation of Homer. Schiller himself translated *Iphigenia in Aulis*. The taste for form and objective beauty thus cultivated is manifested also in the poems *Die Götter Griechenlands* (1788), and *Die Künstler* (1789).

The labors of his professorship, the works which have already been mentioned in anticipation, the poet's betrothal and marriage, a long illness which proved the beginning of his serious sickness fourteen years later, the production of *Die Geschichte des dreissigjährigen Krieges* (1791–93), — these were the main features of Schiller's life until 1796.

Although Schiller had several dramatic plans in contemplation he did not commence serious work on his *Wallenstein* until 1796, and with this a period of supreme activity in the drama began, resulting in the production, within about eight years, of five, or, more fairly estimated, of six great plays, second in the world's literature to Shakespeare's only, if to any. All his careful study of history and philosophy had been a preparation for the artistic work of these dramas. He had been cultivating his taste for form and relf-restraint, and reflecting and debating over æsthetic theory. Thus when he came to the work on *Wallenstein* everything was done with deliberation and conscious judgment. The theory of the dramatic blame (Schuld), the liberties of the creative artist with historical facts, the right relation of the real and the ideal, the place and use of the chorus in the tragedy, — these are some of the problems which he studied, and

his conscientious conclusions find their exemplification in
the dramas : *Wallenstein*, really one play, but consisting of
an introduction in one act, *Wallenstein's Lager*, and the
play proper arbitrarily divided into sections of five acts each,
Die Piccolomini and *Wallenstein's Tod* (finished in 1799) ;
Maria Stuart (1800) ; *Die Jungfrau von Orleans* (1801) ;
Die Braut von Messina (1803) ; and *Wilhelm Tell* (1804).

Wallenstein portrays the end of the career of this famous
general of the Thirty Years' War. Schiller pictures him as
made overconfident by his belief in astrology and by his
reliance upon the fidelity of his officers, especially of his
companion in arms, Octavio Piccolomini. Entrusted by the
emperor with almost supreme power, he enters into am-
biguous negotiations with the enemies of the country and,
by his own confession, dallies with the possibility of treason.
A messenger falls into the emperor's hands, and Wallenstein,
unable to offer plausible explanation of his negotiations, is
forced by circumstances to do what he maintains he had
never seriously intended. When he takes the field against
the emperor, his army falls away from him and his trusted
officers are the ones who execute against him the decree of
deposition and outlawry.

This overtragic material is relieved by the introduction
of the lovers, Thekla, the daughter of Wallenstein, and Max,
the son of Octavio, the favorite of the general, two of the
most ideal of Schiller's creations. *Fiesko* and *Don Karlos*,
though treating historical personages, are not properly historical dramas, because they were not based on careful
study ; the heroes are not of world-wide fame, and the poet
was not controlled by a purpose to be faithful to the truth
of history. In *Wallenstein* Schiller deliberately chose the
historical field because he recognized, as he said, that he
was better adapted to idealizing the real than to realizing
the ideal.

In *Maria Stuart* Schiller treats of the closing days of the unfortunate Scottish queen. The conspiracy of Curl and Nau in her behalf is fictitiously repeated, with some modifications, in the action of Mortimer, the nephew of Paulet, Mary's keeper. He comes to her aid prompted by religious zeal, and continues the plot under her fatal fascination, which had ruined so many, from Rizzio to the end. The chief feature, which is entirely without warrant in history, is a meeting between Elizabeth and Mary, in which the latter has hopes of pardon if she shows herself properly humble. But she was unable to endure Elizabeth's taunts, and gave way to a burst of royal indignation. Thus the fault which had ruined her life and had brought her to her end is ideally expressed in this happily invented scene.

In general, Mary is painted more favorably and Elizabeth less favorably than history approves. Both this play and *Wallenstein* are great favorites on the German stage.

In *Die Jungfrau von Orleans* Schiller departed most widely from traditional accounts, and designated the play, in anticipation of criticism, a "romantic tragedy." The poet ascribes the marvelous feats of the Maid to her consecrated purpose, which inspired herself and her allies with supreme confidence. This purpose is involved with the vow never to love, and to sacrifice to the Virgin every Englishman who falls into her hands. When Johanna meets Lionel on the battlefield and, touched by tenderness and love, violates her vow so far as to spare his life, she loses her self-confidence, and her invincibility leaves her. Thus far Schiller may be close to the truth in his psychological analysis of Johanna's career. But romantic liberty comes in when, after sincere repentance, in captivity, she recovers her marvelous power, breaks massive chains, rushes to the fray and, after a second time saving the cause of the king, perishes on the field of battle.

The dramatic blame or guilt here is similar to that in *Wallenstein*,— the harboring of a wrong thought,— though here it is much more refined, less deliberate and pronounced.

Wallenstein's Lager is written in a sort of irregular
iambic tetrameter, a favorite meter in the popular dramas
and ballads of the late Middle Ages, and known as "Knit-
telverse"; it has, besides, several songs in regular stanzas;
Maria Stuart in one scene departs from the iambic pentameters introduced into the German drama by Lessing in
Nathan der Weise, and accommodates the measure to the
joyful lyric mood; the same is true in *Die Jungfrau von
Orleans,* while in two other scenes the verse assumes a
more ponderous step, the hexameter (so-called trimeters)
for a corresponding reason.

In the next play, *Die Braut von Messina,* Schiller, who
had meanwhile been discussing the Greek drama, and especially the use of the chorus, chose a form which would
give his lyric faculty full play, — that of the Greek tragedy.
At the same time he deserted the historical field and returned to that of free imagination.

The play presents the complications by which two hostile
brothers fall in love, each unknown to the other, with a
maiden who proves in the end to be their sister, though they
had not known they had a sister, and who fall, the elder by
the younger's jealous hand, the latter by his own, at the
moment when their mother was rejoicing over their recon-
ciliation and awaiting the restoration of her long-hidden
daughter and the introduction of the brides of her sons.

Some writers see in this a drama of fate, but it is easy to
find an all-pervading dramatic guilt, to wit, secretiveness,
which brings the curse upon the doomed family.

After *Die Braut von Messina* Schiller translated for the
Weimar theater two French plays, *Der Parasit,* and *Der
Neffe als Onkel,* and then, after a consideration of other
plans, began the studies for *Wilhelm Tell,* in which he re-

turned to the field of history, or at least of legend. The details regarding the composition of this work will be found in the next section. *Tell* was completed in February, 1804, and the poet was already preparing for the next achievement when his health, for years precarious, gave way. Many months were lost to composition, and precious strength was spent on the text of a spectacular piece, *Die Huldigung der Künste*, and then the poet began his last play, *Demetrius*, which was destined to remain a fragment. Only one act was completed. Schiller died May 9th, 1805. *Demetrius* was designed to represent the career of a changeling claimant to the Russian throne, and judging from the one act would have been at least equal to the poet's best.

The last fifteen years of Schiller's life were blessed, in addition to his happy domestic life, with many fine and helpful friendships, among these friends being Wilhelm von Humboldt, Fichte, Herder, his faithful Körner, and Goethe. Goethe, by whom Schiller felt himself at first repelled, was brought into intimate relations with Schiller in 1794 by coöperation on *Die Horen*, and, being counterparts in temperament and methods, each profited much by the other's criticism and advice. Goethe encouraged Schiller through many of the discouraging struggles with *Wallenstein ;* Schiller persuaded Goethe to resume work on *Faust.* In 1797 they took up together the study and composition of ballads, and in this and the three following years Schiller produced some of his most popular poems : *Der Taucher, Der Handschuh, Der Ring des Polykrates, Der Ritter Toggenburg, Die Kraniche des Ibykus, Der Gang nach dem Eisenhammer, Der Kampf mit dem Drachen* and *Das Lied von der Glocke.*

Schiller is less many-sided than Goethe, but more intense. Goethe was more open to all impressions of sensuous beauty, more objective, more lyric; Schiller subordinated the sensuous to the ethical, "his conscience is his Muse." There is no need to institute comparisons of greatness; each of the two poets has his sphere in which he is supreme. But while the majority of critics call Goethe the greater of the two, Schiller is undoubtedly the favorite of the German people. And this is fortunate for Germany and creditable to her people.

THE COMPOSITION OF "WILHELM TELL."

The suggestion of making literary use of the story of Wilhelm Tell came to Schiller from Goethe. Goethe had visited the Forest Cantons three times, in 1775, in 1779, and in 1797. On the last occasion he wrote to Schiller that he was convinced that the story of Tell could be treated as an epic; that he had carefully studied the scene and it now depended on luck whether anything came of it. In the *Tag-und Jahreshefte* Goethe states that he had planned an epic in hexameters, but that he grew tired of the subject, as he always did if he studied too long over form and meter. He had often discussed the subject with Schiller, he tells us, and had described the locality to him, and when it no longer attracted him, some time after 1800, he "gladly and formally" turned it over to Schiller. It should be stated that Goethe's memory is not to be depended upon for details, and especially dates.

During the year 1801 Schiller read Müller's *History of Switzerland*, and as early as in the spring of that year a report somehow got abroad that he was engaged on a *Wilhelm Tell*. Later in the year the rumor became general, though there is no other evidence that Schiller was then actually considering the subject. But on March 16th, 1802, in a letter to Cotta, the publisher, he asked for a detail map of Lake Lucerne, saying that he had so often heard this false rumor that he had finally taken up the subject, and had been studying Tschudi's *Chronicon Helveticum*, and had thereupon seriously purposed to write a play "Wilhelm Tell," which he believed would bring them credit. But he begged Cotta to tell no one, since he lost interest in a subject if he heard too much said about it. After some further reading, the matter was dropped for the work on *Die Braut von Messina*.

After *Die Braut von Messina*, Schiller planned to go to work on *Warbeck*, a long-cherished subject, and then at *Tell*. In September, 1802, he wrote to Körner, that while Tell appeared anything but a tractable subject for dramatic treatment, since the action was so scattered in time and place, and, saving the hat and apple-shooting episode, so ill-adapted to poetic presentation, nevertheless he had already given it so many poetic touches that it was beginning to leave the phase of history and enter that of poetry. He found it "a desperate task, for it consists of representing with the character of utmost consistency and truth a whole locally circumscribed people, a whole remote period and, most difficult of all, an entirely local, indeed almost individual and unique phenomenon." He thought of putting *Tell* into a form similar to that of *Die Braut von Messina*, — that of the Greek tragedy. After finishing the latter, Schiller was forced to occupy himself with other matters,

so that it was in May, 1803, before he could again con-
cern himself seriously with *Tell*. Then he returned to
the study of Tschudi, who gave him "a new light through
his straightforward, Herodotian, almost Homeric tone."
He promised the great actor Iffland, in Berlin, that he
might have the play before the winter was over, and assured him that it would be "a piece for the people, cap-
tivating heart and head." Early in August he wrote to
Cotta requesting more descriptive works on Switzerland,
for the poet himself had never seen that country. On
the 18th of this month he wrote to Wilhelm von Humboldt that the subject was "a tough one" though he hoped
to master it. On the 25th, according to the laconic entry
in his diary, he "went at *Tell*." But several weeks later
he wrote to Körner, again referring to the difficulty of the
subject, and asking for more books to help him with local
color, but adding: "If the gods help me in carrying out
what I have in mind, it will prove a mighty thing and
shake the stages of Germany." Schiller was anything but
conceited about his products, and such confidence as this
was unusual. Later in the month and far into October he
was still seeking and studying works to furnish a setting
for his drama. A large number of sheets are preserved
(see p. liv), on which are Schiller's careful notes to this
end from the various authors he read, the points he used
in many cases methodically checked off. He felt nerved
by the fact that the new play was intended to be given to
greet the return to Weimar of the crown prince and his
young wife. A presentation of *Julius Cæsar* at Weimar on
the 1st of October proved invaluable to the poet, "lifting
his boat" and putting him into the most productive mood.

The first week in November he writes that he is well under way, and tolerably satisfied with what he has done. On the 5th of December he writes to Iffland, who is urging him to early completion, that he expects to have it finished early in March. He is resolved to visit Switzerland before he lets the piece go to press, in order to adjust certain details to fit Swiss national prejudices. To Iffland's request to receive the play an act at a time, Schiller responds: "It is not composed an act at a time, but the matter requires that I carry certain trains of action that belong together through all five acts, and only then take up the others. For instance, Tell stands pretty much by himself in the piece; his cause is a private cause and remains so until, at the close, it is combined with the public cause." He promises the first three acts in the course of January, and sends a scheme of the stage-settings. From this it appears that the first scene of the second act was to follow the second scene of the first act, the setting up of the pole with the hat, now in Act I, scene 3, was to form the first scene of the second act, and be followed by a scene in a room, perhaps the interview between Rudenz and Bertha, now contained in the second scene of the third act, scenes one and two of the fourth act were interchanged, and were to be followed by a wild mountain scene giving perhaps the incident now narrated by Tell in the first scene of the fourth act, while the act was to close with a scene representing the scaling of the Rossberg by Melchthal.

Some progress was made during December, though Schiller was distracted by the presence of Madame de Staël, who spent several months in Weimar, and by the death of

Herder. In spite of the "most vivacious, most disputatious and most talkative French philosopher" (Madame de Staël), the first act was completed on the 12th of January, 1804, and was sent to Goethe, who exclaimed in reply: "This is no first act, but a whole play, and a fine one. At first sight it seems to me to be all right, and that is the chief point in certain pieces which are to produce definite effects." Goethe made two suggestions in minor details. Two days later, Schiller sent him the Rütli scene, which Goethe found worthy of all praise. In sending the first act to Iffland, on the 23rd, Schiller promises the whole piece by the end of February. Johannes von Müller, the Swiss historian, came to Weimar on the 22nd, and while his visits must have consumed some time, intercourse with him must have yielded Schiller profit and inspiration. On the 5th of February the third and fourth acts were done. Iffland wrote, after reading the first act and the Rütli scene: "I have read, devoured and bent my knee, and my heart, my tears, my bounding blood pay rapturous tribute to your mind and heart! O more, very soon more! What a work! what wealth, power, perfection and omnipotence! God preserve you, Amen!" In sending the fourth and part of the fifth acts, on the 13th, Schiller explained those changes in the arrangement of scenes which give us the play as it is at present.

All invitations and interferences were now avoided, and in feverish exaltation the poet hastened to the close. On the 18th of February he wrote in his journal, "*Tell* finished." Goethe wrote after reading the close, "The piece has turned out splendidly and given me an agreeable evening." On the 17th of March the first representation occurred at

Weimar, and though it lasted five hours, it met with immense success, greater, as Schiller said, than any of his other plays. He wrote to Körner that he thought he was gradually acquiring a mastery of the requirements of the stage.

It will interest the student to read a criticism on the first performance which will show that homage was not universal, and that a keen-witted woman saw immediately the defects which have again and again been pointed out by critics. It is the account of Henriette von Knebel, governess of the Princess Caroline of Weimar. "The story of Tell is interesting enough in itself, I think, and the scenery was calculated to transport us to Switzerland. If you ask regarding the dialogues, I must answer, ' Too long, too long!' Tell's story proper does not begin until the third act. The Princess thinks that the piece is not a whole, but consists of several pieces, and she is right. The long (scene of the) conference of the confederates in which not one-third of the words are necessary, and then, in the midst of Tell's story, a tedious Swiss prophet (Attinghausen) whom one would rather have die behind the scenes, since he has to die, we know not just why. And then, in addition, the love affair of a degenerate young Swiss who is brought back by his mistress with many sounding words to reason and his fatherland. Then Duke Albrecht (Johann) is introduced, who murdered the Emperor. And finally, to crown all, Tell, whose strong character is pretty well conceived, as he only acts and speaks little, has to deliver a long monologue, in which, as in all, only Schiller speaks, and not the man himself."

Although designed for the Berlin theater, there was hesita-

tion over the political tone of certain passages, and the
preparation of scenery and music added to the delay, so
that *Tell* was not represented there until the 4th of July,
when it met with the same enthusiastic reception as at
Weimar, and was repeated three times in eight days.
Schiller received 331 thalers for the right of representation in Berlin, the highest fee that the theater had ever
paid for a drama. From Breslau, Hamburg, Mannheim and
Vienna, also, Schiller received considerable sums, and the
play was given at these theaters in March or April. It was
published in October, in an edition of 7,000 copies, and a
second edition of 3,000 was issued the same year. Besides
various verbal improvements the first printed edition added
to the stage version (which is preserved in several manuscripts) the parts of Pfeifer von Luzern, Act I, scene 2, and
Kunz von Gersau, Act IV, scene 1.

It is a curious fact that Goethe again took up his plan
for an epic of Tell in the year following Schiller's death,
but he dropped it without any actual achievement.

Despite all technical faults, *Wilhelm Tell* has remained
one of the most popular pieces on the German stage, and
has had an incalculable effect in the cultivation of national
feeling. Its popularity has always been greatest in periods
of national consciousness, as in 1813–15, 1848, and 1870.

CRITICISMS AND COMMENTS.

The people, the audience, was usually more favorable to
Schiller's plays than the critics. The opinion of Henriette
von Knebel touched technical defects which were often
emphasized by critics to the ignoring of the undisputed
great beauties of the play.

Der Freimüthige, a journal conducted by Merkel and Kotzebue, condemned in its issue of March 29, 1804, the Rütli scene, of which Goethe'thought so highly, as a manifestation of Schiller's passion for the chorus. Such a criticism, it would seem, could spring only from a mind prepared by *Die Braut von Messina* to see the features of that play in all that Schiller produced. It condemns also the fifth act as the work of a courtier, "a bugbear, introduced without any necessity." On the whole it found *Tell* not one of Schiller's better productions.

Die Zeitung für die elegante Welt spoke of *Tell* in a rather perfunctory way as "eine edle Geistesfrucht," but the *Berliner Nachrichten* of July 7, 1805, inspired perhaps by Iffland, is almost as enthusiastic as was the great actor in the praise already quoted. It tells us that after the performance at Weimar the general opinion of the play was cold, even that of Schiller's most pronounced admirers. Schiller had, however, soared in *Tell* to a height which puzzled his critics. In its own view Schiller had never shown himself a greater dramatic poet than in this work. The fifth act, indeed, it found superfluous, though this too possessed great beauties. The dialogue was not so soaringly lyric as was usual in Schiller's dramas.

Der Freimüthige, through the voice of its chief editor, thought better of the play, after knowing it better, and on July 10 characterized it as "the most perfect work of art among Schiller's creations; everything in its place, no gaps and nothing superfluous; free from the long rhetorical meditations which have so strangely disfigured Schiller's pieces from *Don Karlos* on. — A world of real, high-hearted, noble human beings. — The action is not Tell's story, but the liberation of Switzerland. — The fifth act is a supplement and a defect."

The *Berliner Zeitung* of the same date was less enthusiastic : "*Wilhelm Tell*, like other of Schiller's dramas, is not a complete whole ; the parts merely stand side by side, instead of being derived one from another. — The fifth act is superfluous. — Bertha and Rudenz are out of place in a company of country people. Rösselmann is not only superfluous, but in violation of the true spirit of the action. — Only two of all the scenes are powerful : the meeting of Stauffacher, Fürst and Melchthal, and the shooting of the apple. The former deserves unqualified homage, save the almost repulsive rant about the value of the eyes. — There is no unity in Tell's character. — The poet deserves much criticism for Rudenz. — Bertha's is a senseless part."

Despite such criticisms *Tell* was played in Berlin every other day in September.

Die Zeitung für die elegante Welt after reading the play in print, October 13, found it " far below the other products of this great man. It is no whole, but only a mass of beautiful parts. — Tell's monologue is a sermon which seems ridiculous. — The fifth act is a superfluous addition to give the work a moral."

The *Götting'sche Gelehrte Anzeigen* in curious contrast to some of the preceding points finds Tell's son sketched in a masterful way. " The play should be called ' The Liberation of Switzerland,' and not ' Wilhelm Tell.' " And yet, the chief action is Gessler's inhuman act toward Tell and Tell's punishment of it. " There are but few pithy sayings in *Tell.* — There is nowhere any overloading. Only the passage of Melchthal on light will perhaps seem too poetical and far-fetched. — Tell's monologue in the fourth act deserves favorable mention. — The absence of prominent feminine parts is to be regretted. — It is a play especially calculated for the stage."

Perhaps the most curious of contemporary criticisms is that of a Swiss writer in *Isis* for March, 1805. He tells us that this highly lauded work is regarded in Switzerland not without approval, but without enthusiasm, and on the whole as rather mediocre. The criticisms in detail touch alleged offenses against local geography and customs, as in locating the Rütli (cp. the extract from Tschudi, p. xlvii, and note to l. 727) ; having horsemen gallop down to the shore at Treib (Act I, scene 1) ; annihilating the distance from Steinen to Uri (between scenes 2 and 3, Act I) ; describing wide, desolate ice-fields (l. 999) in the Surenne Mountains ; seeing ice-capped mountains eastward from Altorf (SD before scene 3, Act III); having the sirocco blow cold (l. 40), etc. In view of such defects, it would seem, the *Isis* critic concludes that *Tell* cannot count on permanent success. Some of the points here made have been disputed by other writers equally familiar with the locality, but of course such errors, if admitted, are not at all vital.

A. W. Schlegel considered *Tell* Schiller's best work "imbued with the poetry of history, the treatment true to nature and genuine and, considering the poet's unfamiliarity with the country, astonishingly correct in local color."

Tell gives an illustration of the inadequacy of *a priori* critical canons to fully limit and condition a work of creative art. Yet something of this "bankruptcy of criti-

cism " may be only apparent, due to an attempt to apply
to this play the rules of a dramatic form to which it does
not belong.   It should be noted that *Tell* is to all intents
and purposes an historical drama, as Schiller had probably
no doubts of the essential truth of the traditional account.
It is accordingly subject to the natural limitations of an
historical subject.   Criticisms of the chief points of action
and of the traditional character of the persons may, indeed,
lie against the choice of the subject, but not as against the
poet's creative conscience.

Again, *Tell* is not a tragedy, either of the classical or
of the modern type ; it is the only one of Schiller's plays
that ends happily for the hero.   Consequently the subject
of dramatic fault, or " Schuld," falls out entirely in its consideration.   It is also a question whether the traditional
stages of dramatic development : exposition, development,
climax, check, catastrophe, are to be regarded as requirements for a drama without a tragic plot, like *Tell*.

Shakespeare in practice, and Lessing in theory had
broken with the classic requirement of unity in time and
place, but Lessing believed the unity of action to be a
requirement inherent in the nature of the drama.   It may
be that this too belongs only to the tragedy with a plot.
Bulthaupt saves the old requirement by finding in *Tell* a
" unity of spirit," though of dramatic unity there is none.
He says, also, that wherever, as in the Attinghausen scene,
the progress of the dramatic action is interrupted, there
poetry and rhetoric sustain the interest.   Freytag has
pointed out the defects in the dramatic structure of the
play, but he admits in the individual scenes a charm which
compels admiration.   The Rütli scene he calls " a model

which young dramatists need not imitate, but the lofty
beauty of which they should study with care." Similarly
Börne speaks of the defects of the play as "the virtues of
the poet." The student may profitably consider these the-
oretical demands made upon *Tell* in the light of the modern
realistic drama of Ibsen, Sudermann or Herne.

Much offense has been taken at Tell's act in slaying
Gessler, especially in the fact of the deed being done from
ambush. Goethe in *Wahrheit und Dichtung* speaks of it,
with perhaps a touch of sarcasm, as "an assassination which
is regarded by the whole world as commendably heroic and
patriotic." Börne, who was in general an admirer of Schiller,
thought it out of keeping with the character of a hero to
hide behind a bush and commit murder. With the same
feeling Prince Bismarck in his youth could not endure *Tell*.
On an abstract statement of the bare proposition everyone
must agree with Börne. Yet it is a curious fact that the
action of Tell does not present itself in this light on first
reading or first seeing the play. Why this is so, and what
defense can be made for Tell, the student may work out
for himself. On behalf of Schiller it is to be remembered
that this act is one of the permanent features of the tradition.

Scarcely a feature of *Tell* has failed to receive some
criticism. This may be explained by the remark of Börne
about the virtues of the poet. For instance, the poetically
beautiful speeches of Attinghausen, Act II, scene 1, and
Act IV, scene 2, of Melchthal, Act I, scene 4, and of Tell,
Act IV, scene 3, are among those condemned as inartistic.
Attinghausen's whole part, like that of Rudenz, is declared
to be an intrusion and a drag upon the action. Melchthal's

apostrophe is said to be too rhetorical, and out of keeping
with his humble origin and walk in life. Tell's monologue is
criticised on the same ground, and, further, as especially
inconsistent with his character as a man of deeds rather
than of words. In all of these, a constitutional weakness
of Schiller for rhetorical and didactic declamation is discovered. It must be conceded that no peasants were ever
heard to speak as do those in *Tell*, but neither is it likely
that Prince Hamlet talked to himself in pentameters. Many
of these criticisms lose sight of the essential unreality of the
stage, and of the conventional agreement to ignore this
unreality. A monologue is only the speaker's thoughts
uttered aloud for the benefit of the audience. Of like
nature is the criticism of such lines as 210–13, and of
293–94, which are spoken to inform the audience rather
than the person addressed.

The criticisms in which there is most general agreement
are the dispensableness of the Parricide episode, the weakness of Rudenz and Bertha, and the loose connection of
the different threads of the action. Bellermann calls *Tell*
the loosest of all Schiller's compositions and says that the
gloomy figure of Duke Johann is an intrusion and a violation
of the purpose of the play. Rudenz, he says, is weak, and
the scenes in which he appears are the weakest of the play.

Bulthaupt agrees that Rudenz is an egoist, and Bertha
without flesh and blood, but he approves the Parricide
scene, except Tell's description of the way to Rome, which
is "too patriarchal." He also approves Tell's monologue,
saving a few phrases, and Attinghausen, whom Henriette
von Knebel found a "tedious Swiss prophet," Bulthaupt
calls "the most worthy prophet of the fairest and holiest

revelations on freedom and fatherland which ever a poet proclaimed from the mouth of his creatures."

If much space has been given to unfavorable criticisms it is to show the failure of criticism to control popular taste, and because the student may be depended on, as may every reader, to see for himself the beauties of the drama. A few general points may be made in this line, and the student should develop them in detail.

The play depicts a number of heroic deeds, done in a beautiful country by the representatives of an heroic people; it is filled with beautiful descriptions and noble sentiments nobly expressed. On the stage it is found that most of the scenes are exceedingly fascinating and effective. However much better the play might have been with a centralized action, these beauties are sufficient to quite hide the lack of unity, and the total effect, with the majority of people, is a high æsthetic and ethical gratification.

There are really three almost distinct threads of action, the Rütli or popular action, the Tell action, and the Attinghausen-Rudenz-Bertha action. The student will find it interesting to group apart the scenes which carry these threads, and note the points of contact and the devices by which they are connected. There are four avengers among the characters: Baumgarten, Tell, Melchthal, and the Parricide. Here, again, the poet's art is manifested in the ways in which these are compared and contrasted, the causes for their revenge and the differences in their methods of procedure.

Schiller frankly admitted his own limitations in being essentially an idealist. It is common, with Scherer, to regard his youthful dramas as more realistic than those of his later period. It is doubtful, however, whether this realism is more than superficial, whether it is not largely the effect of the prose in which those earlier plays are composed. However this may be, there is more of genuine realism — touches of universal life — in *Tell* than in most of Schiller's work. He admired the greater objectivity of Goethe and sought to acquire this attitude. He was particularly pleased with the subject of *Wallenstein* because he found that he could look at it coolly. In his essay on *Naïve and Sentimental Poetry*, the main thought is that the Greeks and other earlier nations thought and wrote naturally and unconsciously, while the moderns are, as a rule, self-conscious and artificial; they only try to be natural. Goethe, he thought, was one of the few *naïve* poets in the modern world; he, himself, was sentimental, though it was his aim to be natural. No theme could have been found better to encourage objectivity than this story of a simple, freedom-loving people in the pure air of their mountains. Bulthaupt expresses the well-warranted opinion that "there has seldom been a more successful union of idealism and realism, of subjectivity and objectivity," than in *Tell* — realism in motivation, idealism in situation and execution. Among the most striking instances of realism in *Tell* may be noted the conversation, Act I, scene 1, regarding the approaching storm, the fidelity of the parliamentary procedure in the Rütli scene, notably lines 1150–54, 1314 and 1397, and Hedwig's fault-finding in Act III, scene 1.

Schiller was master of the rhetorical device of contrast, and this is one of the great elements of power in *Tell*. A peculiarity of this method when skillfully employed is that it is not noticed. Instances of it may be seen in the in-

troduction of the storm and the tragic episode of Baumgarten upon the supremely peaceful scene of Act I, scene 1 ;
in Melchthal's lines, 590–94, and in Tell's lines, 2568–76 ;
in the presence of the wedding-party and wedding-music at
the death of Gessler ; in the comparison of Tell's deed and
the Parricide's.   In the scene of Rudenz's declaration of
his love for Bertha, which was originally planned to occur
in a parlor (see p. xxiii), we may find a case in which the
contrast was deliberately chosen.

But, after all, the chief charm of *Tell* probably lies in the
universal interest of the theme and the nobility of the
thoughts expressed.   It is noteworthy that Schiller's dramas
without exception introduce the relation of ruler and subject, and discuss more or less prominently the themes of
tyranny and liberty.   The attempt has been made to discover in them a gradual and uniform development of views
on the subject of government.   This goes too far, though,
of course, the later views are in general more conservative
than the earlier.   Yet *Tell* manifests more sympathy for
democracy than *Fiesko*, in which (see p. xi) the disap-
pointed republican Verrina recoils from a revolution prompted
by self-seeking to an enlightened despotism.   In *Tell*, it
should be observed, the movement is not a revolution, but
an insistence upon constitutional rights within the empire.

STYLE AND METER.

Schiller began his *Wallenstein* in prose, but soon became
convinced that he must use a language that was suited to the
heroic theme.   He found, after beginning to write in iam-
bics, that all went better.   The same meter was used in all

his subsequent dramas, with short deviations in most, and
extended deviations in *Die Braut von Messina*. The respects in which the heroic verse in *Wilhelm Tell* differs
from that in the other dramas are chiefly greater simplicity,
greater sententiousness and the presence of archaisms and
local dialect words and expressions. Schiller himself gave
credit for his style to familiarity with the Lutheran Bible,
and some touches of this are recognizable in *Tell*. Much
more marked is the influence of Tschudi, whose Herodotian,
almost Homeric, style charmed Schiller and threw light upon
his task. The influence of Shakespeare, whose *Macbeth*
Schiller had translated, and whose *Julius Cæsar* he saw
(see p. xxii) just after beginning work on *Tell*, is noticeable
in certain passages, while that of Homer shows itself in the
formation of curiously compounded pictorial adjectives.
The student who is familiar with the style of these different
writers will easily recognize their characteristics as he meets
them. To those who are not thus familiar it is of little
profit to point them out.

Contrary to the opinion of the *Götting'sche Gelehrte Anzeigen* (see p. xxviii), there is an extraordinary proportion
of pithy sayings in *Tell*, found especially in the passages
in stichomythic dialogue (see note to l. 136).

Aside from the three lyric diversions, the meter of *Tell*
is rather more uniform than in Schiller's other dramas
(see p. xviii). Still there are a number of lines of six feet,
and some of four and less. As in the other plays, rhyme
is introduced quite freely, especially at the end of scenes,
as in Shakespeare. Rhyming came very easy to Schiller,
and it is possible that in some cases the rhymes crept in
almost unconsciously.

Irregularities in the meter are frequent enough to prevent monotony. The irregular alternation of masculine and feminine endings, the presence of opening anapests and, occasionally, of two unaccented syllables between the accents, are elements which constitute this variety. The carrying over of the thought into a following line without interruption (*enjambement*) is very common and helps to break the sing-song of the meter when the piece is played. There are even a few instances in which compound words are divided between two lines.

On the other hand, to secure a smoother meter letters are freely elided (e and i) and, again, the vowels are restored in endings from which usage has long since dropped them, as „gehet" for „geht." The archaic omission of adjective endings in certain cases (see note to l. 10) is a feature at the same time of the style and of the meter.

The Editor feels that he would be doing the student and his instructor a poor service in enumerating the instances of all these irregularities, but chooses rather to leave this as exercise work for those who may have taste, or wish to cultivate taste, in this direction.

HISTORY AND LEGEND.

For the appreciation and critical judgment of *Wilhelm Tell* as a poetic creation, it is immaterial whether the account which Schiller followed is true or not. Goethe said of the criticism that proposed to show Lucretia and Mutius Scævola to be creatures of fiction : "What use have we for so pitiful a truth? As the Romans were great enough to invent such things, we ought at least to be great enough to believe in them." The remark is applicable to Tell. Yet because the belief in the reality of Tell was once so general, and the interest in the question is still so great, a summary of the matter is here given.

The story of Wilhelm Tell, as it is familiar to the world, and essentially as it is given in Schiller's drama, was regarded as history from 1476, the date of the composition of the chronicle of the parish of Obwalden (part of Unterwalden), known as *Das weisse Buch*, down to 1760, the date of publication of the book of Uriel Freudenberger, *Guillaume Tell, fable danoise.* Within this period doubts of its correctness would have been received much as to-day we should regard doubts of the exploits and execution of Major André or Nathaniel Hale.

I mention 1476 as the earlier limit of this period within which the story was generally accepted, because the chronicle named is the earliest authentic record which reports the life and deeds of Tell. The chief of these deeds, the shooting of the prefect Gessler, is commonly ascribed to the year 1307, one hundred and seventy years before. How far back of the year 1476 the story may have been current, or how, if an imported legend, it crept into this Unterwalden chronicle, are matters which the assailants of an historical Tell have not determined. Rochholz, indeed, believes that the alleged cruelties of Gessler were invented in consequence of a feud between the Swiss cantons and the heirs of Hermann Gessler of Bruneck, waged during the last half of the 15th century, and confused with the blinding of a subject of the city of Zurich, who was in Gessler's service, by the Duke of Austria, in 1412. If Tell is historical, of course the earlier date of 1476 should be moved backward, so as to become identical with the date of the deeds themselves.

It must not be supposed that in the three hundred years preceding 1760 there were absolutely no doubts on the subject. Guilliman, in 1607, expressed a little skepticism, and was severely censured therefor. Iselin, in 1725, called attention to the fact that there is an apple-shooting episode in Danish legends. Voltaire, in his *Sur les Mœurs*, hinted that the Swiss had borrowed a fable to adorn the history of the origin of their independence. But these doubts were isolated, and soon died away. Also the warm discussion that arose over Freudenberger's book seemed to rest in favor of the defenders of Tell, especially after the distinguished historian, Johannes von Müller, in 1787, gave his adherence to the historical verity of the hero. Finally, Schiller's drama seemed to consecrate the episode and to make further doubts doubly heretical. Yet investigations were resumed after some years, and the researches of Ideler, Kopp, Häuser, Huber, Vischer, Rilliet, and Rochholz, added to the points already made by Freudenberger, have just reversed the former situation, so that there remains now but a faint shadow of possibility of the existence of Wilhelm Tell as an historical character.

A résumé of the arguments in the case may leave the student to judge of their weight for himself.

A documentary proof, to which some credence was given in the eighteenth century, was the reported certificate of one hundred and fourteen persons who were present in 1388 at the founding of the Tell chapel on Lake Lucerne, over the Tellplatte, and who had personally known Wilhelm Tell. But the evidence for this certificate rests on a state-

ment of a person in 1758 that he had seen a true copy of
a certificate of the Ammann Zum Brunnen, made in 1460,
to the effect that he had seen a true copy of the original
certificate in question. Hanging by this slender thread,
this certificate falls to the ground when the question is
asked : Why should these good people have taken the trouble
to make such a certificate at a time when presumably there
was no doubt of the existence of Tell? A similar certificate
produced in 1758 is proven by a clumsy discrepancy in the
dates to be a forgery.

All attempts to show the name of Tell in parish or other
records of the Forest Cantons within more than a hundred
years of 1307 have failed, although forgeries have been attempted in this. But from the date of the *White Book* on,
evidence is plentiful. Other chronicles mention the hero.
A popular song reciting his exploits dates from 1477, with
a strong probability of an older original. About 1511 there
was a popular play dealing with the uprising against the
governors and the deeds of Tell. During the last half of
the 16th century all of the three Tell chapels, at Bürglen,
at the Tellplatte, and in the Hohle Gasse, were restored,
this being regarded as good evidence that they were built a
century or more earlier. There is then in behalf of the
legend of Tell a tradition beginning, as has been shown,
about one hundred and fifty years after the events in question, and continuing for three hundred years.

Against this stand the strong, though largely negative
arguments of the iconoclasts : The admitted absence of all
reference in contemporary chronicles to such events and
persons as these is inexplicable ; the absence of all record
of the Tell family in the place and period involved is in-

consistent with the probability of his existence; there was a confederacy formed among the Forest Cantons in 1247, and renewed in 1291, but there is no record of one in 1307; the annals of Austria furnish no record of a governor Gessler, during this period, much less of the assassination of any Austrian bailiff in the Forest Cantons; the existence of the Danish legend of an archer, Toko, compelled by a tyrant, Harald Blatand,* to shoot an apple from his boy's

---

* The chronicler, Saxo Grammaticus, d. 1203, whose account furnished the chief basis for the attack of Freudenberger upon the credibility of the legend, gives the story of the Danish prototype of Tell as follows:

A warrior, Toko, had been some time in the service of the Danish king, Harald Bluetooth, and by his deeds surpassed all his comrades and made many envious. Once at a banquet he boasted that he was so skillful that he could fetch down the smallest apple when placed upon a stick at a distance. Those present repeated this to the king, who was so cruel as to take advantage of the man's rash speech and endanger the life of his little son. He ordered Toko's child to be placed as a mark and that the boaster should pierce an apple on his son's head at the first shot or pay for his rash speech with his life. Now Toko took the child, placed him with his face to the goal and bade him await the whizzing arrow immovable and without turning his head, for the least motion might spoil the best shot. He then took three arrows out of his quiver, put the first on his crossbow and hit the apple. Had he missed and hit the boy, the father would have been held responsible for the murder, and been sent after the boy into eternity. Asked by the king why he had taken the two other arrows, from his quiver, when his safety all depended on one shot, Toko replied: "To avenge the straying of the first upon you with the point of the other two, for innocence shall not be punished and your tyranny go unpunished." After this Toko was obliged to perform the marvelous feat of sliding down a steep mountain on snowshoes into the sea. He was, however, saved by a boat, but Harald concluded from the fragments of the snowshoes, which were rescued from the sea, that Toko was dead. Meantime Harald had gone so far in cruelty toward his

head, and afterward killing the tyrant, and of similar
legends in other Germanic countries, makes it probable
that this episode is not historical, but a borrowed legend;
the Tell chapels were originally not Tell chapels at all, but
were connected with the deeds of the mythical hero after
his story became popular.

In refutation of these arguments the loyal Swiss urges:
Local chronicles in German Switzerland were very few in
the fourteenth century, and it would not be so remarkable
if they overlooked Tell; it is no wonder that the Austrian
annals are silent about so discreditable an episode; that
the apple-shooting might occur more than once in different
countries; and that even if this is a myth, the possibility
of a hero who defended his family against a tyrannical
governor and slew him is not thereby excluded; and, finally,
that the general and enduring national belief in the hero
and his deeds is more valid than any amount of negative
evidence.

PORTIONS OF TSCHUDI USED IN "TELL."

In 1305 the Three Cantons made a protest to the king against
the injustice of their governors. "He referrred them to his
councillors, who replied to them: that they had incurred the
displeasure of the king by their attitude, inasmuch as they were
not willing to do as the cantons of Lucerne, Glarus and other
places; if later they would do this they would doubtless receive

---

subjects as to yoke men and oxen to the plow together. Sweno, the
king's son, headed a rebellion, and Toko was among his retainers.
During the negotiations for a truce, Harald was walking in the forest,
and as he was behind a clump of bushes he was surprised by Toko,
who was still thirsting for revenge, and mortally wounded by an arrow.
Harald died soon after at Julin.

every favor from the king and his sons ; for the present they had better go home, since the king was overwhelmed with business, and they themselves would present the matter at a more convenient time." (ll. 1324-1335.)

From the beginning of 1306 comes the story of Baumgarten. " The king's bailiff in charge of the fortress Rossberg was riding one day to the monastery of Engelberg ; returning the following day, he saw working in a meadow (Matten) the wife of a blameless peasant, Konrad von Baumgarten, who dwelt (sass) at Alzellen, for Alzellen lies 'unter dem Wald' on the highway from Stanz to' Engelberg, on a height (Bühel) not far beyond Wolfenschiessen. The woman was very beautiful ; her beauty inflamed the bailiff to evil desires. * * * He demanded that she should prepare him a bath, for he claimed to be sweaty and weary from travel. The woman began to suspect mischief, and, longing from the bottom of her heart that her husband might soon return, she reluctantly prepared the bath. * * * She was terrified and distressed, for she saw that the bailiff intended to use violence, and * * * slipped quietly out of the back door to escape. At this moment her husband coming from the forest met her, and to him she told, weeping, what the tyrant had tried to do to her, and that he was even now in the bath. The goodman said : ' God be thanked, my dear wife, that he has guarded you and that you have saved your honor ! I will bless the bath for him.' * * * Therewith he entered the house quickly and with his ax struck the bailiff on the head so that he died at the first blow. And he fled directly to Uri, where he remained concealed, although not much pursuit was made because the official had been attempting such a shameful deed." (ll. 90-97.)

The episode of Melchthal comes from the annals of the year 1307. " There was an honest peasant in Unterwalden above the Kernwald (i. e. in Ob dem Wald) who was called Heinrich von Melchthal (ll. 562-64) and dwelt in this valley, a wise, sensible, honorable, well-to-do man and well thought of among the

peasants, who always took care that the privileges of the land
were not impaired, and that there should be no separation from
the Roman Empire. On this account Beringer von Landenberg, the governor over all Unterwalden, was hostile and angry
toward him. This Melchthal had fine oxen. On a slight pre-
text, because his son Arnold had committed some offense and
had thus subjected himself to a fine, the governor sent his servant to take his finest pair of oxen, and in case old Heinrich
von Melchthal should say anything against this, to tell him that
it was the governor's idea that the peasants should pull the
plow themselves, and thereupon to take the oxen and bring
them to him. Now when he was unyoking them, the peasant's
son Arnold, a young fellow, grew angry, and with a stick struck
the servant on the hand so heavily that one of his fingers was
broken. (ll. 466–482.) Straightway he fled from the canton
to Uri, where he remained concealed a long time at the house
of a kinsman. The servant suffered considerably from the blow
and complained to the governor. In anger the governor sent a
message to the father of the youth, in Melchthal, with an order
to take the latter prisoner. But as he was not found, having
left the country, the father so reported to the governor. The
latter summoned the old man with harsh words, and commanded him to produce his son Arnold directly. The goodman
himself did not know where his son was, and he saw besides
that his life would be in peril if he were present. He answered
that he honestly did not know whither he had gone ; for he had
run away from home immediately and had given no hint of
where he was going. Thereupon the governor had both eyes
of this honorable and aged man put out ; for the servant had
reported in his anger that he had declared that the governor
was taking his property unjustly. When the son Arnold heard
how it had fared with his good father he reported his woes to
intimate friends in Uri, hoping thereby to be able to avenge
the wrong done his father." (ll. 565–577.)

"At the same time Gessler, governor of Uri and Schwyz, oppressed the peasants in those cantons no less than Landenberg those of Unterwalden. He determined to build a stronghold in Uri so that he and other governors after him might live there the more safely, in case there should be rebellion, and that the canton might the more easily be kept in fear and obedience. Therefore he had brought to the hill (Bühel) of Solaturn near Altorf, the chief place, stone, lime, sand and timber, and began to get the structure under way, and when they asked him what the name of the stronghold would be, he said : ' Its name shall be Zwing Uri unter den Steg.' * * * (Act I, sc. 3.)

"And on St. James' Day he had a pole set up in Altorf in the square by the linden, where everybody had to go past, and on it put a hat and gave orders that every inhabitant of the canton, under penalty of confiscation of his property and personal punishment, should show honor and respect (Ehre und Reverenz) by bowing and removing his hat (Paret abziehen) as if the king, or the governor in his stead, were personally present. He always kept a watch and guardian beside it in the daytime to observe and report those who did not obey the order. He thought to gain great renown by oppressing severely this active, brave and respected people which had hitherto been highly esteemed by emperors, kings, princes and lords, and had never permitted itself to be forced by anyone. (Act I, sc. 3, and Act III, sc. 1.)

" In these days it came about that the governor, Gessler, proceeding from Uri to his castle at Küssnacht, was riding through the canton of Schwyz, of which also he was governor. Now there dwelt at Steinen, in Schwyz, a wise and honorable man of noble family (Wapens Genossen Geschlecht), Werner von Stauffach, son of the deceased Rudolf von Stauffach, once Landammann in Schwyz. This Werner had built a fine, new house at Steinen, on this side of the bridge. Now when the governor came to this house, and Stauffacher, who was standing before the house, received and welcomed him in a friendly manner as

his lord, the governor asked him whose house this was. He
knew this well ; for he had once made a threat to a third person
that he would take the house from him. Stauffacher noticed
well that he was not asking with good intention ; for he knew
that he was ill-disposed toward him because he had always op-
posed submitting to the princes of Austria, and desired to stand
by the Roman Empire and the old charters ; on this account
Stauffacher had a great following and was in high regard among
the country people. Therefore he answered the governor : ' Sir,
the house is my Lord the Emperor's and yours, and my fief.'
The governor said : ' I am Regent in the land in the stead of
my Lord the King. I do not wish that peasants build houses
without my consent, and do not wish that you live along thus
freely as if you were yourselves masters. I will seek to stop your
doing it (es euch zu wehren).' With this he rode on. This
speech troubled Stauffacher greatly and he took it to heart. Now
he was a reasonable and sensible man and had a wise and prudent
wife, who noticed that he was troubled, and that something lay
heavy on his soul which he was not revealing to her. Now she
would have liked to know what troubled him (im gebrest) and
she spoke of it so often that he told her what the governor had
said to him and that he expected nothing less than that the
governor would some time take from him, house, shelter and
possessions. When she heard this, she said : ' My dear husband (Ehewirth), you know that many a good countryman in
this canton complains of the governor's tyranny (sich ob des
Landvogts Wütherei beklagt). And I doubt not that the tyrant's
yoke oppresses many honest countrymen in Uri, and in Unterwalden also, as we hear daily of their complaints. Therefore it
would be good and useful that some of you who can trust one
another should secretly take counsel and consider how you may
escape from the arrogant power, and that you should promise to
stand by one another and protect one another in your rights.
Thus God will doubtless not desert you but help you to check

the injustice, if you call upon him heartily.' Then she asked
him whether in the cantons of Uri and Unterwalden he had
especial acquaintance with anyone to whom he could confide
and tell his distress, and with whom he could talk of these
things. He answered: ' Yes, I know there prominent leaders
(vornehme Herrenleute) who are especially in my confidence
(mir geheim) and to whom I can confide.'" (Act I, sc. 2.)

Stauffacher took the advice of his wife, went to Uri and met
there Fürst and Melchthal, with whom he planned the League of
the Forest Cantons. They agreed to initiate confederates each
in his own canton and to meet on the Rütli, below Selisberg,
and beside the Mythenstein (vor dem Mythenstein), which
stretches into the lake. (Act I, sc. 4.) In another place the
expression is " neben dem Mythenstein."

Of Duke Johann the historian tells how, while riding across the
fields with his uncle, the emperor, he " demanded that he give
him his paternal and maternal estates, or at least a part of them,
to rule, but received the answer: ' Cousin, why are you so
eager to rule? You are yet too young for that.' Thereupon
the emperor rode to a bush and broke off a branch, made a
wreath from it and placed it on his nephew's head, saying:
' This should give you more pleasure than ruling land and
people.' This remark cut the young duke to the heart, and he
was offended that the emperor let his sons rule, even over his
own estates. Weeping he complained of this to his advisers,
and asked them to vow to avenge this insult on the king. This
King Albrecht was a hard and treacherous man, and many
thought he intended to withhold from the young duke his estates altogether and give them to his own children of whom he
had many, and make him a bishop or an archbishop." (ll.
1336-1348.)

After telling briefly of the meeting of the confederates on the
Rütli, and the decision to destroy the castles and expel the
bailiffs on New Year's Day, Tschudi takes up the account of

Tell. "On Sunday, the 18th of November, a good honest
man of Uri, named Wilhelm Tell, who was also secretly in the
league, went past the hat several times without paying it due
respect as the governor had commanded. Notice of this was
given to the governor. The next day, Monday, he sends for
Tell and asks him haughtily why he refuses obedience to his
commands, by not showing respect to the hat, in contempt of
the king and himself. Tell answered : ' Dear sir, it was done
without design and not from contempt. Pardon me ! If I were
quick witted I should not bear the name of Tell (simpleton). I
beg your mercy ; it shall not happen again.' Now Tell was a
good crossbowman, and a better scarcely could be found ; moreover he had fair children whom he loved.   These the governor
sent for and said : ' Tell, which of the children is dearest to
you?' Tell answered : ' Sir, they are all alike dear.' Then
the governor said : ' Well, then, Tell ! You are a good and
famous archer, as I hear ; now you will have to prove your skill
before me and shoot an apple from the head of one of your
children. Therefore take good care to hit the apple, for if you
do not hit it at the first shot it will cost you your life.' Tell
was horrified and begged the governor for God's sake to excuse
him from the shot; for it was unnatural to shoot at his dear
child ; he would rather die. The governor said : ' You must
do it, or you and the child die.' Tell saw now that he would
have to do it, and prayed ardently to God that he would protect
him and his dear child. He took his crossbow, drew it and
put on the arrow, but stuck another one in behind his jacket.
The governor himself laid the apple on the head of the child
who was not more than six years old. So Tell shot the apple
from the crown of his head without harming him. Now when
the shot was done, the governor marveled at it as a master
shot and praised Tell for his skill. Then he asked him what it
meant that he had put a second arrow into his jerkin. Tell
was dismayed, and thought that the question boded no good,

yet he would gladly have settled the affair without trouble, and
said that this was a hunter's custom. The governor saw that
Tell was evading him and said: 'Tell, now tell me frankly
(frölich) and do not be afraid; you shall be sure of your life;
for I will not accept the answer you have given; it must have
meant something else.' Then spoke Wilhelm Tell: 'Well,
sir, since you have assured me of my life I will tell you the
truth thoroughly (gründlich), that my final purpose was this,
that if I had hit my child I should have shot you with the
second arrow, and doubtless I should not have missed you.'
When the governor heard this he said: 'Very well, Tell, I
have assured you of your life (dich dins Lebens gesichert) and
that I will keep. But because I have learned your evil purpose
toward me, I will have you taken to a place and locked up
there so that you shall never again see sun or moon, that I may
be safe from you.' Herewith he bade his servants take him
prisoner and bring him bound directly to Flüelen. (Act III, sc.
3.) And he went with them and took along Tell's weapons,
his quiver, arrows and crossbow, intending to keep them for
himself. Thereupon the governor took ship along with his servants and with Tell bound, purposing to sail to Brunnen and
then bring Tell over land through Schwyz to his castle at
Küssnacht and there cause him to end his life in a gloomy
tower; Tell's bow and quiver lay in the stern of the ship near
the rudder. Now, when they had gone forth upon the lake and had
sailed as far as the Axen, God ordained it that a cruel, violent
storm arose so that they all prepared to perish miserably. Now
Tell was a strong man and well acquainted with the water. So
one of the servants said to the governor: 'Sir, you see your
and our distress, and the mortal peril we are in, and that the
shipmasters are terrified and not well posted (bericht) in sailing; but here is Tell, a strong man who can steer well. We
ought now to use him in our need.' The governor was fright-
ened by the danger of drowning and said to Tell: 'If you will

undertake (getruwtist) to save us out of this danger, I would
free you from your bonds.' Tell gave answer: 'Yes, sir, I
will undertake to help us out of this (hiedannen).' So he was
released, took his place at the rudder and steered skillfully
(redlich, probably with this older meaning in Tschudi) along,
but kept looking at the bow which lay near him, and for an
opportunity to spring off. And when he came to a ledge, which
has since kept the name of Tellsplatte, and a chapel is built
beside it, it seemed to him that he could there leap from the
boat and escape. So he shouted to the rowers to row vigorously
(hantlich zugind, a verb which Schiller took for zugingen, instead of the preterit of ziehen) till they should be past this
ledge, when they would have escaped the worst. And as he
came beside this ledge, being a powerful man, he crowded the
stern with force against the ledge, seized his weapons, sprang out
upon the ledge, thrust the vessel back with violence, and left it
to rock and drift upon the waves. (Act IV, sc. 1.) But Tell
ran up the mountain toward the north, for as yet no snow had
fallen, past Morschach, through the canton of Schwyz to the
highest point on the highway between Arth and Küssnacht
where is a sunken road (hohle Gasse) with bushes overshadow-
ing it. There he concealed himself; for he knew that the
governor would ride by there to his castle at Küssnacht. The
governor and his servants with great difficulty got as far on the
lake as Brunnen. They then rode through the land of Schwyz,
and as they came near the above-mentioned sunken road he
(Tell) heard all manner of devices of the governor against him ;
but he had his crossbow strung, and with an arrow shot the
governor through so that he fell from his horse and died on the
spot. Thereupon Tell hastened back, as night was approaching.
(Act IV, sc. 3.) He notified Stauffacher, in passing, of the
whole affair, how it had occurred, and then went forward by
night to Brunnen, where he was hastily brought in a boat to
Uri by one who was secretly in the conspiracy ; it was still

night when he arrived, as at that time the nights are longest. He kept himself hidden, but informed Walther Fürst and other confederates that he had shot the governor. And this was secretly reported to the confederates in Unterwalden. At the place above the Hohle Gasse where Wilhelm Tell shot the governor a chapel was afterwards built, which still stands. The authorities at that time took no steps in the matter because the king was just then in Lower Austria, and waited until he could appoint a new governor."

Portions of the account of the taking of the castle and of the assassination of the emperor here follow.

" In the fortress of Rossberg, which stood on a high mountain below the Kernwald, was a maid, the sweetheart of a man of Stanz, who was also in the league. He agreed to visit her on New Year's eve, and she was to draw him up by a rope to a window which he pointed out. The man climbed thus into the castle, and then one after another of the confederates drew himself up till all were in the castle. (Cp. ll. 1413-17.) * * Now the governor, Landenberg, who dwelt in the castle of Sarnen above the wood, had forcibly accustomed the people to bring him presents at New Year's. So fifty of those that were in the league had agreed that thirty of their number should hide themselves before dawn, well armed, in the alders below the mill; the others were to procure staves and fit spearheads to them : every one was to carry such sharp irons beneath his blouse, and so bring the New Year's presents into the castle, for no arms were allowed there. But when they were all in, one on the hill in front was to blow a horn, whereupon the twenty would quickly put the spearheads on their staves and try to keep the gate open by force, while those in the alders were to hasten to the aid of the others as soon as they heard the horn blown. (Cp. ll. 1400– 1412.) This was done, and the castle was razed to the ground ; Rossberg was destroyed in like manner. When the governor with his attendants in the church heard this, they attempted to

flee over the mountains ; but as the snow prevented this, they
fled along the mountains by the way of Alpnach to Lucerne.
They were seen, indeed, but allowed to go unharmed as had
been agreed. (Cp. l. 2902.)

"At the same time those of Uri also freed their land and destroyed the half-finished fortress which the tyrant Gessler intended to name Zwing Uri unter die Stegen, and all swore together, nobles and commons, to help and protect one another.
(Act. V, sc. 1.)   All this took place on New Year's Day, 1308,
a Monday, as had been previously agreed.   The following Sunday each land sent honorable messengers to the others and they
swore the league for ten years to help and protect one another,
with all the points which in the beginning Walther Fürst of Uri,
Werner Stauffacher of Schwyz and Arnold von Melchthal had
sworn."

After telling the curious tale of the knight and the hornets
(see text, lines 2668–74) Tschudi proceeds to the account of
Duke Johann. "So on the before-mentioned May evening he
appealed again to the king : Would he not turn over to him his
paternal and maternal inheritance of land and people, which
belonged to him, as he wished to rule henceforth for himself.
The king answered him : ' The time will probably come,' and
gave him no further satisfaction.   This speech and arrogant
answer pained Duke Johann, and he reported it weeping to his
advisers.   The next morning, May Day, the king rode out from
Baden to visit his consort, Queen Elsbeth, whom he had left at
Rheinfelden.   When he came to the ferry at Windisch, Duke
Johann of Austria and the four mentioned : Wart, Eschenbach,
Palm and Tegerfelden, purposely kept together, and managed
so that they were the first to cross over the waters of the Reuss ;
the rest of the retinue came slowly after.   And as the king was
riding among the grain-fields between Windisch and Brugg,
speaking with Walther von Casteln and suspecting no ill, he was
assailed by his cousin Duke Johann and his accomplices.   Duke

Johann stabbed the king in the throat, exclaiming : ' You dog,
I shall now pay you for the insult you gave me, and see whether
I may get my inheritance.' Walther von Eschenbach split the
king's head, and Rudolf von Palm ran him through. So the
king lost his life because of his great avarice and niggardliness,
slain by his own, in and upon his own, in the county of Habsburg, on his own inheritance, the territory of his family and his
name. And by chance as the deed was done a poor girl was at
hand ; she took the king in her arms as he fell from his horse,
and he passed away in her lap. (Cp. ll. 2954–87.) And when
Duke Johann and his accomplices had finished the deed they all
fled away, each whither he might ; Duke Johann rode by hidden
.paths through the territory of Zug and by night reached the
monastery of Einsiedeln, where no one knew him, and remained
there several days. (Cp. ll. 3006–10.) When King Albrecht
was slain there was everywhere great uneasiness ; the whole
country was in fear — they anticipated great disturbances, and yet
the country had more repose than had been expected, almost
more than before. (Cp. l. 2990.) As soon as the news of the
king's death was spread in the land, the cities and fortresses in
all the cantons were fortified, the gates kept well locked at night
and guarded by soldiers. The gates of Zurich had been open
for thirty years, so that they had been locked neither by day
nor night, though they had had enemies during this time ; but
now they had them locked so that no one of those who were
guilty of the murder might take refuge in their city. (Cp. ll.
2991–95.) The representatives of the Forest Cantons, in re-
sponse to the queen's appeal for aid in punishing the murderers,
promised to take no advantage of this opportunity to avenge
their own wrongs, but as for helping to avenge the king's death,
from whom they never received any benefit, and pursuing the
murderers who had done them no harm, they deemed it unbe-
coming to them. Duke Johann and the perpetrators of the
deed actually applied to the Forest Cantons for aid and protec-

tion, but it was refused them, as the people did not wish to become involved in the affair." (Cp. ll. 3040-76.)

THE POLITICAL SITUATION.

The political situation in the Forest Cantons, as assumed at the beginning of the play, is this : The Cantons are immediate dependencies of the Empire, and are so treated by the emperor (king). But the house of Habsburg, hereditary dukes of Austria, whose representative is also at present emperor by election, claims the Cantons as feudal dependencies. The emperor is harrying the Cantons by sending cruel governors to represent him, hoping thus to drive them to seek the protection of some powerful hereditary family and make themselves thus mediate vassals of the empire. As representative of the Austrian house of Habsburg, he expects to offer this protection against himself as emperor, and thus to secure the Cantons as permanent dependencies of his own family, which will always be rulers of Austria, but may at any time be supplanted in the office of emperor. The same conditions make it the policy of the cantons to cling tenaciously to the Empire.

SPECIMENS OF SCHILLER'S NOTES FOR "TELL."

From Müller.

Die Heerde fährt zu Berg (l. 17). — Meister Hirt (l. 1774).

Hohes Joch der Berge, mit ewigem Eis, goldroth von der Sonne beschienen, wenn schwarze Nacht die Thäler bedeckt. NB. Mit dieser Erscheinung kann sich der Akt wo man im Rütli ist, endigen (ll. 1439-43).

Der Volksstamm kommt aus Norden, wo eine Theuerung ihn auszuwandern zwang (ll. 1167 ff). NB. Kann im Rütli erzählt werden.

Obmann, Schiedsrichter (l. 701).

From Fäsi.

Die mittleren Theile der Berge haben kurze Kräuter, diess die kräftigsten. Ende Junis fahren die Sennen auf diese höheren Alpen. Dort die Sennhütten. Um S. Bartholomä ziehen sie ab (ll. 13-24).

Anblick von oben wenn man über den Wolken steht. Die Gegend scheint wie ein grosser See vor einem zu liegen. Inseln ragen daraus hervor : öfnen sich die Wolken irgendwo, so kann man ins Menschen bewohnte Thal auf Häuser und Kirchen hinabsehen (ll. 31-36).

Bergquellen (l. 1016).

Lämmergeier (l. 1000).

Tells Blatten oder Tells Sprung. Das Felsenstück hängt an der Seite des grossen Axenbergs eine starke Stunde unter Flüelen. Vor der Platten sind einige Felsenschiefer, wo die Schiffe länden können. Die ganze Ebene der Blatte hält 18 quadrat Schuh. Hinter der Blatten steigt der Axenberg hoch in die Wolken (ll. 2227-70).

From Scheuchzer.

Vorboten des Regens. Schwalben fliegen niedrig, Wasservögel tauchen unter, Schafe fressen begierig Grass, Hunde scharren die Erde auf, Fische springen aus dem Wasser heraus.— der graue Thalvogt kommt — wenn der oder der Berg eine Kappe auf hat, so wirf die Sense hin und nimm den Rechen. Der Firn brüllt, die Gemsen lassen sich in die Tiefe herab (ll. 37-45).

These specimens are from the Introduction to the edition of "Wilhelm Tell" in Vol. 14 of the Historisch-kritische Ausgabe edited by Gödeke.

CHRONOLOGY.

DATES OF AUTHENTIC SWISS HISTORY.

Alamannic invasion. . . . 264

Alamannic dominion . . . 406

Burgundian conquest of West
    Switzerland 443

Franks conquer Alamannic
    Switzerland 496

Franks conquer Burgundian
    Switzerland 534

Uri dependency of the mon-
    astery of Zürich, before . 853

Uri combined with Zürich into
    an Imperial Prefecture, un-
    der the Lords of Zähringen 1098

Schwyz a community of free-
    men under the protection
    of the Counts of Habsburg,
    before 1100

Unterwalden, under the mon-
    astery of Engelberg . . . 1120

Freiburg founded 1177

Bern founded. 1191

Unterwalden, under Counts
    of Habsburg 1200

Schwyz in contention with the
    monastery of Einsiedeln,
    1114, 1144, and 1217

Bern, Zurich, Solothurn, and
    other cities become 'reichs-
    frei,' soon after 1218

Uri made an immediate de-
    pendency of the empire
    (reichsunmittelbar) . . . 1231

Schwyz made 'reichsfrei' by
    Friedrich II, not recognized
    however by the Habsburgs . 1240

Schwyz rebels against the
    Habsburgs, and is subdued,
    losing its independence, 1245–50

Unterwalden (Obwalden) re-
    bels 1245–50

Rudolph, d. 1291, refuses to
    recognize the charters of the
    Forest Cantons 1291

Uri takes part in forming the
    League 1291

Unterwalden helps form (or
    renew) League 1291

Schwyz joins Uri and Unter-
    walden in League . . . 1291

Albrecht I, d. . . . May 1, 1308

Heinrich VII confirms charters
    of the Forest Cantons . . 1309

Battle of Morgarten, defeat of
    Leopold and of the Habs-
    burg claims to the Forest
    Cantons . . . Nov. 15, 1315

Renewal of the League of the
    Forest Cantons, at Brunnen, 1315

Luzern joins the League . . 1332

Zurich joins the League . . 1351

Glarus and Zug join the
    League 1352

Bern joins the League . . . 1353

Battle of Sempach 1386

Battle of Näfels 1388
Independence of Switzerland
  recognized by Austria . . 1394

Switzerland an independent
  country 1499
Switzerland, recognized as such
  in the Treaty of Westphalia, 1648

DATES ACCORDING TO LEGENDARY HISTORY (TSCHUDI).

Earlier dates not essentially different from accepted dates, save as to the migration from Sweden.

Forest Cantons 'reichsfrei,' governed by bailiffs not residing in the cantons . . 1301
Embassies to Albrecht to protest against the tyranny of the bailiffs 1304
Gessler and Landenberg appointed Governors . . . 1304
Embassies to complain of these 1305
Wolfenschiessen's offense. . 1306
Herzog Johann's vain request for his estates 1306
Blinding of Heinrich von der Halden, early in 1307
Gessler builds the fortress in Altorf 1307
Gessler sets up hat, July 25th.
Gessler threatens Stauffacher, soon after.

Compact of the Three Leaders, early in the autumn . . . 1307
Meeting on the Rütli, November 7th–8th.
Tell's contempt of the hat, November 18th.
The apple-shooting, November 19th.
Gessler's death, November 19th.
Capture of Rossberg, Sarnen, Lowerz, Zwing Uri, January 1st, ... 1308
The adventure of the knight with the hornets, April 28th.
Herzog Johann's last appeal, April 30th.
Murder of Albrecht I, May 1st.
Tell takes part at Morgarten . 1315
Tell drowned in the Schächen, 1354

TIME AND DATES ACCORDING TO THE PLAY.

Act I,   Scene 1, afternoon, October 28th.

Scene 2, same afternoon.

Scene 3, probably the same afternoon, though if the distance from Steinen to Altorf is considered, it may be the following day.

Scene 4, same day as preceding.

Act II,   Scene 1, morning, no lapse of time indicated.

Scene 2, some days must intervene after Act I, Scene 4, to allow for Melchthal's trip; it is the traditional 8th of November.

Act III, Scene 1, probably afternoon, the traditional 18th of November; some time must have elapsed since Hedwig has had time to hear rumors of the Rütli meeting.

Scene 2, the same day, time of day not indicated.

Scene 3, same day, probably afternoon.

Act IV, Scene 1, same day as Act III, Scene 3.

Scene 2, no indication of time, but presumably the same day as Scene 1.

Scene 3, same day as Scene 1, though if the distance is considered the events might have occurred on the following day.

Act V,   Scene 1, the next or the second day after Act IV, Scene 3; the distances, the deeds accomplished, and the spread of the news, would take in reason two days; if the murder of the emperor were taken into account, it would be May 1st, 1308, or a few days later.

Scene 2, same day, no time of day indicated.

Scene 3, same day, no time of day indicated.

LIST OF PERSONS.

Appearances are given by act and scene; references by lines.

Agnes, der Ungarn Königin, daughter of the emperor Albrecht, Ref., l. 2997ff.

Albrecht (I), king (emperor) of Germany. Ref., l. 2943ff. (Other references are to the office merely and are not enumerated.)

Armgard, poor peasant woman, appears, IV, 3.

Arnold von Sewa, citizen of Unterwalden, appears, II, 2.

Attinghausen, Werner, Freiherr von, a native noble of Uri, appears, II, 1; IV, 2. Ref., ll. 52, 337, 542, 2114.

Ausrufer, herald, appears, I, 3.

Barmherzigen Brüder, Die, appear, IV, 3.

Baumgarten, Konrad, citizen of Alzellen in Unterwalden, appears, I, 1; I, 2; II, 2; IV, 2; V, 1. Ref., ll. 549ff, 717 (der Alzeller), 1525 (der Unterwaldner).

Bertha von Bruneck, Austrian noblewoman, in Gessler's suite, appears, I, 3; III, 2; III, 3; V, 3. Ref., ll. 936, 2525, 2880ff.

Burkhardt am Bühel, citizen of Unterwalden, appears, II, 2.

Diethelm, Gessler's squire, Ref., l. 2879.

Elsbeth, peasant woman, appears, III, 3.

Elsbeth, Königin, wife of emperor Albrecht, Ref., l. 3033ff.

Eschenbach, Herr von, an accomplice of Johannes Parricida, Ref., l. 2960.

Friesshardt, a soldier of Gessler, guardian of the hat, appears, III, 3; IV, 3.

Fronvogt, appears, I, 3.

Fürst, Walther, citizen of Uri, father-in-law of Tell, appears, I, 4; II, 2; III, 3; IV, 2; V, 1; V, 3. Ref., l. 334ff.

Gessler, Hermann, Landvogt in Uri and Schwyz, appears, III, 3; IV, 3. Ref., ll. 220ff, 355, 396, 1428, 1540, 1555ff, 1610, 2173, 2224ff, 2560ff.

Hans auf der Mauer, citizen of Schwyz, appears, II, 2.

Hans, Herzog, see Johannes Parricida.

Hedwig, wife of Tell, appears, III, 1; IV, 2; V, 2.

Heinrich von der Halden, citizen of Unterwalden, father of Arnold vom Melchthal. Ref., ll. 462ff, 561ff, 744, 988.

Hildegard, peasant woman, appears III, 3.

Iberg, father of Gertrud Stauffacher, Ref., ll. 240ff, 517.

Jenni, Fischerknabe, son of Ruodi, appears, I, 1; IV, 1.

Johannes Parricida, duke of Suabia, nephew of emperor Albrecht, appears, V, 2. Ref., ll. 1337 (Herzog Hans), 2951ff.

Jörg im Hofe, citizen of Schwyz, appears, II, 2.

Jost von Weiler, citizen of Schwyz, appears, II, 2.

Kaiser (König) Der, see Albrecht I.

Klaus von der Flüe, citizen of Unterwalden, appears, II, 2.

Klostermeier von Mörlischachen, Ref., l. 2651.

Konrad Hunn, citizen of Schwyz, appears, II, 2.

Kunz von Gersau, appears, IV, 1.

Kuoni der Hirte, citizen of Uri, appears, I, 1; II, 1; II, 2; V, 1.

Landenberg, Berengar von, Landvogt in Unterwalden. Ref., ll. 170, 282, 486ff, 1963, 2902.

Leopold, Herzog von Oesterreich, Ref., ll. 2967, 3200.

Leuthold, soldier of Gessler, guardian of the hat, appears, III, 3.

Luxemburg, Graf von (Emperor Heinrich VII), Ref., l. 3023.

Mechthild, peasant woman, appears, III, 3.

Meier von Sarnen, citizen of Unterwalden, appears, II, 2.

Melchthal Arnold vom, citizen of Unterwalden, appears, I, 4; II, 2; III, 3; IV, 2; V, 1. Ref., l. 565ff.

Müller, Johannes von, Ref., l. 2-948.

Palm, Herr von, accomplice of Johannes Parricida, Ref., l. 2-961.

Petermann der Sigrist, citizen of Uri, appears, II, 2; III, 3; V, 1. Ref., l. 1749.

Pfeifer von Luzern, appears, I, 2.

Reding, Itel, citizen of Schwyz, appears, II, 2.

Rösselmann der Pfarrer, of Uri, appears, II, 2; III, 3; V, 1. Ref., l. 1746.

Rudenz, Ulrich von, a Swiss noble, nephew of Attinghausen, appears, II, 1; III, 2; III, 3; IV, 2; V, 3. Ref., ll. 2373ff, 2873.

Rudolph, emperor, Ref., ll. 3049, 3192, 3263.

Rudolph der Harras, Gessler's master of the horse, appears, III, 3; IV, 3. Ref., l. 2224.

Ruodi der Fischer, citizen of Uri, appears, I, 1; II, 2; IV, 1; V, 1.

Seppi, attendant of Kuoni, appears, I, 1.

Sillinen, Herr von, a native noble of Uri, Ref., l. 685.

Stauffacher, Gertrud, wife of Werner, appears, I, 2. Ref., l. 516ff.

Stauffacher, Werner, citizen of Steinen in Schwyz, appears, I, 2; I, 3; I, 4; II, 2; III, 3; IV, 2; V, 1; V, 3. Ref., ll. 351, 982.

Steinmetz, mason, appears, I, 3; V, 1.

Stier von Uri, der, appears, V, 1.

Stüssi der Flurschütz, appears, IV, 3.

Tegerfeld, Herr von, accomplice of Johannes Parricida, Ref., l. 1339; 2961.

Tell, Wilhelm, citizen of Bürglen in Uri, appears, I, 1; I, 2; I, 3; III, 1; III, 3; IV, 1; IV, 3; V, 2; V, 3. Ref., ll. 555, 1434, 2100, 2316ff, 3082.

Ulrich, see Rudenz.

Ulrich, der Schmid, citizen of Schwyz, appears, II, 2.

Walther, Tell's son, appears, III, 1; III, 3; IV, 2; V, 2; V, 3.

Wandrer, traveler, appears, IV, 3.

Wart, Herr von der, accomplice of Johannes Parricida, Ref., ll. 1339, 2961.

Werni der Alpenjäger, citizen of Uri, appears, I, 1; II, 2; V, 1.

Wilhelm, Tell's son, appears, III, 1; V, 2; V, 3.

Winkelried, Struth von, citizen of Unterwalden, appears, II, 2.

Wolfenschiessen der, Burgvogt at Rossberg in Unterwalden, Ref., ll. 77, 546, 945.

Wilhelm Tell

Schauspiel

von

Schiller

Zum Neujahrsgeschenk auf 1805

————◆————

Tübingen

in der J. G. Cotta'schen Buchhandlung

1804

Personen.

Hermann Geßler, Reichsvogt in Schwyz und Uri.
Werner, Freiherr von Attinghausen, Bannerherr.
Ulrich von Rudenz, sein Neffe.

Werner Stauffacher,
Konrad Hunn,
Itel Reding,
Hans auf der Mauer, } Landleute aus Schwyz.
Jörg im Hofe,
Ulrich der Schmid,
Jost von Weiler,

Walther Fürst,
Wilhelm Tell,
Rösselmann, der Pfarrer,
Petermann, der Sigrist, } aus Uri.
Kuoni, der Hirte,
Werni, der Jäger,
Ruodi, der Fischer,

Arnold vom Melchthal,
Konrad Baumgarten,
Meier von Sarnen,
Struth von Winkelried, } aus Unterwalden.
Klaus von der Flüe,
Burkhardt am Bühel,
Arnold von Sewa,

Pfeifer von Luzern.
Kunz von Gersau.
Jenni, Fischerknabe.
Seppi, Hirtenknabe.
Gertrud, Stauffachers Gattin.
Hedwig, Tells Gattin, Fürsts Tochter.
Bertha von Bruneck, eine reiche Erbin.
Armgard,
Mechthild, } Bäuerinnen.
Elsbeth,
Hildegard,
Walther, } Tells Knaben.
Wilhelm,
Frießhardt, } Söldner.
Leuthold,
Rudolf der Harras, Geßlers Stallmeister.
Johannes Parricida, Herzog von Schwaben.
Stüßi, der Flurschütz.
Der Stier von Uri.
Ein Reichsbote.
Fronvogt.
Meister Steinmetz, Gesellen und Handlanger.
Öffentliche Ausrufer.
Barmherzige Brüder.
Geßlerische und Landenbergische Reiter.
Viele Landleute, Männer und Weiber aus den Waldstätten.

3

Erster Aufzug.

Erste Szene.

Hohes Felsenufer des Vierwaldstättensees, Schwyz gegenüber.

Der See macht eine Bucht ins Land, eine Hütte ist unweit dem Ufer; Fischer-
knabe fährt sich in einem Kahn. Über den See hinweg sieht man die grünen
Matten, Dörfer und Höfe von Schwyz im hellen Sonnenschein liegen. Zur
Linken des Zuschauers zeigen sich die Spitzen des Haken, mit Wolken umgeben;
zur Rechten im fernen Hintergrund sieht man die Eisgebirge. Noch ehe der
Vorhang aufgeht, hört man den Kuhreihen und das harmonische Geläut der
Herdenglocken, welches sich auch bei eröffneter Szene noch eine Zeitlang fortsetzt.

Fischerknabe, singt im Kahn.
Melodie des Kuhreihens.

Es lächelt der See, er ladet zum Bade,
Der Knabe schlief ein am grünen Gestade,
Da hört er ein Klingen,
Wie Flöten so süß,
5   Wie Stimmen der Engel
Im Paradies.
Und wie er erwachet in seliger Lust,
Da spülen die Wasser ihm um die Brust,
Und es ruft aus den Tiefen:
10   Lieb Knabe, bist mein;
Ich locke den Schläfer,
Ich zieh' ihn herein.

Hirte, auf dem Berge.
Variation des Kuhreihens.

Ihr Matten, lebt wohl!
Ihr sonnigen Weiden!
15   Der Senne muß scheiden,
Der Sommer ist hin.

Wir fahren zu Berg, wir kommen wieder,
Wenn der Kuckuck ruft, wenn erwachen die Lieder,
Wenn mit Blumen die Erde sich kleidet neu,
20　Wenn die Brünnlein fließen im lieblichen Mai.
　　　　Ihr Matten, lebt wohl!
　　　　Ihr sonnigen Weiden!
　　　　Der Senne muß scheiden,
　　　　Der Sommer ist hin.

Alpenjäger

erscheint gegenüber auf der Höhe des Felsen.

zweite Variation.

25　Es donnern die Höhen, es zittert der Steg,
　Nicht grauet dem Schützen auf schwindlichtem Weg.
　　　　Er schreitet verwegen
　　　　Auf Feldern von Eis,
　　　　Da pranget kein Frühling,
30　　　Da grünet kein Reis;
　Und unter den Füßen ein neblichtes Meer,
　Erkennt er die Städte der Menschen nicht mehr;
　　　　Durch den Riß nur der Wolken
　　　　Erblickt er die Welt,
35　　　Tief unter den Wassern
　　　　Das grünende Feld.

Die Landschaft verändert sich; man hört ein dumpfes Krachen von den Bergen;
Schatten von Wolken laufen über die Gegend.

Ruodi, der Fischer, kommt aus der Hütte. Werni, der Jäger, steigt
vom Felsen. Kuoni, der Hirt, kommt mit dem Mellnapf auf der Schulter;
Seppi, sein Handbube, folgt ihm.

Ruodi

Mach' hurtig, Jenni. Zieh' die Naue ein.
Der graue Thalvogt kommt, dumpf brüllt der Firn;

Der Mythenstein zieht seine Haube an,
40 Und kalt her bläst es aus dem Wetterloch;
Der Sturm, ich mein', wird da sein, eh' wir's denken.

Kuoni

's kommt Regen, Fährmann. Meine Schafe fressen
Mit Begierde Gras, und Wächter scharrt die Erde.

Werni

Die Fische springen, und das Wasserhuhn
45 Taucht unter. Ein Gewitter ist im Anzug.

Kuoni, zum Buben.

Lug', Seppi, ob das Vieh sich nicht verlaufen.

Seppi

Die braune Lisel kenn' ich am Geläut.

Kuoni

So fehlt uns keine mehr, die geht am weitsten.

Ruodi

Ihr habt ein schön Geläute, Meister Hirt.

Werni

50 Und schmuckes Vieh; ist's euer eignes, Landsmann?

Kuoni

Bin nit so reich; 's ist meines gnäd'gen Herrn,
Des Attinghäusers, und mir zugezählt.

Ruodi

Wie schön der Kuh das Band zu Halse steht.

Kuoni

Das weiß sie auch, daß sie den Reihen führt,
55 Und, nähm' ich ihr's, sie hörte auf zu fressen.

Ruodi

Ihr seid nicht klug; ein unvernünft'ges Vieh —

Werni

Ist bald gesagt. Das Tier hat auch Vernunft;
Das wissen **wir**, die wir die Gemsen jagen.
Die stellen klug, **wo** sie zur Weide gehn,
60 'ne Vorhut aus, **die** spitzt **das** Ohr und **warnet**
Mit heller Pfeife, wenn der Jäger naht.

Ruodi, zum Hirten.

Treibt ihr jetzt heim?

Kuoni

       Die Alp ist abgeweidet.

Werni

Glücksel'ge Heimkehr, Senn'!

Kuoni

          Die wünsch' ich euch;
Von eurer Fahrt kehrt sich's nicht immer wieder.

Ruodi

65 Dort kommt ein Mann in voller Hast gelaufen.

Werni

Ich kenn' ihn, 's ist der Baumgart von Alzellen.

Konrad **Baumgarten**, atemlos hereinstürzend.

Baumgarten

Um Gottes willen, Fährmann, euren Kahn!

Ruodi

Nun, nun, was giebt's so eilig?

Baumgarten

          Bindet los!
Ihr rettet mich vom Tode. Setzt mich **über**!

Kuoni

70 Landsmann, was habt ihr?

Werni

Wer verfolgt euch denn?

Baumgarten, zum Fischer.

Eilt, eilt, sie sind mir dicht schon an den Fersen.
Des Landvogts Reiter kommen hinter mir.
Ich bin ein Mann des Tods, wenn sie mich greifen.

Ruodi

Warum verfolgen euch die Reisigen?

Baumgarten

75 Erst rettet mich, und dann steh' ich euch Rede.

Werni

Ihr seid mit Blut befleckt; was hat's gegeben?

Baumgarten

Des Kaisers Burgvogt, der auf Roßberg saß —

Kuoni

Der Wolfenschießen? Läßt euch der verfolgen?

Baumgarten

Der schadet nicht mehr; ich hab' ihn erschlagen.

Alle, fahren zurück,

80 Gott sei euch gnädig! Was habt ihr gethan?

Baumgarten

Was jeder freie Mann an meinem Platz, —
Mein gutes Hausrecht hab' ich ausgeübt
Am Schänder meiner Ehr' und meines Weibes.

Kuoni

Hat euch der Burgvogt an der Ehr' geschädigt?

Baumgarten

85 Daß er sein bös Gelüsten nicht vollbracht,
Hat Gott und meine gute Art verhütet.

Werni

Ihr habt ihm mit der Art den Kopf zerspalten?

Kuoni

O laßt uns alles hören; ihr habt Zeit,
Bis er den Kahn vom Ufer losgebunden.

Baumgarten

90 Ich hatte Holz gefällt im Wald; da kommt
Mein Weib gelaufen in der Angst des Todes:
„Der Burgvogt lieg' in meinem Haus; er hab'
Ihr anbefohlen, ihm ein Bad zu rüsten.
Drauf hab' er Ungebührliches von ihr
95 Verlangt; sie sei entsprungen, mich zu suchen."
Da lief ich frisch hinzu, so wie ich war,
Und mit der Art hab' ich ihm 's Bad gesegnet.

Werni

Ihr thatet wohl; kein Mensch kann euch drum schelten.

Kuoni

Der Wüterich! Der hat nun seinen Lohn
100 Hat 's lang verdient ums Volk von Unterwalden.

Baumgarten

Die That ward ruchtbar; mir wird nachgesetzt.
Indem wir sprechen, Gott! verrinnt die Zeit.

Es fängt an zu donnern.

Kuoni

Frisch, Fährmann, schaff' den Biedermann hinüber.

Ruodi

Geht nicht. Ein schweres Ungewitter ist
105 Im Anzug. Ihr müßt warten.

Baumgarten

Heil'ger Gott!
Ich kann nicht warten. Jeder Aufschub tötet.

Kuoni, zum Fischer.

Greif' an mit Gott! Dem Nächsten muß man helfen.
Es kann uns allen Gleiches ja begegnen.

Brausen und Donnern.

Ruodi

Der Föhn ist los; ihr seht, wie hoch der See geht;
110 Ich kann nicht steuern gegen Sturm und Wellen.

Baumgarten, umfaßt seine Kniee.

So helf' euch Gott, wie ihr euch mein erbarmet.

Werni

Es geht uns Leben. Sei barmherzig, Fährmann.

Kuoni

's ist ein Hausvater und hat Weib und Kinder.

Wiederholte Donnerschläge.

Ruodi

Was! Ich hab' auch ein Leben zu verlieren,
115 Hab' Weib und Kind daheim, wie er. Seht hin,
Wie's brandet, wie es wogt und Wirbel zieht,
Und alle Wasser aufrührt in der Tiefe.
Ich wollte gern den Biedermann erretten;
Doch es ist rein unmöglich, ihr seht selbst.

Baumgarten, noch auf den Knieen.

120 So muß ich fallen in des Feindes Hand,
Das nahe Rettungsufer im Gesichte.

Dort liegt's, ich kann's erreichen mit den Augen;
Hinüberdringen kann der Stimme Schall;
Da ist der Kahn, der mich hinübertrüge,
125 Und muß hier liegen, hilflos, und verzagen.

Kuoni

Seht, wer da kommt.

Werni

Es ist der Tell aus Bürglen.

Tell mit der Armbrust.

Tell

Wer ist der Mann, der hier um Hilfe fleht?

Kuoni

's ist ein Alzeller Mann; er hat sein' Ehr'
Verteidigt und den Wolfenschieß erschlagen,
130 Des Königs Burgvogt, der auf Roßberg saß;
Des Landvogts Reiter sind ihm auf den Fersen;
Er fleht den Schiffer um die Überfahrt;
Der fürcht't sich vor dem Sturm und will nicht fahren.

Ruodi

Da ist der Tell, er führt das Ruder auch,
135 Der soll mir's zeugen, ob die Fahrt zu wagen.

Tell

Wo's not thut, Fährmann, läßt sich alles wagen.

Heftige Donnerschläge; der See rauscht auf.

Ruodi

Ich soll mich in den Höllenrachen stürzen?
Das thäte keiner, der bei Sinnen ist.

Tell

Der brave Mann denkt an sich selbst zuletzt;
140 Vertrau' auf Gott und rette den Bedrängten.

Ruodi

Vom sichern Port läßt sich's gemächlich raten.
Da ist der Kahn und dort der See. Versucht's.

Tell

Der See kann sich, der Landvogt nicht erbarmen.
Versuch' es, Fährmann.

Hirten und Jäger

Rett' ihn! Rett' ihn! Rett' ihn!

Ruodi

145 Und wär's mein Bruder und mein leiblich Kind,
Es kann nicht sein; 's ist heut Simons und Judä;
Da rast der See und will sein Opfer haben.

Tell

Mit eitler Rede wird hier nichts geschafft;
Die Stunde dringt, dem Mann muß Hilfe werden.
150 Sprich, Fährmann, willst du fahren?

Ruodi

Nein, nicht ich!

Tell

In Gottes Namen, denn, gieb her den Kahn;
Ich will's mit meiner schwachen Kraft versuchen.

Kuoni

Ha, wackrer Tell!

Werni

Das gleicht dem Weidgesellen.

Baumgarten

Mein Retter seid ihr und mein Engel, Tell.

Tell

155 Wohl aus des Vogts Gewalt errett' ich euch;
Aus Sturmes Nöten muß ein andrer helfen.

Doch beſſer iſt's, ihr fallt in Gottes Hand,
Als in der Menſchen. Zu dem Hirten: Landsmann, tröſtet ihr
Mein Weib, wenn mir was Menſchliches begegnet;
160 Ich hab' gethan, was ich nicht laſſen konnte.

Er ſpringt in den Kahn.

Kuoni, zum Fiſcher.

Ihr ſeid ein Meiſter Steuermann! Was ſich
Der Tell getraut, das konntet ihr nicht wagen?

Ruodi

Wohl beßre Männer thun's dem Tell nicht nach;
Es giebt nicht zwei, wie der iſt, im Gebirge.

Werni, iſt auf den Fels geſtiegen.

165 Er ſtößt ſchon ab. Gott helf' dir, braver Schwimmer!
Sieh, wie das Schifflein auf den Wellen ſchwankt!

Kuoni, am Ufer.

Die Flut geht drüber weg, — ich ſeh's nicht mehr, —
Doch halt! da iſt es wieder. Kräftiglich
Arbeitet ſich der Wackre durch die Brandung.

Seppi

170 Des Landvogts Reiter kommen angeſprengt.

Kuoni

Weiß Gott, ſie ſind's! Das war Hilf' in der Not.

Ein Trupp Landenbergiſcher Reiter.

Erſter Reiter

Den Mörder gebt heraus, den ihr verborgen.

Zweiter

Des Wegs kam er; umſonſt verhehlt ihr ihn.

Kuoni und Ruodi

Wen meint ihr, Reiter?

Erster Reiter, entdeckt den Nachen.

Ha, was seh' ich? Teufel!

Werni, oben.

175 Ist's der im Nachen, den ihr sucht? — Reit zu;
Wenn ihr frisch beilegt, holt ihr ihn noch ein.

Zweiter

Verwünscht! Er ist entwischt.

Erster, zum Hirten und Fischer.

Ihr habt ihm fortgeholfen.

Ihr sollt uns büßen. — Fallt in ihre Herde.
Die Hütte reißet ein, brennt und schlagt nieder. Eilen fort.

Seppi, stürzt nach.

180 O meine Lämmer!

Kuoni, folgt.

Weh mir! Meine Herde!

Werni

Die Wütriche!

Ruodi, ringt die Hände.

Gerechtigkeit des Himmels!
Wann wird der Retter kommen diesem Lande? Folgt ihnen.

Zweite Szene.

Zu Steinen in Schwyz; eine Linde vor des Stauffachers Hause an
der Landstraße, nächst der Brücke.

Werner Stauffacher, Pfeifer von Luzern kommen im Gespräch.

Pfeifer

Ja, ja, Herr Stauffacher, wie ich euch sagte,
Schwört nicht zu Östreich, wenn ihr's könnt vermeiden.

185 Haltet fest am Reich und wacker, wie bisher;
Gott schirme euch bei eurer alten Freiheit.
Drückt ihm herzlich die Hand und will gehen.

Stauffacher

Bleibt doch, bis meine Wirtin kommt. Ihr seid
Mein Gast zu Schwyz, ich in Luzern der eure.

Pfeifer

Viel Dank. Muß heute Gersau noch erreichen.
190 — Was ihr auch Schweres mögt zu leiden haben
Von eurer Vögte Geiz und Übermut,
Tragt's in Geduld. Es kann sich ändern, schnell,
Ein andrer Kaiser kann ans Reich gelangen.
Seid ihr erst Österreichs, seid ihr's auf immer.

Er geht ab. Stauffacher setzt sich kummervoll auf eine Bank unter der Linde.
So findet ihn Gertrud, seine Frau, die sich neben ihn stellt und ihn eine
Zeitlang schweigend betrachtet.

Gertrud

195 So ernst, mein Freund? Ich kenne dich nicht mehr.
Schon viele Tage seh' ich's schweigend an,
Wie finstrer Trübsinn deine Stirne furcht.
Auf deinem Herzen drückt ein still Gebresten;
Vertrau' es mir; ich bin dein treues Weib,
200 Und meine Hälfte fordr' ich deines Grams.
Stauffacher reicht ihr die Hand und schweigt.
Was kann dein Herz beklemmen, sag' es mir.
Gesegnet ist dein Fleiß, dein Glücksstand blüht;
Voll sind die Scheunen und der Rinder Scharen,
Der glatten Pferde wohlgenährte Zucht
205 Ist von den Bergen glücklich heimgebracht
Zur Winterung in den bequemen Ställen.
Da steht dein Haus, reich wie ein Edelsitz;
Von schönem Stammholz ist es neu gezimmert,

Und nach dem Richtmaß ordentlich gefügt;
210 Von vielen Fenstern glänzt es wohnlich, hell;
Mit bunten Wappenschildern ist's bemalt,
Und weisen Sprüchen, die der Wandersmann
Verweilend liest und ihren Sinn bewundert.

Stauffacher

Wohl steht das Haus gezimmert und gefügt,
215 Doch, ach! es wankt der Grund, auf den wir bauten.

Gertrud

Mein Werner, sage, wie verstehst du das?

Stauffacher

Vor dieser Linde saß ich jüngst, wie heut,
Das schön Vollbrachte freudig überdenkend;
Da kam daher von Küßnacht, seiner Burg,
220 Der Vogt mit seinen Reisigen geritten.
Vor diesem Hause hielt er wundernd an,
Doch ich erhub mich schnell, und unterwürfig,
Wie sich's gebührt, trat ich dem Herrn entgegen,
Der uns des Kaisers richterliche Macht
225 Vorstellt im Lande. Wessen ist dies Haus?
Fragt' er bösmeinend, denn er wußt' es wohl.
Doch schnell besonnen ich entgegn' ihm so:
Dies Haus, Herr Vogt, ist meines Herrn des Kaisers
Und eures, und mein Lehen. Da versetzt' er:
230 „Ich bin Regent im Land an Kaisers Statt,
Und will nicht, daß der Bauer Häuser baue
Auf seine eigne Hand, und also frei
Hinleb', als ob er Herr wär' in dem Lande;
Ich werd' mich unterstehn, euch das zu wehren."
235 Dies sagend, ritt er trutziglich von dannen,

Ich aber blieb mit kummervoller Seele,
Das Wort bedenkend, das der Böse sprach.

Gertrud

Mein lieber Herr und Ehewirt, magst du
Ein redlich Wort von deinem Weib vernehmen?
240 Des edeln Jbergs Tochter rühm' ich mich,
Des vielerfahrnen Manns. Wir Schwestern saßen,
Die Wolle spinnend, in den langen Nächten,
Wenn bei dem Vater sich des Volkes Häupter
Versammelten, die Pergamente lasen
245 Der alten Kaiser, und des Landes Wohl
Bedachten in vernünftigem Gespräch.
Aufmerkend hört' ich da manch kluges Wort,
Was der Verständ'ge denkt, der Gute wünscht, —
Und still im Herzen hab' ich mir's bewahrt;
250 So höre denn und acht' auf meine Rede;
Denn, was dich preßte, sieh, das wußt' ich längst.
Dir grollt der Landvogt, möchte gern dir schaden,
Denn du bist ihm ein Hindernis, daß sich
Der Schwyzer nicht dem neuen Fürstenhaus
255 Will unterwerfen, sondern treu und fest
Beim Reich beharren, wie die würdigen
Altvordern es gehalten und gethan.
Ist's nicht so, Werner? Sag' es, wenn ich lüge.

Stauffacher

So ist's, das ist des Geßlers Groll auf mich.

Gertrud

260 Er ist dir neidisch, weil du glücklich wohnst,
Ein freier Mann auf deinem eignen Erb',
Denn er hat keins. Vom Kaiser selbst und Reich

Trägſt du dies Haus zu Lehn; du darfſt es zeigen,
So gut der Reichsfürſt ſeine Länder zeigt;
265 Denn über dir erkennſt du keinen Herrn,
Als nur den Höchſten in der Chriſtenheit.
Er iſt ein jüngrer Sohn nur ſeines Hauſes,
Nichts nennt er ſein, als ſeinen Rittermantel;
Drum ſieht er jedes Biedermannes Glück
270 Mit ſcheelen Augen gift'ger Mißgunſt an.
Dir hat er längſt den Untergang geſchworen;
Noch ſtehſt du unverſehrt. Willſt du erwarten,
Bis er die böſe Luſt an dir gebüßt?
[Der kluge Mann baut vor.]

Stauffacher

Was iſt zu thun?

Gertrud, tritt näher.

275 So höre meinen Rat. Du weißt, wie hier
Zu Schwyz ſich alle Redlichen beklagen
Ob dieſes Landvogts Geiz und Wüterei.
So zweifle nicht, daß ſie dort drüben auch,
In Unterwalden und im Urner Land
Des Dranges müd' ſind und des harten Jochs;
Denn, wie der Geßler hier, ſo ſchafft es frech
Der Landenberger drüben überm See.
Es kommt kein Fiſcherkahn zu uns herüber,
Der nicht ein neues Unheil und Gewalt=
285 Beginnen von den Vögten uns verkündet.
Drum thät' es gut, daß euer etliche,
Die's redlich meinen, ſtill zu Rate gingen,
Wie man des Drucks ſich möcht' erledigen;
So acht' ich wohl, Gott würd' euch nicht verlaſſen

290 Und der gerechten Sache gnädig sein.
     Hast du in Uri keinen Gastfreund, sprich,
     Dem du dein Herz magst redlich offenbaren?

                    Stauffacher

     Der wackern Männer kenn' ich viele dort,
     Und angesehen große Herrenleute,
295 Die mir geheim sind und gar wohl vertraut. Er steht auf.
     Frau, welchen Sturm gefährlicher Gedanken
     Weckst du mir in der stillen Brust! Mein Innerstes
     Kehrst du ans Licht des Tages mir entgegen;
     Und was ich mir zu denken still verbot,
300 Du sprichst's mit leichter Zunge fecklich aus.
     — Hast du auch wohl bedacht, was du mir rätst?
     Die wilde Zwietracht und den Klang der Waffen
     Rufst du in dieses friedgewohnte Thal.
     Wir wagten es, ein schwaches Volk der Hirten,
305 In Kampf zu gehen mit dem Herrn der Welt?
     Der gute Schein nur ist's, worauf sie warten,
     Um loszulassen auf dies arme Land
     Die wilden Horden ihrer Kriegesmacht,
     Darin zu schalten mit des Siegers Rechten,
310 Und unterm Schein gerechter Züchtigung
     Die alten Freiheitsbriefe zu vertilgen.

                    Gertrud

     Ihr seid auch Männer, wisset eure Art
     Zu führen, und dem Mutigen hilft Gott.

                    Stauffacher

     O Weib! ein furchtbar wütend Schrecknis ist
315 Der Krieg; die Herde schlägt er und den Hirten.

Gertrud

Ertragen muß man, was der Himmel sendet;
Unbilliges erträgt kein edles Herz.

Stauffacher

Dies Haus erfreut dich, das wir neu erbauten;
Der Krieg, der ungeheure, brennt es nieder.

Gertrud

320 Wüßt' ich mein Herz an zeitlich Gut gefesselt,
Den Brand wärf' ich hinein mit eigner Hand.

Stauffacher

Du glaubst an Menschlichkeit. Es schont der Krieg
Auch nicht das zarte Kindlein in der Wiege.

Gertrud

Die Unschuld hat im Himmel einen Freund.
325 — Sieh vorwärts, Werner, und nicht hinter dich.

Stauffacher

Wir Männer können tapfer fechtend sterben,
Welch Schicksal aber wird das eure sein?

Gertrud

Die letzte Wahl steht auch dem Schwächsten offen;
Ein Sprung von dieser Brücke macht mich frei.

Stauffacher, stürzt in ihre Arme,

330 Wer solch ein Herz an seinen Busen drückt,
Der kann für Herd und Hof mit Freuden fechten,
Und keines Königs Heermacht fürchtet er.
Nach Uri fahr' ich stehnden Fußes gleich;
Dort lebt ein Gastfreund mir, Herr Walther Fürst,
335 Der über diese Zeiten denkt, wie ich.
Auch find' ich dort den edeln Bannerherrn
Von Attinghaus; obgleich von hohem Stamm,

Liebt er das Volk und ehrt die alten Sitten.
Mit ihnen beiden pfleg' ich Rats, wie man
340 Der Landesfeinde mutig sich erwehrt.
Leb' wohl! und, weil ich fern bin, führe du
Mit klugem Sinn das Regiment des Hauses:
Dem Pilger, der zum Gotteshause wallt,
Dem frommen Mönch, der für sein Kloster sammelt,
345 Gieb reichlich und entlaß ihn wohlgepflegt.
Stauffachers Haus verbirgt sich nicht; zu äußerst
Am offnen Heerweg steht's, ein wirtlich Dach
Für alle Wandrer, die des Weges fahren.

Indem sie nach dem Hintergrund abgehen, tritt Wilhelm Tell mit
Baumgarten vorn auf die Szene.

Tell, zu Baumgarten.

Ihr habt jetzt meiner weiter nicht vonnöten.
350 Zu jenem Hause gehet ein; dort wohnt
Der Stauffacher, ein Vater der Bedrängten.
— Doch sieh, da ist er selber. Folgt mir, kommt.

Gehen auf ihn zu; die Szene verwandelt sich.

Dritte Szene.

Öffentlicher Platz bei Altorf.

Auf einer Anhöhe im Hintergrunde sieht man eine Feste bauen, welche schon so
weit gediehen, daß sich die Form des Ganzen darstellt. Die hintere Seite ist
fertig, an der vordern wird eben gebaut; das Gerüste steht noch, an welchem
die Werkleute auf und nieder steigen; auf dem höchsten Dach hängt der
Schieferdecker. Alles ist in Bewegung und Arbeit.

Fronvogt, Meister Steinmetz, Gesellen und Handlanger.

Fronvogt, mit dem Stabe, treibt die Arbeiter.

Nicht lang gefeiert! Frisch! Die Mauersteine
Herbei! Den Kalk, den Mörtel zugefahren!

355 Wenn der Herr Landvogt kommt, daß er das Werk
Gewachsen sieht. Das schlendert wie die Schnecken.

Zu zwei Handlangern, welche tragen.

Heißt das geladen? Gleich das Doppelte!
Wie die Tagdiebe ihre Pflicht bestehlen!

Erster Gesell

Das ist doch hart, daß wir die Steine selbst
360 Zu unserm Twing und Kerker sollen fahren.

Fronvogt

Was murret ihr? Das ist ein schlechtes Volk,
Zu nichts anstellig, als das Vieh zu melken
Und faul herum zu schlendern auf den Bergen.

Alter Mann, *ruht aus.*

Ich kann nicht mehr.

Fronvogt, *schüttelt ihn.*

Frisch, Alter, an die Arbeit!

Erster Gesell

365 Habt ihr denn gar kein Eingeweid', daß ihr
Den Greis, der kaum sich selber schleppen kann,
Zum harten Frondienst treibt?

Meister Steinmetz und Gesellen

's ist himmelschreiend.

Fronvogt

Sorgt ihr für euch; ich thu' was meines Amts.

Zweiter Gesell

Fronvogt, wie wird die Feste denn sich nennen,
370 Die wir da baun?

Fronvogt

Zwing Uri soll sie heißen,
Denn unter dieses Joch wird man euch beugen.

Gesellen

Zwing Uri!

Fronvogt

Nun, was giebt's dabei zu lachen?

Zweiter Gesell

Mit diesem Häuslein wollt ihr Uri zwingen?

Erster Gesell

Laß sehn, wie viel man solcher Maulwurfshaufen
375 Muß über 'nander setzen, bis ein Berg
Draus wird, wie der geringste nur in Uri.

Fronvogt geht nach dem Hintergrund.

Meister Steinmetz

Den Hammer werf' ich in den tiefsten See,
Der mir gedient bei diesem Fluchgebäude.

Tell und Stauffacher kommen.

Stauffacher

O, hätt' ich nie gelebt, um das zu schauen!

Tell

380 Hier ist nicht gut sein. Laßt uns weiter gehn.

Stauffacher

Bin ich zu Uri, in der Freiheit Land?

Meister Steinmetz

O Herr, wenn ihr die Keller erst gesehn
Unter den Türmen! Ja, wer die bewohnt,
Der wird den Hahn nicht fürder krähen hören.

Stauffacher

385 O Gott!

Steinmetz

Seht diese Flanken, diese Strebepfeiler;
Die stehn, wie für die Ewigkeit gebaut.

Tell

(Was Hände bauten, können Hände stürzen.)

Nach den Bergen zeigend,

(Das Haus der Freiheit hat uns Gott gegründet.)

Man hört eine Trommel; es kommen Leute, die einen Hut auf einer Stange tragen;
ein Ausrufer folgt ihnen; Weiber und Kinder dringen tumultuarisch nach.

Erster Gesell

Was will die Trommel? Gebet acht!

Meister Steinmetz

Was für

390 Ein Faßnachtsaufzug, und was soll der Hut?

Ausrufer

In des Kaisers Namen! Höret.

Gesellen

Still doch! Höret.

Ausrufer

Ihr sehet diesen Hut, Männer von Uri.
Aufrichten wird man ihn auf hoher Säule,
Mitten in Altorf, an dem höchsten Ort;
395 Und dieses ist des Landvogts Will' und Meinung:
Dem Hut soll gleiche Ehre, wie ihm selbst, geschehn.
Man soll ihn mit gebognem Knie und mit
Entblößtem Haupt verehren. Daran will
Der König die Gehorsamen erkennen.
400 Verfallen ist mit seinem Leib und Gut
Dem Könige, wer das Gebot verachtet.

Das Volk lacht laut auf; die Trommel wird gerührt; sie gehen vorüber.

Erster Gesell

Welch neues Unerhörtes hat der Vogt
Sich ausgesonnen! Wir 'nen Hut verehren?
Sagt, hat man je vernommen von dergleichen?

Meister Steinmetz

405 Wir unsre Kniee beugen einem Hut?
Treibt er sein Spiel mit ernsthaft würd'gen Leuten?

Erster Gesell

Wär's noch die kaiserliche Kron'! So ist's
Der Hut von Österreich; ich sah ihn hangen
über dem Thron, wo man die Lehen giebt.

Meister Steinmetz

410 Der Hut von Österreich! Gebt acht, es ist
Ein Fallstrick, uns an Östreich zu verraten.

Gesellen

Kein Ehrenmann wird sich der Schmach bequemen.

Meister Steinmetz

Kommt, laßt uns mit den andern Abred' nehmen.

Sie gehen nach der Tiefe.

Tell, zum Stauffacher.

Ihr wisset nun Bescheid. Lebt wohl, Herr Werner.

Stauffacher

415 Wo wollt ihr hin? O eilt nicht so von dannen.

Tell

Mein Haus entbehrt des Vaters. Lebet wohl!

Stauffacher

Mir ist das Herz so voll, mit euch zu reden.

Tell

Das schwere Herz wird nicht durch Worte leicht.

Stauffacher

Doch könnten Worte uns zu Thaten führen.

Tell

420 Die einz'ge That ist jetzt Geduld und Schweigen.

Stauffacher

Soll man ertragen, was unleidlich ist?

Tell

(Die schnellen Herrscher sind's, die kurz regieren.)
Wenn sich der Föhn erhebt aus seinen Schlünden,
Löscht man die Feuer aus, die Schiffe suchen
425 Eilends den Hafen, und der mächt'ge Geist
Geht ohne Schaden spurlos über die Erde.
Ein jeder lebe still bei sich daheim;
(Dem Friedlichen gewährt man gern den Frieden.

Stauffacher

Meint ihr?

Tell

(Die Schlange sticht nicht ungereizt.)
430 Sie werden endlich doch von selbst ermüden,
Wenn sie die Lande ruhig bleiben sehn.

Stauffacher

Wir könnten viel, wenn wir zusammenstünden.

Tell

Beim Schiffbruch hilft der einzelne sich leichter.

Stauffacher

So kalt verlaßt ihr die gemeine Sache?

Tell

435 Ein jeder zählt nur sicher auf sich selbst.

Stauffacher

Verbunden werden auch die Schwachen mächtig.

Tell

Der Starke ist am mächtigsten allein.

Stauffacher

So kann das Vaterland auf euch nicht zählen,
Wenn es verzweiflungsvoll zur Notwehr greift?

Tell, giebt ihm die Hand.

440 Der Tell holt ein verlornes Lamm vom Abgrund,
Und sollte seinen Freunden sich entziehen?
Doch, was ihr thut, laßt mich aus eurem Rat;
Ich kann nicht lange prüfen oder wählen;
Bedürft ihr meiner zu bestimmter That,
445 Dann ruft den Tell, es soll an mir nicht fehlen.

Gehen ab zu verschiedenen Seiten. Ein plötzlicher Auflauf entsteht um das Gerüste.

Meister Steinmetz, eilt hin.

Was giebt's?

Erster Gesell, kommt vor, rufend,

Der Schieferdecker ist vom Dach gestürzt.

Bertha mit Gefolge.

Bertha, stürzt herein,

Ist er zerschmettert? Rennet; rettet; helft,—
Wenn Hilfe möglich; rettet, hier ist Gold.

Wirft ihr Geschmeide unter das Volk.

Meister

450 Mit eurem Golde! — Alles ist euch feil
Um Gold. Wenn ihr den Vater von den Kindern
Gerissen und den Mann von seinem Weibe
Und Jammer habt gebracht über die Welt,
Denkt ihr's mit Golde zu vergüten. Geht!
455 Wir waren frohe Menschen, eh' ihr kamt;
Mit euch ist die Verzweiflung eingezogen.

Bertha, zu dem Fronvogt, der zurückkommt.

Lebt er?

Fronvogt giebt ein Zeichen des Gegenteils.

O unglücksel'ges Schloß, mit Flüchen
Erbaut, und Flüche werden dich bewohnen! Geht ab.

Vierte Szene.

Walther Fürsts Wohnung.

Walther Fürst und Arnold vom Melchthal treten zugleich
ein von verschiedenen Seiten.

Melchthal

Herr Walther Fürst, —

Walther Fürst

Wenn man uns überraschte!

460 Bleibt, wo ihr seid; wir sind umringt von Spähern.

Melchthal

Bringt ihr mir nichts von Unterwalden? nichts
Von meinem Vater? Nicht ertrag' ich's länger
Als ein Gefangner müßig hier zu liegen.
Was hab' ich denn so Sträfliches gethan,
465 Um mich gleich einem Mörder zu verbergen?
Dem frechen Buben, der die Ochsen mir
Das trefflichste Gespann, vor meinen Augen
Weg wollte treiben auf des Vogts Geheiß,
Hab' ich den Finger mit dem Stab gebrochen.

Walther Fürst

470 Ihr seid zu rasch. Der Bube war des Vogts;
Von eurer Obrigkeit war er gesendet.
Ihr wart in Straf' gefallen; mußtet euch,
Wie schwer sie war, der Buße schweigend fügen.

Melchthal

Ertragen sollt' ich die leichtfert'ge Rede
475 Des Unverschämten: „Wenn der Bauer Brot
Wollt' essen, mög' er selbst am Pfluge ziehn!"
In die Seele schnitt mir's, als der Bub die Ochsen,

Die schönen Tiere, von dem Pfluge spannte.
Dumpf brüllten sie, als hätten sie Gefühl
480 Der Ungebühr, und stießen mit den Hörnern;
Da übernahm mich der gerechte Zorn,
Und, meiner selbst nicht Herr, schlug ich den Boten.

Walther Fürst

O kaum bezwingen wir das eigne Herz;
Wie soll die rasche Jugend sich bezähmen!

Melchthal

485 Mich jammert nur der Vater. Er bedarf
So sehr der Pflege, und sein Sohn ist fern.
Der Vogt ist ihm gehässig, weil er stets
Für Recht und Freiheit redlich hat gestritten.
Drum werden sie den alten Mann bedrängen,
490 Und niemand ist, der ihn vor Unglimpf schütze.
Werde mit mir, was will, ich muß hinüber.

Walther Fürst

Erwartet nur und faßt euch in Geduld,
Bis Nachricht uns herüberkommt vom Walde.
— Ich höre klopfen, geht. Vielleicht ein Bote
495 Vom Landvogt. Geht hinein. Ihr seid in Uri
Nicht sicher vor des Landenbergers Arm,
Denn die Tyrannen reichen sich die Hände.

Melchthal

Sie lehren uns, was wir thun sollten.

Walther Fürst

Geht.

Ich ruf' euch wieder, wenn's hier sicher ist.

Melchthal geht hinein.

500 Der Unglückselige! ich darf ihm nicht

Gestehen, was mir Böses schwant. Wer klopft?
So oft die Thüre rauscht, erwart' ich Unglück.
Verrat und Argwohn lauscht in allen Ecken;
Bis in das Innerste der Häuser dringen
505 Die Boten der Gewalt; bald thät' es not
Wir hätten Schloß und Riegel an den Thüren.

Er öffnet und tritt erstaunt zurück, da Werner Stauffacher hereintritt.

Was seh' ich? Ihr, Herr Werner! Nun, bei Gott!
Ein werter, teurer Gast; kein beßrer Mann
Ist über diese Schwelle noch gegangen.
510 Seid hoch willkommen unter meinem Dach.
Was führt euch her? Was sucht ihr hier in Uri?

Stauffacher, ihm die Hand reichend.

Die alten Zeiten und die alte Schweiz.

Walther Fürst

Die bringt ihr mit euch. Sieh, mir wird so wohl!
Warm geht das Herz mir auf bei eurem Anblick.
515 Setzt euch, Herr Werner. Wie verließet ihr
Frau Gertrud, eure angenehme Wirtin,
Des weisen Ibergs hochverständ'ge Tochter?
Von allen Wandrern aus dem deutschen Land,
Die über Meinrads Zell nach Welschland fahren,
520 Rühmt jeder euer gastlich Haus. Doch, sagt,
Kommt ihr soeben frisch von Flüelen her?
Und habt euch nirgends sonst noch umgesehn,
Eh' ihr den Fuß gesetzt auf diese Schwelle?

Stauffacher, setzt sich.

Wohl ein erstaunlich neues Werk hab' ich
525 Bereiten sehen, das mich nicht erfreute.

Walther Fürst

O Freund, da habt ihr's gleich mit e i n e m Blicke!

Stauffacher

Ein solches ist in Uri nie gewesen;
Seit Menschendenken war kein Twinghof hier,
Und fest war keine Wohnung, als das Grab.

[margin: within the memory of men]

Walther Fürst

530 Ein Grab der Freiheit ist's; ihr nennt's mit Namen.

Stauffacher

Herr Walther Fürst, ich will euch nicht verhalten,
Nicht eine müß'ge Neugier führt mich her;
Mich drücken schwere Sorgen. Drangsal hab' ich
Zu Haus verlassen, Drangsal find' ich hier.
535 Denn ganz unleidlich ist's, was wir erdulden,
Und dieses Dranges ist kein Ziel zu sehn.
Frei war der Schweizer von uralters her;
Wir sind's gewohnt, daß man uns gut begegnet.
Ein solches war im Lande nie erlebt,
540 Solang ein Hirte trieb auf diesen Bergen.

[margin: character]

Walther Fürst

Ja, es ist ohne Beispiel, wie sie's treiben.
Auch unser edler Herr von Attinghausen,
Der noch die alten Zeiten hat gesehn,
Meint selber, es sei nicht mehr zu ertragen.

[margin: acts of violence]

Stauffacher

545 Auch drüben unterm Wald geht Schweres vor,
Und blutig wird's gebüßt. Der Wolfenschießen,
Des Kaisers Vogt, der auf dem Roßberg hauste,
Gelüsten trug er nach verbotner Frucht:

[margin: desire]

Baumgartens Weib, der haushält zu Alzellen,
550 Wollt' er zu frecher Ungebühr mißbrauchen,
Und mit der Axt hat ihn der Mann erschlagen.

Walther Fürst

(O die Gerichte Gottes sind gerecht!)
Baumgarten, sagt ihr? ein bescheidner Mann;
Er ist gerettet doch und wohl geborgen?

Stauffacher

555 Euer Eidam hat ihn übern See geflüchtet;
Bei mir zu Steinen halt' ich ihn verborgen.
Noch Greulichers hat mir derselbe Mann
Berichtet, was zu Sarnen ist geschehn;
Das Herz muß jedem Biedermanne bluten.

Walther Fürst, aufmerksam.

560 Sagt an, was ist's?

Stauffacher

Im Melchthal, da wo man
Eintritt bei Kerns, wohnt ein gerechter Mann,
Sie nennen ihn den Heinrich von der Halden,
Und seine Stimm' gilt was in der Gemeinde.

Walther Fürst

Wer kennt ihn nicht? Was ist's mit ihm? Vollendet.

Stauffacher

565 Der Landenberger büßte seinen Sohn
Um kleinen Fehlers willen; ließ die Ochsen,
Das beste Paar ihm aus dem Pfluge spannen;
Da schlug der Knab' den Knecht und wurde flüchtig.

Walther Fürst, in höchster Spannung.

Der Vater aber, sagt, wie steht's um den?

Stauffacher

570 Den Vater läßt der Landenberger fodern:
Zur Stelle schaffen soll er ihm den Sohn;
Und da der alte Mann mit Wahrheit schwört,
Er habe von dem Flüchtling keine Kunde,
Da läßt der Vogt die Folterknechte kommen —

Walther Fürst,
springt auf und will ihn auf die andere Seite führen.

575 O still! nichts mehr!

Stauffacher, mit steigendem Ton.

„Ist mir der Sohn entgangen,
So hab' ich dich;" läßt ihn zu Boden werfen,
Den spitz'gen Stahl ihm in die Augen bohren.

Walther Fürst

Barmherz'ger Himmel!

Melchthal, stürzt heraus.

In die Augen, sagt ihr?

Stauffacher, erstaunt zu Walther Fürst.

Wer ist der Jüngling?

Melchthal, faßt ihn mit krampfhafter Heftigkeit.

In die Augen? Redet.

Walther Fürst

580 O der Bejammernswürdige!

Stauffacher

Wer ist's?

Da Walther Fürst ihm ein Zeichen giebt.

Der Sohn ist's? Allgerechter Gott!

Melchthal

Und ich

Muß ferne sein! — In seine beiden Augen?

Walther Fürst

Bezwinget euch. Ertragt es, wie ein Mann.

Melchthal

Um meiner Schuld, um meines Frevels willen!
585 Blind also! Wirklich blind und ganz geblendet?

Stauffacher

Ich sagt's. Der Quell des Seh'ns ist ausgeflossen;
Das Licht der Sonne schaut er niemals wieder.

Walther Fürst

Schont seines Schmerzens.

Melchthal

Niemals, niemals wieder!

Er drückt die Hand vor die Augen und schweigt einige Momente; dann wendet er sich
von dem einen zu dem andern und spricht mit sanfter, von Thränen erstickter Stimme.

O, eine edle Himmelsgabe ist
590 Das Licht des Auges. (Alle Wesen leben
Vom Lichte, jedes glückliche Geschöpf;)
Die Pflanze selbst kehrt freudig sich zum Lichte,
Und er muß sitzen, fühlend in der Nacht,
Im ewig Finstern; ihn erquickt nicht mehr
595 Der Matten warmes Grün, der Blumen Schmelz;
Die roten Firnen kann er nicht mehr schauen.
Sterben ist nichts, doch leben und nicht sehen,
Das ist ein Unglück. — Warum seht ihr mich
So jammernd an? Ich hab' zwei frische Augen
600 Und kann dem blinden Vater keines geben, —
Nicht einen Schimmer von dem Meer des Lichts,
Das glanzvoll, blendend mir ins Auge bringt.

Stauffacher

Ach! ich muß euren Jammer noch vergrößern,
Statt ihn zu heilen. Er bedarf noch mehr,

605 Denn alles hat der Landvogt ihm geraubt;
Nichts hat er ihm gelassen als den Stab,
Um nackt und blind von Thür zu Thür zu wandern.

Melchthal

Nichts als den Stab dem augenlosen Greis!
Alles geraubt und auch das Licht der Sonne,
610 Des Ärmsten allgemeines Gut! Jetzt rede
— Mir keiner mehr von Bleiben, von Verbergen.
Was für ein feiger Elender bin ich,
Daß ich auf meine Sicherheit gedacht
Und nicht auf deine; dein geliebtes Haupt
615 Als Pfand gelassen in des Wütrichs Händen.
Feigherz'ge Vorsicht, fahre hin! Auf nichts
Als blutige Vergeltung will ich denken.
Hinüber will ich, keiner soll mich halten,
Des Vaters Auge von dem Landvogt fodern.
620 Aus allen seinen Reisigen heraus
Will ich ihn finden. Nichts liegt mir am Leben,
Wenn ich den heißen, ungeheuren Schmerz
In seinem Lebensblute kühle. *Er will gehen.*

Walther Fürst
Bleibt.

Was könnt ihr gegen ihn? Er sitzt zu Sarnen
625 Auf seiner hohen Herrenburg und spottet
Ohnmächt'gen Zorns in seiner sichern Feste.

Melchthal

Und wohnt er droben auf dem Eispalast
Des Schreckhorns, oder höher, wo die Jungfrau
Seit Ewigkeit verschleiert sitzt, ich mache
630 Mir Bahn zu ihm; mit zwanzig Jünglingen,

Gesinnt wie ich, zerbrech' ich seine Feste.
Und wenn mir niemand folgt, und wenn ihr alle,
Für eure Hütten bang und eure Herden,
Euch dem Tyrannenjoche beugt, die Hirten
635 Will ich zusammenrufen im Gebirg,
Dort, unterm freien Himmelsdache, wo
Der Sinn noch frisch ist und das Herz gesund,
Das ungeheuer Gräßliche erzählen.

Stauffacher, zu Walter Fürst.

Es ist auf seinem Gipfel. Wollen wir
640 Erwarten, bis das Äußerste —

Melchthal

Welch Äußerstes
Ist noch zu fürchten, wenn der Stern des Auges
In seiner Höhle nicht mehr sicher ist?
Sind wir denn wehrlos? Wozu lernten wir
Die Armbrust spannen und die schwere Wucht
645 Der Streitart schwingen? Jedem Wesen ward
Ein Notgewehr in der Verzweiflungsangst.
Es stellt sich der erschöpfte Hirsch und zeigt
Der Meute sein gefürchtetes Geweih;
Die Gemse reißt den Jäger in den Abgrund;
650 Der Pflugstier selbst, der sanfte Hausgenoß
Des Menschen, der die ungeheure Kraft
Des Halses duldsam unters Joch gebogen,
Springt auf, gereizt, wetzt sein gewaltig Horn
Und schleudert seinen Feind den Wolken zu.

Walther Fürst

655 Wenn die drei Lande dächten wie wir drei,
So möchten wir vielleicht etwas vermögen.

Stauffacher

Wenn Uri ruft, wenn Unterwalden hilft,
Der Schwyzer wird die alten Bünde ehren.

Melchthal

Groß ist in Unterwalden meine Freundschaft
660 Und jeder wagt mit Freuden Leib und Blut,
Wenn er am andern einen Rücken hat
Und Schirm. — O fromme Väter dieses Landes!
Ich stehe, nur ein Jüngling, zwischen euch,
Den Vielerfahrnen; meine Stimme muß
665 Bescheiden schweigen in der Landsgemeinde.
Nicht, weil ich jung bin und nicht viel erlebte,
Verachtet meinen Rat und meine Rede;
Nicht lüstern jugendliches Blut, mich treibt
Des höchsten Jammers schmerzliche Gewalt,
670 Was auch den Stein des Felsen muß erbarmen.
Ihr selbst seid Väter, Häupter eines Hauses,
Und wünscht euch einen tugendhaften Sohn,
Der eures Hauptes heil'ge Locken ehre,
Und euch den Stern des Auges fromm bewache;
675 O, weil ihr selbst an eurem Leib und Gut
Noch nichts erlitten, eure Augen sich
Noch frisch und hell in ihren Kreisen regen,
So sei euch darum unsre Not nicht fremd.
Auch über euch hängt das Tyrannenschwert;
680 Ihr habt das Land von Östreich abgewendet;
Kein anderes war meines Vaters Unrecht?
Ihr seid in gleicher Mitschuld und Verdammnis.

Stauffacher, zu Walter Fürst.

Beschließet ihr; ich bin bereit, zu folgen.

Walther Fürst

Wir wollen hören, was die edeln Herrn
685 Von Sillinen, von Attinghausen raten.
(Ihr Name, denk' ich, wird uns Freunde werben.)

Melchthal

Wo ist ein Name in dem Waldgebirg'
Ehrwürdiger, als eurer und der eure?
An solcher Namen echte Währung glaubt
690 Das Volk, sie haben guten Klang im Lande.
Ihr habt ein reiches Erb' von Vätertugend
Und habt es selber reich vermehrt. — Was braucht's
Des Edelmanns? Laßt's uns allein vollenden.
Wären wir doch allein im Land! Ich meine,
695 Wir wollten uns schon selbst zu schirmen wissen.

Stauffacher

Die Edeln drängt nicht gleiche Not mit uns;
Der Strom, der in den Niederungen wütet,
Bis jetzt hat er die Höhn noch nicht erreicht.
Doch ihre Hilfe wird uns nicht entstehn,
700 Wenn sie das Land in Waffen erst erblicken.

Walther Fürst

Wäre ein Obmann zwischen uns und Östreich,
So möchte Recht entscheiden und Gesetz;
Doch der uns unterdrückt, ist unser Kaiser
Und höchster Richter; so muß Gott uns helfen
705 Durch unsern Arm. Erforschet ihr die Männer
Von Schwyz, ich will in Uri Freunde werben.
Wen aber senden wir nach Unterwalden? —

Melchthal

Mich sendet hin. Wem läg' es näher an?

Walther Fürst

Ich geb's nicht zu; ihr seid mein Gast, ich muß
710 Für eure Sicherheit gewähren.

Melchthal

Laßt mich;
Die Schliche kenn' ich und die Felsensteige;
Auch Freunde find' ich gnug, die mich dem Feind
Verhehlen und ein Obdach gern gewähren.

Stauffacher

Laßt ihn mit Gott hinübergehn. Dort drüben
715 Ist kein Verräter. So verabscheut ist
Die Tyrannei, daß sie kein Werkzeug findet.
Auch der Alzeller soll uns nid dem Wald
Genossen werben und das Land erregen.

Melchthal

Wie bringen wir uns sichre Kunde zu,
720 Daß wir den Argwohn der Tyrannen täuschen?

Stauffacher

Wir könnten uns zu B r u n n e n oder T r e i b
Versammeln, wo die Kaufmannsschiffe landen.

Walther Fürst

So offen dürfen wir das Werk nicht treiben.
Hört meine Meinung. Links am See, wenn man
725 Nach Brunnen fährt, dem Mythenstein grad' über,
Liegt eine Matte heimlich im Gehölz;
Das N ü t l i heißt sie bei dem Volk der Hirten,
Weil dort die Waldung ausgereutet ward.
Dort ist's, wo unsre Landmark und die eure, zu Melchthal.
730 Zusammen grenzen, und in kurzer Fahrt, zu Stauffacher.

Trägt euch der leichte Kahn von Schwyz herüber.
Auf öden Pfaden können wir dahin
Bei Nachtzeit wandern und uns still beraten.
Dahin mag jeder zehn vertraute Männer
735 Mitbringen, die herzeinig sind mit uns;
So können wir gemeinsam das Gemeine
Besprechen und mit Gott es frisch beschließen.

Stauffacher

So sei's. Jetzt reicht mir eure biedre Rechte;
Reicht ihr die eure her, und so, wie wir
740 Drei Männer jetzo unter uns die Hände
Zusammenflechten, redlich, ohne Falsch,
So wollen wir drei Länder auch zu Schutz
Und Trutz zusammen stehn auf Tod und Leben.

Walther Fürst und Melchthal

Auf Tod und Leben!

Sie halten die Hände noch einige Pausen lang zusammengeflochten und schweigen.

Melchthal

Blinder, alter Vater!
745 Du kannst den Tag der Freiheit nicht mehr schauen;
Du sollst ihn hören. Wenn von Alp zu Alp
Die Feuerzeichen flammend sich erheben,
Die festen Schlösser der Tyrannen fallen,
In deine Hütte soll der Schweizer wallen,
750 Zu deinem Ohr die Freudenkunde tragen,
Und hell in deiner Nacht soll es dir tagen.

Sie gehen auseinander.

Zweiter Aufzug.

Erste Szene.

Edelhof des Freiherrn von Attinghausen.

Ein gotischer Saal, mit Wappenschildern und Helmen verziert. Der Freiherr, ein Greis von fünfundachtzig Jahren, von hoher edler Statur, an
einem Stabe, worauf ein Gemsenhorn, und in ein Pelzwams gekleidet.
Kuoni und noch sechs Knechte stehen um ihn her mit Rechen und Sensen.
Ulrich von Rudenz tritt ein in Ritterkleidung.

Rudenz

Hier bin ich, Oheim. Was ist euer Wille?

Attinghausen

Erlaubt, daß ich nach altem Hausgebrauch
Den Frühtrunk erst mit meinen Knechten teile.

Er trinkt aus einem Becher, der dann in der Reihe herumgeht.

755 Sonst war ich selber mit in Feld und Wald,
Mit meinem Auge ihren Fleiß regierend,
Wie sie mein Banner führte in der Schlacht;
Jetzt kann ich nichts mehr, als den Schaffner machen,
Und kommt die warme Sonne nicht zu mir,
760 Ich kann sie nicht mehr suchen auf den Bergen.
Und so, in enger stets und engerm Kreis,
Beweg' ich mich dem engesten und letzten,
Wo alles Leben stillsteht, langsam zu.
Mein Schatte bin ich nur, bald nur mein Name.

Kuoni, *zu Rudenz mit dem Becher.*

765 Ich bring's euch, Junker;

Da Rudenz zaudert, den Becher zu nehmen.

Trinket frisch. Es geht
Aus einem Becher und aus einem Herzen.

42

Attinghausen

Geht, Kinder, und wenn's Feierabend ist,
Dann reden wir auch von des Lands Geschäften.

Knechte gehen ab.

Attinghausen und Rudenz.

Attinghausen

Ich sehe dich gegürtet und gerüstet;
770 Du willst nach Altorf in die Herrenburg?

Rudenz

Ja, Oheim, und ich darf nicht länger säumen.

Attinghausen, *setzt sich.*

Hast du's so eilig? Wie! Ist deiner Jugend
Die Zeit so karg gemessen, daß du sie
An deinem alten Oheim mußt ersparen?

Rudenz

775 Ich sehe, daß ihr meiner nicht bedürft;
Ich bin ein Fremdling nur in diesem Hause.

Attinghausen, *hat ihn lange mit den Augen gemustert.*

Ja leider bist du's. Leider ist die Heimat
Zur Fremde dir geworden. Uli! Uli!
Ich kenne dich nicht mehr. In Seide prangst du,
780 Die Pfauenfeder trägst du stolz zur Schau,
Und schlägst den Purpurmantel um die Schultern;
Den Landmann blickst du mit Verachtung an,
Und schämst dich seiner traulichen Begrüßung.

Rudenz

Die Ehr', die ihm gebührt, geb' ich ihm gern;
785 Das Recht, das er sich nimmt, verweigr' ich ihm.

Attinghausen

Das ganze Land liegt unterm schweren Zorn
Des Königs; jedes Biedermannes Herz
Ist kummervoll ob der tyrannischen Gewalt,
Die wir erdulden; dich allein rührt nicht
790 Der allgemeine Schmerz; dich siehet man,
Abtrünnig von den Deinen, auf der Seite
Des Landesfeindes stehen, unsrer Not
Hohnsprechend, nach der leichten Freude jagen,
Und buhlen um die Fürstengunst, indes
795 Dein Vaterland von schwerer Geißel blutet.

Rudenz

Das Land ist schwer bedrängt. Warum, mein Oheim?
Wer ist's, der es gestürzt in diese Not?
Es kostete ein einzig leichtes Wort,
Um augenblicks des Dranges los zu sein
800 Und einen gnäd'gen Kaiser zu gewinnen.
Weh ihnen, die dem Volk die Augen halten,
Daß es dem wahren Besten widerstrebt.
Um eignen Vorteils willen hindern sie,
Daß die Waldstätte nicht zu Östreich schwören,
805 Wie ringsum alle Lande doch gethan.
Wohl thut es ihnen, auf der Herrenbank
Zu sitzen mit dem Edelmann; den Kaiser
Will man zum Herrn, um keinen Herrn zu haben.

Attinghausen

Muß ich das hören und aus deinem Munde?

Rudenz

810 Ihr habt mich aufgefodert; laßt mich enden.
Welche Person ist's, Oheim, die ihr selbst
Hier spielt? Habt ihr nicht höhern Stolz, als hier

Landammann oder Bannerherr, zu sein,
Und neben diesen Hirten zu regieren?
815 Wie! Ist's nicht eine rühmlichere Wahl,
Zu huldigen dem königlichen Herrn,
Sich an sein glänzend Lager anzuschließen,
Als eurer eignen Knechte Pair zu sein,
Und zu Gericht zu sitzen mit dem Bauer?

Attinghausen

820 Ach, Uli! Uli! Ich erkenne sie,
Die Stimme der Verführung; sie ergriff
Dein offnes Ohr, sie hat dein Herz vergiftet.

Rudenz

Ja, ich verberg' es nicht; in tiefer Seele
Schmerzt mich der Spott der Fremdlinge, die uns
825 Den Baurenadel schelten. Nicht ertrag' ich's,
Indes die edle Jugend rings umher
Sich Ehre sammelt unter Habsburgs Fahnen,
Auf meinem Erb' hier müßig still zu liegen
Und bei gemeinem Tagewerk den Lenz
830 Des Lebens zu verlieren. — Anderswo
Geschehen Thaten; eine Welt des Ruhms
Bewegt sich glänzend jenseits dieser Berge;
Mir rosten in der Halle Helm und Schild.
Der Kriegstrommete mutiges Getön,
835 Der Heroldsruf, der zum Turniere ladet,
Er dringt in diese Thäler nicht herein;
Nichts als den Kuhreihn und der Herdeglocken
Einförmiges Geläut' vernehm' ich hier.

Attinghausen

Verblendeter! vom eiteln Glanz verführt,
840 Verachte dein Geburtsland! Schäme dich

Der uralt frommen Sitte deiner Väter!
Mit heißen Thränen wirst du dich dereinst
Heim sehnen nach den väterlichen Bergen,
Und dieses Herdenreihens Melodie,
845 Die du in stolzem Überdruß verschmähst,
Mit Schmerzenssehnsucht wird sie dich ergreifen,
Wenn sie dir anklingt auf der fremden Erde.
O, mächtig ist der Trieb des Vaterlands.
Die fremde, falsche Welt ist nicht für dich.
850 Dort an dem stolzen Kaiserhof bleibst du
Dir ewig fremd mit deinem treuen Herzen.
Die Welt, sie fodert andre Tugenden,
Als du in diesen Thälern dir erworben.
Geh' hin, verkaufe deine freie Seele,
855 Nimm Land zu Lehen, werd' ein Fürstenknecht,
Da du ein Selbstherr sein kannst und ein Fürst
Auf deinem eignen Erb' und freien Boden.
Ach, Uli! Uli! Bleibe bei den Deinen.
Geh' nicht nach Altorf. O, verlaß sie nicht,
860 Die heil'ge Sache deines Vaterlands.
Ich bin der Letzte meines Stamms; mein Name
Endet mit mir. Da hängen Helm und Schild;
Die werden sie mir in das Grab mitgeben.
Und muß ich denken bei dem letztem Hauch,
865 Daß du mein brechend Auge nur erwartest,
Um hinzugehn vor diesen neuen Lehenhof
Und meine edeln Güter, die ich frei
Von Gott empfing, von Östreich zu empfangen?

Rudenz

Vergebens widerstreben wir dem König;
870 Die Welt gehört ihm; wollen wir allein

Uns eigensinnig steifen und verstocken,
Die Länderkette ihm zu unterbrechen,
Die er gewaltig rings um uns gezogen?
Sein sind die Märkte, die Gerichte, sein
875 Die Kaufmannsstraßen, und das Saumroß selbst,
Das auf dem Gotthard zieret, muß ihm zollen.
Von seinen Ländern wie mit einem Netz
Sind wir umgarnet rings und eingeschlossen.
Wird uns das Reich beschützen? Kann es selbst
880 Sich schützen gegen Östreichs wachsende Gewalt?
Hilft Gott uns nicht, kein Kaiser kann uns helfen.
Was ist zu geben auf der Kaiser Wort,
Wenn sie in Geld= und Kriegesnot die Städte,
Die untern Schirm des Adlers sich geflüchtet,
885 Verpfänden dürfen und dem Reich veräußern?
Nein, Oheim; Wohlthat ist's und weise Vorsicht,
In diesen schweren Zeiten der Parteiung,
Sich anzuschließen an ein mächtig Haupt.
Die Kaiserkrone geht von Stamm zu Stamm;
890 Die hat für treue Dienste kein Gedächtnis.
Doch, um den mächt'gen Erbherrn wohl verdienen,
Heißt Saaten in die Zukunft streun.

Attinghausen

Bist du so weise?
Willst heller sehn, als deine edeln Väter,
Die um der Freiheit kostbarn Edelstein
895 Mit Gut und Blut und Heldenkraft gestritten?
Schiff' nach Luzern hinunter, frage dort,
Wie Östreichs Herrschaft lastet auf den Ländern.
Sie werden kommen, unsre Schaf' und Rinder
Zu zählen, unsre Alpen abzumessen,

900 Den Hochflug und das Hochgewilde bannen
In unsern freien Wäldern, ihren Schlagbaum
An unsre Brücken, unsre Thore setzen,
Mit unsrer Armut ihre Länderläufe,
Mit unserm Blute ihre Kriege zahlen.
905 Nein, wenn wir unser Blut dran setzen sollen,
So sei's für uns; wohlfeiler kaufen wir
Die Freiheit als die Knechtschaft ein.

Rudenz
Was können wir,
Ein Volk der Hirten, gegen Albrechts Heere?

Attinghausen
Lern' dieses Volk der Hirten kennen, Knabe.
910 Ich kenn's, ich hab' es angeführt in Schlachten;
Ich hab' es fechten sehen bei Favenz.
Sie sollen kommen, uns ein Joch aufzwingen,
Das wir entschlossen sind nicht zu ertragen!
O, lerne fühlen, welches Stamms du bist.
915 Wirf nicht für eiteln Glanz und Flitterschein
Die echte Perle deines Wertes hin.
Das Haupt zu heißen eines freien Volks,
Das dir aus Liebe nur sich herzlich weiht,
Das treulich zu dir steht in Kampf und Tod,
920 Das sei dein Stolz, des Adels rühme dich.
Die angebornen Bande knüpfe fest;
Ans Vaterland, ans teure, schließ' dich an,
Das halte fest mit deinem ganzen Herzen.
Hier sind die starken Wurzeln deiner Kraft;
925 Dort in der fremden Welt stehst du allein,
Ein schwankes Rohr, das jeder Sturm zerknickt.
O komm', — du hast uns lang nicht mehr gesehn, —

Versuch's mit uns nur einen Tag; nur heute
Geh' nicht nach Altorf, — hörst du? — heute nicht;
930 Den einen Tag nur schenke dich den Deinen.

Er faßt seine Hand.

Rudenz

Ich gab mein Wort. Laßt mich; ich bin gebunden.

Attinghausen, *läßt seine Hand los, mit Ernst.*

Du bist gebunden; ja, Unglücklicher,
Du bist's, doch nicht durch Wort und Schwur;
Gebunden bist du durch der Liebe Seile.

Rudenz wendet sich weg.

935 Verbirg dich, wie du willst. Das Fräulein ist's,
Bertha von Bruneck, die zur Herrenburg
Dich zieht, dich fesselt an des Kaisers Dienst.
Das Ritterfräulein willst du dir erwerben
Mit deinem Abfall von dem Land. Betrüg' dich nicht.
940 Dich anzulocken, zeigt man dir die Braut;
Doch deiner Unschuld ist sie nicht beschieden.

Rudenz

Genug hab' ich gehört. Gehabt euch wohl. *Er geht ab.*

Attinghausen

Wahnsinn'ger Jüngling! bleib'. — Er geht dahin;
Ich kann ihn nicht erhalten, nicht erretten.
945 So ist der Wolfenschießen abgefallen
Von seinem Land; so werden andre folgen.
Der fremde Zauber reißt die Jugend fort,
Gewaltsam strebend über unsre Berge.
O unglücksel'ge Stunde, da das Fremde
950 In diese still beglückten Thäler kam,
Der Sitten fromme Unschuld zu zerstören.

Das Neue dringt herein mit Macht; das Alte,
Das Würd'ge scheidet; andre Zeiten kommen,
Es lebt ein anders denkendes Geschlecht.
955　Was thu' ich hier? Sie sind begraben alle,
Mit denen ich gewaltet und gelebt.
Unter der Erde schon liegt meine Zeit;
Wohl dem, der mit der neuen nicht mehr braucht zu leben!

Geht ab.

Zweite Szene.

Eine Wiese von hohen Felsen und Wald umgeben.

Auf den Felsen sind Steige mit Geländern, auch Leitern, von denen man
nachher die Landleute herabsteigen sieht. Im Hintergrunde zeigt sich der See,
über welchem anfangs ein Mondregenbogen zu sehen ist. Den Prospekt schließen
hohe Berge, hinter welchen noch höhere Eisgebirge ragen. Es ist völlig Nacht
auf der Szene; nur der See und die weißen Gletscher leuchten im Mondenlicht.

Melchthal, Baumgarten, Winkelried, Meier von Sarnen,
Burkhardt am Bühel, Arnold von Sewa, Klaus von der
Flüe und noch vier andere Landleute, alle bewaffnet.

Melchthal, noch hinter der Szene.

Der Bergweg öffnet sich; nur frisch mir nach.
960　Den Fels erkenn' ich und das Kreuzlein drauf;
Wir sind am Ziel, hier ist das Rütli.

Treten auf mit Windlichtern.

Winkelried

Horch!

Sewa

Ganz leer.

Meier

's ist noch kein Landmann da. Wir sind
Die ersten auf dem Platz, wir Unterwaldner.

THE RÜTLI.   Act II. Sc. 2.

Melchthal

Wie weit ist's in der Nacht?

Baumgarten

Der Feuerwächter

965 Vom Selisberg hat eben zwei gerufen.

Man hört in der Ferne läuten.

Meier

Still! Horch!

Am Bühel

Das Mettenglöcklein in der Waldkapelle

Klingt hell herüber aus dem Schwyzerland.

Von der Flüe

Die Luft ist rein und trägt den Schall so weit.

Melchthal

Gehn einige und zünden Reisholz an,

970 Daß es loh brenne, wenn die Männer kommen.

Zwei Landleute gehen.

Sewa

's ist eine schöne Mondennacht. Der See

Liegt ruhig da, als wie ein ebner Spiegel.

Am Bühel

Sie haben eine leichte Fahrt.

Winkelried, *zeigt nach dem See.*

Ha! seht;

Seht dorthin. Seht ihr nichts?

Meier

Was denn? Ja wahrlich!

975 Ein Regenbogen mitten in der Nacht.

Melchthal

Es ist das Licht des Mondes, das ihn bildet.

Von der Flüe

Das ist ein seltsam wunderbares Zeichen.
Es leben viele, die das nicht gesehn.

Sewa

Er ist doppelt; seht, ein bläfferer steht drüber.

Baumgarten

980　Ein Nachen fährt soeben drunter weg.

Melchthal

Das ist der Stauffacher mit seinem Kahn;
Der Biedermann läßt sich nicht lang erwarten.

Geht mit Baumgarten nach dem Ufer.

Meier

Die Urner sind es, die am längsten säumen.

Am Bühel

Sie müssen weit umgehen durchs Gebirg,
985　Daß sie des Landvogts Kundschaft hintergehen.

*Unterdessen haben die zwei Landleute in der Mitte des Platzes ein Feuer
angezündet.*

Melchthal, am Ufer,

Wer ist da? Gebt das Wort.

Stauffacher, von unten,

Freunde des Landes.

*Alle gehen nach der Tiefe, den Kommenden entgegen. Aus dem Kahn steigen
Stauffacher, Itel Reding, Hans auf der Mauer, Jörg im
Hofe, Konrad Hunn, Ulrich der Schmid, Jost von Weiler
und noch drei andere Landleute, gleichfalls bewaffnet.*

Alle rufen

Willkommen!

*Indem die Übrigen in der Tiefe verweilen und sich begrüßen, kommt Melchthal mit
Stauffacher vorwärts.*

Melchthal

O Herr Stauffacher, ich hab' ihn
Gesehn, der mich nicht wiederseſhen konnte.
Die Hand hab' ich gelegt auf seine Augen,
990 Und glühend Rachgefühl hab' ich gesogen
Aus der erloschnen Sonne seines Blicks.

Stauffacher

Sprecht nicht von Rache. Nicht Geschehnes rächen,
Gedrohtem Übel wollen wir begegnen.
Jetzt sagt, was ihr im Unterwaldner Land
995 Geschafft und für gemeine Sach' geworben;
Wie die Landleute denken; wie ihr selbst
Den Stricken des Verrats entgangen seid.

Melchthal

Durch der Surennen furchtbares Gebirg,
Auf weit verbreitet öden Eisesfeldern,
1000 Wo nur der heisre Lämmergeier krächzt,
Gelangt' ich zu der Alpentrift, wo sich
Aus Uri und vom Engelberg die Hirten
Anrufend grüßen und gemeinsam weiden,
Den Durst mir stillend mit der Gletscher Milch,
1005 Die in den Runsen schäumend niederquillt.
In den einsamen Sennhütten kehrt' ich ein,
Mein eigner Wirt und Gast, bis daß ich kam
Zu Wohnungen gesellig lebender Menschen.
Erschollen war in diesen Thälern schon
1010 Der Ruf des neuen Greuels, der geschehn,
Und fromme Ehrfurcht schaffte mir mein Unglück
Vor jeder Pforte, wo ich wandernd klopfte.
Entrüstet fand ich diese graden Seelen
Ob dem gewaltsam neuen Regiment;

1015 Denn so wie ihre Alpen fort und fort
     Dieselben Kräuter nähren, ihre Brunnen
     Gleichförmig fließen, Wolken selbst und Winde
     Den gleichen Strich unwandelbar befolgen,
     So hat die alte Sitte hier vom Ahn
1020 Zum Enkel unverändert fort bestanden.
     Nicht tragen sie verwegne Neuerung
     Im altgewohnten gleichen Gang des Lebens.
     Die harten Hände reichten sie mir dar;
     Von den Wänden langten sie die rost'gen Schwerter,
1025 Und aus den Augen blitzte freudiges
     Gefühl des Muts, als ich die Namen nannte,
     Die im Gebirg dem Landmann heilig sind, —
     Den eurigen und Walther Fürsts. Was euch
     Recht würde dünken, schwuren sie zu thun;
1030 Euch schwuren sie bis in den Tod zu folgen.
     So eilt' ich sicher unterm heil'gen Schirm
     Des Gastrechts von Gehöfte zu Gehöfte,
     Und als ich kam ins heimatliche Thal,
     Wo mir die Vettern viel verbreitet wohnen,
1035 Als ich den Vater fand, beraubt und blind,
     Auf fremdem Stroh, von der Barmherzigkeit
     Mildthät'ger Menschen lebend —

                    Stauffacher

                              Herr im Himmel!

               Melchthal

     Da weint' ich nicht. Nicht in ohnmächt'gen Thränen
     Goß ich die Kraft des heißen Schmerzens aus;
1040 In tiefer Brust, wie einen teuren Schatz,
     Verschloß ich ihn und dachte nur auf Thaten.
     Ich kroch durch alle Krümmen des Gebirgs;

Kein Thal war so versteckt, ich späht' es aus;
Bis an der Gletscher eisbedeckten Fuß
1045 Erwartet' ich und fand bewohnte Hütten,
Und überall, wohin mein Fuß mich trug,
Fand ich den gleichen Haß der Tyrannei;
Denn bis an diese letzte Grenze selbst
Belebter Schöpfung, wo der starre Boden
1050 Aufhört zu geben, raubt der Vögte Geiz.
Die Herzen alle dieses biedern Volks
Erregt' ich mit dem Stachel meiner Worte,
Und unser sind sie all' mit Herz und Mund.

Stauffacher
Großes habt ihr in kurzer Frist geleistet.

Melchthal
1055 Ich that noch mehr. Die beiden Festen sind's,
- Roßberg und - Sarnen, die der Landmann fürchtet;
Denn hinter ihren Felsenwällen schirmt
Der Feind sich leicht und schädiget das Land.
Mit eignen Augen wollt' ich es erkunden;
1060 Ich war zu Sarnen und besah die Burg.

Stauffacher
Ihr wagtet euch bis in des Tigers Höhle?

Melchthal
Ich war verkleidet dort in Pilgerstracht;
Ich sah den Landvogt an der Tafel schwelgen.
Urteilt, ob ich mein Herz bezwingen kann;
1065 Ich sah den Feind, und ich erschlug ihn nicht.

Stauffacher
Fürwahr, das Glück war eurer Kühnheit hold.

Unterdessen sind die andern Landleute vorwärts gekommen und nähern sich
den beiden.

Doch jetzo sagt mir, wer die Freunde sind
Und die gerechten Männer, die euch folgten?
Macht mich bekannt mit ihnen, daß wir uns
1070 Zutraulich nahen und die Herzen öffnen.

Meier

Wer kennte euch nicht, Herr, in den drei Landen?
Ich bin der Mei'r von Sarnen; dies hier ist
Mein Schwestersohn, der Struth von Winkelried.

Stauffacher

Ihr nennt mir keinen unbekannten Namen.
1075 Ein Winkelried war's, der den Drachen schlug
Im Sumpf bei Weiler und sein Leben ließ
In diesem Strauß.

Winkelried

Das war mein Ahn, Herr Werner.

Melchthal, zeigt auf zwei Landleute,

Die wohnen hinterm Wald, sind Klosterleute
Vom Engelberg. Ihr werdet sie drum nicht
1080 Verachten, weil sie eigne Leute sind
Und nicht, wie wir, frei sitzen auf dem Erbe.
Sie lieben's Land, sind sonst auch wohl berufen.

Stauffacher, zu den beiden,

Gebt mir die Hand. (Es preise sich, wer keinem
Mit seinem Leibe pflichtig ist auf Erden;
1085 Doch Redlichkeit gedeiht in jedem Stande.)

Konrad Hunn

Das ist Herr Reding, unser Altlandammann.

Meier

Ich kenn' ihn wohl. Er ist mein Widerpart
Der um ein altes Erbstück mit mir rechtet.

Herr Reding, wir sind Feinde vor Gericht;
1090 Hier sind wir einig. *Schüttelt ihm die Hand.*

Stauffacher
Das ist brav gesprochen.

Winkelried
Hört ihr? Sie kommen. Hört das Horn von Uri.

*Rechts und links sieht man bewaffnete Männer mit Windlichtern die Felsen herab-
steigen.*

Auf der Mauer
Seht! Steigt nicht selbst der fromme Diener Gottes,
Der würd'ge Pfarrer, mit herab? Nicht scheut er
Des Weges Mühen und das Graun der Nacht,
1095 Ein treuer Hirte, für das Volk zu sorgen.

Baumgarten
Der Sigrist folgt ihm und Herr Walther Fürst;
Doch nicht den Tell erblick' ich in der Menge.

*Walther Fürst, Rösselmann, der Pfarrer, Petermann, der Sigrist,
Kuoni, der Hirt, Werni, der Jäger, Ruodi, der Fischer, und noch fünf
andere Landleute. Alle zusammen, dreiunddreißig an der Zahl, treten
vorwärts und stellen sich um das Feuer.*

Walther Fürst
So müssen wir auf unserm eignen Erb'
Und väterlichen Boden uns verstohlen
1100 Zusammen schleichen, wie die Mörder thun,
Und bei der Nacht, die ihren schwarzen Mantel
Nur dem Verbrechen und der sonnenscheuen
Verschwörung leihet, unser gutes Recht
Uns holen, das doch lauter ist und klar,
1105 Gleichwie der glanzvoll offne Schoß des Tages.

Melchthal
Laßt's gut sein. Was die dunkle Nacht gesponnen,
Soll frei und fröhlich an das Licht der Sonnen.

Rösselmann

Hört, was mir Gott ins Herz giebt, Eidgenossen.
Wir stehen hier statt einer Landsgemeinde
1110 Und können gelten für ein ganzes Volk.
So laßt uns tagen nach den alten Bräuchen
Des Lands, wie wir's in ruhigen Zeiten pflegen;
Was ungesetzlich ist in der Versammlung,
Entschuldige die Not der Zeit. (Doch Gott
1115 Ist überall, wo man das Recht verwaltet,)
Und unter seinem Himmel stehen wir.

Stauffacher

Wohl, laßt uns tagen nach der alten Sitte;
Ist es gleich Nacht, so leuchtet unser Recht.

Melchthal

Ist gleich die Zahl nicht voll, das H e r z ist hier
1120 Des ganzen Volks; die B e s t e n sind zugegen.

Konrad Hunn

Sind auch die alten Bücher nicht zur Hand,
Sie sind in unsre Herzen eingeschrieben.

Rösselmann

Wohlan, so sei der Ring sogleich gebildet.
Man pflanze a u f die Schwerter der Gewalt.

Auf der Mauer

1125 Der Landesammann nehme seinen Platz,
Und seine Weibel stehen ihm zur Seite.

Sigrist

Es sind der Völker dreie. Welchem nun
Gebührt's, das Haupt zu geben der Gemeinde?

Meier

Um diese Ehr' mag Schwyz mit Uri streiten;
1130 Wir Unterwaldner stehen frei zurück.

Melchthal

Wir stehn zurück; wir sind die Flehenden,
Die Hilfe heischen von den mächt'gen Freunden.

Stauffacher

So nehme Uri denn das Schwert; sein Banner
Zieht bei den Römerzügen uns voran.

Walther Fürst

1135 Des Schwertes Ehre werde Schwyz zu teil;
Denn seines Stammes rühmen wir uns alle.

Rösselmann

Den edeln Wettstreit laßt mich freundlich schlichten;
Schwyz soll im Rat, Uri im Felde führen.

Walther Fürst, reicht dem Stauffacher die Schwerter.

So nehmt.

Stauffacher

Nicht mir, dem Alter sei die Ehre.

Im Hofe

1140 Die meisten Jahre zählt Ulrich der Schmid.

Auf der Mauer

Der Mann ist wacker, doch nicht freien Stands;
Kein eigner Mann kann Richter sein in Schwyz.

Stauffacher

Steht nicht Herr Reding hier, der Altlandammann?
Was suchen wir noch einen Würdigern?

Walther Fürst

1145 Er sei der Ammann und des Tages Haupt.
Wer dazu stimmt, erhebe seine Hände.

Alle heben die rechte Hand auf.

Reding, tritt in die Mitte.

Ich kann die Hand nicht auf die Bücher legen,
So schwör' ich droben bei den ew'gen Sternen,
Daß ich mich nimmer will vom Recht entfernen.

Man richtet die zwei Schwerter vor ihm auf; der Ring bildet sich um ihn her; Schwyz hält die Mitte, rechts stellt sich Uri und links Unterwalden. Er steht auf sein Schlachtschwert gestützt.

1150 Was ist's, das die drei Völker des Gebirgs
Hier an des Sees unwirtlichem Gestade
Zusammenführte in der Geisterstunde?
Was soll der Inhalt sein des neuen Bunds,
Den wir hier unterm Sternenhimmel stiften?

Stauffacher, tritt in den Ring.

1155 Wir stiften keinen neuen Bund; es ist
Ein uralt Bündnis nur von Väter Zeit,
Das wir erneuern. Wisset, Eidgenossen,
Ob uns der See, ob uns die Berge scheiden
Und jedes Volk sich für sich selbst regiert,
1160 So sind wir eines Stammes doch und Bluts,
Und eine Heimat ist's, aus der wir zogen.

Winkelried

So ist es wahr, wie's in den Liedern lautet,
Daß wir von fernher in das Land gewallt?
O, teilt's uns mit, was euch davon bekannt,
1165 Daß sich der neue Bund am alten stärke.

Stauffacher

Hört, was die alten Hirten sich erzählen:
Es war ein großes Volk, hinten im Lande
Nach Mitternacht, das litt von schwerer Teurung.
In dieser Not beschloß die Landsgemeinde,

1170 Daß je der zehnte Bürger nach dem Los
Der Väter Land verlasse. Das geschah;
Und zogen aus, wehklagend, Männer und Weiber,
Ein großer Heerzug, nach der Mittagsonne,
Mit dem Schwert sich schlagend durch das deutsche Land,
1175 Bis an das Hochland dieser Waldgebirge.
Und eher nicht ermüdete der Zug,
Bis daß sie kamen in das wilde Thal,
Wo jetzt die Muotta zwischen Wiesen rinnt;
Nicht Menschenspuren waren hier zu sehen,
1180 Nur eine Hütte stand am Ufer einsam.
Da saß ein Mann und wartete der Fähre.
Doch heftig wogte der See und war
Nicht fahrbar; da besahen sie das Land
Sich näher und gewahrten schöne Fülle
1185 Des Holzes und entdeckten gute Brunnen,
Und meinten, sich im lieben Vaterland
Zu finden. Da beschlossen sie zu bleiben;
Erbaueten den alten Flecken Schwyz,
Und hatten manchen sauren Tag, den Wald
1190 Mit weitverschlungnen Wurzeln auszuroden.
Drauf, als der Boden nicht mehr Gnügen that
Der Zahl des Volks, da zogen sie hinüber
Zum schwarzen Berg, ja, bis ans Weißland hin,
Wo, hinter ew'gem Eiswall verborgen,
1195 Ein andres Volk in andern Zungen spricht.
Den Flecken Stanz erbauten sie am Kernwald,
Den Flecken Altorf in dem Thal der Reuß;
Doch blieben sie des Ursprungs stets gedenk.
Aus all den fremden Stämmen, die seitdem
1200 In Mitte ihres Lands sich angesiedelt,

Finden die Schwyzer Männer sich heraus;
(Es giebt das Herz, das Blut sich zu erkennen.)

Reicht rechts und links die Hand hin.

Auf der Mauer

Ja, wir sind e i n e s Herzens, e i n e s Bluts.

Alle, sich die Hände reichend,

Wir sind e i n Volk, und einig wollen wir handeln.

Stauffacher

1205 Die andern Völker tragen fremdes Joch;
Sie haben sich dem Sieger unterworfen.
Es leben selbst in unsern Landesmarken
Der Saffen viel, die fremde Pflichten tragen,
Und ihre Knechtschaft erbt auf ihre Kinder.
1210 Doch w i r, der alten Schweizer echter Stamm,
Wir haben stets die Freiheit uns bewahrt.
Nicht unter Fürsten bogen wir das Knie,
Freiwillig wählten wir den Schirm der Kaiser.

Rösselmann

Frei wählten wir des Reiches Schutz und Schirm;
1215 So steht's bemerkt in Kaiser Friedrichs Brief.

Stauffacher

(Denn herrenlos ist auch der Freiste nicht.
Ein Oberhaupt muß sein, ein höchster Richter,
Wo man das Recht mag schöpfen in dem Streit.)
Drum haben unsre Väter für den Boden,
1220 Den sie der alten Wildnis abgewonnen,
Die Ehr' gegönnt dem Kaiser, der den Herrn
Sich nennt der deutschen und der welschen Erde,
Und, wie die andern Freien seines Reichs,

Sich ihm zu edelm Waffendienst gelobt;
1225 Denn dieses ist der Freien einz'ge Pflicht:
Das Reich zu schirmen, das sie selbst beschirmt.

Melchthal

Was drüber ist, ist Merkmal eines Knechts.

Stauffacher

Sie folgten, wenn der Heribann erging,
Dem Reichspanier und schlugen seine Schlachten.
1230 Nach Welschland zogen sie gewappnet mit,
Die Römerkron' ihm auf das Haupt zu setzen.
Daheim regierten sie sich fröhlich selbst
Nach altem Brauch und eigenem Gesetz;
Der höchste Blutbann war allein des Kaisers,
1235 Und dazu ward bestellt ein großer Graf,
Der hatte seinen Sitz nicht in dem Lande;
Wenn Blutschuld kam, so rief man ihn herein,
Und unter offnem Himmel, schlicht und klar,
Sprach er das Recht und ohne Furcht der Menschen.
1240 Wo sind hier Spuren, daß wir Knechte sind?
Ist einer, der es anders weiß, der rede.

Im Hofe

Nein, so verhält sich alles, wie ihr sprecht;
Gewaltherrschaft ward nie bei uns geduldet.

Stauffacher

Dem Kaiser selbst versagten wir Gehorsam,
1245 Da er das Recht zu Gunst der Pfaffen bog.
Denn als die Leute von dem Gotteshaus
Einsiedeln uns die Alp in Anspruch nahmen,
Die wir beweidet seit der Väter Zeit,
Der Abt herfürzog einen alten Brief,

1250 Der ihm die herrenlose Wüste schenkte —
Denn unser Dasein hatte man verhehlt —
Da sprachen wir: „Erschlichen ist der Brief.
Kein Kaiser kann, was unser ist, verschenken;
Und wird uns Recht versagt vom Reich, wir können
1255 In unsern Bergen auch des Reichs entbehren."
So sprachen unsre Väter. Sollen wir
Des neuen Joches Schändlichkeit erdulden?
Erleiden von dem fremden Knecht, was uns
In seiner Macht kein Kaiser durfte bieten?
1260 Wir haben diesen Boden uns erschaffen
Durch unsrer Hände Fleiß, den alten Wald,
Der sonst der Bären wilde Wohnung war,
Zu einem Sitz für Menschen umgewandelt;
Die Brut des Drachen haben wir getötet,
1265 Der aus den Sümpfen giftgeschwollen stieg;
Die Nebeldecke haben wir zerrissen,
Die ewig grau um diese Wildnis hing;
Den harten Fels gesprengt, über den Abgrund
Dem Wandersmann den sichern Steg geleitet;
1270 Unser ist durch tausendjährigen Besitz
Der Boden, und der fremde Herrenknecht
Soll kommen dürfen und uns Ketten schmieden
Und Schmach anthun auf unsrer eignen Erde?
Ist keine Hilfe gegen solchen Drang?

Eine große Bewegung unter den Landleuten.

1275 Nein, eine Grenze hat Tyrannenmacht:
Wenn der Gedrückte nirgends Recht kann finden,
Wenn unerträglich wird die Last, greift er
Hinauf getrosten Mutes in den Himmel
Und holt herunter seine ew'gen Rechte,

1280 Die droben hangen unveräußerlich
Und unzerbrechlich, wie die Sterne selbst;)
Der alte Urstand der Natur kehrt wieder,
Wo Mensch dem Menschen gegenüber steht;
Zum letzten Mittel, wenn kein andres mehr
1285 Verfangen will, ist ihm das Schwert gegeben.
Der Güter höchstes dürfen wir verteid'gen
Gegen Gewalt. Wir stehn vor unser Land,
Wir stehn vor unsre Weiber, unsre Kinder.

Alle, an ihre Schwerter schlagend.

Wir stehn vor unsre Weiber, unsre Kinder.

Rösselmann, tritt in den Ring.

1290 Eh' ihr zum Schwerte greift, bedenkt es wohl.
Ihr könnt es friedlich mit dem Kaiser schlichten.
Es kostet euch ein Wort, und die Tyrannen,
Die euch jetzt schwer bedrängen, schmeicheln euch.
Ergreift, was man euch oft geboten hat,
1295 Trennt euch vom Reich; erkennet Östreichs Hoheit.

Auf der Mauer

Was sagt der Pfarrer? Wir zu Östreich schwören?

Am Bühel

Hört ihn nicht an.

Winkelried

Das rät uns ein Verräter,
Ein Feind des Landes.

Reding

Ruhig, Eidgenossen!

Sewa

Wir Östreich huldigen, nach solcher Schmach?

Von der Flüe

1300 Wir uns abtrotzen laffen durch Gewalt
Was wir der Güte weigerten?

Meier

Dann wären
Wir Sklaven und verdienten, es zu sein.

Auf der Mauer

Der sei gestoßen aus dem Recht der Schweizer,
Wer von Ergebung spricht an Österreich.
1305 Landammann, ich bestehe drauf, dies sei
Das erste Landsgesetz, das wir hier geben.

Melchthal

So sei's. Wer von Ergebung spricht an Östreich,
Soll rechtlos sein und aller Ehren bar;
Kein Landmann nehm' ihn auf an seinem Feuer.

Alle, heben die rechte Hand auf.

1310 Wir wollen es, das sei Gesetz.

Reding, nach einer Pause.

Es ist's.

Rösselmann

Jetzt seid ihr frei, ihr seid's durch dies Gesetz.
Nicht durch Gewalt soll Österreich ertrotzen
Was es durch freundlich Werben nicht erhielt.

Jost von Weiler

Zur Tagesordnung, weiter.

Reding

Eidgenossen,
1315 Sind alle sanften Mittel auch versucht?
Vielleicht weiß es der König nicht; es ist

Wohl gar sein Wille nicht, was wir erdulden.
Auch dieses Letzte sollten wir versuchen,
Erst unsre Klage bringen vor sein Ohr,
1320 Eh' wir zum Schwerte greifen. (Schrecklich immer,
Auch in gerechter Sache, ist Gewalt.
Gott hilft nur dann, wenn Menschen nicht mehr helfen.)

Stauffacher, zu Konrad Hunn.

Nun ist's an euch, Bericht zu geben.　Redet.

Konrad Hunn

Ich war zu Rheinfeld an des Kaisers Pfalz,
1325 Wider der Vögte harten Druck zu klagen,
Den Brief zu holen unsrer alten Freiheit,
Den jeder neue König sonst bestätigt.
Die Boten vieler Städte fand ich dort,
Vom schwäb'schen Lande und vom Lauf des Rheins,
1330 Die all' erhielten ihre Pergamente,
Und kehrten freudig wieder in ihr Land.
Mich, euren Boten, wies man an die Räte,
Und die entließen mich mit leerem Trost:
„Der Kaiser habe diesmal keine Zeit;
1335 Er würde sonst einmal wohl an uns denken."
Und als ich traurig durch die Säle ging
Der Königsburg, da sah ich Herzog Hansen
In einem Erker weinend stehn, um ihn
Die edeln Herrn von Wart und Tegerfeld.
1340 Die riefen mir und sagten: „Helft euch selbst;
Gerechtigkeit erwartet nicht vom König.
Beraubt er nicht des eignen Bruders Kind
Und hinterhält ihm sein gerechtes Erbe?
Der Herzog fleht' ihn um sein Mütterliches:

1345 Er habe seine Jahre voll, es wäre
     Nun Zeit, auch Land und Leute zu regieren.
     Was ward ihm zum Bescheid? Ein Kränzlein setz
     Der Kaiser auf: das sei die Zier der Jugend."

Auf der Mauer

     Ihr habt's gehört. Recht und Gerechtigkeit
1350 Erwartet nicht vom Kaiser. Helft euch selbst.

Reding

     Nichts Andres bleibt uns übrig. Nun gebt Rat,
     Wie wir es klug zum frohen Ende leiten.

Walther Fürst, tritt in den Ring.

     Abtreiben wollen wir verhaßten Zwang;
     Die alten Rechte, wie wir sie ererbt
1355 Von unsern Vätern, wollen wir bewahren;
     Nicht ungezügelt nach dem Neuen greifen.
     Dem Kaiser bleibe, was des Kaisers ist;
     Wer einen Herrn hat, dien' ihm pflichtgemäß.

Meier

     Ich trage Gut von Österreich zu Lehen.

Walther Fürst

1360 Ihr fahret fort, Östreich die Pflicht zu leisten.

Jost von Weiler

     Ich steure an die Herrn von Rappersweil.

Walther Fürst

     Ihr fahret fort zu zinsen und zu steuern.

Rösselmann

     Der großen Frau zu Zürch bin ich vereidet.

Walther Fürst

     Ihr gebt dem Kloster, was des Klosters ist.

Stauffacher

1365 Ich trage keine Lehen, als des Reichs.

Walther Fürst

(Was sein muß, das geschehe, doch nicht drüber.)
Die Vögte wollen wir mit ihren Knechten
Verjagen, und die festen Schlösser brechen;
Doch, wenn es sein mag, ohne Blut. Es sehe
1370 Der Kaiser, daß wir notgedrungen nur
Der Ehrfurcht fromme Pflichten abgeworfen.
Und sieht er uns in unsern Schranken bleiben,
Vielleicht besiegt er staatsklug seinen Zorn;
Denn bill'ge Furcht erwecket sich ein Volk,
1375 Das mit dem Schwerte in der Faust sich mäßigt.)

Reding

Doch lasset hören, w i e vollenden wir's?
Es hat der Feind die Waffen in der Hand,
Und nicht fürwahr in Frieden wird er weichen.

Stauffacher

Er wird's, wenn er in Waffen uns erblickt;
1380 Wir überraschen ihn, eh' er sich rüstet.

Meier

Ist bald gesprochen, aber schwer gethan.
Uns ragen in dem Land zwei feste Schlösser,
Die geben Schirm dem Feind und werden furchtbar,
Wenn uns der König in das Land sollt' fallen.
1385 Roßberg und Sarnen muß bezwungen sein,
Eh' man ein Schwert erhebt in den drei Landen.

Stauffacher

Säumt man so lang, so wird der Feind gewarnt;
Zu viele sind's, die das Geheimnis teilen.

Meier

In den Waldstätten find't sich kein Verräter.

Rösselmann

1390 Der Eifer auch, der gute, kann verraten.

Walther Fürst

Schiebt man es auf, so wird der Twing vollendet
In Altorf, und der Vogt befestigt sich.

Meier

Ihr denkt an e u ch.

Sigrist

Und ihr seid ungerecht.

Meier, auffahrend.

Wir ungerecht? Das darf uns Uri bieten?

Reding

1395 Bei eurem Eide, Ruh'!

Meier

Ja, wenn sich Schwyz
Versteht mit Uri, müssen w i r wohl schweigen.

Reding

Ich muß euch weisen vor der Landsgemeinde,
Daß ihr mit heft'gem Sinn den Frieden stört.
Stehn wir nicht alle für dieselbe Sache?

Winkelried

1400 Wenn wir's verschieben bis zum Fest des Herrn,
Dann bringt's die Sitte mit, daß alle Sassen
Dem Vogt Geschenke bringen auf das Schloß.
So können zehen Männer oder zwölf
Sich unverdächtig in der Burg versammeln,
1405 Die führen heimlich spitz'ge Eisen mit,
Die man geschwind kann an die Stäbe stecken,

Denn niemand kommt mit Waffen in die Burg.
Zunächst im Wald hält dann der große Haufe,
Und wenn die andern glücklich sich des Thors
1410 Ermächtiget, so wird ein Horn geblasen,
Und jene brechen aus dem Hinterhalt.
So wird das Schloß mit leichter Arbeit unser.

Melchthal

Den Roßberg übernehm' ich zu ersteigen,
Denn eine Dirn des Schlosses ist mir hold,
1415 Und leicht bethör' ich sie, zum nächtlichen
Besuch die schwanke Leiter mir zu reichen;
Bin ich droben erst, zieh' ich die Freunde nach.

Reding

Ist's aller Wille, daß verschoben werde?
Die Mehrheit erhebt die Hand.

Stauffacher, zählt die Stimmen,

Es ist ein Mehr von zwanzig gegen zwölf.

Walther Fürst

1420 Wenn am bestimmten Tag die Burgen fallen,
So geben wir von einem Berg zum andern
Das Zeichen mit dem Rauch; der Landsturm wird
Aufgeboten, schnell, im Hauptort jedes Landes;
Wenn dann die Vögte sehn der Waffen Ernst,
1425 Glaubt mir, sie werden sich des Streits begeben
Und gern ergreifen friedliches Geleit,
Aus unsern Landesmarken zu entweichen.

Stauffacher

Nur mit dem Geßler fürcht' ich schweren Stand;
Furchtbar ist er mit Reisigen umgeben;

1430 Nicht ohne Blut räumt er das Feld; ja, selbst
Vertrieben bleibt er furchtbar noch dem Land.
Schwer ist's und fast gefährlich, ihn zu schonen.

Baumgarten

Wo's halsgefährlich ist, da stellt mich hin.
Dem Tell verdank' ich mein gerettet Leben;
1435 Gern schlag' ich's in die Schanze für das Land.
Mein' Ehr' hab' ich beschützt, mein Herz befriedigt.

Reding

(Die Zeit bringt Rat.) Erwartet's in Geduld.
(Man muß dem Augenblick auch was vertrauen.)
— Doch seht, indes wir nächtlich hier noch tagen,
1440 Stellt auf den höchsten Bergen schon der Morgen
Die glühnde Hochwacht aus. Kommt, laßt uns scheiden,
Eh' uns des Tages Leuchten überrascht.

Walther Fürst

Sorgt nicht; die Nacht weicht langsam aus den Thälern.

Alle haben unwillkürlich die Hüte abgenommen und betrachten mit stiller Sammlung
die Morgenröte.

Rösselmann

Bei diesem Licht, das uns zuerst begrüßt
1445 Von allen Völkern, die tief unter uns
Schweratmend wohnen in dem Qualm der Städte,
Laßt uns den Eid des neuen Bundes schwören:
(Wir wollen sein ein einzig Volk von Brüdern,
In keiner Not uns trennen und Gefahr

Alle sprechen es nach mit erhobenen drei Fingern.

1450 Wir wollen frei sein, wie die Väter waren,
Eher den Tod, als in der Knechtschaft leben. Wie oben.

Wir wollen trauen auf den höchsten Gott
Und uns nicht fürchten vor der Macht der Menschen.)

Wie oben. Die Landleute umarmen einander.

Stauffacher

Jetzt gehe jeder seines Weges still
1455 Zu seiner Freundschaft und Genoßfame.
Wer Hirt ist, wintre ruhig seine Herde
Und werb' im stillen Freunde für den Bund.
Was noch bis dahin muß erduldet werden,
Erduldet's. Laßt die Rechnung der Tyrannen
1460 Anwachsen, bis ein Tag die allgemeine
Und die besondre Schuld auf einmal zahlt.
Bezähme jeder die gerechte Wut
Und spare für das Ganze seine Rache;
(Denn Raub begeht am allgemeinen Gut,
1465 Wer selbst sich hilft in seiner eignen Sache.)

Indem sie zu drei verschiedenen Seiten in größter Ruhe abgehen, fällt das Orchester
mit einem prachtvollen Schwung ein; die leere Szene bleibt noch eine Zeitlang offen
und zeigt das Schauspiel der aufgehenden Sonne über den Eisgebirgen.

Dritter Aufzug.

Erste Szene.

Hof vor Tells Hause.

Er ist mit der Zimmeraxt, Hedwig mit einer häuslichen Arbeit beschäftigt.
Walther und Wilhelm in der Tiefe spielen mit einer kleinen Armbrust.

Walther, singt.

Mit dem Pfeil, dem Bogen,
Durch Gebirg und Thal
Kommt der Schütz gezogen
Früh am Morgenstrahl.

1470 Wie im Reich der Lüfte
König ist der Weih,
Durch Gebirg und Klüfte
Herrscht der Schütze frei.

Ihm gehört das Weite,
1475 Was sein Pfeil erreicht;
Das ist seine Beute,
Was da fleugt und kreucht.

Kommt gesprungen.

Der Strang ist mir entzwei. Mach' mir ihn, Vater.

Tell

Ich nicht. Ein rechter Schütze hilft sich selbst.

Knaben entfernen sich.

Hedwig

1480 Die Knaben fangen zeitig an zu schießen.

Tell

Früh übt sich, was ein Meister werden will.

Hedwig

Ach, wollte Gott, sie lernten's nie!

Tell

Sie sollen alles lernen. Wer durchs Leben
Sich frisch will schlagen, muß zu Schutz und Trutz
1485 Gerüstet sein.

Hedwig

Ach! es wird keiner seine Ruh'
Zu Hause finden.

Tell

Mutter, ich kann's auch nicht;
Zum Hirten hat Natur mich nicht gebildet;
Rastlos muß ich ein flüchtig Ziel verfolgen.
Dann erst genieß' ich meines Lebens recht,
1490 Wenn ich mir's jeden Tag aufs neu' erbeute.

Hedwig

Und an die Angst der Hausfrau denkst du nicht,
Die sich indessen, deiner wartend, härmt.
Denn mich erfüllt's mit Grausen, was die Knechte
Von euren Wagefahrten sich erzählen.
1495 Bei jedem Abschied zittert mir das Herz,
Daß du mir nimmer werdest wiederkehren.
Ich sehe dich, im wilden Eisgebirg
Verirrt, von einer Klippe zu der andern
Den Fehlsprung thun; seh', wie die Gemse dich
1500 Rückspringend mit sich in den Abgrund reißt;
Wie eine Windlawine dich verschüttet;
Wie unter dir der trügerische Firn
Einbricht und du hinabsinkst, ein lebendig
Begrabner, in die schauerliche Gruft.
1505 Ach! den verwegnen Alpenjäger hascht

Der Tod in hundert wechselnden Gestalten.
Das ist ein unglückseliges Gewerb',
Das halsgefährlich führt am Abgrund hin.

Tell

(Wer frisch umherspäht mit gesunden Sinnen,)
1510 Auf Gott vertraut und die gelenke Kraft,
Der ringt sich leicht aus jeder Fahr und Not;
Den schreckt der Berg nicht, der darauf geboren.

Er hat seine Arbeit vollendet, legt das Gerät hinweg.

Jetzt, mein' ich, hält das Thor auf Jahr und Tag.
(Die Axt im Haus erspart den Zimmermann. Nimmt den Hut.

Hedwig

1515 Wo gehst du hin?

Tell

Nach Altorf zu dem Vater.

Hedwig

Sinnst du auch nichts Gefährliches? Gesteh' mir's.

Tell

Wie kommst du darauf, Frau?

Hedwig

Es spinnt sich etwas
Gegen die Vögte. Auf dem Rütli ward
Getagt; ich weiß, und du bist auch im Bunde.

Tell

1520 Ich war nicht mit dabei, doch werd' ich mich
Dem Lande nicht entziehen, wenn es ruft.

Hedwig

Sie werden dich hinstellen, wo Gefahr ist;
Das Schwerste wird dein Anteil sein wie immer.

Tell

(Ein jeder wird besteuert nach Vermögen.

Hedwig

1525 Den Unterwaldner hast du auch im Sturme
Über den See geschafft. Ein Wunder war's,
Daß ihr entkommen. Dachtest du denn gar nicht
An Kind und Weib?

Tell

Lieb Weib, ich dacht' an euch;
Drum rettet' ich den Vater seinen Kindern.

Hedwig

1530 Zu schiffen in dem wüt'gen See! Das heißt
Nicht Gott vertrauen; das heißt Gott versuchen.

Tell

Wer gar zu viel bedenkt, wird wenig leisten.

Hedwig

Ja, du bist gut und hilfreich, dienest allen,
Und wenn du selbst in Not kommst, hilft dir keiner.

Tell

1535 Verhüt' es Gott, daß ich nicht Hilfe brauche!

Er nimmt die Armbrust und Pfeile.

Hedwig

Was willst du mit der Armbrust? Laß sie hier.

Tell

Mir fehlt der Arm, wenn mir die Waffe fehlt.

Die Knaben kommen zurück.

Walther

Vater, wo gehst du hin?

Tell

Nach Altorf, Knabe,
Zum Ehni. Willst du mit?

Walther

Ja, freilich will ich.

Hedwig

1540 Der Landvogt ist jetzt dort.   Bleib' weg von Altorf.

Tell

Er g e h t, noch heute.

Hedwig

Drum laß ihn erst fort sein.
Gemahn' ihn nicht an dich; du weißt, er grollt uns.

Tell

Mir soll sein böser Wille nicht viel schaden;
Ich thue recht und scheue keinen Feind.

Hedwig

1545 Die recht thun, eben die haßt er am meisten.

Tell

Weil er nicht an sie kommen kann.   M i c h wird
Der Ritter wohl in Frieden lassen, mein' ich.

Hedwig

So, weißt du das?

Tell

Es ist nicht lange her,
Da ging ich jagen durch die wilden Gründe
1550 Des Schächenthals, auf menschenleerer Spur,
Und da ich einsam einen Felsensteig
Verfolgte, wo nicht auszuweichen war, —
Denn über mir hing schroff die Felswand her,
Und unten rauschte fürchterlich der Schächen, —

*Die Knaben drängen sich rechts und links an ihn und sehen mit gespannter Neugier
an ihm hinauf.*

1555 Da kam der Landvogt gegen mich daher,
      Er ganz allein mit mir, der auch allein war,
      Bloß Mensch zu Mensch, und neben uns der Abgrund;
      Und als der Herre mein ansichtig ward
      Und mich erkannte, den er kurz zuvor
1560 Um kleiner Ursach' willen schwer gebüßt,
      Und sah mich mit dem stattlichen Gewehr
      Daher geschritten kommen, da verblaßt' er;
      Die Knie' versagten ihm; ich sah es kommen,
      Daß er jetzt an die Felswand würde sinken.
1565 Da jammerte mich sein; ich trat zu ihm
      Bescheidentlich und sprach: Ich bin's, Herr Landvogt.
      Er aber konnte keinen armen Laut
      Aus seinem Munde geben. Mit der Hand nur
      Winkt' er mir schweigend, meines Wegs zu gehn;
1570 Da ging ich fort und sandt' ihm sein Gefolge.

                  Hedwig
      Er hat vor dir gezittert; wehe dir!
      Daß du ihn schwach gesehn, vergiebt er nie.

                    Tell
      Drum meid' ich ihn, und er wird mich nicht suchen.

                  Hedwig
      Bleib' heute nur dort weg. Geh' lieber jagen.

                    Tell
1575 Was fällt dir ein?

                  Hedwig
                     Mich ängstigt's. Bleibe weg.

                    Tell
      Wie kannst du dich so ohne Ursach' quälen?

Hedwig
Weil's keine Ursach' hat. Tell, bleibe hier!

Tell
Ich hab's versprochen, liebes Weib, zu kommen.

Hedwig
Mußt du, so geh', nur lasse mir den Knaben.

Walther
1580 Nein, Mütterchen. Ich gehe mit dem Vater.

Hedwig
Wälty, verlassen willst du deine Mutter?

Walther
Ich bring' dir auch was Hübsches mit vom Ehni.

Geht mit dem Vater.

Wilhelm
Mutter, ich bleibe bei dir.

Hedwig, *umarmt ihn,*

Ja, du bist
Mein liebes Kind, du bleibst mir noch allein.

Sie geht an das Hofthor und folgt den Abgehenden lange mit den Augen.

Zweite Szene.

Eine eingeschlossene wilde Waldgegend; Staubbäche stürzen von den Felsen.

Bertha *im Jagdkleid. Gleich darauf Rudenz.*

Bertha
1585 Er folgt mir. Endlich kann ich mich erklären.

Rudenz, *tritt rasch ein,*

Fräulein, jetzt endlich sind' ich euch allein;
Abgründe schließen rings umher uns ein;

In dieser Wildnis fürcht' ich keinen Zeugen;
Vom Herzen wälz' ich dieses lange Schweigen.

Bertha

1590 Seid ihr gewiß, daß uns die Jagd nicht folgt?

Rudenz

Die Jagd ist dort hinaus. Jetzt oder nie.
Ich muß den teuren Augenblick ergreifen;
Entschieden sehen muß ich mein Geschick,
Und sollt' es mich auf ewig von euch scheiden.
1595 O waffnet eure güt'gen Blicke nicht
Mit dieser finstern Strenge. Wer bin ich,
Daß ich den kühnen Wunsch zu euch erhebe?
Mich hat der Ruhm noch nicht genannt; ich darf
Mich in die Reih' nicht stellen mit den Rittern,
1600 Die siegberühmt und glänzend euch umwerben.
Nichts hab' ich, als mein Herz voll Treu' und Liebe.

Bertha, ernst und streng.

Dürft ihr von Liebe reden und von Treue,
Der treulos wird an seinen nächsten Pflichten?

Rudenz tritt zurück.

Der Sklave Österreichs, der sich dem Frembling
1605 Verkauft, dem Unterdrücker seines Volks?

Rudenz

Von euch, mein Fräulein, hör' ich diesen Vorwurf?
Wen such' ich denn, als euch, auf jener Seite?

Bertha

Mich denkt ihr auf der Seite des Verrats
Zu finden? Eher wollt' ich meine Hand
1610 Dem Geßler selbst, dem Unterdrücker, schenken,
Als dem naturvergeß'nen Sohn der Schweiz,
Der sich zu seinem Werkzeug machen kann.

Rudenz

O Gott, was muß ich hören?

Bertha

Wie! was liegt
Dem guten Menschen näher, als die Seinen?
1615 Giebt's schönre Pflichten für ein edles Herz,
Als ein Verteidiger der Unschuld sein,
Das Recht der Unterdrückten zu beschirmen?
Die Seele blutet mir um euer Volk;
Ich leide mit ihm, denn ich muß es lieben,
1620 Das so bescheiden ist und doch voll Kraft;
Es zieht mein ganzes Herz mich zu ihm hin;
Mit jedem Tage lern' ich's mehr verehren.
Ihr aber, den Natur und Ritterpflicht
Ihm zum geborenen Beschützer gaben,
1625 Und der's verläßt, der treulos übertritt
Zum Feind, und Ketten schmiedet seinem Land,
Ihr seid's, der mich verletzt und kränkt; ich muß
Mein Herz bezwingen, daß ich euch nicht hasse.

Rudenz

Will ich denn nicht das Beste meines Volks?
1630 Ihm unter Östreichs mächt'gem Zepter nicht
Den Frieden —

Bertha

Knechtschaft wollt ihr ihm bereiten.
Die Freiheit wollt' ihr aus dem letzten Schloß,
Das ihr noch auf der Erde blieb, verjagen.
Das Volk versteht sich besser auf sein Glück;
1635 Kein Schein verführt sein sicheres Gefühl.
Euch haben sie das Netz ums Haupt geworfen.

Rudenz

Bertha! Ihr haßt mich, ihr verachtet mich.

Bertha

Thät' ich's, mir wäre besser. Aber den
Berachtet s e h e n und verachtungswert,
1640 Den man gern lieben möchte —

Rudenz

Bertha! Bertha!
Ihr zeiget mir das höchste Himmelsglück
Und stürzt mich tief in e i n e m Augenblick.

Bertha

Nein, nein, das Edle ist nicht ganz erstickt
In euch. Es schlummert nur, ich will es wecken;
1645 Ihr müßt Gewalt ausüben an euch selbst,
Die angestammte Tugend zu ertöten;
Doch, wohl euch, sie ist mächtiger als ihr,
Und trotz euch selber seid ihr gut und edel.

Rudenz

Ihr glaubt an mich? O Bertha, alles läßt
1650 Mich eure Liebe sein und werden.

Bertha

Seid,
Wozu die herrliche Natur euch machte.
Erfüllt den Platz, wohin sie euch gestellt;
Zu eurem Volke steht und eurem Lande
Und kämpft für euer heilig Recht.

Rudenz

Weh' mir!
1655 Wie kann ich euch erringen, euch besitzen,
Wenn ich der Macht des Kaisers widerstrebe?
Ist's der Verwandten mächt'ger Wille nicht,
Der über eure Hand tyrannisch waltet?

Bertha

　　　In den Waldstätten liegen meine Güter,
1660　Und ist der Schweizer frei, so bin auch ich's.

Rudenz

　　　Bertha, welch einen Blick thut ihr mir auf!

Bertha

　　　Hofft nicht, durch Östreichs Gunst mich zu erringen;
　　　Nach meinem Erbe strecken sie die Hand;
　　　Das will man mit dem großen Erb' vereinen.
1665　Dieselbe Ländergier, die eure Freiheit
　　　Verschlingen will, sie drohet auch der meinen.
　　　O Freund, zum Opfer bin ich ausersehn,
　　　Vielleicht, um einen Günstling zu belohnen.
　　　Dort, wo die Falschheit und die Ränke wohnen,
1670　Hin an den Kaiserhof will man mich ziehn;
　　　Dort harren mein verhaßter Ehe Ketten;
　　　Die Liebe nur, die eure, kann mich retten.

Rudenz

　　　Ihr könntet euch entschließen, hier zu leben,
　　　In meinem Vaterlande mein zu sein?
1675　O Bertha, all mein Sehnen in das Weite,
　　　Was war es, als ein Streben nur nach euch?
　　　Euch sucht' ich einzig auf dem Weg des Ruhms,
　　　Und all mein Ehrgeiz war nur meine Liebe.
　　　Könnt ihr mit mir euch in dies stille Thal
1680　Einschließen und der Erde Glanz entsagen,
　　　O dann ist meines Strebens Ziel gefunden;
　　　Dann mag der Strom der wildbewegten Welt
　　　Ans sichre Ufer dieser Berge schlagen.
　　　Kein flüchtiges Verlangen hab' ich mehr

1685 Hinaus zu senden in des Lebens Weiten;
Dann mögen diese Felsen um uns her
Die undurchdringlich feste Mauer breiten,
Und dies verschloß'ne sel'ge Thal allein
Zum Himmel offen und gelichtet sein.

Bertha

1690 Jetzt bist du ganz, wie dich mein ahnend Herz
Geträumt, mich hat mein Glaube nicht betrogen.

Rudenz

Fahr' hin, du eitler Wahn, der mich bethört!
Ich soll das Glück in meiner Heimat finden.
Hier, wo der Knabe fröhlich aufgeblüht,
1695 Wo tausend Freudespuren mich umgeben,
Wo alle Quellen mir und Bäume leben,
Im Vaterland willst du die Meine werden.
Ach! wohl hab' ich es stets geliebt. Ich fühl's,
Es fehlte mir zu jedem Glück der Erden.

Bertha

1700 Wo wär' die sel'ge Insel aufzufinden,
Wenn sie nicht hier ist, in der Unschuld Land?
Hier, wo die alte Treue heimisch wohnt,
Wo sich die Falschheit noch nicht hingefunden,
Da trübt kein Neid die Quelle unsers Glücks,
1705 Und ewig hell entfliehen uns die Stunden.
Da seh' ich dich im echten Männerwert,
Den ersten von den Freien und den Gleichen,
Mit reiner, freier Huldigung verehrt,
Groß, wie ein König wirkt in seinen Reichen.

Rudenz

1710 Da seh' ich dich, die Krone aller Frauen,

In weiblich reizender Geschäftigkeit,
In meinem Haus den Himmel mir erbauen,
Und wie der Frühling seine Blumen streut,
Mit schöner Anmut mir das Leben schmücken
1715 Und alles rings beleben und beglücken.

Bertha

Sieh, teurer Freund, warum ich trauerte,
Als ich dies höchste Lebensglück dich selbst
Zerstören sah. — Weh mir! Wie stünd's um mich,
Wenn ich dem stolzen Ritter müßte folgen,
1720 Dem Landbedrücker auf sein finstres Schloß!
Hier ist kein Schloß. Mich scheiden keine Mauern
Von einem Volk, das ich beglücken kann.

Rudenz

Doch, wie mich retten? wie die Schlinge lösen,
Die ich mir thöricht selbst ums Haupt gelegt?

Bertha

1725 Zerreiße sie mit männlichem Entschluß.
Was auch draus werde, steh' zu deinem Volk.
Es ist dein angeborner Platz. Jagdhörner in der Ferne.

Die Jagd

Kommt näher. Fort, wir müssen scheiden. Kämpfe
Fürs Vaterland, du kämpfst für deine Liebe.
1730 Es ist ein Feind, vor dem wir alle zittern,
Und eine Freiheit macht uns alle frei. Gehen ab.

Feb. 9 - 1909 - Skeet.

THE TELL STATUE AT ALTORF. Act III, Sc. 3.

Dritte Szene.

Wiese bei Altorf. Im Vordergrund Bäume; in der Tiefe der Hut auf
einer Stange. Der Prospekt wird begrenzt durch den Bannberg, über
welchem ein Schneegebirg emporragt. *town above*

Frießhardt und Leuthold halten Wache.

Frießhardt

Wir passen auf umsonst. Es will sich niemand
Heran begeben und dem Hut sein' Reverenz
Erzeigen. 's war doch sonst wie Jahrmarkt hier;
1735 Jetzt ist der ganze Anger wie verödet,
Seitdem der Popanz auf der Stange hängt.

Leuthold

Nur schlecht Gesindel läßt sich sehn und schwingt
Uns zum Verdrieße die zerlumpten Mützen.
Was rechte Leute sind, die machen lieber
1740 Den langen Umweg um den halben Flecken,
Eh' sie den Rücken beugten vor dem Hut.

Frießhardt

Sie müssen über diesen Platz, wenn sie
Vom Rathaus kommen um die Mittagsstunde.
Da meint' ich schon, 'nen guten Fang zu thun,
1745 Denn keiner dachte dran, den Hut zu grüßen;
Da sieht's der Pfaff', der Rösselmann, — kam just
Von einem Kranken her, — und stellt' sich hin
Mit dem Hochwürdigen, grad' vor die Stange.
Der Sigrist mußte mit dem Glöcklein schellen;
1750 Da fielen all' aufs Knie, ich selber mit,
Und grüßten die Monstranz, doch nicht den Hut.

Leuthold

Höre, Gesell, es fängt mir an zu deuchten,
Wir stehen hier am Pranger vor dem Hut;
's ist doch ein Schimpf für einen Reitersmann,
1755 Schildwach' zu stehn vor einem leeren Hut,
Und jeder rechte Kerl muß uns verachten.
Die Reverenz zu machen einem Hut,
Es ist doch, traun, ein närrischer Befehl.

Frießhardt

Warum nicht einem leeren, hohlen Hut?
1760 Bückst du dich doch vor manchem hohlen Schädel.

Hildegard, Mechthild und Elsbeth treten auf mit Kindern und stellen
sich um die Stange.

Leuthold

Und du bist auch so ein dienstfert'ger Schurke,
Und brächtest wackre Leute gern ins Unglück.
Mag, wer da will, am Hut vorübergehn,
Ich drück' die Augen zu und seh' nicht hin.

Mechthild

1765 Da hängt der Landvogt; habt Respekt, ihr Buben!

Elsbeth

Wollt's Gott, er ging' und ließ' uns seinen Hut!
Es sollte drum nicht schlechter stehn ums Land.

Frießhardt, verscheucht sie.

Wollt ihr vom Platz! Verwünschtes Volk der Weiber!
Wer fragt nach euch? Schickt eure Männer her,
1770 Wenn sie der Mut sticht, dem Befehl zu trotzen.

Weiber gehen.

Tell mit der Armbrust tritt auf, den Knaben an der Hand führend: sie gehen
an dem Hut vorbei gegen die vordere Szene, ohne darauf zu achten.

Walther, zeigt nach dem Bannberg.

Vater, ist's wahr, daß auf dem Berge dort
Die Bäume bluten, wenn man einen Streich
Drauf führte mit der Axt?

Tell

Wer sagt das, Knabe?

Walther

Der Meister Hirt erzählt's. Die Bäume seien
1775 Gebannt, sagt er, und wer sie schädige,
Dem wachse seine Hand heraus zum Grabe.

Tell

Die Bäume sind gebannt, das ist die Wahrheit.
Siehst du die Firnen dort, die weißen Hörner,
Die hoch bis in den Himmel sich verlieren?

Walther

1780 Das sind die Gletscher, die des Nachts so donnern
Und uns die Schlaglawinen niedersenden.

Tell

So ist's, und die Lawinen hätten längst
Den Flecken Altorf unter ihrer Last
Verschüttet, wenn der Wald dort oben nicht
1785 Als eine Landwehr sich dagegen stellte.

Walther, nach einigem Besinnen.

Giebt's Länder, Vater, wo nicht Berge sind?

Tell

Wenn man hinunter steigt von unsern Höhen,
Und immer tiefer steigt, den Strömen nach,
Gelangt man in ein großes, eb'nes Land,
1790 Wo die Waldwasser nicht mehr brausend schäumen,

Die Flüsse ruhig und gemächlich ziehn;
Da sieht man frei nach allen Himmelsräumen;
Das Korn wächst dort in langen, schönen Auen,
Und wie ein Garten ist das Land zu schauen.

Walther
1795 Ei, Vater, warum steigen wir denn nicht
Geschwind hinab in dieses schöne Land,
Statt daß wir uns hier ängstigen und plagen?

Tell
Das Land ist schön und gütig, wie der Himmel;
Doch, die's bebauen, sie genießen nicht
1800 Den Segen, den sie pflanzen.

Walther
                        Wohnen sie
Nicht frei, wie du, auf ihrem eignen Erbe?

Tell
Das Feld gehört dem Bischof und dem König.

Walther
So dürfen sie doch frei in Wäldern jagen?

Tell
Dem Herrn gehört das Wild und das Gefieder.

Walther
1805 Sie dürfen doch frei fischen in dem Strom?

Tell
Der Strom, das Meer, das Salz gehört dem König.

Walther
Wer ist der König denn, den alle fürchten?

Tell
Es ist der eine, der sie schützt und nährt.

Walther

Sie können sich nicht mutig selbst beschützen?

Tell

1810 Dort darf der Nachbar nicht dem Nachbar trauen.

Walther

Vater, es wird mir eng im weiten Land;
Da wohn' ich lieber unter den Lawinen.

Tell

Ja, wohl ist's besser, Kind, die Gletscherberge
Im Rücken haben, als die bösen Menschen.

Sie wollen vorübergehen.

Walther

1815 Ei, Vater, sieh den Hut dort auf der Stange.

Tell

Was kümmert uns der Hut? Komm', laß uns gehen.

Indem er abgehen will, tritt ihm Frießhardt mit vorgehaltener Pike entgegen.

Frießhardt

In des Kaisers Namen! Haltet an und steht.

Tell, *greift in die Pike.*

Was wollt ihr? Warum haltet ihr mich auf?

Frießhardt

Ihr habt's Mandat verletzt; ihr müßt uns folgen.

Leuthold

1820 Ihr habt dem Hut nicht Reverenz bewiesen..

Tell

Freund, laß mich gehen.

Frießhardt

Fort, fort ins Gefängnis!

Walther

Den Vater ins Gefängnis! Hilfe! Hilfe! In die Szene rufend,
Herbei, ihr Männer, gute Leute, helft!
Gewalt! Gewalt! Sie führen ihn gefangen.

Rösselmann, der Pfarrer, und Petermann, der Sigrist, kommen
herbei, mit drei andern Männern.

Sigrist

1825 Was giebt's?

Rösselmann

Was legst du Hand an diesen Mann?

Frießhardt

Er ist ein Feind des Kaisers, ein Verräter.

Tell, faßt ihn heftig,

Ein Verräter, ich?

Rösselmann

Du irrst dich, Freund. Das ist
Der Tell, ein Ehrenmann und guter Bürger.

Walther, erblickt Walther Fürsten und eilt ihm entgegen,

Großvater, hilf! Gewalt geschieht dem Vater.

Frießhardt

1830 Ins Gefängnis, fort!

Walther Fürst, herbeieilend,

Ich leiste Bürgschaft, haltet.
Um Gottes willen, Tell, was ist geschehen?

Melchthal und Stauffacher kommen

Frießhardt

Des Landvogts oberherrliche Gewalt
Verachtet er und will sie nicht erkennen.

Stauffacher

Das hätt' der Tell gethan?

Melchthal

Das lügst du, Bube!

Leuthold

1835 Er hat dem Hut nicht Reverenz bewiesen.

Walther Fürst

Und darum soll er ins Gefängnis? Freund,
Nimm meine Bürgschaft an und laß ihn ledig.

Frießhardt

Bürg' du für dich und deinen eignen Leib.
Wir thun, was unsers Amtes. Fort mit ihm!

Melchthal, zu den Landleuten,

1840 Nein, das ist schreiende Gewalt. Ertragen wir's,
Daß man ihn fortführt, frech, vor unsern Augen?

Sigrist

Wir sind die Stärkern. Freunde, duldet's nicht.
Wir haben einen Rücken an den andern.

Frießhardt

Wer widersetzt sich dem Befehl des Vogts?

Noch drei Landleute, herbeieilend.

1845 Wir helfen euch. Was giebt's? Schlagt sie zu Boden.

Hildegard, Mechthild und Elsbeth kommen zurück.

Tell

Ich helfe mir schon selbst. Geht, gute Leute.
Meint ihr, wenn ich die Kraft gebrauchen wollte,
Ich würde mich vor ihren Spießen fürchten?

Melchthal, zu Frießhardt,

Wag's, ihn aus unsrer Mitte wegzuführen!

Walther Fürst und **Stauffacher**

1850 Gelassen! Ruhig!

Frießhardt, schreit,

　　Aufruhr und Empörung!

Man hört Jagdhörner.

Weiber

Da kommt der Landvogt.

Frießhardt, erhebt die Stimme,

　　　　Meuterei!　Empörung!

Stauffacher

Schrei', bis du berstest, Schurke!

Rösselmann und Melchthal

　　　　Willst du schweigen?

Frießhardt, ruft noch lauter,

Zu Hilf', zu Hilf' den Dienern des Gesetzes!

Walther Fürst

Da ist der Vogt.　Weh uns, was wird das werden?

Geßler zu Pferd, den Falken auf der Faust, Rudolf der Harras,
Bertha und Rudenz, ein großes Gefolge von bewaffneten Knechten,
welche einen Kreis von Piken um die ganze Szene schließen.

Rudolf der Harras

1855　Platz, Platz dem Landvogt!

Geßler

　　　　Treibt sie auseinander.

Was läuft das Volk zusammen?　Wer ruft Hilfe?

Allgemeine Stille.

Wer war's?　Ich will es wissen; zu Frießhardt.

　　　　Du tritt vor.

Wer bist du, und was hältst du diesen Mann?

Er giebt den Falken einem Diener.

Frießhardt

Gestrenger Herr, ich bin dein Waffenknecht

1860　Und wohlbestellter Wächter bei dem Hut.

Diesen Mann ergriff ich über frischer That,
Wie er dem Hut den Ehrengruß versagte.
Verhaften wollt' ich ihn, wie du befahlst,
Und mit Gewalt will ihn das Volk entreißen.

Geßler, nach einer Pause.

1865 Verachtest du so deinen Kaiser, Tell,
Und mich, der hier an seiner Statt gebietet,
Daß du die Ehr' versagst dem Hut, den ich
Zur Prüfung des Gehorsams aufgehangen?
Dein böses Trachten hast du mir verraten.

Tell

1870 Verzeiht mir, lieber Herr. Aus Unbedacht,
Nicht aus Verachtung eurer ist's geschehn.
Wär' ich besonnen, hieß' ich nicht der Tell;
Ich bitt' um Gnad', es soll nicht mehr begegnen.

Geßler, nach einigem Stillschweigen.

Du bist ein Meister auf der Armbrust, Tell;
1875 Man sagt, du nehmst es auf mit jedem Schützen?

Walther Tell

Und das muß wahr sein, Herr; 'nen Apfel schießt
Der Vater dir vom Baum auf hundert Schritte.

Geßler

Ist das dein Knabe, Tell?

Tell

Ja, lieber Herr.

Geßler

Hast du der Kinder mehr?

Tell

Zwei Knaben, Herr.

Geßler

1880 Und welcher ist's, den du am meisten liebst?

Tell

Herr, beide sind sie mir gleich liebe Kinder.

Geßler

Nun, Tell, weil du den Apfel triffst vom Baume
Auf hundert Schritte, so wirst du deine Kunst
Vor mir bewähren müssen. Nimm die Armbrust, —
1885 Du hast sie gleich zur Hand, — und mach' dich fertig,
Einen Apfel von des Knaben Kopf zu schießen.
Doch, will ich raten, ziele gut, daß du
Den Apfel treffest auf den ersten Schuß;
Denn fehlst du ihn, so ist dein Kopf verloren.

Alle geben Zeichen des Schreckens.

Tell

1890 Herr, welches Ungeheure sinnet ihr
Mir an? Ich soll vom Haupte meines Kindes —
Nein, nein doch, lieber Herr, das kömmt euch nicht
Zu Sinn. Verhüt's der gnäd'ge Gott! Das kömmt ihr
Im Ernst von einem Vater nicht begehren.

Geßler

1895 Du wirst den Apfel schießen von dem Kopf
Des Knaben; ich begehr's und will's.

Tell

                    Ich soll
Mit meiner Armbrust auf das liebe Haupt
Des eignen Kindes zielen? Eher sterb' ich.

Geßler

Du schießest, oder stirbst mit deinem Knaben.

Tell

1900 Ich soll der Mörder werden meines Kinds?
Herr, ihr habt keine Kinder, wisset nicht,
Was sich bewegt in eines Vaters Herzen.

Geßler

Ei, Tell, du bist ja plötzlich so besonnen.
Man sagte mir, daß du ein Träumer seist
1905 Und dich entfernst von andrer Menschen Weise.
Du liebst das Seltsame; drum hab' ich jetzt
Ein eigen Wagstück für dich ausgesucht.
Ein andrer wohl bedächte sich; du drückst
Die Augen zu und greifst es herzhaft an.

Bertha

1910 Scherzt nicht, o Herr, mit diesen armen Leuten.
Ihr seht sie bleich und zitternd stehn; so wenig
Sind sie Kurzweils gewohnt aus eurem Munde.

Geßler

Wer sagt euch, daß ich scherze?

Greift nach einem Baumzweige, der über ihn herhängt.

Hier ist der Apfel.

Man mache Raum; er nehme seine Weite,
1915 Wie's Brauch ist; achtzig Schritte geb' ich ihm, —
Nicht weniger, noch mehr. Er rühmte sich,
Auf ihrer hundert seinen Mann zu treffen.
Jetzt, Schütze, triff und fehle nicht das Ziel.

Rudolf der Harras

Gott, das wird ernsthaft. Falle nieder, Knabe,
1920 Es gilt, und fleh' den Landvogt um dein Leben!

Walther Fürst

Beiseite zu Melchthal, der kaum seine Ungeduld bezwingt,

Haltet an euch, ich fleh' euch drum, bleibt ruhig.

Bertha, zum Landvogt.

Laßt es genug sein, Herr. Unmenschlich ist's,
Mit eines Vaters Angst also zu spielen.
Wenn dieser arme Mann auch Leib und Leben
1925   Verwirkt durch seine leichte Schuld, bei Gott!
Er hätte jetzt zehnfachen Tod empfunden.
Entlaßt ihn ungekränkt in seine Hütte;
Er hat euch kennen lernen; dieser Stunde
Wird er und seine Kindeskinder denken.

Geßler

1930   Öffnet die Gasse. — Frisch, was zauderst du?
Dein Leben ist verwirkt, ich kann dich töten;
Und sieh, ich lege gnädig dein Geschick
In deine eigne kunstgeübte Hand.
Der kann nicht klagen über harten Spruch,
1935   Den man zum Meister seines Schicksals macht.
Du rühmst dich deines sichern Blicks. Wohlan!
Hier gilt es, S ch ü tz e, deine Kunst zu zeigen;
Das Ziel ist würdig, und der Preis ist groß.
Das Schwarze treffen in der Scheibe, d a s
1940   Kann auch ein andrer; d e r ist mir der Meister,
Der seiner Kunst gewiß ist überall,
Dem 's Herz nicht in die Hand tritt, noch ins Auge.

Walther Fürst, wirft sich vor ihm nieder,

Herr Landvogt, wir erkennen eure Hoheit;
Doch lasset Gnad' vor Recht ergehen; nehmt
1945   Die Hälfte meiner Habe, nehmt sie ganz.
Nur dieses Gräßliche erlasset einem Vater.

Walther Tell

Großvater, knie' nicht vor dem falschen Mann.
Sagt, wo ich hinstehn soll. Ich fürcht' mich nicht.

Der Vater trifft den Vogel ja im Flug;
1950 Er wird nicht fehlen auf das Herz des Kindes.

Stauffacher

Herr Landvogt, rührt euch nicht des Kindes Unschuld?

Rösselmann

O denket, daß ein Gott im Himmel ist,
Dem ihr müßt Rede stehn für eure Thaten.

Geßler, zeigt auf den Knaben,

Man bind' ihn an die Linde dort.

Walther Tell

Mich binden?
1955 Nein, ich will nicht gebunden sein. Ich will
Still halten, wie ein Lamm, und auch nicht atmen.
Wenn ihr mich bindet, nein, so kann ich's nicht,
So werd' ich toben gegen meine Bande.

Rudolf der Harras

Die Augen nur laß dir verbinden, Knabe.

Walther Tell

1960 Warum die Augen? Denket ihr, ich fürchte
Den Pfeil von Vaters Hand? Ich will ihn fest
Erwarten und nicht zucken mit den Wimpern.
Frisch, Vater, zeig's, daß du ein Schütze bist.
Er glaubt dir's nicht; er denkt uns zu verderben.
1965 Dem Wütrich zum Verdrusse schieß' und triff.

Er geht an die Linde, man legt ihm den Apfel auf.

Melchthal, zu den Landleuten,

Was? Soll der Frevel sich vor unsern Augen
Vollenden? Wozu haben wir geschworen?

Stauffacher

Es ist umsonst. Wir haben keine Waffen;
Ihr seht den Wald von Lanzen um uns her.

Melchthal

1970 O, hätten wir's mit frischer That vollendet!
Verzeih's Gott denen, die zum Aufschub rieten!

Geßler, zum Tell,

Ans Werk! Man führt die Waffen nicht vergebens.
Gefährlich ist's, ein Mordgewehr zu tragen,
Und auf den Schützen springt der Pfeil zurück.
1975 Dies stolze Recht, das sich der Bauer nimmt,
Beleidiget den höchsten Herrn des Landes.
Gewaffnet sei niemand, als wer gebietet.
Freut's euch, den Pfeil zu führen und den Bogen,
Wohl, so will ich das Ziel euch dazu geben.

Tell, spannt die Armbrust und legt den Pfeil auf.

1980 Öffnet die Gasse. Platz!

Stauffacher

Was, Tell? Ihr wolltet? Nimmermehr! Ihr zittert,
Die Hand erbebt euch; eure Kniee wanken.

Tell, läßt die Armbrust sinken.

Mir schwimmt es vor den Augen.

Weiber

Gott im Himmel!

Tell, zum Landvogt,

Erlasset mir den Schuß. Hier ist mein Herz.

Er reißt die Brust auf.

1985 Ruft eure Reisigen und stoßt mich nieder.

Geßler

Ich will dein Leben nicht, ich will den Schuß.
Du kannst ja alles, Tell, an nichts verzagst du;
Das Steuerruder führst du wie den Bogen;
Dich schreckt kein Sturm, wenn es zu retten gilt.
1990 Jetzt, Retter, hilf dir selbst; du rettest alle.

Tell steht in fürchterlichem Kampf, mit den Händen zuckend und die rollenden Augen bald auf den Landvogt, bald zum Himmel gerichtet. Plötzlich greift er in seinen Köcher, nimmt einen zweiten Pfeil heraus und steckt ihn in seinen Goller. Der Landvogt bemerkt alle diese Bewegungen.

Walther Tell, unter der Linde,

Vater, schieß' du. Ich fürcht' mich nicht.

Tell

                    Es muß.

Er rafft sich zusammen und legt an.

Rudenz,

der die ganze Zeit über in der heftigsten Spannung gestanden und mit Gewalt an sich gehalten, tritt hervor,

Herr Landvogt, weiter werdet ihr's nicht treiben;
Ihr werdet nicht. Es war nur eine Prüfung;
Den Zweck habt ihr erreicht. Zu weit getrieben,
1995 Verfehlt die Strenge ihres weisen Zwecks,
Und allzustraff gespannt, zerspringt der Bogen

Geßler

Ihr schweigt, bis man euch aufruft.

Rudenz

                    Ich will reden.

Ich darf's. Des Königs Ehre ist mir heilig;
Doch solches Regiment muß Haß erwerben.
2000 Das ist des Königs Wille nicht, ich darf's

Behaupten.   Solche Grausamkeit verdient
Mein Volk nicht; dazu habt ihr keine Vollmacht.

Geßler

Ha, ihr erkühnt euch!

Rudenz

Ich hab' still geschwiegen
Zu allen schweren Thaten, die ich sah;
2005 Mein sehend Auge hab' ich zugeschlossen;
Mein überschwellend und empörtes Herz
Hab' ich hinabgedrückt in meinen Busen;
Doch länger schweigen wär' Verrat zugleich
An meinem Vaterland und an dem Kaiser.

Bertha, wirft sich zwischen ihn und den Landvogt.

2010 O Gott! ihr reizt den Wütenden noch mehr.

Rudenz

Mein Volk verließ ich; meinen Blutsverwandten
Entsagt' ich, alle Bande der Natur
Zerriß ich, um an euch mich anzuschließen.
Das Beste aller glaubt' ich zu befördern,
2015 Da ich des Kaisers Macht befestigte.
Die Binde fällt von meinen Augen. Schaudernd
Seh' ich an einen Abgrund mich geführt,
Mein freies Urteil habt ihr irr geleitet,
Mein redlich Herz verführt. Ich war daran,
2020 Mein Volk in bester Meinung zu verderben.

Geßler

Verwegner, diese Sprache deinem Herrn?

Rudenz

Der Kaiser ist mein Herr, nicht ihr. — Frei bin ich
Wie ihr geboren, und ich messe mich

Mit euch in jeder ritterlichen Tugend.

2025 Und stündet ihr nicht hier in Kaisers Namen,
Den ich verehre, selbst wo man ihn schändet,
Den Handschuh wärf' ich vor euch hin, ihr solltet
Nach ritterlichem Brauch mir Antwort geben.
Ja, winkt nur euren Reisigen. Ich stehe

2030 Nicht wehrlos da, wie die. *Auf das Volk zeigend.*

Ich hab' ein Schwert,
Und wer mir naht —

Stauffacher, ruft,

Der Apfel ist gefallen.

Indem sich alle nach dieser Seite gewendet und Bertha zwischen Rudenz und den Landvogt sich geworfen, hat Tell den Pfeil abgedrückt.

Rösselmann

Der Knabe lebt.

Viele Stimmen

Der Apfel ist getroffen.

Walther Fürst schwankt und droht zu sinken, Bertha hält ihn.

Geßler, erstaunt,

Er hat geschossen? Wie? Der Rasende!

Bertha

Der Knabe lebt. Kommt zu euch, guter Vater.

Walther Tell, kommt mit dem Apfel gesprungen,

2035 Vater hier ist der Apfel. Wußt' ich's ja,
Du würdest deinen Knaben nicht verletzen.

Tell stand mit vorgebognem Leib, als wollt' er dem Pfeil folgen; die Armbrust entsinkt seiner Hand; wie er den Knaben kommen sieht, eilt er ihm mit ausgebreiteten Armen entgegen und hebt ihn mit heftiger Inbrunst zu seinem Herzen hinauf; in dieser Stellung sinkt er kraftlos zusammen. Alle stehen gerührt.

Bertha

O güt'ger Himmel!

Walther Fürst, zu Vater und Sohn.

Kinder! meine Kinder!

Stauffacher

Gott sei gelobt!

Leuthold

Das war ein Schuß! Davon
Wird man noch reden in den spätsten Zeiten.

Rudolf der Harras

2040 Erzählen wird man von dem Schützen Tell,
Solang die Berge stehn auf ihrem Grunde.

Reicht dem Landvogt den Apfel.

Geßler

Bei Gott! der Apfel mitten durch geschossen.
Es war ein Meisterschuß, ich muß ihn loben.

Rösselmann

Der Schuß war gut; doch wehe dem, der ihn
2045 Dazu getrieben, daß er Gott versuchte.

Stauffacher

Kommt zu euch, Tell, steht auf, ihr habt euch männlich
Gelöst, und frei könnt ihr nach Hause gehen.

Rösselmann

Kommt, kommt und bringt der Mutter ihren Sohn.

Sie wollen ihn wegführen.

Geßler

Tell, höre.

Tell, kommt zurück.

Was befehlt ihr, Herr?

Geßler

Du stecktest

2050 Noch einen zweiten Pfeil zu dir. — Ja, ja,
Ich sah es wohl. Was meintest du damit?

Tell, verlegen.

Herr, das ist also bräuchlich bei den Schützen.

Geßler

Nein, Tell, die Antwort laß' ich dir nicht gelten;
Es wird was Anders wohl bedeutet haben.
2055 Sag' mir die Wahrheit frisch und fröhlich, Tell;
Was es auch sei, dein Leben sichr' ich dir.
Wozu der zweite Pfeil?

Tell

Wohlan! o Herr
Weil ihr mich meines Lebens habt gesichert,
So will ich euch die Wahrheit gründlich sagen.

Er zieht den Pfeil aus dem Goller und sieht den Landvogt mit einem furcht-
baren Blick an.

2060 Mit diesem zweiten Pfeil durchschoß ich — euch,
Wenn ich mein liebes Kind getroffen hätte,
Und eurer, wahrlich, hätt' ich nicht gefehlt.

Geßler

Wohl, Tell. Des Lebens hab' ich dich gesichert;
Ich gab mein Ritterwort, das will ich halten.
2065 Doch weil ich deinen bösen Sinn erkannt,
Will ich dich führen lassen und verwahren,
Wo weder Mond noch Sonne dich bescheint,
Damit ich sicher sei vor deinen Pfeilen.
Ergreift ihn, Knechte. Bindet ihn. Tell wird gebunden.

Stauffacher

Wie, Herr?

2070 So könntet ihr an einem Manne handeln,
An dem sich Gottes Hand sichtbar verkündigt?

Geßler

Laß sehn, ob sie ihn zweimal retten wird.
Man bring' ihn auf mein Schiff. Ich folge nach
Sogleich; ich selbst will ihn nach Küßnacht führen?

Rösselmann

2075 Das dürft ihr nicht, das darf der Kaiser nicht;
Das widerstreitet unsern Freiheitsbriefen.

Geßler

Wo sind sie? Hat der Kaiser sie bestätigt?
Er hat sie nicht bestätigt. Diese Gunst
Muß erst erworben werden durch Gehorsam.
2080 Rebellen seid ihr alle gegen Kaisers
Gericht und nährt verwegene Empörung.
Ich kenn' euch alle; ich durchschau' euch ganz.
Den nehm' ich jetzt heraus aus eurer Mitte;
Doch alle seid ihr teilhaft seiner Schuld.
2085 Wer klug ist, lerne schweigen und gehorchen.

Er entfernt sich; Bertha, Rudenz, Harras und Knechte folgen, Frießhardt und
Leuthold bleiben zurück.

Walther Fürst, in heftigem Schmerz.

Es ist vorbei; er hat's beschlossen, mich
Mit meinem ganzen Hause zu verderben.

Stauffacher, zum Tell.

O warum mußtet ihr den Wütrich reizen?

Tell

Bezwinge sich, wer meinen Schmerz gefühlt.

Stauffacher

2090 O nun ist alles, alles hin. Mit euch
Sind wir gefesselt alle und gebunden.

Landleute, umringen den Tell,

Mit euch geht unser letzter Trost dahin.

Leuthold, nähert sich,

Tell, es erbarmt mich; doch ich muß gehorchen.

Tell

Lebt wohl!

Walther Tell,
sich mit heftigem Schmerz an ihn schmiegend,

O Vater! Vater! lieber Vater!

Tell, hebt die Arme zum Himmel,

2095 Dort droben ist dein Vater. Den ruf' an.

Stauffacher

Tell, sag' ich eurem Weibe nichts von euch?

Tell,
hebt den Knaben mit Inbrunst an seine Brust.

Der Knab' ist unverletzt; mir wird Gott helfen.
Reißt sich schnell los und folgt den Waffenknechten.

Vierter Aufzug.

Erste Szene.

Östliches Ufer des Vierwaldstättensees.

Die seltsam gestalteten schroffen Felsen im Westen schließen den Prospekt. Der See ist bewegt; heftiges Rauschen und Tosen, dazwischen Blitze und Donnerschläge.

Kunz von Gersau. Fischer und Fischerknabe.

Kunz

Ich sah's mit Augen an, ihr könnt mir's glauben;
's ist alles so geschehn, wie ich euch sagte.

Fischer

2100 Der Tell gefangen abgeführt nach Küßnacht,
Der beste Mann im Land, der bravste Arm,
Wenn's einmal gelten sollte für die Freiheit.

Kunz

Der Landvogt führt ihn selbst den See herauf;
Sie waren eben dran, sich einzuschiffen,
2105 Als ich von Flüelen abfuhr; doch der Sturm,
Der eben jetzt im Anzug ist, und der
Auch mich gezwungen, eilends hier zu landen,
Mag ihre Abfahrt wohl verhindert haben.

Fischer

Der Tell in Fesseln, in des Vogts Gewalt.
2110 O glaubt, er wird ihn tief genug vergraben,
Daß er des Tages Licht nicht wieder sieht.
Denn fürchten muß er die gerechte Rache
Des freien Mannes, den er schwer gereizt.

THE AXENSTRASSE, WITH FLÜELEN IN THE DISTANCE.   Act IV. Sc. 1.

Kunz

Der Altlandammann auch, der edle Herr
2115 Von Attinghausen, sagt man, lieg' am Tode.

Fischer

So bricht der letzte Anker unsrer Hoffnung.
Der war es noch allein, der seine Stimme
Erheben durfte für des Volkes Rechte.

Kunz

Der Sturm nimmt überhand. Gehabt euch wohl.
2120 Ich nehme Herberg' in dem Dorf; denn heut'
Ist doch an keine Abfahrt mehr zu denken. Geht ab.

Fischer

Der Tell gefangen und der Freiherr tot:
Erheb' die freche Stirne, Tyrannei,
Wirf alle Scham hinweg! Der Mund der Wahrheit
2125 Ist stumm, das sehnde Auge ist geblendet,
Der Arm, der retten sollte, ist gefesselt.

Knabe

Es hagelt schwer. Kommt in die Hütte, Vater;
Es ist nicht kommlich, hier im Freien hausen.

Fischer

Raset, ihr Winde! Flammt herab, ihr Blitze!
2130 Ihr Wolken, berstet! Gießt herunter, Ströme
Des Himmels, und ersäuft das Land! Zerstört
Im Keim die ungeborenen Geschlechter!
Ihr wilden Elemente, werdet Herr!
Ihr Bären, kommt, ihr alten Wölfe wieder
2135 Der großen Wüste! euch gehört das Land.
Wer wird hier leben wollen ohne Freiheit!

Knabe

Hört, wie der Abgrund tost, der Wirbel brüllt;
So hat's noch nie gerast in diesem Schlunde.

Fischer

Zu zielen auf des eignen Kindes Haupt,
2140 Solches ward keinem Vater noch geboten.
Und die Natur soll nicht in wildem Grimm
Sich drob empören? O mich soll's nicht wundern,
Wenn sich die Felsen bücken in den See;
Wenn jene Zacken, jene Eisestürme,
2145 Die nie auftauten seit dem Schöpfungstag,
Von ihren hohen Kulmen niederschmelzen;
Wenn die Berge brechen; wenn die alten Klüfte
Einstürzen, eine zweite Sündflut alle
Wohnstätten der Lebendigen verschlingt. Man hört läuten.

Knabe

2150 Hört ihr, sie läuten droben auf dem Berg.
Gewiß hat man ein Schiff in Not gesehn
Und zieht die Glocke, daß gebetet werde. Steigt auf eine Anhöhe.

Fischer

Wehe dem Fahrzeug, das, jetzt unterwegs,
In dieser furchtbarn Wiege wird gewiegt!
2155 Hier ist das Steuer unnütz und der Steurer;
Der Sturm ist Meister; Wind und Welle spielen
Ball mit dem Menschen. Da ist nah und fern
Kein Busen, der ihm freundlich Schutz gewährte.
Handlos und schroff ansteigend starren ihm
2160 Die Felsen, die unwirtlichen, entgegen,
Und weisen ihm nur ihre steinern schroffe Brust.

Knabe, deutet links.

Vater, ein Schiff; es kommt von Flüelen her.

Fischer

Gott helf' den armen Leuten! Wenn der Sturm
In dieser Wasserkluft sich erst verfangen,
2165 Dann rast er um sich mit des Raubtiers Angst,
Das an des Gitters Eisenstäbe schlägt.
Die Pforte sucht er heulend sich vergebens,
Denn ringsum schränken ihn die Felsen ein,
Die himmelhoch den engen Paß vermauren.

Er steigt auf die Anhöhe.

Knabe

2170 Es ist das Herrenschiff von Uri, Vater;
Ich kenn's am roten Dach und an der Fahne.

Fischer

Gerichte Gottes! Ja, er ist es selbst,
Der Landvogt, der da fährt. Dort schifft er hin
Und führt im Schiffe sein Verbrechen mit.
2175 Schnell hat der Arm des Rächers ihn gefunden;
Jetzt kennt er über sich den stärkern Herrn.
Diese Wellen geben nicht auf seine Stimme;
Diese Felsen bücken ihre Häupter nicht
Vor seinem Hute. Knabe, bete nicht;
2180 Greif' nicht dem Richter in den Arm.

Knabe

Ich bete für den Landvogt nicht; ich bete
Für den Tell, der auf dem Schiff sich mit befindet.

Fischer

O Unvernunft des blinden Elements!
Mußt du, um einen Schuldigen zu treffen,
2185 Das Schiff mitsamt dem Steuermann verderben?

Knabe

Sieh, sieh, sie waren glücklich schon vorbei
Am Buggisgrat; doch die Gewalt des Sturmes,
Der von dem Teufelsmünster widerprallt,
Wirft sie zum großen Axenberg zurück.
2190 Ich seh' sie nicht mehr.

Fischer

Dort ist das Hackmesser,
Wo schon der Schiffe mehrere gebrochen.
Wenn sie nicht weislich dort vorüberlenken,
So wird das Schiff zerschmettert an der Fluh,
Die sich gähstotzig absenkt in die Tiefe.
2195 Sie haben einen guten Steuermann
Am Bord; könnt einer retten, wär's der Tell;
Doch dem sind Arm' und Hände ja gefesselt.

Wilhelm Tell mit der Armbrust.

Er kommt mit raschen Schritten, blickt erstaunt umher und zeigt die heftigste Bewegung. Wenn er mitten auf der Szene ist, wirft er sich nieder, die Hände zu der Erde und dann zum Himmel ausbreitend.

Knabe, bemerkt ihn.

Sieh, Vater, wer der Mann ist der dort kniet?

Fischer

Er faßt die Erde an mit seinen Händen
2200 Und scheint wie außer sich zu sein.

Knabe, kommt vorwärts.

Was seh' ich! Vater, Vater, kommt und seht.

Fischer, nähert sich.

Wer ist es? — Gott im Himmel! Was? der Tell?
Wie kommt ihr hieher? Redet.

Knabe

Wart ihr nicht
Dort auf dem Schiff gefangen und gebunden?

Fischer

2205 Ihr wurdet nicht nach Küßnacht abgeführt?

Tell, steht auf.

Ich bin befreit.

Fischer und Knabe

Befreit? O Wunder Gottes!

Knabe

Wo kommt ihr her?

Tell

Dort aus dem Schiffe.

Fischer

Was!

Knabe, zugleich.

Wo ist der Landvogt?

Tell

Auf den Wellen treibt er.

Fischer

Ist's möglich? Aber ihr? Wie seid ihr hier,
2210 Seid euren Banden und dem Sturm entkommen?

Tell

Durch Gottes gnäd'ge Fürsehung. Hört an.

Fischer und Knabe

O redet, redet.

Tell

Was in Altorf sich
Begeben, wißt ihr's?

Fischer

Alles weiß ich; redet.

Tell

Daß mich der Landvogt fahen ließ und binden,
2215 Nach seiner Burg zu Küßnacht wollte führen?

Fischer

Und sich mit euch zu Flüelen eingeschifft.
Wir wissen alles. Sprecht, wie ihr entkommen?

Tell

Ich lag im Schiff, mit Stricken fest gebunden,
Wehrlos, ein aufgegebner Mann. Nicht hofft' ich,
2220 Das frohe Licht der Sonne mehr zu sehn,
Der Gattin und der Kinder liebes Antlitz,
Und trostlos blickt' ich in die Wasserwüste.

Fischer

O armer Mann!

Tell

So fuhren wir dahin,
Der Vogt, Rudolf der Harras und die Knechte.
2225 Mein Köcher aber mit der Armbrust lag
Am hintern Graußen bei dem Steuerruder.
Und als wir an die Ecke jetzt gelangt
Beim kleinen Axen, da verhängt' es Gott,
Daß solch ein grausam mördrisch Ungewitter
2230 Gählings herfürbrach aus des Gotthards Schlünden,
Das allen Ruderern das Herz entsank,
Und meinten alle, elend zu ertrinken.
Da hört' ich's, wie der Diener einer sich
Zum Landvogt wendet' und die Worte sprach:
2235 Ihr sehet eure Not und unsre, Herr,
Und daß wir all' am Rand des Todes schweben;
Die Steuerleute aber wissen sich
Für großer Furcht nicht Rat und sind des Fahrens

Nicht wohl berichtet. Nun aber ist der Tell

2240 Ein starker Mann und weiß ein Schiff zu steuern.
Wie, wenn wir sein jetzt brauchten in der Not?
Da sprach der Vogt zu mir: Tell, wenn du dir's
Getrautest, uns zu helfen aus dem Sturm,
So möcht' ich dich der Bande wohl entled'gen.

2245 Ich aber sprach: Ja, Herr, mit Gottes Hilfe
Getrau' ich mir's und helf' uns wohl hiedannen.
So ward ich meiner Bande los und stand
Am Steuerruder und fuhr redlich hin.
Doch schielt' ich seitwärts, wo mein Schießzeug lag,

2250 Und an dem Ufer merkt' ich scharf umher,
Wo sich ein Vorteil aufthät' zum Entspringen.
Und wie ich eines Felsenriffs gewahre,
Das abgeplattet vorsprang in den See —

Fischer

Ich kenn's, es ist am Fuß des großen Axen,

2255 Doch nicht für möglich acht' ich's, so gar steil
Geht's an, vom Schiff es springend abzureichen. —

Tell

Schrie ich den Knechten, handlich zuzugehn,
Bis daß wir vor die Felsenplatte kämen;
Dort, rief ich, sei das Ärgste überstanden.

2260 Und als wir sie frischrudernd bald erreicht,
Fleh' ich die Gnade Gottes an und drücke,
Mit allen Leibeskräften angestemmt,
Den hintern Gransen an die Felswand hin.
Jetzt, schnell mein Schießzeug fassend, schwing' ich selbst

2265 Hochspringend auf die Platte mich hinauf,
Und mit gewalt'gem Fußstoß hinter mich

Schleudr' ich das Schifflein in den Schlund der Wasser.
Dort mag's, wie Gott will, auf den Wellen treiben.
So bin ich hier, gerettet aus des Sturms
2270 Gewalt und aus der schlimmeren der Menschen.

Fischer

Tell, Tell, ein sichtbar Wunder hat der Herr
An euch gethan; kaum glaub' ich's meinen Sinnen.
Doch saget: Wo gedenket ihr jetzt hin?
Denn Sicherheit ist nicht für euch, wofern
2275 Der Landvogt lebend diesem Sturm entkommt.

Tell

Ich hört' ihn sagen, da ich noch im Schiff
Gebunden lag, er woll' bei Brunnen landen
Und über Schwytz nach seiner Burg mich führen.

Fischer

Will er den Weg dahin zu Lande nehmen?

Tell

2280 Er denkt's.

Fischer

    O so verbergt euch ohne Säumen.
Nicht zweimal hilft euch Gott aus seiner Hand.

Tell

Nennt mir den nächsten Weg nach Arth und Küßnacht.

Fischer

Die offne Straße zieht sich über Steinen;
Doch einen kürzern Weg und heimlichern
2285 Kann euch mein Knabe über Lowerz führen.

Tell, giebt ihm die Hand,

Gott lohn' euch eure Gutthat. Lebet wohl.

Geht und kehrt wieder um,

Habt ihr nicht auch im Rütli mitgeschworen?
Mir deucht, man nannt' euch mir.

Fischer

                        Ich war dabei,
Und hab' den Eid des Bundes mit beschworen.

Tell

2290 So eilt nach Bürglen, thut die Lieb mir an;
Mein Weib verzagt um mich; verkündet ihr,
Daß ich gerettet sei und wohl geborgen.

Fischer

Doch wohin sag' ich ihr, daß ihr geflohn?

Tell

Ihr werdet meinen Schwäher bei ihr finden,
2295 Und andre, die im Rütli mit geschworen:
Sie sollen wacker sein und gutes Muts;
Der Tell sei frei und seines Armes mächtig;
Bald werden sie ein Weitres von mir hören.

Fischer

Was habt ihr im Gemüt? Entdeckt mir's frei.

Tell

2300 Ist es gethan, wird's auch zur Rede kommen. Geht ab.

Fischer

Zeig' ihm den Weg, Jenni. Gott steh' ihm bei!
Er führt's zum Ziel, was er auch unternommen. Geht ab.

Zweite Szene.

Edelhof zu Attinghausen.

Der Freiherr, in einem Armsessel, sterbend. Walther Fürst, Stauffacher, Melchthal und Baumgarten um ihn beschäftigt. Walther Tell, knieend vor dem Sterbenden.

Walther Fürst

Es ist vorbei mit ihm, er ist hinüber.

Stauffacher

Er liegt nicht wie ein Toter. Seht, die Feder
2305 Auf seinen Lippen regt sich. Ruhig ist
Sein Schlaf, und friedlich lächeln seine Züge.

Baumgarten geht an die Thüre und spricht mit jemand.

Walther Fürst, zu Baumgarten,

Wer ist's?

Baumgarten, kommt zurück,

Es ist Frau Hedwig, eure Tochter;
Sie will euch sprechen, will den Knaben sehn.

Walther Tell richtet sich auf.

Walther Fürst

Kann ich sie trösten? Hab' ich selber Trost?
2310 Häuft alles Leiden sich auf meinem Haupt?

Hedwig, hereindringend,

Wo ist mein Kind? Laßt mich, ich muß es sehn.

Stauffacher

Faßt euch. Bedenkt, daß ihr im Haus des Todes.

Hedwig, stürzt auf den Knaben,

Mein Wälty! O! er lebt mir.

Walther Tell, hängt an ihr.

Arme Mutter!

Hedwig

Ist's auch gewiß? Bist du mir unverletzt?

Betrachtet ihn mit ängstlicher Sorgfalt.

2315 Und ist es möglich? Konnt' er auf dich zielen?
Wie konnt' er's? O! er hat kein Herz. Er konnte
Den Pfeil abdrücken auf sein eignes Kind!

Walther Fürst

Er that's mit Angst, mit schmerzzerriß'ner Seele;
Gezwungen that er's, denn es galt das Leben.

Hedwig

2320 O hätt' er eines Vaters Herz, eh' er's
Gethan, er wäre tausendmal gestorben.

Stauffacher

Ihr solltet Gottes gnäd'ge Schickung preisen,
Die es so gut gelenkt.

Hedwig

Kann ich vergessen,
Wie's hätte kommen können? Gott des Himmels!
2325 Und lebt' ich achtzig Jahr, ich seh' den Knaben ewig
Gebunden stehn, den Vater auf ihn zielen,
Und ewig fliegt der Pfeil mir in das Herz.

Melchthal

Frau, wüßtet ihr, wie ihn der Vogt gereizt.

Hedwig

O rohes Herz der Männer! Wenn ihr Stolz
2330 Beleidigt wird, dann achten sie nichts mehr;
Sie setzen in der blinden Wut des Spiels
Das Haupt des Kindes und das Herz der Mutter.

Baumgarten

Ist eures Mannes Los nicht hart genug,
Daß ihr mit schwerem Tadel ihn noch kränkt?
2335 Für s e i n e Leiden habt ihr kein Gefühl?

Hedwig,

kehrt sich nach ihm um und sieht ihn mit einem großen Blick an,

Hast du nur Thränen für des Freundes Unglück?
Wo waret ihr, da man den Trefflichen
In Bande schlug? Wo war da eure Hilfe?
Ihr sahet zu, ihr ließt das Gräßliche geschehn;
2340 Geduldig littet ihr's, daß man den Freund
Aus eurer Mitte führte. Hat der Tell
Auch so an euch gehandelt? Stand er auch
Bedaurend da, als hinter dir die Reiter
Des Landvogts drangen, als der wüt'ge See
2345 Vor dir erbrauste? Nicht mit müß'gen Thränen
Beklagt' er dich; in den Nachen sprang er; Weib
Und Kind vergaß er und befreite dich.

Walther Fürst

Was konnten wir zu seiner Rettung wagen,
Die kleine Zahl, die unbewaffnet war?

Hedwig, wirft sich an seine Brust,

2350 O Vater! Und auch du hast ihn verloren
Das Land, wir alle haben ihn verloren.
Uns allen fehlt er, ach, wir fehlen ihm.
Gott rette seine Seele vor Verzweiflung!
Zu ihm hinab ins öde Burgverlies
2355 Dringt keines Freundes Trost. Wenn er erkrankt!
Ach, in des Kerkers feuchter Finsternis
Muß er erkranken. Wie die Alpenrose

Bleicht und verkümmert in der Sumpfesluft, *swamp*
So ist für ihn kein Leben als im Licht
2360 Der Sonne, in dem Balsamstrom der Lüfte.
Gefangen! Er! Sein Atem ist die Freiheit;
Er kann nicht leben in dem Hauch der Grüfte.

Stauffacher

Beruhigt euch. Wir alle wollen handeln,
Um seinen Kerker aufzuthun.

Hedwig

2365 Was könnt i h r schaffen ohne ihn? So lang
Der Tell noch frei war, ja, da war noch Hoffnung,
Da hatte noch die Unschuld einen Freund,
Da hatte einen Helfer der Verfolgte;
Euch alle rettete der Tell; ihr alle
2370 Zusammen könnt nicht s e i n e Fesseln lösen.

Der Freiherr erwacht.

Baumgarten

Er regt sich. Still!

Attinghausen, sich aufrichtend,
Wo ist er?

Stauffacher
Wer?

Attinghausen
Er fehlt mir,

Verläßt mich in dem letzten Augenblick.

Stauffacher

Er meint den Junker. Schickte man nach ihm?

Walther Fürst

Es ist nach ihm gesendet. Tröstet euch.
2375 Er hat sein Herz gefunden, er ist unser.

Attinghausen

Hat er gesprochen für sein Vaterland?

Stauffacher

Mit Heldenkühnheit.

Attinghausen

Warum kommt er nicht,
Um meinen letzten Segen zu empfangen?
Ich fühle, daß es schleunig mit mir endet.

Stauffacher

2380 Nicht also, edler Herr. Der kurze Schlaf
Hat euch erquickt, und hell ist euer Blick.

Attinghausen

Der Schmerz ist Leben, er verließ mich auch.
Das Leiden ist, so wie die Hoffnung, aus.

Er bemerkt den Knaben.

Wer ist der Knabe?

Walther Fürst,

Segnet ihn, o Herr!
2385 Er ist mein Enkel und ist vaterlos.

Hedwig sinkt mit dem Knaben vor dem Sterbenden nieder.

Attinghausen

Und vaterlos laß' ich euch alle, alle
Zurück. Weh' mir, daß meine letzten Blicke
Den Untergang des Vaterlands gesehn!
Mußt' ich des Lebens höchstes Maß erreichen,
2390 Um ganz mit allen Hoffnungen zu sterben?

Stauffacher, zu Walther Fürst.

Soll er in diesem finstern Kummer scheiden?
Erhellen wir ihm nicht die letzte Stunde

Mit schönem Strahl der Hoffnung? — Edler Freiherr,
Erhebet euren Geist. Wir sind nicht ganz
2395 Verlassen, sind nicht rettungslos verloren.

Attinghausen

Wer soll euch retten?

Walther Fürst

      Wir uns selbst. Vernehmt:
Es haben die drei Lande sich das Wort
Gegeben, die Tyrannen zu verjagen.
Geschlossen ist der Bund; ein heil'ger Schwur
2400 Verbindet uns. Es wird gehandelt werden,
Eh' noch das Jahr den neuen Kreis beginnt.
Euer Staub wird ruhn in einem freien Lande.

Attinghausen

O saget mir: Geschlossen ist der Bund?

Melchthal

Am gleichen Tage werden alle drei
2405 Waldstätte sich erheben. Alles ist
Bereit und das Geheimnis wohlbewahrt
Bis jetzt, obgleich viel hunderte es teilen.
Hohl ist der Boden unter den Tyrannen;
Die Tage ihrer Herrschaft sind gezählt,
2410 Und bald ist ihre Spur nicht mehr zu finden.

Attinghausen

Die festen Burgen aber in den Landen?

Melchthal

Sie fallen alle an dem gleichen Tag.

Attinghausen

Und sind die Edeln dieses Bunds teilhaftig?

Stauffacher

Wir harren ihres Beistands, wenn es gilt;
2415 Jetzt aber hat der Landmann nur geschworen.

Attinghausen, *richtet sich langsam in die Höhe, mit großem Erstaunen.*

Hat sich der Landmann solcher That verwogen,
Aus eignem Mittel, ohne Hilf' der Edeln,
Hat er der eignen Kraft so viel vertraut,
Ja, dann bedarf es unserer nicht mehr,
2420 Getröstet können wir zu Grabe steigen,
Es lebt n a ch uns, durch andre Kräfte will
Das Herrliche der Menschheit sich erhalten.

Er legt seine Hand auf das Haupt des Kindes, das vor ihm auf den Knieen liegt.

Aus diesem Haupte, wo der Apfel lag,
Wird euch die neue beß're Freiheit grünen;
2425 Das Alte stürzt, es ändert sich die Zeit,
Und neues Leben blüht aus den Ruinen.

Stauffacher, zu Walther Fürst.

Seht, welcher Glanz sich um sein Aug' ergießt!
Das ist nicht das Erlöschen der Natur;
Das ist der Strahl schon eines neuen Lebens.

Attinghausen

2430 Der Adel steigt von seinen alten Burgen
Und schwört den Städten seinen Bürgereid;
Im Üchtland schon, im Thurgau hat's begonnen;
Die edle Bern erhebt ihr herrschend Haupt;
Freiburg ist eine sichre Burg der Freien;
2435 Die rege Zürich waffnet ihre Zünfte
Zum kriegerischen Heer; es bricht die Macht
Der Könige sich an ihren ew'gen Wällen.

Er spricht das Folgende mit dem Ton eines Sehers; seine Rede steigt bis zur
Begeisterung.

Die Fürsten seh' ich und die edeln Herrn
In Harnischen herangezogen kommen,
2440 Ein harmlos Volk von Hirten zu bekriegen.
Auf Tod und Leben wird gekämpft, und herrlich
Wird mancher Paß durch blutige Entscheidung.
Der Landmann stürzt sich mit der nackten Brust,
Ein freies Opfer, in die Schar der Lanzen.
2445 Er bricht sie, und des Adels Blüte fällt;
Es hebt die Freiheit siegend ihre Fahne.

Walther Fürsts und Stauffachers Hände fassend.

Drum haltet fest zusammen, fest und ewig;
Kein Ort der Freiheit sei dem andern fremd.
Hochwachten stellet aus auf euren Bergen,
2450 Daß sich der Bund zum Bunde rasch versammle.
Seid einig — einig — einig —

Er fällt in das Kissen zurück; seine Hände halten entseelt noch die andern gefaßt.
Fürst und Stauffacher betrachten ihn noch eine Zeitlang schweigend; dann treten sie
hinweg, jeder seinem Schmerz überlassen. Unterdessen sind die Knechte still herein-
gedrungen; sie nähern sich mit Zeichen eines stillern oder heftigern Schmerzens;
einige knieen bei ihm nieder und weinen auf seine Hand; während dieser stummen
Szene wird die Burgglocke geläutet.

Rudenz zu den Vorigen.

Rudenz, rasch eintretend.

Lebt er? O saget: kann er mich noch hören?

Walther Fürst, deutet hin mit weggewandtem Gesicht.

Ihr seid jetzt unser Lehensherr und Schirmer,
Und dieses Schloß hat einen andern Namen.

Rudenz, erblickt den Leichnam und steht von heftigem Schmerz ergriffen.

2455 O güt'ger Gott! Kommt meine Reu' zu spät?
Kommt' er nicht wen'ge Pulse länger leben,

Um mein geändert Herz zu sehn?
Verachtet hab' ich seine treue Stimme,
Da er noch wandelte im Licht; — er ist
2460 Dahin, ist fort auf immerdar, und läßt mir
Die schwere, unbezahlte Schuld. O saget:
Schied er dahin im Unmut gegen mich?

Stauffacher

Er hörte sterbend noch, was ihr gethan,
Und segnete den Mut, mit dem ihr spracht.

Rudenz, kniet an dem Toten nieder.

2465 Ja, heil'ge Reste eines teuren Mannes,
Entseelter Leichnam, hier gelob' ich dir's
In deine kalte Totenhand: zerrissen
Hab' ich auf ewig alle fremden Bande;
Zurückgegeben bin ich meinem Volk;
2470 Ein Schweizer bin ich, und ich will es sein
Von ganzer Seele. Aufstehend.
Trauert um den Freund,
Den Vater aller, doch verzaget nicht.
Nicht bloß sein Erbe ist mir zugefallen;
Es steigt sein Herz, sein Geist auf mich herab,
2475 Und leisten soll euch meine frische Jugend,
Was euch sein greises Alter schuldig blieb.
Ehrwürd'ger Vater, gebt mir eure Hand.
Gebt mir die eurige. Melchthal, auch ihr.
Bedenkt euch nicht. O wendet euch nicht weg.
2480 Empfanget meinen Schwur und mein Gelübde.

Walther Fürst

Gebt ihm die Hand. Sein wiederkehrend Herz
Verdient Vertraun.

Melchthal

Ihr habt den Landmann nichts geachtet.
Sprecht, wessen soll man sich zu euch versehn?

Rudenz

O denket nicht des Irrtums meiner Jugend.

Stauffacher, zu Melchthal,

2485 Seid einig, war das letzte Wort des Vaters.
Gedenket dessen.

Melchthal

Hier ist meine Hand.
Des Bauern Handschlag, edler Herr, ist auch
Ein Manneswort. Was ist der Ritter ohne uns?
Und unser Stand ist älter, als der eure.

Rudenz

2490 Ich ehr' ihn, und mein Schwert soll ihn beschützen.

Melchthal

Der Arm, Herr Freiherr, der die harte Erde
Sich unterwirft und ihren Schoß befruchtet,
Kann auch des Mannes Brust beschützen.

Rudenz

Ihr
Sollt meine Brust, ich will die eure schützen;
2495 So sind wir einer durch den andern stark.
Doch wozu reden, da das Vaterland
Ein Raub noch ist der fremden Tyrannei?
Wenn erst der Boden rein ist von dem Feind,
Dann wollen wir's in Frieden schon vergleichen.

Nachdem er einen Augenblick inne gehalten.

2500 Ihr schweigt? Ihr habt mir nichts zu sagen? Wie?

Verdien' ich's **noch nicht, daß** ihr mir **vertraut?**
So muß ich wider euren **Willen mich**
In das Geheimnis eures Bundes **drängen.**
Ihr habt **getagt,** geschworen **auf dem** Rütli.
2505 Ich weiß, weiß alles was ihr dort verhandelt;
Und, was mir nicht von **euch** vertrauet ward,
Ich hab's bewahrt gleichwie ein **heilig Pfand.**
Nie war ich meines Landes Feind, glaubt mir,
Und niemals hätt' ich gegen **euch** gehandelt.
2510 Doch übel thatet ihr, es zu verschieben;
Die Stunde bringt, und rascher That bedarf's.
Der Tell ward schon das Opfer eures **Säumens.**

Stauffacher
Das Christfest abzuwarten, schwuren wir.

Rudenz
Ich war nicht dort, ich hab' **nicht mitgeschworen.**
2515 Wartet ihr **ab;** ich handle.

Melchthal
                    Was? Ihr wolltet —

Rudenz
Des Landes Vätern zähl' ich **mich jetzt** bei,
Und meine erste Pflicht ist, **euch** zu schützen.

Walther Fürst
Der Erde diesen teuren Staub zu geben,
Ist eure nächste Pflicht und heiligste.

Rudenz
2520 Wenn wir das Land befreit, dann **legen wir**
Den frischen Kranz des Siegs ihm auf **die** Bahre.
O Freunde, eure Sache nicht allein,
Ich habe meine eigne auszufechten

Mit dem Tyrannen.   Hört und wißt: Verschwunden
2525 Ist meine Bertha, heimlich weggeraubt,
Mit lecker Frevelthat, aus unsrer Mitte.

Stauffacher

Solcher Gewaltthat hätte der Tyrann
Wider die freie Edle sich verwogen?

Rudenz

O meine Freunde, euch versprach ich Hilfe,
2530 Und ich zuerst muß sie von euch erflehn.
Geraubt, entrissen ist mir die Geliebte.
Wer weiß, wo sie der Wütende verbirgt,
Welcher Gewalt sie frevelnd sich erkühnen,
Ihr Herz zu zwingen zum verhaßten Band!
2535 Verlaßt mich nicht; o helft mir sie erretten.
Sie liebt euch; o sie hat's verdient ums Land,
Daß alle Arme sich für sie bewaffnen.

Walther Fürst

Was wollt ihr unternehmen?

Rudenz

                              Weiß ich's?   Ach,
In dieser Nacht, die ihr Geschick umhüllt,
2540 In dieses Zweifels ungeheurer Angst,
Wo ich nichts Festes zu erfassen weiß,
Ist mir nur dieses in der Seele klar:
Unter den Trümmern der Tyrannenmacht
Allein kann sie hervorgegraben werden;
2545 Die Festen alle müssen wir bezwingen,
Ob wir vielleicht in ihren Kerker dringen.

Melchthal

Kommt, führt uns an.   Wir folgen euch.   Warum
Bis morgen sparen, was wir heut' vermögen?

Frei war der Tell, als wir im Rütli schwuren;
2550 Das Ungeheure war noch nicht geschehen.
Es bringt die Zeit ein anderes Gesetz;
Wer ist so feig, der jetzt noch könnte zagen?

Rudenz, zu Stauffacher und Walther Fürst.

Indes bewaffnet und zum Werk bereit,
Erwartet ihr der Berge Feuerzeichen;
2555 Denn schneller als ein Botensegel fliegt,
Soll euch die Botschaft unsers Siegs erreichen;
Und seht ihr leuchten die willkommnen Flammen,
Dann auf die Feinde stürzt, wie Wetters Strahl,
Und brecht den Bau der Thrannei zusammen. Geht ab.

Dritte Szene.

Die hohle Gasse bei Küßnacht.

Man steigt von hinten zwischen Felsen herunter, und die Wanderer werden, ehe sie auf der Szene erscheinen, schon von der Höhe gesehen. Felsen umschließen die ganze Szene; auf einem der vordersten ist ein Vorsprung mit Gesträuch bewachsen.

Tell, tritt auf mit der Armbrust.

2560 Durch diese hohle Gasse muß er kommen;
Es führt kein andrer Weg nach Küßnacht. Hier
Vollend' ich's. Die Gelegenheit ist günstig:
Dort der Hollunderstrauch verbirgt mich ihm;
Von dort herab kann ihn mein Pfeil erlangen;
2565 Des Weges Enge wehret den Verfolgern.
Mach' deine Rechnung mit dem Himmel, Vogt;
Fort mußt du, deine Uhr ist abgelaufen.

Ich lebte still und harmlos. Das Geschoß
War auf des Waldes Tiere nur gerichtet;

THE TELL CHAPEL AT KÜSSNACHT. Act IV, Sc. 3.

2570 Meine Gedanken waren rein von Mord.
Du hast aus meinem Frieden mich heraus=
Geschreckt; in gährend Drachengift hast du
Die Milch der frommen Denkart mir verwandelt;
Zum Ungeheuren hast du mich gewöhnt.
2575 Wer sich des Kindes Haupt zum Ziele setzte,
Der kann auch treffen in das Herz des Feinds.

Die armen Kindlein, die unschuldigen,
Das treue Weib muß ich vor deiner Wut
Beschützen, Landvogt. Da, als ich den Bogenstrang
2580 Anzog, als mir die Hand erzitterte,
Als du mit grausam teuflischer Lust
Mich zwangst, aufs Haupt des Kindes anzulegen,
Als ich ohnmächtig flehend rang vor dir,
Damals gelobt' ich mir in meinem Innern
2585 Mit furchtbarm Eidschwur, den nur Gott gehört,
Daß meines näch sten Schusses erstes Ziel
Dein Herz sein sollte. Was ich mir gelobt
In jenes Augenblickes Höllenqualen,
Ist eine heil'ge Schuld; ich will sie zahlen.

2590 Du bist mein Herr und meines Kaisers Vogt;
Doch nicht der Kaiser hätte sich erlaubt,
Was du. Er sandte dich in diese Lande,
Um Recht zu sprechen, — strenges, denn er zürnet, —
Doch nicht, um mit der mörderischen Lust
2595 Dich jedes Greuels straflos zu erfrechen; *commit these with impunity*.
Es lebt ein Gott, zu strafen und zu rächen.

Komm' du hervor, du Bringer bittrer Schmerzen,
Mein teures Kleinod jetzt, mein höchster Schatz!
Ein Ziel will ich dir geben, das bis jetzt

2600 Der frommen Bitte undurchdringlich war,
Doch dir soll es nicht widerstehn. Und du,
Vertraute Bogensehne, die so oft
Mir treu gedient hat in der Freude Spielen,
Verlaß' mich nicht im fürchterlichen Ernst.
2605 Nur jetzt noch halte fest, du treuer Strang,
Der mir so oft den herben Pfeil beflügelt.
Entränn' er jetzo kraftlos meinen Händen,
Ich habe keinen zweiten zu versenden.

Wanderer gehen über die Szene.

Auf dieser Bank von Stein will ich mich setzen,
2610 Dem Wanderer zur kurzen Ruh' bereitet;
Denn hier ist keine Heimat. Jeder treibt
Sich an dem andern rasch und fremd vorüber
Und fraget nicht nach seinem Schmerz. Hier geht
Der sorgenvolle Kaufmann und der leicht=
2615 Geschürzte Pilger, der andächt'ge Mönch,
Der düstre Räuber und der heitre Spielmann,
Der Säumer mit dem schwerbeladnen Roß,
Der ferne herkommt von der Menschen Ländern;
Denn jede Straße führt ans End' der Welt.
2620 Sie alle ziehen ihres Weges fort
An ihr Geschäft, — und meines ist der Mord! Setzt sich.

Sonst, wenn der Vater auszog, liebe Kinder,
Da war ein Freuen, wenn er wieder kam;
Denn niemals kehrt' er heim, er bracht' euch etwas,
2625 War's eine schöne Alpenblume, war's
Ein seltner Vogel oder Ammonshorn,
Wie es der Wandrer findet auf den Bergen.
Jetzt geht er einem andern Weidwerk nach;

Am wilden Weg sitzt er mit Mordgedanken;
2630 Des Feindes Leben ist's, worauf er lauert.
Und doch an euch nur denkt er, lieben Kinder,
Auch jetzt; euch zu verteib'gen, eure holde Unschuld
Zu schützen vor der Rache des Tyrannen,
Will er zum Morde jetzt den Bogen spannen. Steht auf.

2635   Ich laure auf ein edles Wild. Läßt sich's
Der Jäger nicht verdrießen, tagelang
Umher zu streifen in des Winters Strenge,
Von Fels zu Fels den Wagesprung zu thun,
Hinan zu klimmen an den glatten Wänden,
2640 Wo er sich anleimt mit dem eignen Blut,
Um ein armselig Grättier zu erjagen.
Hier gilt es einen köstlicheren Preis:
Das Herz des Todfeinds, der mich will verderben.

Man hört von ferne eine heitre Musik, welche sich nähert.

Mein ganzes Leben lang hab' ich den Bogen
2645 Gehandhabt, mich geübt nach Schützenregel;
Ich habe oft geschossen in das Schwarze,
Und manchen schönen Preis mir heimgebracht
Vom Freudenschießen. Aber heute will ich
Den Meisterschuß thun und das Beste mir
2650 Im ganzen Umkreis des Gebirgs gewinnen.

Eine Hochzeit zieht über die Szene und durch den Hohlweg hinauf. Tell
betrachtet sie, auf seinen Bogen gelehnt; S t ü f s i , der Flurschütz, gesellt
sich zu ihm.

Stüfsi

Das ist der Klostermei'r von Mörlischachen,
Der hier den Brautlauf hält; ein reicher Mann,
Er hat wohl zehen Senten auf den Alpen.

Die Braut holt er jetzt ab zu Imisee,
2655 Und diese Nacht wird hoch geschwelgt zu Küßnacht.
Kommt mit; 's ist jeder Biedermann geladen.

Tell

Ein ernster Gast stimmt nicht zum Hochzeithaus.

Stüssi

Drückt euch ein Kummer, werft ihn frisch vom Herzen.
Nehmt mit, was kommt; die Zeiten sind jetzt schwer;
2660 Drum muß der Mensch die Freude leicht ergreifen.
Hier wird gefreit und anderswo begraben.

Tell

Und oft kommt gar das eine zu dem andern.

Stüssi

So geht die Welt nun. Es giebt allerwegen
Unglücks genug. Ein Russi ist gegangen
2665 Im Glarner Land, und eine ganze Seite
Vom Glärnisch eingesunken.

Tell

Wanken auch
Die Berge selbst? Es steht nichts fest auf Erden.

Stüssi

Auch anderswo vernimmt man Wunderdinge.
Da sprach ich einen, der von Baden kam:
2670 Ein Ritter wollte zu dem König reiten,
Und unterwegs begegnet ihm ein Schwarm
Von Hornissen; die fallen auf sein Roß,
Daß es für Marter tot zu Boden sinkt,
Und er zu Fuße ankommt bei dem König.

Tell

2675 Dem Schwachen ist sein Stachel auch gegeben.

Armgard kommt mit mehreren Kindern und stellt sich an den Eingang
des Hohlwegs.

Stüssi

Man deutet's auf ein großes Landesunglück,
Auf schwere Thaten wider die Natur.

Tell

Dergleichen Thaten bringet jeder Tag;
Kein Wunderzeichen braucht sie zu verkünden.

Stüssi

2680 Ja, wohl dem, der sein Feld bestellt in Ruh',
Und ungekränkt daheim sitzt bei den Seinen.

Tell

Es kann der Frömmste nicht im Frieden bleiben,
Wenn es dem bösen Nachbar nicht gefällt.

Tell sieht oft mit unruhiger Erwartung nach der Höhe des Weges.

Stüssi

Gehabt euch wohl. Ihr wartet hier auf jemand?

Tell

2685 Das thu' ich.

Stüssi

Frohe Heimkehr zu den Euren!
Ihr seid aus Uri? Unser gnäb'ger Herr,
Der Landvogt, wird noch heut' von dort erwartet.

Wandrer, kommt,

Den Vogt erwartet heut' nicht mehr. Die Wasser
Sind ausgetreten von dem großen Regen,
2690 Und alle Brücken hat der Strom zerrissen.

Tell steht auf.

Armgard, kommt vorwärts,

Der Landvogt kommt nicht?

Stüssi

Sucht ihr was an ihm?

Armgard

Ach freilich!

Stüssi

Warum stellet ihr euch denn
In dieser hohlen Gass' ihm in den Weg?

Armgard

Hier weicht er mir nicht aus, er muß mich hören.

Frießhardt

kommt eilfertig den Hohlweg herab und ruft in die Szene.

2695 Man fahre aus dem Weg. Mein gnäd'ger Herr,
Der Landvogt, kommt dicht hinter mir geritten. *Tell geht ab.*

Armgard, *lebhaft.*

Der Landvogt kommt.

Sie geht mit ihren Kindern nach der vorderen Szene. Geßler und Rudolf der Harras zeigen sich zu Pferd auf der Höhe des Wegs.

Stüssi, *zum Frießhardt.*

Wie kamt ihr durch das Wasser,
Da doch der Strom die Brücken fortgeführt?

Frießhardt

Wir haben mit dem See gefochten, Freund,
2700 Und fürchten uns vor keinem Alpenwasser.

Stüssi

Ihr wart zu Schiff in dem gewalt'gen Sturm?

Frießhardt

Das waren wir. Mein Lebtag denk' ich dran.

Stüssi

O bleibt, erzählt.

Frießhardt

Laßt mich, ich muß voraus,
Den Landvogt muß ich in der Burg verkünden. Ab.

Stüffi

2705 Wär'n gute Leute auf dem Schiff gewesen,
In Grund gesunken wär's mit Mann und Maus;
Dem Volk kann weder Wasser bei noch Feuer. Er sieht sich um.
Wo kam der Weidmann hin, mit dem ich sprach? Geht ab.
Geßler und Rudolf der Harras zu Pferd.

Geßler

Sagt, was ihr wollt, ich bin des Kaisers Diener,
2710 Und muß drauf denken, wie ich ihm gefalle.
Er hat mich nicht ins Land geschickt, dem Volk
Zu schmeicheln und ihm sanft zu thun. Gehorsam
Erwartet er; der Streit ist, ob der Bauer
Soll Herr sein in dem Lande, oder der Kaiser.

Armgard

2715 Jetzt ist der Augenblick. Jetzt bring' ich's an.
Nähert sich furchtsam.

Geßler

Ich hab' den Hut nicht aufgesteckt zu Altorf
Des Scherzes wegen, oder um die Herzen
Des Volks zu prüfen; diese kenn' ich längst.
Ich hab' ihn aufgesteckt, daß sie den Nacken
2720 Mir lernen beugen, den sie aufrecht tragen;
Das Unbequeme hab' ich hingepflanzt
Auf ihren Weg, wo sie vorbeigehn müssen,
Daß sie draufstoßen mit dem Aug' und sich
Erinnern ihres Herrn, den sie vergessen.

Rudolf der Harras

2725 Das Volk hat aber doch gewisse Rechte.

Geßler

Die abzuwägen, ist jetzt keine Zeit.
Weitschicht'ge Dinge sind im Werk und Werden;
Das Kaiserhaus will wachsen; was der Vater
Glorreich begonnen, will der Sohn vollenden.
2730 Dies kleine Volk ist uns ein Stein im Weg;
So oder so, es muß sich unterwerfen.

Sie wollen vorüber. Die Frau wirft sich vor dem Landvogt nieder.

Armgard

Barmherzigkeit! Herr Landvogt. Gnade! Gnade!

Geßler

Was bringt ihr euch auf offner Straße mir
In Weg? Zurück!

Armgard

   Mein Mann liegt im Gefängnis;
2735 Die armen Waisen schrein nach Brot. Habt Mitleid,
Gestrenger Herr, mit unserm großen Elend.

Rudolf der Harras

Wer seid ihr? Wer ist euer Mann?

Armgard

       Ein armer
Wildheuer, guter Herr, vom Rigiberge,
Der überm Abgrund weg das freie Gras
2740 Abmähet von den schroffen Felsenwänden,
Wohin das Vieh sich nicht getraut zu steigen.

Rudolf der Harras, *zum Landvogt.*

Bei Gott! ein elend und erbärmlich Leben!
Ich bitt' euch, gebt ihn los, den armen Mann.
Was er auch Schweres mag verschuldet haben,
2745 Strafe genug ist sein entsetzlich Handwerk. *Zu der Frau.*

Euch soll Recht werden.   Drinnen auf der Burg
Nennt eure Bitte; hier ist nicht der Ort.

Armgard

Nein, nein, ich weiche nicht von diesem Platz,
Bis mir der Vogt den Mann zurückgegeben.
2750 Schon in den sechsten Mond liegt er im Turm
Und harret auf den Richterspruch vergebens.

Geßler

Weib, wollt ihr mir Gewalt anthun? Hinweg!

Armgard

Gerechtigkeit! Landvogt.   Du bist der Richter
Im Lande an des Kaisers Statt und Gottes.
2755 Thu' deine Pflicht. So du Gerechtigkeit
Vom Himmel hoffest, so erzeig' sie uns.

Geßler

Fort! Schafft das freche Volk mir aus den Augen.

Armgard, greift in die Zügel des Pferdes.

Nein, nein, ich habe nichts mehr zu verlieren.
Du kommst nicht von der Stelle, Vogt, bis du
2760 Mir Recht gesprochen. Falte deine Stirne,
Rolle die Augen, wie du willst. Wir sind
So grenzenlos unglücklich, daß wir nichts.
Nach deinem Zorn mehr fragen.

Geßler

Weib, mach' Platz,
Oder mein Roß geht über dich hinweg.

Armgard

2765 Laß' es über mich dahin gehn.   Da!

Sie reißt ihre Kinder zu Boden und wirft sich mit ihnen ihm in den Weg.

Hier lieg' ich

Mit meinen Kindern. Laß' die armen Waisen
Von deines Pferdes Huf zertreten werden.
Es ist das Ärgste nicht, was du gethan.

Rudolf der Harras

Weib, seid ihr rasend?

Armgard, heftiger fortfahrend,

           Tratest du doch längst
2770 Das Land des Kaisers unter deine Füße!
O, ich bin nur ein Weib. Wär' ich ein Mann,
Ich wüßte wohl was Besseres, als hier
Im Staub zu liegen.

Man hört die vorige Musik wieder auf der Höhe des Wegs, aber gedämpft.

Geßler

       Wo sind meine Knechte?
Man reiße sie von hinnen, oder ich
2775 Vergesse mich und thue, was mich reuet.

Rudolf der Harras

Die Knechte können nicht hindurch, o Herr,
Der Hohlweg ist gesperrt durch eine Hochzeit.

Geßler

Ein allzu milder Herrscher bin ich noch
Gegen dies Volk; die Zungen sind noch frei;
2780 Es ist noch nicht ganz, wie es soll, gebändigt.
Doch es soll anders werden, ich gelob' es.
Ich will ihn brechen, diesen starren Sinn;
Den kecken Geist der Freiheit will ich beugen;
Ein neu Gesetz will ich in diesen Landen
2785 Verkündigen. Ich will —

Ein Pfeil durchbohrt ihn; er fährt mit der Hand aus Herz und will sinken. Mit matter Stimme,

           Gott sei mir gnädig!

Rudolf der Harras

Herr Landvogt! Gott! Was ist das? Woher kam das?

Armgard, absterbend,

Mord! Mord! Er taumelt, sinkt. Er ist getroffen.
Mitten ins Herz hat ihn der Pfeil getroffen.

Rudolf der Harras, springt vom Pferde.

Welch gräßliches Ereignis! Gott! Herr Ritter,
2790 Ruft die Erbarmung Gottes an; ihr seid
Ein Mann des Todes.

Geßler

                    Das ist Tells Geschoß.

*Ist vom Pferd herab dem Rudolf Harras in den Arm gegleitet und wird auf der
Bank niedergelassen.*

Tell, erscheint oben auf der Höhe des Felsen,

Du kennst den Schützen, suche keinen andern.
Frei sind die Hütten; sicher ist die Unschuld
Vor dir; du wirst dem Lande nicht mehr schaden.

Verschwindet von der Höhe. Volk stürzt herein.

Stüssi, voran,

2795 Was giebt es hier. Was hat sich zugetragen?

Armgard

Der Landvogt ist von einem Pfeil durchschossen.

Volk, im Hereinstürzen,

Wer ist erschossen?

*Indem die Vordersten von dem Brautzug auf die Szene kommen, sind die Hin-
tersten noch auf der Höhe, und die Musik geht fort.*

Rudolf der Harras

Fort! Schaffet Hilfe. Setzt dem Mörder nach.

— Verlorner Mann, so muß es mit dir enden;
2800 Doch meine Warnung wolltest du nicht hören.

Stüssi

Bei Gott! da liegt er bleich und ohne Leben.

Viele Stimmen

Wer hat die That gethan?

Rudolf der Harras

Rast dieses Volk,
Daß es dem Mord Musik macht? Laßt sie schweigen.

Musik bricht plötzlich ab; es kommt noch mehr Volk nach.

Herr Landvogt, redet, wenn ihr könnt. — Habt ihr
2805 Mir nichts mehr zu vertraun?

*Geßler giebt Zeichen mit der Hand, die er mit Heftigkeit wiederholt, da sie nicht
gleich verstanden werden.*

Wo soll ich hin?
— Nach Küßnacht? Ich versteh' euch nicht. O werdet
Nicht ungeduldig. Laßt das Irdische;
Denkt jetzt, euch mit dem Himmel zu versöhnen.

Die ganze Hochzeitsgesellschaft umsteht den Sterbenden mit einem fühllosen Grausen.

Stüssi

Sieh, wie er bleich wird! Jetzt, jetzt tritt der Tod
2810 Ihm an das Herz; die Augen sind gebrochen.

Armgard, hebt ein Kind empor,

Seht, Kinder, wie ein Wüterich verscheidet.

Rudolf der Harras

Wahnsinn'ge Weiber, habt ihr kein Gefühl,
Daß ihr den Blick an diesem Schrecknis weidet?
Helft. Leget Hand an. Steht mir niemand bei,
2815 Den Schmerzenspfeil ihm aus der Brust zu ziehn?

Weiber, treten zurück.

Wir ihn berühren, welchen Gott geschlagen?

Rudolf der Harras

Fluch treff' euch und Verdammnis!

Zieht das Schwert.

Stüssi, fällt ihm in den Arm.

Wagt es, Herr!

Eu'r Walten hat ein Ende. Der Tyrann

Des Landes ist gefallen. Wir erdulden

2820 Keine Gewalt mehr. Wir sind freie Menschen.

Alle, tumultuarisch.

Das Land ist frei!

Rudolf der Harras

Ist es dahin gekommen?

Endet die Furcht so schnell und der Gehorsam?

Zu den Waffenknechten, die hereindringen.

Ihr seht die grausenvolle That des Mords,

Die hier geschehen. Hilfe ist umsonst;

2825 Vergeblich ist's, dem Mörder nachzusetzen.

Uns drängen andre Sorgen. Auf nach Küßnacht!

Daß wir dem Kaiser seine Feste retten!

Denn aufgelöst in diesem Augenblick

Sind aller Ordnung, aller Pflichten Bande,

2830 Und keines Mannes Treu' ist zu vertrauen.

Indem er mit den Waffenknechten abgeht, erscheinen sechs b a r m h e r z i g e
Brüder.

Armgard

Platz! Platz! Da kommen die barmherz'gen Brüder.

Stüssi

Das Opfer liegt, die Raben steigen nieder.

Barmherzige Brüder,

schließen einen Halbkreis um den Toten und singen in tiefem Ton.

Rasch tritt der Tod den Menschen an;
　　Es ist ihm keine Frist gegeben;
2835　　Es stürzt ihn mitten in der Bahn,
　　Es reißt ihn fort vom vollen Leben.
Bereitet oder nicht, zu gehen,
Er muß vor seinen Richter stehen.

Indem die letzten Zeilen wiederholt werden, fällt der Vorhang.

Fünfter Aufzug.

Erste Szene.

Öffentlicher Platz bei Altorf.

Im Hintergrunde rechts die Feste Zwing Uri mit dem noch stehenden Bauge-
rüste wie in der dritten Szene des ersten Aufzugs; links eine Aussicht in
viele Berge hinein, auf welchen allen Signalfeuer brennen. Es ist eben
Tagesanbruch, Glocken ertönen aus verschiedenen Fernen.

Ruodi, Kuoni, Werni, Meister Steinmetz und viele andere
Landleute, auch Weiber und Kinder.

Ruodi

Seht ihr die Feursignale auf den Bergen?

Steinmetz

2840 Hört ihr die Glocken drüben überm Wald?

Ruodi

Die Feinde sind verjagt.

Steinmetz

      Die Burgen sind erobert.

Ruodi

Und wir im Lande Uri dulden noch
Auf unserm Boden das Tyrannenschloß?
Sind wir die Letzten, die sich frei erklären?

Steinmetz

2845 Das Joch soll stehen, das uns zwingen wollte?
Auf! Reißt es nieder.

Alle

      Nieder! nieder! nieder!

145

Ruodi

Wo ist der Stier von Uri?

Stier von Uri

Hier. Was soll ich?

Ruodi

Steigt auf die Hochwacht, blast in euer Horn,
Daß es weitschmetternd in die Berge schalle,
2850 Und, jedes Echo in den Felsenklüften
Aufweckend, schnell die Männer des Gebirgs
Zusammenrufe.

Stier von Uri geht ab. Walther Fürst kommt.

Walther Fürst

Haltet! Freunde. Haltet!
Noch fehlt uns Kunde, was in Unterwalden
Und Schwyz geschehen. Laßt uns Boten erst
2855 Erwarten.

Ruodi

Was erwarten? Der Tyrann
Ist tot; der Tag der Freiheit ist erschienen.

Steinmetz

Ist's nicht genug an diesen flammenden Boten,
Die rings herum auf allen Bergen leuchten?

Ruodi

Kommt alle, kommt; legt Hand an, Männer und Weiber.
2860 Brecht das Gerüste. Sprengt die Bogen. Reißt
Die Mauern ein. Kein Stein bleib' auf dem andern.

Steinmetz

Gesellen, kommt. Wir haben's aufgebaut,
Wir wissen's zu zerstören.

Alle

Kommt, reißt nieder.

Sie stürzen sich von allen Seiten auf den Bau.

Walther Fürst

Es ist im Lauf. Ich kann sie nicht mehr halten.

Melchthal und Baumgarten kommen.

Melchthal

2865 Was? Steht die Burg noch, und Schloß Sarnen liegt
In Asche, und der Roßberg ist gebrochen?

Walther Fürst

Seid ihr es, Melchthal? Bringt ihr uns die Freiheit?
Sagt, sind die Lande alle rein vom Feind?

Melchthal, *umarmt ihn.*

Rein ist der Boden. Freut euch, alter Vater.
2870 In diesem Augenblicke, da wir reden,
Ist kein Tyrann mehr in der Schweizer Land.

Walther Fürst

O sprecht, wie wurdet ihr der Burgen mächtig?

Melchthal

Der Rudenz war es, der das Sarner Schloß
Mit mannlich kühner Waffenthat gewann.
2875 Den Roßberg hatt' ich nachts zuvor erstiegen.
Doch höret, was geschah. Als wir das Schloß
Vom Feind geleert, nun freudig angezündet,
Die Flamme prasselnd schon zum Himmel schlug,
Da stürzt der Diethelm, Geßlers Bub', hervor,
2880 Und ruft, daß die Bruneckerin verbrenne.

Walther Fürst

Gerechter Gott!

Man hört die Balken des Gerüstes stürzen.

Melchthal

Sie war es selbst, war heimlich
Hier eingeschlossen auf des Vogts Geheiß.
Rasend erhub sich Rudenz; denn wir hörten
Die Balken schon, die festen Pfosten stürzen
2885 Und aus dem Rauch hervor den Jammerruf
Der Unglückseligen.

Walther Fürst

Sie ist gerettet?

Melchthal

Da galt Geschwindsein und Entschlossenheit.
Wär' er nur unser Edelmann gewesen,
Wir hätten unser Leben wohl geliebt;
2890 Doch er war unser Eidgenoß, und Bertha
Ehrte das Volk. So setzten wir getrost
Das Leben dran und stürzten in das Feuer.

Walther Fürst

Sie ist gerettet?

Melchthal

Sie ist's. Rudenz und ich,
Wir trugen sie selbander aus den Flammen
2895 Und hinter uns fiel krachend das Gebälk.
Und jetzt, als sie gerettet sich erkannte,
Die Augen aufschlug zu dem Himmelslicht,
Jetzt stürzte mir der Freiherr an das Herz,
Und schweigend ward ein Bündnis jetzt beschworen,
2900 Das, fest gehärtet in des Feuers Glut,
Bestehen wird in allen Schicksalsproben.

Walther Fürst

Wo ist der Landenberg?

Melchthal

Über den Brünig.

Nicht lag's an mir, daß er das Licht der Augen
Davontrug, der den Vater mir geblendet.
2905 Nach jagt' ich ihm, erreicht' ihn auf der Flucht
Und riß ihn zu den Füßen meines Vaters.
Geschwungen über ihm war schon das Schwert;
Von der Barmherzigkeit des blinden Greises
Erhielt er flehend das Geschenk des Lebens;
2910 Urphede schwur er, nie zurück zu kehren;
Er wird sie halten; unsern Arm hat er
Gefühlt.

Walther Fürst

Wohl euch, daß ihr den reinen Sieg
Mit Blute nicht geschändet.

Kinder, eilen mit Trümmern des Gerüstes über die Szene.

Freiheit! Freiheit!

Das Horn von Uri wird mit Macht geblasen.

Walther Fürst

Seht, welch ein Fest! Des Tages werden sich
2915 Die Kinder spät als Greise noch erinnern.

Mädchen bringen den Hut auf einer Stange getragen; die ganze Szene füllt sich
mit Volk an.

Ruodi

Hier ist der Hut, dem wir uns beugen mußten.

Baumgarten

Gebt uns Bescheid, was damit werden soll.

Walther Fürst

Gott! Unter diesem Hute stand mein Enkel.

Mehrere Stimmen

Zerstört das Denkmal der Tyrannenmacht.
2920 Ins Feuer mit ihm!

Walther Fürst
Nein, laßt ihn aufbewahren.
Der Tyrannei mußt' er zum Werkzeug dienen;
Er soll der Freiheit ewig Zeichen sein.

Die Landleute, Männer, Weiber und Kinder stehen und sitzen auf den Balken des
zerbrochenen Gerüstes malerisch gruppiert in einem großen Halbkreis umher.

Melchthal
So stehen wir nun fröhlich auf den Trümmern
Der Tyrannei, und herrlich ist's erfüllt,
2925 Was wir im Rütli schwuren, Eidgenossen.

Walther Fürst
Das Werk ist angefangen, nicht vollendet.
Jetzt ist uns Mut und feste Eintracht not;
Denn, seid gewiß, nicht säumen wird der König,
Den Tod zu rächen seines Vogts, und den
2930 Vertriebnen mit Gewalt zurück zu führen.

Melchthal
Er zieh' heran mit seiner Heeresmacht;
Ist aus dem Innern doch der Feind verjagt,
Dem Feind von außen wollen wir begegnen.

Ruodi
Nur wen'ge Pässe öffnen ihm das Land;
2935 Die wollen wir mit unsern Leibern decken.

Baumgarten
Wir sind vereinigt durch ein ewig Band,
Und seine Heere sollen uns nicht schrecken.

Rösselmann und Stauffacher kommen

Rösselmann, im Eintreten,
Das sind des Himmels furchtbare Gerichte.

Landleute
Was giebt's?

Rösselmann
In welchen Zeiten leben wir!

Walther Fürst
2940 Sagt an, was ist es? Ha, seid ihr's, Herr Werner?
Was bringt ihr uns?

Landleute
Was giebt's?

Rösselmann
Hört und erstaunet.

Stauffacher
Von einer großen Furcht sind wir befreit.

Rösselmann
Der Kaiser ist ermordet.

Walther Fürst
Gnäd'ger Gott!

Landleute machen einen Aufstand und umdrängen den Stauffacher.

Alle
Ermordet? Was! Der Kaiser? Hört! Der Kaiser?

Melchthal
2945 Nicht möglich. Woher kam euch diese Kunde?

Stauffacher
Es ist gewiß. Bei Bruck fiel König Albrecht
Durch Mörders Hand; ein glaubenwerter Mann,
Johannes Müller, bracht' es von Schaffhausen.

Walther Fürst
Wer wagte solche grauenvolle That?

Stauffacher
2950 Sie wird noch grauenvoller durch den Thäter.
Es war sein Neffe, seines Bruders Kind,
Herzog Johann von Schwaben, der's vollbrachte,

Melchthal

Was trieb ihn zu der That des Vatermords?

Stauffacher

Der Kaiser hielt das väterliche Erbe
2955 Dem ungeduldig Mahnenden zurück;
Es hieß, er denk' ihn ganz darum zu kürzen,
Mit einem Bischofshut ihn abzufinden.
Wie dem auch sei, der Jüngling öffnete
Der Waffenfreunde bösem Rat sein Ohr,
2960 Und mit den edeln Herrn von Eschenbach,
Von Tegerfelden, von der Wart und Palm
Beschloß er, da er Recht nicht konnte finden,
Sich Rach' zu holen mit der eignen Hand.

Walther Fürst

O sprecht, wie ward das Gräßliche vollendet?

Stauffacher

2965 Der König ritt herab vom Stein zu Baden,
Gen Rheinfeld, wo die Hofstatt war, zu ziehn,
Mit ihm die Fürsten Hans und Leopold
Und ein Gefolge hochgeborner Herren.
Und als sie kamen an die Reuß, wo man
2970 Auf einer Fähre sich läßt übersetzen,
Da drängten sich die Mörder in das Schiff,
Daß sie den Kaiser vom Gefolge trennten.
Drauf, als der Fürst durch ein geackert Feld
Hinreitet, — eine alte große Stadt
2975 Soll drunter liegen aus der Heiden Zeit, —
Die alte Feste Habsburg im Gesicht,
Wo seines Stammes Hoheit ausgegangen,
Stößt Herzog Hans den Dolch ihm in die Kehle,

Rudolf von Palm durchrennt ihn mit dem Speer,
2980 Und Eschenbach zerspaltet ihm das Haupt,
Daß er heruntersinkt in seinem Blut,
Gemordet von den Seinen, auf dem Seinen.
Am andern Ufer sahen sie die That;
Doch, durch den Strom geschieden, konnten sie
2985 Nur ein ohnmächtig Wehgeschrei erheben;
Am Wege aber saß ein armes Weib,
In ihrem Schoß verblutete der Kaiser.

Melchthal
So hat er nur sein frühes Grab gegraben,
Der unersättlich alles wollte haben.

Stauffacher
2990 Ein ungeheurer Schrecken ist im Land umher;
Gesperrt sind alle Pässe des Gebirgs;
Jedweder Stand verwahret seine Grenzen;
Die alte Zürich selbst schloß ihre Thore,
Die dreißig Jahr' lang offen standen, zu,
2995 Die Mörder fürchtend und, noch mehr, die Rächer;
Denn, mit des Bannes Fluch bewaffnet, kommt
Der Ungarn Königin, die strenge Agnes,
Die nicht die Milde kennet ihres zarten
Geschlechts, des Vaters königliches Blut
3000 Zu rächen an der Mörder ganzem Stamm,
An ihren Knechten, Kindern, Kindeskindern,
Ja, an den Steinen ihrer Schlösser selbst.
Geschworen hat sie, ganze Zeugungen
Hinabzusenden in des Vaters Grab,
3005 In Blut sich, wie in Maientau, zu baden.

Melchthal
Weiß man, wo sich die Mörder hingeflüchtet?

Stauffacher

Sie flohen alsbald nach vollbrachter That
Auf fünf verschiednen Straßen auseinander,
Und trennten sich, um nie sich mehr zu sehn.
3010 Herzog Johann soll irren im Gebirge.

Walther Fürst

So trägt die Unthat ihnen keine Frucht.
Rache trägt keine Frucht. Sich selbst ist sie
Die fürchterliche Nahrung; ihr Genuß
Ist Mord und ihre Sättigung das Grausen.

Stauffacher

3015 Den Mördern bringt die Unthat nicht Gewinn;
Wir aber brechen mit der reinen Hand
Des blut'gen Frevels segenvolle Frucht;
Denn einer großen Furcht sind wir entledigt;
Gefallen ist der Freiheit größter Feind,
3020 Und wie verlautet, wird das Scepter gehn
Aus Habsburgs Haus zu einem andern Stamm;
Das Reich will seine Wahlfreiheit behaupten.

Walther Fürst und Mehrere

Vernahmt ihr was?

Stauffacher

        Der Graf von Luxemburg
Ist von den mehrsten Stimmen schon bezeichnet.

Walther Fürst

3025 Wohl uns, daß wir beim Reiche treu gehalten;
Jetzt ist zu hoffen auf Gerechtigkeit.

Stauffacher

Dem neuen Herrn thun tapfre Freunde not;
Er wird uns schirmen gegen Östreichs Rache.

     Die Landleute umarmen einander.

Sigrist mit einem Reichsboten.

Sigrist

Hier sind des Landes würd'ge Oberhäupter.

Rösselmann und Mehrere

3030 Sigrist, was giebt's?

Sigrist

Ein Reichsbot' bringt dies Schreiben.

Alle, zu Walther Fürst.

Erbrecht und leset.

Walther Fürst, liest.

„Den bescheidnen Männern
„Von Uri, Schwyz und Unterwalden bietet
„Die Königin Elsbeth Gnad' und alles Gutes."

Viele Stimmen

Was will die Königin? Ihr Reich ist aus.

Walther Fürst, liest.

3035 „In ihrem großen Schmerz und Wittwenleid,
„Worein der blut'ge Hinscheid ihres Herrn
„Die Königin versetzt, gedenkt sie noch
„Der alten Treu' und Lieb' der Schweizerlande."

Melchthal

In ihrem Glück hat sie das nie gethan.

Rösselmann

3040 Still! Lasset hören.

Walther Fürst, liest.

„Und sie versieht sich zu dem treuen Volk,
„Daß es gerechten Abscheu werde tragen
„Vor den verfluchten Thätern dieser That;
„Darum erwartet sie von den drei Landen,

3045 „Daß sie den Mördern nimmer Vorschub thun,
„Vielmehr getreulich dazu helfen werden,
„Sie auszuliefern in des Rächers Hand,
„Der Lieb' gedenkend und der alten Gunst,
„Die sie von Rudolfs Fürstenhaus empfangen."

Zeichen des Unwillens unter den Landleuten.

Viele Stimmen
3050 Der Lieb' und Gunst!

Stauffacher
Wir haben Gunst empfangen von dem Vater;
Doch wessen rühmen wir uns von dem Sohn?
Hat er den Brief der Freiheit uns bestätigt,
Wie vor ihm alle Kaiser doch gethan?
3055 Hat er gerichtet nach gerechtem Spruch,
Und der bedrängten Unschuld Schutz verliehn?
Hat er auch nur die Boten wollen hören,
Die wir in unsrer Angst zu ihm gesendet?
Nicht eins von diesem allen hat der König
3060 An uns gethan, und hätten wir nicht selbst
Uns Recht verschafft mit eigner mut'ger Hand,
Ihn rührte unsre Not nicht an. Ihm Dank?
Nicht Dank hat er gesät in diesen Thälern.
Er stand auf einem hohen Platz; er konnte
3065 Ein Vater seiner Völker sein; doch ihm
Gefiel es, nur zu sorgen für die Seinen.
Die er gemehrt hat, mögen um ihn weinen!

Walther Fürst
Wir wollen nicht frohlocken seines Falls,
Nicht des empfangnen Bösen jetzt gedenken;
3070 Fern sei's von uns. Doch, daß wir rächen sollten

THE REUSS WITH THE TEUFELSBRÜCKE. Act V, Sc. 2.

Des Königs Tod, der nie uns Gutes that,
Und die verfolgen, die uns nie betrübten,
Das ziemt uns nicht und will uns nicht gebühren.
Die Liebe will ein freies Opfer sein;
3075 Der Tod entbindet von erzwungnen Pflichten.
Ihm haben wir nichts weiter zu entrichten.

Melchthal

Und weint die Königin in ihrer Kammer,
Und klagt ihr wilder Schmerz den Himmel an,
So seht ihr hier ein angstbefreites Volk
3080 Zu eben diesem Himmel dankend flehen.
Wer Thränen ernten will, muß Liebe säen.

Reichsbote geht ab.

Stauffacher, zu dem Volk.

Wo ist der Tell? Soll e r allein uns fehlen,
Der unsrer Freiheit Stifter ist? Das Größte
Hat e r gethan, das Härteste erduldet.
3085 Kommt alle, kommt, nach seinem Haus zu wallen,
Und rufet Heil dem Retter von uns allen.

Alle gehen ab.

Zweite Szene.

Tells Hausflur.

Ein Feuer brennt auf dem Herd. Die offenstehende Thüre zeigt ins Freie.

Hedwig. Walther und Wilhelm.

Hedwig

Heut' kommt der Vater. Kinder, liebe Kinder,
Er lebt, ist frei, und wir sind frei und alles.
Und euer Vater ist's, der's Land gerettet.

Walther

3090 Und ich bin auch dabei gewesen, Mutter.
Mich muß man auch mit nennen. Vaters Pfeil
Ging mir am Leben hart vorbei, und ich
Hab' nicht gezittert.

Hedwig, umarmt ihn.

Ja, du bist mir wieder
Gegeben. Zweimal hab' ich dich geboren.
3095 Zweimal litt ich den Mutterschmerz um dich.
Es ist vorbei; ich hab' euch beide, beide.
Und heute kommt der liebe Vater wieder.

Ein Mönch erscheint an der Hausthüre.

Wilhelm

Sieh, Mutter, sieh; dort steht ein frommer Bruder.
Gewiß wird er um eine Gabe flehn.

Hedwig

3100 Führ' ihn herein, damit wir ihn erquicken;
Er fühl's, daß er ins Freudenhaus gekommen.

Geht hinein und kommt bald mit einem Becher wieder.

Wilhelm, zum Mönch,

Kommt, guter Mann. Die Mutter will euch laben.

Walther

Kommt, ruht euch aus und geht gestärkt von dannen.

Mönch, scheu umherblickend mit zerstörten Zügen.

Wo bin ich? Saget an, in welchem Lande?

Walther

3105 Seid ihr verirret, daß ihr das nicht wißt?
Ihr seid zu Bürglen, Herr, im Lande Uri,
Wo man hineingeht in das Schächenthal.

Mönch, zur Hedwig, welche zurückkommt,

Seid ihr allein? Ist euer Herr zu Hause?

Hedwig

Ich erwart' ihn eben; doch was ist euch, Mann?
3110 Ihr seht nicht aus, als ob ihr Gutes brächtet.
Wer ihr auch seid, ihr seid bedürftig; nehmt.

Reicht ihm den Becher.

Mönch

Wie auch mein lechzend Herz nach Labung schmachtet,
Nichts rühr' ich an, bis ihr mir zugesagt —

Hedwig

Berührt mein Kleid nicht; tretet mir nicht nah;
3115 Bleibt ferne stehn, wenn ich euch hören soll.

Mönch

Bei diesem Feuer, das hier gastlich lodert,
Bei eurer Kinder teurem Haupt, das ich
Umfasse — Ergreift die Knaben.

Hedwig

Mann, was sinnet ihr? Zurück
Von meinen Kindern! Ihr seid kein Mönch! Ihr seid
3120 Es nicht! Der Friede wohnt in diesem Kleide;
In euren Zügen wohnt der Friede nicht.

Mönch

Ich bin der unglückseligste der Menschen.

Hedwig

Das Unglück spricht gewaltig zu dem Herzen;
Doch euer Blick schnürt mir das Innre zu.

Walther, aufspringend,

3125 Mutter, der Vater! Eilt hinaus.

Hedwig

O mein Gott!

Will nach, zittert und hält sich an.

Wilhelm, *eilt nach.*

Der Vater!

Walther, *draußen.*

Da bist du wieder.

Wilhelm, *draußen.*

Vater, lieber Vater!

Tell, *draußen.*

Da bin ich wieder. Wo ist eure Mutter? *Treten herein*

Walther

Da steht sie an der Thür und kann nicht weiter;
So zittert sie für Schrecken und für Freude.

Tell

3130 O Hedwig! Hedwig! Mutter meiner Kinder;
Gott hat geholfen; uns trennt kein Tyrann mehr.

Hedwig, *an seinem Halse.*

O Tell! Tell! Welche Angst litt ich um dich!

Mönch wird aufmerksam.

Tell

Vergiß sie jetzt und lebe nur der Freude.
3135 Da bin ich wieder. Das ist meine Hütte.
Ich stehe wieder auf dem Meinigen.

Wilhelm

Wo aber hast du deine Armbrust, Vater?
Ich seh' sie nicht.

Tell

Du wirst sie nie mehr sehn.

An heil'ger Stätte ist sie aufbewahrt;
Sie wird hinfort zu keiner Jagd mehr dienen.

Hedwig

3140 O Tell! Tell! Tritt zurück, läßt seine Hand los.

Tell

Was erschreckt dich, liebes Weib?

Hedwig

Wie, wie kommst du mir wieder? Diese Hand —
Darf ich sie fassen? — diese Hand — o Gott!

Tell, herzlich und mutig.

Hat euch verteidigt und das Land gerettet;
Ich darf sie frei hinauf zum Himmel heben.

Mönch macht eine rasche Bewegung; er erblickt ihn.

3145 Wer ist der Bruder hier?

Hedwig

Ach, ich vergaß ihn.
Sprich du mit ihm, mir graut in seiner Nähe.

Mönch, tritt näher.

Seid ihr der Tell, durch den der Landvogt fiel?

Tell

Der bin ich, ich verberg' es keinem Menschen.

Mönch

Ihr seid der Tell! Ach, es ist Gottes Hand,
3150 Die unter euer Dach mich hat geführt.

Tell, mißt ihn mit den Augen.

Ihr seid kein Mönch! Wer seid ihr?

Mönch

Ihr erschlugt
Den Landvogt, der euch Böses that. Auch ich

Hab' einen Feind erschlagen, der mir Recht
Versagte. Er war euer Feind, wie meiner;
3155 Ich hab' das Land von ihm befreit.

Tell, zurückfahrend.

Ihr seid —
Entsetzen! Kinder, Kinder, geht hinein.
Geh', liebes Weib. Geh', geh'! — Unglücklicher,
Ihr wäret —

Hedwig
Gott, wer ist es?

Tell

Frage nicht.
Fort, fort! Die Kinder dürfen es nicht hören.
3160 Geh' aus dem Hause, weit hinweg; du darfst
Nicht unter einem Dach mit diesem wohnen.

Hedwig
Weh mir, was ist das? Kommt. Geht mit den Kindern.

Tell, zu dem Mönch,

Ihr seid der Herzog
Von Österreich. Ihr seid's! Ihr habt den Kaiser
Erschlagen, euern Ohm und Herrn.

Johannes Parricida

Er war
3165 Der Räuber meines Erbes.

Tell

Euern Ohm
Erschlagen, euern Kaiser! Und euch trägt
Die Erde noch! Euch leuchtet noch die Sonne!

Parricida
Tell, hört mich, eh' ihr —

Tell

       Von dem Blute triefend
Des Vatermordes und des Kaisermords,
3170 Wagst du zu treten in mein reines Haus?
Du wagst's, dein Antlitz einem guten Menschen
Zu zeigen und das Gastrecht zu begehren?

Parricida

Bei euch hofft' ich Barmherzigkeit zu finden;
Auch ihr nahmt Rach' an euerm Feind.

Tell

          Unglücklicher,
3175 Darfst du der Ehrsucht blut'ge Schuld vermengen
Mit der gerechten Notwehr eines Vaters?
Hast du der Kinder liebes Haupt verteidigt?
Des Herdes Heiligtum beschützt? das Schrecklichste,
Das Letzte von den Deinen abgewehrt?
3180 Zum Himmel heb' ich meine reinen Hände,
Verfluche dich und deine That. Gerächt
Hab' ich die heilige Natur, die du
Geschändet. Nichts teil' ich mit dir. Gemordet
Hast du, ich hab' mein Teuerstes verteidigt.

Parricida

3185 Ihr stoßt mich von euch, trostlos, in Verzweiflung?

Tell

Mich faßt ein Grausen, da ich mit dir rede.
Fort! Wandle deine fürchterliche Straße.
Laß rein die Hütte, wo die Unschuld wohnt.

Parricida, wendet sich zu gehen.

So kann ich, und so will ich nicht mehr leben.

Tell

3190 Und doch erbarmt mich deiner; Gott des Himmels!
So jung, von solchem adelichen Stamm,
Der Enkel Rudolfs, meines Herrn und Kaisers,
Als Mörder flüchtig, hier an meiner Schwelle,
Des armen Mannes, — flehend und verzweifelnd!

Verhüllt sich das Gesicht.

Parricida

3195 O, wenn ihr weinen könnt, laßt mein Geschick
Euch jammern; es ist fürchterlich. Ich bin
Ein Fürst — ich war's; ich konnte glücklich werden,
Wenn ich der Wünsche Ungeduld bezwang.
Der Neid zernagte mir das Herz. Ich sah
3200 Die Jugend meines Vetters Leopold
Gekrönt mit Ehre und mit Land belohnt,
Und mich, der gleiches Alters mit ihm war,
In sklavischer Unmündigkeit gehalten.

Tell

Unglücklicher, wohl kannte dich dein Ohm.
3205 Da er dir Land und Leute weigerte.
Du selbst mit rascher, wilder Wahnsinnsthat
Rechtfertigst furchtbar seinen weisen Schluß.
Wo sind die blut'gen Helfer deines Mords?

Parricida

Wohin die Rachegeister sie geführt;
3210 Ich sah sie seit der Unglücksthat nicht wieder.

Tell

Weißt du, daß dich die Acht verfolgt; daß du
Dem Freund verboten und dem Feind erlaubt?

Parricida

Darum vermeid' ich alle offne-Straßen;
An keine Hütte wag' ich anzupochen;
3215 Der Wüste kehr' ich meine Schritte zu;
Mein eignes Schrecknis, irr' ich durch die Berge
Und fahre schaudernd vor mir selbst zurück,
Zeigt mir ein Bach mein unglückselig Bild.
O, wenn ihr Mitleid fühlt und Menschlichkeit, —

Fällt vor ihm nieder.

Tell, *abgewendet,*

3220 Steht auf. Steht auf.

Parricida

Nicht, bis ihr mir die Hand gereicht zur Hilfe.

Tell

Kann ich euch helfen? Kann's ein Mensch der Sünde?
Doch stehet auf. Was ihr auch Gräßliches
Verübt, ihr seid ein Mensch; ich bin es auch.
3225 Vom Tell soll keiner ungetröstet scheiden.
Was ich vermag, das will ich thun.

Parricida, *aufspringend und seine Hand mit Heftigkeit ergreifend,*

O Tell,
Ihr rettet meine Seele von Verzweiflung.

Tell

Laßt meine Hand los. Ihr müßt fort. Hier könnt
Ihr unentdeckt nicht bleiben, könnt entdeckt
3230 Auf Schutz nicht rechnen. Wo gedenkt ihr hin?
Wo hofft ihr Ruh' zu finden?

Parricida

Weiß ich's? Ach!

Tell

Hört, was mir Gott ins Herz giebt: ihr müßt fort
Ins Land Italien, nach Sankt Peters Stadt;
Dort werft ihr euch dem Papst zu Füßen, beichtet
3235 Ihm eure Schuld und löset eure Seele.

Parricida

Wird er mich nicht dem Rächer überliefern?

Tell

Was er euch thut, das nehmet an von Gott.

Parricida

Wie komm' ich in das unbekannte Land?
Ich bin des Wegs nicht kundig, wage nicht
3240 Zu Wanderern die Schritte zu gesellen.

Tell

Den Weg will ich euch nennen; merket wohl:
Ihr steigt hinauf, dem Strom der Reuß entgegen,
Die wildes Laufes von dem Berge stürzt —

Parricida, erschrickt.

Seh' ich die Reuß? Sie floß bei meiner That.

Tell

3245 Am Abgrund geht der Weg, und viele Kreuze
Bezeichnen ihn, errichtet zum Gedächtnis
Der Wanderer, die die Lawine begraben.

Parricida

Ich fürchte nicht die Schrecken der Natur,
Wenn ich des Herzens wilde Qualen zähme.

Tell

3250 Vor jedem Kreuze fallet hin und büßet
Mit heißen Reuethränen eure Schuld.

Und seid ihr glücklich durch die Schreckensstraße,
Sendet der Berg nicht seine Windeswehen
Auf euch herab von dem beeisten Joch,
3255 So kommt ihr auf die Brücke, welche stäubet.
Wenn sie nicht einbricht unter eurer Schuld,
Wenn ihr sie glücklich hinter euch gelassen,
So reißt ein schwarzes Felsenthor sich auf;
Kein Tag hat's noch erhellt. Da geht ihr durch;
3260 Es führt euch in ein heitres Thal der Freude;
Doch schnellen Schritts müßt ihr vorüber eilen;
Ihr dürft nicht weilen, wo die Ruhe wohnt.

Parricida

O Rudolf! Rudolf! Königlicher Ahn!
So zieht dein Enkel ein auf deines Reiches Boden.

Tell

3265 So immer steigend, kommt ihr auf die Höhen
Des Gotthards, wo die ew'gen Seen sind,
Die von des Himmels Strömen selbst sich füllen.
Dort nehmt ihr Abschied von der deutschen Erde,
Und muntern Laufs führt euch ein andrer Strom
3270 Ins Land Italien hinab, euch das gelobte.

Man hört den Kuhreihen von vielen Alphörnern geblasen.

Ich höre Stimmen. Fort!

Hedwig, *eilt herein,*

Wo bist du, Tell?
Der Vater kommt. Es nahn in frohem Zug
Die Eidgenossen alle.

Parricida, *verhüllt sich,*

Wehe mir!
Ich darf nicht weilen bei den Glücklichen.

Tell

3275 Geh', liebes Weib. Erfrische diesen Mann;
Belad' ihn reich mit Gaben, denn sein Weg
Ist weit, und keine Herberg' findet er.
Eile.   Sie nahn.

Hedwig

Wer ist es?

Tell

Forsche nicht;
Und wenn er geht, so wende deine Augen,
3280 Daß sie nicht sehen, welchen Weg er wandelt.

Parricida geht auf den Tell zu mit einer raschen Bewegung; dieser aber bedeutet
ihn mit der Hand und geht. Wenn beide zu verschiedenen Seiten abgegangen,
veränbert sich der Schauplatz, und man sieht in der

Letzten Szene

den ganzen Thalgrund vor Tells Wohnung, nebst den Anhöhen, welche ihn
einschließen, mit Landleuten besetzt, welche sich zu einem malerischen Ganzen
gruppieren. Andere kommen über einen hohen Steg, der über den Schächen
führt, gezogen. Walther Fürst mit den beiden Knaben, Melchthal und Stauffacher kommen vorwärts, andere drängen nach; wie Tell heraustritt, empfangen sie ihn alle mit lautem Frohlocken.

Alle

Es lebe Tell! der Schütz und der Erretter!

Indem sich die Vordersten um den Tell drängen und ihn umarmen, erscheinen
noch Rudenz und Bertha, jener die Landleute, diese die Hedwig umar-
mend. Die Musik vom Berge begleitet diese stumme Szene. Wenn sie ge-
endigt, tritt Bertha in die Mitte des Volks.

Bertha

Landleute, Eidgenossen, nehmt mich auf
In euern Bund, die erste Glückliche,

THE SCHILLER STONE. Act V, Last Scene.

Die Schutz gefunden in der Freiheit Land.
3285 In eure tapfre Hand leg' ich mein Recht;
Wollt ihr als eure Bürgerin mich schützen?

Landleute

Das wollen wir mit Gut und Blut.

Bertha

Wohlan!
So reich' ich diesem Jüngling meine Rechte,
Die freie Schweizerin dem freien Mann.

Rudenz

3290 Und frei erklär' ich alle meine Knechte.

Indem die Musik von neuem rasch einfällt, fällt der Vorhang.

NOTES.

ABBREVIATIONS.

cp., compare.

comp., compound.

dimin., diminutive.

explet., expletive.

ff., and following pages.

impers., impersonal.

Introd., Introduction.

l., line; *ll.*, lines.

lit., literally.

pr., pronounce.

sc., supply.

SD., Stage Directions.

subj., subject.

tr., translate.

NOTES.

ACT I. SCENE 1.

SD. Szene. In most of the dramas of his second period, and in Fiesko, Schiller uses Aufzug and Auftritt; in Die Räuber and Kabale und Liebe he uses Akt and Szene; in Don Karlos and the translation of Iphigenie in Aulis he combines Akt and Auftritt; in Tell, Aufzug and Szene. There is no significance in the selection. Vierwaldstättensees, the Hamburg Theatre MS. has Vierwaldstätterssee, now the established spelling. The place indicated is on the southern arm of the lake, called the Urner See, near the Mythenstein and the cape where the shore turns to the west. Let the student gather the evidence for this from the map and the text. unweit, usually with genitive. Haken, see map. Noch, *yet*, omit in translation. Kuhreihen, a simple bit of melody, sung or played on a pipe or horn, ancient and inimitable, varying according to the canton.

Page 5. — line 1. Es, explet.; ladet = ladet ein.

l. 2. schlief ein, but for the metre we should probably have ist eingeschlafen.

l. 4. read: so süß wie Flöten.

l. 8. spülen, *wash, dash*; ihm, dative of possession.

l. 9. es, impers., *there comes a voice.*

l. 10. Lieb, in older German the neuter and sometimes the masculine singular nominative adjective, strong declension, might be without ending. Here the license favors the meter.

l. 11-12. Schiller found in Scheuchzer a legend of a certain lake that draws people even from quite a distance into its waters.

l. 14. After personal pronouns the adjective is strong in the singular, weak in the plural.

l. 16. The shepherds leave the high Alps about the last week in August.

Page 6. — line 17. fahren zu Berg, *come up*, the verbs may be read as future.

l. 20.   The herds are taken into the high Alps as late as June.

l. 25.   **Es**, explet.; **Steg**, *foot-bridge*.

l. 26.   **grauet**, impers. (**es** understood), the order due to the meter; **schwindlicht = schwindlig** (the t is unorganic, i.e. is not accounted for by regular rules of derivation and declension).

l. 31.   **neblicht = neblig** (see l. 26); **unter den Füßen**, *beneath his feet;* **Meer** is absolute nominative, as though subj. of **liegt** or **ist** understood, dependent on **Da** (understood) at beginning of line.

l. 35.   **Wassern**, i.e. of the misty sea.

l. 36.   **das grünende Feld**, *the field growing green*, **Feld** in same construction as **Welt**.

SD.   **verändert sich**, *changes its aspect*.

SD.   **Melknapf**, *milk-pail*.   **Ruodi** (pr. Rú-ŏ-di; a closer approximation to the Swiss pronunciation is expressed by Rúᵒ-di, where the small o represents the faint portion of a vanishing diphthong.   Cp. also Kuoni, and Muotta, l. 1178), nickname of **Rudolf; Werni**, of **Werner; Kuoni** (pr. Kú-ŏ-ni), of **Konrad; Seppi**, of **Joseph. Handbube**, *attendant*.

l. 37.   **Jenni**, dimin. of **Johannes. Naue**, *boat, skiff*, applies to same thing as **Kahn** (before l. 1), from Latin navis, through M.H.G. nawe.

l. 38.   **Thalvogt**, a word reported by Scheuchzer as used in the monastery Engelberg, (lit. valley-governor), *storm-cloud*.   **Firn**, tr. *snow-field*, field of half-melted and frozen snow in loose, coarse grains or masses, not yet packed enough to become glacier-ice.   Such fields feed glaciers, and their masses sliding or rolling down *roar* (**brüllt**).

Page 7. — line 39.   **Mythenstein**, see map.   The mountain called **der große Mythen** is probably meant, and not the natural obelisk near the Rütli; **Haube**, here *cloud-cap*.

l. 40.   In prose **her** would be at the end; **Wetterloch**, *weather-quarter* (lit. hole), i.e. the south, the Gotthard pass.

l. 41.   **mein'**, *think*.   **meinen** is think = *judge*, have an opinion; **glauben** is think = *believe*, conjecture; **denken** = *expect*.

l. 43.   **Wächter**, Watch, a dog's name; these and the following signs of approaching rain Schiller found in Scheuchzer.

l. 46.   **Lug**, *look* (South German and Swiss dialect); **sich verlaufen**, *strayed*, supply **habe**, or **hat**.

l. 47.   **Lisel**, dimin. of **Elsa**, or **Elisabeth**, *Lizzie* (the cow's name);

Geläut, here = Laut, but in l. 49, and perhaps here, *chime*, several bells tuned in chord.

l. 48. So = alſo, *then;* die, *she;* der, die, das demonstrative is to be distinguished from der, die, das relative by the position of the verb.

l. 49. ſchön, see note to l. 10.

l. 50. Landsmann, cp. with Landmann, l. 1056.

l. 51. nit = nicht (common South German dialect form).

l. 52. Des Attinghäuſers, the baron of Attinghausen (see map), genitive in apposition with Herrn; zugezählt, *entrusted,* perhaps *let on shares.*

l. 53. der Kuh, indirect object of ſteht; zu Halſe, as to her neck, tr. *looks on the cow's neck.*

l. 54. Das, i.e. what is in l. 53; since the following clause, beginning daß, is in the herdman's mind equivalent to l. 53, das may refer to this also; Reihen, confusion with der R. the dance.

l. 55. ihr, *from her;* hörte auf, imperfect subjunctive for conditional.

Page 8. — line 56. nicht klug, *foolish;* with Vieh understand either iſt es or kann das nicht.

l. 57. Iſt bald geſagt, *that is easy to say;* das Tier, not ' this animal,' but *animals.* The definite article, with a noun in either the singular or the plural, has a generalizing force; compare English usage.

l. 58. die wir, when the antecedent of the relative pronoun der, die, das, is of the 1st or 2nd person, the relative is usually followed by the personal pronoun, as here; when not so followed the verb is in the 3rd person.

l. 59. Die, demonstrative pronoun, *They.*

l. 60. 'ne = eine; die, *it*, not ' which.'

l. 61. Pfeife, *call.*

l. 62. abgeweidet, *grazed bare.*

l. 63. Die, *that;* tr. *I wish you the same.*

l. 64. Kehrt ſich's, an extreme case of the impersonal reflexive, *one does not always return.*

l. 65. gelaufen, *running,* thus always after kommen and gehen, the past participle of the verb indicating the mode of motion.

l. 66. der, colloquially and familiarly the definite article is used with surnames as in the family it is used with Christian names; Baumgart, short for meter's sake; Alzellen, see map.

l. 68. was giebt's ſo eilig? *what is the hurry?*

Page 9. — line 71. dicht fchon, read fchon dicht.

l. 72. Landvogt, *governor* (see l. 131), in this case, Landenberg, see Introd. xliv

l. 73. ein Mann des Tods, *a dead man.*

l. 76. Was hat's gegeben, *what has happened.*

l. 77. Des Kaisers, cp. l. 130, Albrecht was not in fact emperor. But the titles are used indifferently in "Tell"; Burgvogt, *castellan*, see l. 130; faß, *had his seat.*

l. 78. Wolfenschießen (see Introd. xliii) is also the name of a place ; see map; cp. l. 131; Läßt euch der verfolgen? *Is he having you pursued.*

l. 81. jeder, *any;* at the end of the line supply gethan hätte.

l. 82. Mein gutes Hausrecht, *my domestic rights.*

l. 83. Am, *against.*

Page 10. — line 85. bös, see note to l. 10; Gelüsten, infinitive as noun = Gelüst.

l. 87. ihm, dative of possession.

l. 89. Bis, *before.*

l. 90. See Introd. xliii; hatte gefällt, *had been felling;* da, 'then,' tr. *when.*

l. 91. in der Angst des Todes, *in deadly fear*, not ' in the anguish of death.'

l. 92. lieg', subjunctive of indirect discourse, about which the Germans often use quotation-marks.

l. 94. Ungebührliches von ihr verlangt, *made improper demands of her.*

l. 95. frisch, *promptly.*

l. 97. 's = das ; gesegnet, *blessed.* The expression is from Tschudi (gesegnen) and of course ironical. See Introd. xliii.

l. 98. schelten = tadeln.

l. 101. ruchtbar = ruchbar ; mir wird nachgesetzt (subject es understood). Note that an indirect object cannot properly be used as subject in a passive voice, but remains in the oblique case, as here; tr. *I am pursued.*

Page 11. — line 104. Geht nicht, 3rd person singular with es understood.

l. 106. tötet, *is death.*

l. 107. mit Gott, *in God's name.*

l. 108. Gleiches, *the like;* ja, *why,* at beginning, or *you know,* at end.   The student should make a point of getting good idiomatic renderings for doch, ja, schon, wohl and auch.

l. 109. Föhn, *south-wind,* on lake Lucerne usually a dangerous storm-wind, cp. l. 423 ff.

l. 111. mein (an historically correct form) = meiner; the line is meant as an appeal, not as a threat.

l. 112. Es geht um's Leben, *it's a matter of life and death.*

l. 116. *How the breakers roll, how it seethes and eddies.*

l. 121. Rettungsufer, analyze and translate accordingly.

Page 12. — line 123. This is possible at the narrowest point indicated.

l. 124. hinübertrüge, conditional, with suppressed condition: wenn ihr es wagen wolltet.

l. 125. Before muß sc. sich; verzagen, infinitive, same construction as liegen.

l. 127. Observe that the abrupt question from Tell implies assured superiority and mastery.

l. 128. Alzeller, *of Alzellen,* accent on penult, cp. l. 66.

l. 130. König's, here and often instead of Kaiser.

l. 131. Landvogt, see l. 72; the Burgvogt (see l. 77) was subordinate to the Landvogt.   See also Wolfenschießen, l. 945.

l. 135. After wagen sc. sei.

l. 136. läßt sich, *may;* wagen, passive infinitive; the dialogue that here follows is a specimen of what is called in the Greek drama 'stichomythy,' (lit. dialogue in lines).   It is marked by its brevity, and by being cast in general terms.   See Introd. xxxvi.   Let the student observe its recurrence, and note who uses it.

l. 137. Höllenrachen, analyze and translate accordingly.

l. 141. läßt sich's gemächlich raten, *it is easy to advise.*

Page 13. — line 143. Note the difficulty of well translating kann, though it has the same meaning in both clauses: possibility.

l. 146. Simons und Judä (sc. Tag), the 28th of October, the common anniversary of Simon the Canaanite and Judas the son of James, not Simon Peter and Judas Iscariot.   Perhaps such a confusion led Schiller to transfer to this day a superstition belonging to St. John's Day.

l. 149. dem Mann muß Hilfe werden, *the man must be helped;* werden = zu Teil werden, was formerly widely used in this sense, cp. ll. 645 and 1347.

l. 152. ſchwach, not in comparison with Ruodi, but with the storm.

l. 153. Weidgeſellen = Weidmann.

l. 155. Wohl, *indeed*, read after Gewalt.

Page 14. — line 158. der Menſchen, genitive plural, sc. Hand; Landsmann, all of the men are Tell's countrymen, but it must be inferred that Kuoni is from near Tell's home.

l. 159. Menſchliches, *fatal* (lit. human); was = etwas.

l. 160. laſſen = unterlaſſen, tr. *help doing.*

l. 161. Meiſter, probably ironical. Note the change in pronoun used by Kuoni to Ruodi going back to the formal ihr used previous to l. 103.

l. 162. ſich getraut, *venture*, cp. l. 2244.

l. 163. Wohl, *indeed*, read after Männer.

l. 164. im Gebirge, i.e. the Forest Cantons.

l. 170. angeſprengt, cp. note to l. 65.

l. 171. Weiß Gott, inverted; inversion caused by an impersonal es understood is quite common.

l. 172. After verborgen sc. habt ; this omission of the auxiliary at the end of subordinate clause is so common that it will not be pointed out again.

l. 173. Des = dieſes, adverbial genitive.

Page 15. — line 176. beilegt, *push on ;* this the evident meaning is not found in most standard dictionaries; perhaps Schiller misunderstood the nautical term beilegen = to lay by.

l. 179. Reißet ein, *break open.*

l. 181. Wütriche, *monsters.*

l. 182. dieſem Lande, i.e. the Forest Cantons, not merely Uri. The reference to *one land* is justified by the „uralt Bündnis" cited l. 1156.

ACT I. SCENE 2.

SD. des Stauffachers. The article with personal names indicates intimacy or wide repute, but usage is fluctuant; cp. ll. 126, 134, 162, etc., and the opening of Act III, Scene 1.

SD. Pfeifer is a name, not an office.

l. 183. ſagte, *was saying.*

l. 184. Schwört nicht zu Öſtreich, *Do not swear allegiance to Austria*, i.e. the Duchy of Austria, hereditary with the house of Habsburg; the imperial office was elective, but was held at this time by the Duke of Austria.

Page 16. — line 185. am Reich, i.e. to their (assumed) immediate relation to the Empire.

SD. will, *is about to.*

l. 187. Wirtin, *wife*, archaic, modern only 'hostess'; Bleibt doch, *pray* or *do remain.* The quality of conversational German is greatly affected by the use of the words: doch, ja, schon, auch, and wohl; no dictionary will give universal equivalents, but the student should make a point of feeling and rendering the special force of each.

l. 189. Viel, accusative but undeclined, as is usual with viel and wenig in the nominative and accusative, masculine and neuter.

l. 190. Schweres, tr. *hardships.*

l. 193. ans Reich gelangen, *come to the throne;* the imperial office was elective.

l. 194. Seid ihr erst, *If you are once;* Österreichs, the regular form, that in l. 184 being a contraction; seid ihr es, *you are hers.*

l. 196. *For many days I have observed in silence,* the present with schon or seit is used for the present perfect when the action or condition continues in present time.

l. 198. Gebresten, *grief,* an unusual word suggested by Tschudi's Chronicle, from the verb gebresten, 'to be lacking.'

l. 202. Glücksstand, *condition.*

l. 203. Scheunen, *sheds,* for hay and grain; after Scharen sc. sind voll.

l. 204. Zucht, *herd.*

l. 208. Stammholz, *massive timber* (lit. trunk-wood).

Page 17. — line 209. *Symmetrically put together according to the standard;* the line could have been spared. It is said to be due to an attempt to imitate Homer whom Schiller as well as Goethe studied as a model.

l. 210. Von, *with,* not 'from.'

l. 211. Wappenschildern. It is not likely that the house had more than one *escutcheon* or possibly two, one for Stauffacher and one for his wife's family (Müller, from whom the description is imitated, mentions none), but it might have various scenes, or mottoes, as may still be seen on old buildings in Switzerland.

l. 214. Wohl, modifies gezimmert and gefügt.

l. 215. den, the accusative is very unusual.

l. 218. das schön Vollbrachte, Haus is not distinctly understood; tr. *what is so beautifully finished.*

l. 220. **geritten** with fam, cp. note to l. 65.

l. 223. **trat entgegen,** *advanced to meet.*

l. 226. **bösmeinend,** *with evil intent.*

l. 227. **befonnen,** past participle of befinnen, tr. by present participle *reflecting ;* not quite like the petrified past participle in l. 1872.

l. 229. **eures,** agrees with Herrn understood; cp. the language in Tschudi, Introd. xlvi.

l. 232. **Auf seine eigne Hand,** *on his own motion ;* **also frei,** *thus freely.* Observe that German „also" is never ' also.'

l. 234. **Euch das zu wehren,** *to prevent you (from doing) that.*

l. 235. **trutziglich,** archaic for trotzig, cp., l. 168, **kräftiglich** for kräftig.

Page 18. — line 238. **Ehewirt,** *husband,* cp. note to l. 187; **Magst du,** *Are you willing.*

l. 240. **Jbergs.** Gertrude's family name according to the chronicle was Herlobig, but Schiller found the name Iberg in Müller, and it pleased him better; **rühm' ich mich,** tr. *I am proud to say I am.*

l. 241. **vielerfahrnen,** **much** *experienced;* this adjective is suggestive of the Homeric method of composition; **certain commentators** discover a great deal of Homeric suggestion in "Tell," but it is well to remember that word-composition is in the genius of the German language as much as in the Greek; **saßen,** *used to sit.*

l. 244. **Pergamente,** tr. *charters.*

l. 251. **preßte** == drückte; **wußt' ich längst,** *I have long known.*

l. 253. **Ein Hindernis, daß** etc., **an obstacle** (tr.) *preventing the Swiss etc.,* **but** *(leading them to)* etc. Or tr. **Hindernis,** *cause,* and proceed literally.

l. 254. **dem neuen Fürstenhaus,** i e. the Habsburgs.

l. 257. **Altvordern,** *forefathers.*

l. 258. **lüge, am wrong,** often thus, and not ' lie.'

l. 259. **Groll auf,** more commonly gegen.

l. 260. **dir neidisch,** more commonly auf dich neidisch.

Page 19. — line 264. **So gut,** *as well* or *freely as ;* note that in adverbial comparisons of equality, like this, the second *as* (**wie or als**) is not commonly expressed.

l. 266. **den Höchsten in der Christenheit,** i.e. the Emperor, as head of the " Holy Roman Empire."

l. 270. *With envious looks of spiteful jealousy.*

l. **272.** nod), the student should be careful in translating nod) not to put *still* at beginning of sentence, as the word is then the equivalent of bod).

l. **273.** die böfe £uft an bir gebügt, *has accomplished his evil purpose against you.*

l. **275.** Cp. this portion of Gertrude's speech with that attributed to her by Tschudi, Introd. xlvi.

l. **277.** Ob, archaic for über. Schiller has added „(Beij" to the „Wüterei" attributed to Gessler by Tschudi.

l. **279.** Urner, genitive plural, lit., of the inhabitants of Uri, tr. *the land of Uri.*

l. **281.** fd)afft es fred), *acts highhandedly.*

l. **282.** brüben überm See, *yonder across the lake.*

l. **284.** (Bewalt=Beginnen, *deed of violence.* Beginnen as noun is commonly not 'beginning,' but has the sense of act, undertaking; cp. Wallenfteins Tob, Act I, Scene 4: Was ift bein Beginnen?

l. **285.** This is one of three instances in "Tell" where a word is divided between two lines (cp. ll. 2571 and 2614); there are many more in Schiller's earlier dramas; see Introd. xxxvii; non, *by.*

l. **286.** tl)ät' es gut = wäre es gut.

l. **287.** reblid) meinen, *are in earnest.*

l. **289.** So ad)t' id) wol)l, *And I fully believe.*

Page 20. — line **291.** Baftfreunb, *friend* (with whom one exchanges visits).

l. **293.** Cp. again the extracts from Tschudi, Introd. xlvii.

l. **294.** angefel)en, *respected,* same construction as große, but ending dropped for meter's sake; Herrenleute, *leaders.*

l. **295.** gel)eim, *devoted;* gar wol)l vertraut, *thoroughly trusted* (by me).

l. **297.** Innerftes, *inmost soul.*

l. **298.** mir entgegen, *before me.*

l. **299.** ftill, modifies benfen.

l. **300.** fedflid) = led, cp. ll. 168 and 235.

l. **301.** aud), *moreover,* at beginning of line.

l. **303.** friedgewol)nt, *peacewonted,* or simply *peaceful.*

l. **304.** wagten, subjunctive dependent on rätft, *should venture.*

l. **309.** Darin fd)alten, 'hold sway in it,' tr. *rule it.*

l. 315. ſchlägt, *strikes down.* There is a resemblance between this line and Matthew 26, 31.

Page 21. — line 316. Cp. note to l. 136.

l. 319. der ungeheure, 'the monstrous,' tr. *the monster.*

l. 331. Herd und Hof, *hearth and* farm, tr. *home.* Freuden, dative plural; this usage is old and still common, but one may also say, mit Freude.

l. 333. ſtehnden Fußes, adverbial genitive, *without delay;* perhaps the idea of the peculiar phrase 'with standing foot' is 'on my feet as I am'; gleich is redundant.

l. 334. mir, dative of interest; the natural order is: Dort lebt mir e. G., tr. *I have there a friend.*

l. 336. Bannerherrn, *banneret,* military title of honor rather than title of nobility.

Page 22. — line 341. weil = dieweil, während.

l. 343. zum Gotteshauſe. Probably Stauffacher refers to the *monastery* of Einsiedeln about nine miles northeast of Steinen.

l. 346. Zu äußerſt am, *Right out on.*

l. 347. Heerweg = Heerſtraße.

l. 348. fahren, more commonly gehen.

l. 349. *You have now no further need of me;* the phrase is more commonly nötig haben (with accusative).

ACT I. SCENE 3.

SD. bauen, passive infinitive in sense; gediehen, past participle, supply iſt, tr. *is advanced;* wird eben gebaut (lit. is just being built), tr. *work is in progress;* hängt, *clings.* Fronvogt (Fron = lord or master, as in Fronleichnam, Corpus Christi, lit. the Lord's body), *taskmaster,* the representative of Gessler.

l. 353. gefeiert, past participle, a substitute for the imperative, *Don't rest long!* so also zugefahren in the next line; the accusatives Kalk and Mörtel show that the full construction is: Laßt den Kalk zugefahren werden.

Page 23. — line 355. daß = damit.

l. 356. ſieht, indicative to express certain expectancy where the subjunctive would be more common. Das, i.e. dieſes Volk (contemptuous).

l. 357. Heißt das geladen? 'Is that called loaded'? tr. *Do you call that a load?*

l. 358. ihre Pflicht bestehlen, 'rob,' tr. *shirk their duty.*

l. 360. Twing, archaic for Zwing, which occurs in l. 370; the latter word, usually in the phrase Zwing und Bann, now means jurisdiction, while the meaning of the present text, *fortress* or *keep*, has been transferred to the newer word Zwinger.

l. 361. Was = warum.

l. 362. anstellig, dialect, *fit.*

l. 364. After mehr sc. arbeiten.

l. 365. Eingeweid', *bowels of mercy.*

l. 367. Frondienst, *forced labor.*

l. 368. After Amts sc. ist, *what belongs to my office.*

l. 370. Zwing, *Hold* or *Keep* Uri, gives an imperfect reproduction of the play on the word.

Page 24. — line 372. was giebt's dabei zu lachen, *what occasion is there in that to laugh.*

l. 374. viel, for viele.

l. 375. bis ein Berg draus wird, *till they make a mountain.*

l. 377. in den tiefsten See, *into the depths of the lake.*

l. 382. erst, *once;* after gesehn sc. hättet.

l. 383. wer, *whoever,* the Der, at the beginning of next line, is unnecessary but the repetition is quite common.

l. 384. fürder, archaic, = weiter.

l. 386. Flanken, *walls,* lit. the retreating walls of a bastion, but probably used here loosely for the *bastions* themselves.

l. 389. Was will die Trommel? *What does the drum mean?*

Page 25. — line 390. Faßnachtsaufzug, now commonly printed incorrectly, Fastnachtsaufzug, *carnival-masquerade*; was soll, *what means.*

l. 393. Aufrichten. The word applies rather to the pole on which the hat was set.

l. 395. Meinung, *purpose.*

l. 396. geschehn, tr. *be shown.*

l. 400-401. *Whoever disregards the command shall forfeit,* lit. is forfeit. Leib, tr. *life.*

l. 402. Unerhörtes, *atrocity,* lit. unheard of (thing).

l. 404. dergleichen, this is the genitive plural, the real object of von being Dingen understood.

Page 26. — line 407. So, *As it is*.

l. 408. Der Hut, the emblem of the ducal office.

l. 409. Probably not at Vienna, but at Baden in Aargau where Albrecht sometimes held court. Lehen giebt, *distributes the fiefs*.

l. 414. wisset Bescheid, *are posted*, lit. know definite information.

l. 415. Cp. note to l. 136.

Page 27. — line 422. schnell, *rash* or *violent*.

l. 423. Föhn, see note to l. 109.

l. 427. *Let each*, tr. *every one live quietly at home by himself* (without interfering).

l. 429. Meint ihr, *Do you think so*. Die Schlange sticht nicht ungereizt, *The snake does not bite*, lit. sting, *unless irritated*.

l. 430. doch, *certainly*.

l. 431. Lande ; this plural is poetic, and more common in the meaning 'estates,' Länder being the regular form for 'states' or *cantons*. Schiller did not discriminate; cp. ll. 655 and 742.

l. 433. der einzelne, *a man alone*.

l. 439. zur Notwehr greift, *resorts to* self-defense, tr. *arms*.

Page 28. — line 441. sollte, *should* (i.e. is it to be expected that he will).

l. 442. was = was auch), *whatever*.

l. 443. Cp. this with ll. 2561–2651.

l. 444. bestimmter, *a definite*.

l. 448–9. Bertha's act was not wise but perhaps natural; feeling rather than deliberate judgment often controls in such circumstances.

l. 450. Mit eurem Golde, expression of impatience, tr. *Away with your gold* (in German sc. Geht before Mit). Alles ist euch feil um Gold (euch, ethical dative), *You think everything is to be had for gold*.

l. 455. eh' ihr kannt, thus unjustly identifying Bertha with her kinsman Gessler.

ACT I. SCENE 4.

Page 29. — line 459. Wenn, tr. *What if*.

l. 461. It is not necessary to assume, as does Düntzer, that Fürst is just returning from a trip to Unterwalden.

l. 462. The order of Nicht ertrag' ich's länger is unusual and not to be accounted for by the necessities of meter.

l. 465. Um, etc., tr. *That I should*.

l. 466. For the following recital cp. the account of Tschudi, Introd. xliv. Dem frechen Buben, and mir, datives of possession; in translation begin with l. 469. Buben, *servant*.

l. 472. in Straf' gefallen, more commonly der Strafe verfallen, *incurred a penalty*; mußtet, *were compelled* (i.e. by prudence); more natural would seem hättet...fügen sollen.

l. 473. Wie schwer sie (sc. auch) war, *however severe it was*.

l. 476. mög', *let*.

Page 30. — line 478. spannte, *unyoked*.

l. 480. stießen, *hooked*.

l. 487. gehässig, in active sense, tr. *hates him*.

l. 490. niemand ist = es ist niemand (sc. da) ; schütze, a delicate subjunctive, common in French in such a case (relative after negative), but rare in German.

l. 491. hinüber, *across*, i.e. the mountains, not the lake, which does not lie between Uri and Melchthal, see map.

l. 493. vom Walde, i.e. Unterwalden.

l. 497. reichen sich die Hände, *join hands*.

Page 31. — line 501. schwant, dialect for ahnt, tr. *what evil I forebode*.

l. 503. lauscht; the use of a singular verb with two singular subjects is quite common in German, where English usage would not permit it.

l. 505. thät' es not, *it would be necessary* (sc. as condition, 'if it kept on this way').

SD. da, *as;* the student should learn to discriminate between da, adverb = then or there (verb immediately following), and da, conjunction = as or since (verb at end of clause).

l. 507. bei Gott! The German uses the titles of the divinity with much greater freedom than the English, yet without any sense of irreverence, tr. *by Heaven*, or *I declare*.

l. 508. werter, not 'worthy,' but *dear*, synonymous with teurer, which tr. *valued*.

l. 513. Die, *those;* mir wird so wohl, for es thut mir so wohl.

l. 514. geht auf, *swells*; eurem Anblick, *the sight of you*.

l. 516. Wirtin, cp. l. 187.

l. 517. Cp. note to ll. 240 and 241.

l. 519. über Meinrads Zell, *by the way of Meinrad's hermitage*, i.e. Einsiedeln, which is on the old highway that leads over the Gotthard pass. It is on the spot where St. Meinrad was murdered in 861, cp. note to l. 343.

l. 522. nirgends fonſt noch, *nowhere else besides.*

l. 524. Wohl, *indeed,* the natural order would be : Wohl hab' ich, etc.

Page 32. — line 526. da habt ihr's, *there you have it* ('the whole story').

l. 528. feit Menſchendenken (= gedenten), *within the memory of men.*

l. 529. feſt, *impregnable.*

l. 530. mit Namen, *by its* (sc. *right*) *name.*

l. 531. ich will euch, etc., either sc. es as direct object, or daß at beginning of l. 532.

l. 536. Ziel = Ende.

l. 537. von uralters her, *from primitive times down :* uralters, an adverbial genitive, is here used substantively.

l. 539. Ein ſolches, sc. Ding. war = ward.

l. 540. trieb, *has driven,* sc. as object ſeine Herde.

l. 541. es treiben, *carry on.*

l. 543. noch, *(though) still (alive).* It may be as well to omit altogether in translation.

l. 544. To give the proper meter to the line the nicht must be stressed

l. 545. unterm Wald, Unterwalden, or perhaps the phrase is used for the part of Unterwalden called nid (i.e. unter) dem Wald. Schweres, *deeds of violence.*

l. 548. Gelüſten trug er, *he longed.*

Page 33. — line 549. haushält, *dwells.*

l. 550. zu frecher Ungebühr, tr. *in highhanded outrage.*

l. 551. der Mann, *the husband.*

l. 554. doch, tr. *I hope.*

l. 555. Euer Eidam, i.e. Tell ; übern = über den ; geflüchtet, *aided — in flight.*

l. 557. derſelbe Mann, i.e. Baumgarten.

l. 560. Melchthal, see map.

l. 561. eintritt, i.e. into the valley.

l. 562. Halden, lit. slope, but do not translate. See Introd. xlii.

l. 563. gilt was (= etwas), *has some weight.*

l. 565. büßte, *fined.*

l. 566. After Um sc. eines.

l. 567. ihm, dative of possesion with Ochsen.

l. 568. Da, *thereupon;* wurde flüchtig, *fled.*

Page 34. — line 571. fodern, archaic for fordern. *He* (the father) *is required to bring in to him* (the governor) *his son.*

l. 574. Da, *therefore,* or leave untranslated.

SD. will, *tries to.*

l. 577. bohren, *thrust.*

Page 35. — line 585. The spacing (Sperrschrift) shows the emphasis. geblendet adds nothing to blind, tr. *really and wholly blind.*

l. 586. sagt's = sagte es; ausgeflossen, *gone dry.*

l. 593. fühlend, *groping.*

l. 594. Finstern, unusual for Finsternis. erquickt, present for future.

l. 595. Schmelz, *lustre.*

l. 596. Die roten Firnen, tr. *rosy ice-peaks,* see note to l. 38; whole peaks are sometimes covered with „Firneis,“ and receive thence the name Firn; the refracted and reflected light from such peaks causes what is called Alpenglühen.

l. 599. frische, *sound.*

l. 600. keines, *neither.*

l. 602. mir ins Auge dringt, *enters my eyes.*

Page 36. — line 609. Alles, same construction as in l. 605; note that rauben takes accusative of the thing and dative of the person ; the compound berauben has government like the English.

l. 614. Haupt, tr. *life.*

l. 615. gelassen, same construction as gedacht, l. 613.

l. 618. hinüber, see note to l. 491.

l. 620. heraus, separable particle with finden.

l. 625. Herrenburg, *lordly* castle, tr. *seat.*

l. 628. Schreckhorn, a peak in the Bernese Alps southeast of Lucerne and about equidistant from Bern and Lucerne; die Jungfrau, a famous peak about nine miles southeast of the Schreckhorn.

l. 629. verschleiert, the figure does not apply literally, as the mountain is by no means always *veiled.* mache, present instead of machte, which would correspond to wohnt', to express greater reality in the conclusion.

Page 37. — line 632. ihr alle, i.e. men of means and leaders.

l. **637.** Sinn, *mind.*

l. **639.** Es ist auf seinem Gipfel, *it is at its height,* i.e. Melchthal's passion. Wollen wir erwarten bis das Äußerste sc. vorüber ist, *let us wait until the extreme* (or tr. *worst*) *is past.*

l. **640.** Welch Äußerstes. Melchthal, to whom the remark was not addressed, overhears it, and misunderstands its application, thinking it to refer to the general state of affairs.

l. **645.** Jedem Wesen ward, cp. note to l. 149.

l. **646.** Notgewehr, weapon in need, tr. *means of defence.*

l. **647.** Es, expletive; stellt sich, *stands at bay.*

l. **649.** reißt, *drags* or *hurls.*

l. **650.** Hausgenoß, lit. house-companion, which was true in old German houses where the whole establishment was under one roof; tr. *helpmeet,* or with Des Menschen, tr. simply, *domestic animal.*

l. **652.** gebogen (hat), *has subjected to.*

l. **653.** gereizt, absolute past participle, *when irritated.* wetzt sein gewaltig Horn, a fancy derived from the bull's habit of tearing the ground with his horns.

l. **654.** zu, separable particle with schleudert, *towards.*

l. **656.** vermögen, *accomplish.*

Page 38. — line 658. See Introd. xlii.

l. **660.** Leib und Blut, tr. *life and limb.*

l. **661.** am andern, *from others.* einen Rücken, *backing.*

l. **666.** Nicht; the natural order to give the correct sense would be: Verachtet nicht, weil, etc., tr. *Do not, because,* etc.

l. **668.** lüstern jugendliches Blut, *wanton, youthful* blood, tr. *spirits.*

l. **670.** Was, has no definite antecedent, tr. *a case which.* Stein des Felsen, tr. *a heart of stone.*

l. **671.** Hauses, and l. **672,** Sohn, tr. in plural.

l. **673.** ehre, and l. **674,** bewache, delicate uses of the subjunctive, influenced by wünscht, as though the sentence were: wünscht, daß ein tugendhafter Sohn . . . ehre, etc.

l. **675.** Read l. 678 first, omitting darum.

l. **680.** Cp. ll. 252–257. No details for this charge are given.

l. **682.** Mitschuld und Verdammnis, *guilt and condemnation.*

Page 39. — line 684. Herrn, usually Herren in plural.

l. **685.** Sillinen, a family mentioned by Tschudi; the estate was on the Reuss, nine miles above Altorf.

l. 688. eurer, to Fürst; der eure, to Stauffacher.

l. 689. echte Währung, *the genuine worth.*

l. 690. Klang = Ruf.

l. 694. Wären wir doch, *O would we were.*

l. 695. schon, *all right.*

l. 696. tr. in passive; mit uns, *as we.*

l. 698. Bis jetzt, *Thus far.*

l. 699. entstehn = fehlen.

l. 703. After Doch, sc. der ; the omission of the first element of the correlative is quite common in poetry. Kaifer, rather König, see note to l. 77.

l. 708. läg', conditional or potential subjunctive.

Page 40. — line 710. Laßt mich, sc. gehen.

l. 714. mit Gott, *in God's name.*

l. 717. der Alzeller, i.e. Baumgarten. nid dem Wald, cp. note to l. 545; see map.

l. 719. uns, reciprocal, *to one another.*

l. 721. Brunnen oder Treib, Brunnen in Schwyz, Treib in Uri, just opposite, see map.

l. 725. nach Brunnen, i.e. northward. dem Mythenstein grad' über, *just above the Mythenstein,* a natural obelisk 100 feet high, in the lake around a point southward from Treib; see map, also Introd. xlvii.

l. 727. Rütli (lit. 'clearing,' from stem reuten, to root out), written also Grütli, is above, but a mile south of the Mythenstein; grad' über, may = grad' gegenüber, just opposite, in which case the Mythenstein would seem to mean the mountain Mythen in Schwyz, as in l. 39. But the Rütli is more properly *just above* the Mythenstein than 'just opposite' the Mythen. Volk der Hirten, genitive of identity, tr. *the shepherds.*

l. 729. Dort ist's, in fact the Rütli is over a mile from the border of the two cantons; the border may once have been different.

Page 41. — line 732. öden, *secret, solitary.*

l. 734. mag, *let;* cp. l. 476.

l. 735. herzeinig, *of one heart.*

l. 737. frisch, *promptly.*

l. 738. eure (to Fürst).

l. 739. die eure (to Melchthal).

l. 741. falsch, *guile,* archaic.

l. 742. **Länder**, see note to l. 431.

SD. einige Pausen lang, *for a few moments.*

l. 749. wallen, *make pilgrimages.*

l. 751. soll es dir tagen, *shall the day dawn for you.*

ACT II. SCENE 1.

Some days must intervene between the first act and the second, to allow for Melchthal's journey, and the arrangements for Scene 2.

Page 42. — line 754. Frühtrunk, *morning-drink*, perhaps a light breakfast of which beer was the chief element.

SD. The custom of drinking round was very common formerly, cp. the description in "Faust," ll. 725-28.

l. 757. Wie = sowie.

l. 758. den Schaffner machen, *play the steward.*

l. 761. enger, for engerm.   Körner regarded this as a mistake, and corrected it in his edition of Schiller's works.   But there are numerous examples in the classic writers where the second of two adjectives is declined while the first is not; where both are logically comparative Goethe sometimes left the first in the positive degree, as Nun glühte seine Wange roth und röther, l. 49, Epilog zu „Das Lied von der Glocke."

l. 764. Schatte, older form for Schatten.

l. 765. bring's euch, with both literal and derived meanings : *I bring it to you*, and *I drink to you.*

l. 765. geht, *comes.*

Page 43. — line 770. It is assumed that there is a castle at Altorf aside from the Keep that we see building in Act I, Scene 3; Tschudi mentions a tower there, see Introd. xlv.

l. 772. Haft du's so eilig, for Haft du solche Eile, or Bist du so eilig.

l. 774. An, *at the expense of.*

l. 778. Zur Fremde, *a strange place.*   Uli, pet form of Ulrich.

l. 780. trägst zur Schau, *you display.*

Page 44. — line 787. Königs, and just below, l. 800, Kaiser, see note to l. 77.

l. 788. ob = über.

l. 793. Hohnsprechend, *mocking*, not, as usual, 'defying.'

l. 794. indes, for indem.

l. 798. kostete, *would cost*, subjunctive for conditional.

l. 801. ihnen, for denen. halten = zu halten.

l. 802. Daß, *so that.*

l. 803. hindern ... Daß nicht, *prevent from*, cp. l. 253 and note.

l. 806. Wohl thut es ihnen, *it flatters them.* Herrenbank, *bench of lords* (in the council).

Page 45. — line 813. Landammann (= L.-amtman), *judge*, an officer in the cantons corresponding to that of Bürgermeifter in a city.

l. 817. sich an ... anzuschließen, *to join.*

l. 818. Pair, *the equal.*

l. 819. zu Gericht sitzen, *to sit in judgment;* the local assembly had both judicial and legislative powers.

l. 822. Sie ergriff dein offnes Ohr, tr. *It found your ear open.*

l. 825. Den Bauernadel schelten, *call us in ridicule peasant nobility.* schelten in this sense, like nennen and heißen, takes two accusatives.

l. 828. müßig still, tr. *idle and silent.*

l. 829. bei, *in.*

l. 831. Geschehen, *are being done.*

l. 832. glänzend, tr. as adjective with Welt.

l. 833. Mir, dative of possession.

l. 834. Kriegstrommete = K.-trompete.

l. 836. Er, as agreeing with Ruf; we might expect, Sie bringen.

Page 46. — line 843. Heim sehnen nach, lit. *long home for*, tr. *long for your home in;* väterlichen, *ancestral.*

l. 847. sie dir anklingt, *you hear it.*

l. 848. der Trieb des Vaterlands, *the instinct for*, or *the love of fatherland.*

l. 850. bleibst du, etc., tr. *you with*, etc., *will remain forever a stranger.* The effect of Dir is: *it will seem so to you.*

l. 855. ein Fürstenknecht, *a prince's vassal.*

l. 856. Da, *when.* ein Selbstherr, *your own master.*

l. 863. Die, *these.*

l. 865. mein brechend Auge, *my* breaking, tr. *closing eyes*, or better, *the closing of my eyes;* the idiom comes from a misunderstanding of the discharge of the tear-glands at death; thus, sein Auge brach = he died.

l. 868. von Östreich zu empfangen, the man who wished to become the vassal of another first gave him his estates and then received them back in fee.

Page 47. — line 872. **die Länderkette**; Schiller had jotted down a memorandum of this *chain of lands* as follows: —

Zug   Einſiedeln
        Unterwalden   Schweiz
Luzern   Glarus
                        Uri
Entlibuchern   Diſentis
                Wald Urſern

l. 873. **gewaltig, tr.** as adjective with **Länderkette.**

l. 874. The details of the situation here given are taken from Müller and Tschudi, though only words and occasional phrases are borrowed.

l. 875. **Kaufmannsſtraßen,** *commercial highways.*

l. 879. **das Reich,** *the* estates of the *Empire* apart from the emperor.

l. 882. **Was iſt zu geben auf,** *What dependence* is to *be placed in.*

l. 883. **Geld= und Kriegesnot,** *need of money and the stress* of war.

l. 884. **des Adlers,** *of the eagle,* i.e. as emblem of the empire.

l. 885. *dare pawn and alienate from the empire,* the practice was a common one; of course it affected only the imperial revenues and the feudal allegiance of the cities.

l. 889. Cp. note to l. 184 and Introd. liv.

l. 891. *But to deserve well of a powerful hereditary lord* (such as the Habsburg Duke of Austria).

l. 892. **Heißt,** *is.*

l. 893. **Willſt,** *Do you claim to.*

l. 899. **zählen,** *enumerate* (in census for taxation).

Page 48. — line 900. **Hochflug,** *game birds;* **Hochwild,** *large game;* **bannen,** *preserve,* reserve for imperial use.

l. 904. **zahlen = bezahlen.**

l. 911. **bei Favenz,** *Faenza,* which was taken in 1241, after an eight months' siege by Emperor Frederick II.

l. 912. **Sie ſollen kommen,** spoken in defiance.

l. 915. **Flitterſchein,** *glittering tinsel.*

l. 919. **zu,** *by.*

l. 920. **des = dieſes.**

l. 922. **aus teure, tr.** as standing before **Vaterland**; notice that the declined adjective is capitalized only when no noun agreeing is present in the context.

l. 927. **Du haſt uns lang' nicht mehr geſehn,** *it is long since we* have seen you.

Page 49. — line 939. Mit, burch was rather to be expected.

l. 940. die Braut, *a* (possible) *betrothed;* the word is not used for 'bride,' save on the wedding-day.

l. 941. deiner Unſchuld, *for your inexperience,* i.e. for you, inexperienced fellow; beſchieden, *destined.*

l. 944. erhalten, here *restrain.*

l. 948. Gewaltſam ſtrebend (i.e. der Zauber), *working powerfully.*

l. 950. ſtill beglückt, *blessed in being quiet,* but tr. *blessed with peace.*

Page 50. — line 954. anders denkendes, *with other thoughts.*

ACT II. SCENE 2.

SD. Steige, *paths* with steps cut; Jm Hintergrunde; we are supposed to stand with our backs to the mountain (the Selisberg), looking across the Rütli toward the lake; the hohe Berge must be those of Schwyz — the Haken; the Eisgebirge are those of Glarus. For comments on this scene, see Introd. xxiv, xxvii, xxx.

l. 961. Before nur sc. kommt.

l. 964. Feuerwächter, a poetic and less common form for Nacht-wächter.

l. 965. Vom Selisberg, i.e. from the village on the Selisberg.

SD. Man hört läuten, *the ringing of a bell is heard.*

l. 966. Mettenglöcklein, *matin-bell,* though the regular hour for that is three.

l. 969. Gehn, subjunctive for imperative.

l. 972. als wie, unusual for wie.

l. 975. A lunar rainbow is rare, but the secondary bow at night is extraordinary. Schiller found the suggestion in Scheuchzer.

Page 52. — line 978. nicht = nie.

l. 980. fährt . . . weg, *is sailing along.*

l. 982. ſich . . . erwarten, more usual: auf ſich warten.

SD. nach dem Ufer. The Rütli is on a promontory a hundred feet or more above the water's edge.

l. 985. Kundſchaft = Kundſchafter, *spies.*

SD. drei, as Stauffacher was to bring ten, this should be four.

Page 53. — line 990. geſogen; the figure is neither clear nor pleasant, tr. *And the sight of the extinguished sun of his vision filled me with,* etc.

l. 992. Geſchehnes, *what is done;* rächen, dependent on wollen wir (l. 993) *let us.*

l. 995. geſchafft, *done;* gemeine Sach', the omission of the article is due to the meter.

l. 998. durch der Surennen, i.e. going from Walther Fürst's, in Uri, where they had last met. The Surenne or Surner Alps, see map, with peaks over 10000 feet high and considerable glaciers, lie on the west of Uri adjoining Unterwalden.

l. 1000. Lämmergeier, a large vulture, same name in English.

l. 1001. Alpentrift, *highland pasture.*

l. 1002. Engelberg, the monastery of Engelberg (see map), built in 1083.

l. 1004. der Gletſcher Milch, *the glacier milk,* so called from the bluish white color of the water from the melted ice.

l. 1005. Runſen, *runlets.*

l. 1007. It was so late in the fall that the huts were deserted.

l. 1008. geſellig lebend, *gregarious.*

l. 1011. Ehrfurcht, object; ſchaffte = verſchaffte, *procured.*

Page 54. — line 1018. In the long narrow alpine valleys this is really the case in large measure.

l. 1020. fortbeſtanden, *continued.*

l. 1021. tragen, for ertragen, *tolerate.*

l. 1022. altgewohnt, *long wonted;* gleich, *uniform.*

l. 1024. langten, *took.*

l. 1033. heimatliche, *home* or *native.*

l. 1034. mir, dative of possession; viel has the effect of ſehr and also of viele with Wettern.

l. 1042. froch, perhaps with reference to stealthy manner, perhaps influenced by alliteration with Krümmen.

Page 55. — line 1043. After es sc. denn, the resulting construction, very common in the Bible = daß ich es nicht ausſpähte. This peculiar construction is the relic of a M.H.G. construction in which there was regularly the negative particle ne ; thus 'ez ne si denne ' meant ' unless it be.' The particle vanished but the negative force remained. Another relic of the construction is the word nur which is the contraction of (ez) ne wære.

l. 1045. After ich sc. zu finden.

l. 1049. ſtarre, *frozen.*

l. 1051. Though alle agrees with Herzen, tr. with Volt.

l. 1060. Sarnen, Landenberg's residence.

Page 56. — line 1071. kennte, potential subjunctive.

l. 1075. See note to l. 1264.

l. 1078. hinterm Wald, = ob dem Wald, hinter from Melchthal's point of view, living in nid dem Wald; Klosterleute, *dependents of the monastery, serfs*, see note to l. 1002.

l. 1080. eigne Leute, lit. owned people, *serfs*.

l. 1081. auf dem Erbe, *on their own inheritance*.

l. 1082. wohl berufen, *of good repute*.

l. 1083. Es preise sich sc. glücklich; wer, comp. relative, logical subject of preise.

l. 1084. mit seinem Leibe pflichtig, lit. bound with his body, tr. *in personal bondage*.

l. 1086. Altlandammann, *ex-magistrate*, see note to l. 813.

Page 57. — line 1090. brav, observe that brav is rarely 'brave,' here *well*.

l. 1091. das Horn von Uri, the head of the aurochs is the emblem of Uri, the canton claiming its name from the animal.

l. 1094. das Graun = Grauen, tr. *the terrors*.

l. 1095. Before Ein sc. Um als.

l. 1096. Sigrist, sexton (both words from Middle Latin sacrista).

l. 1102. sonnenscheuen, lit. sunshunning, *which avoids the light*.

l. 1104. uns holen, *secure*.

l. 1105. der . . . Schoß des Tages, tr. *the brilliant open face* (lit. bosom) *of day*, i.e. the sun.

l. 1106. Laßt's gut sein, *Never mind*.

l. 1107. At end sc. kommen.

Page 58. — line 1108. Eidgenossen, it is strange that the priest thus addresses them before they have formed the confederacy. Perhaps he is justified by l. 1156.

l. 1109. Landsgemeinde, *general assembly*, town meeting, the political assembly of the whole body of voters in a pure democracy, cp. Landgemeinde = country congregation.

l. 1111. tagen, *hold session*, same meaning as in Landtag, Reichstag; cp. *diet*.

l. 1114. Entschuldige, imperative subjunctive of which Not is the subject.

l. 1117. Wohl = wohlan.

l. 1118. gleidy with wenn implied by inverted position of verb, *although;* so in 1119, and with audy in 1121.

l. 1121. die alten Büchyer, the popular laws, such for instance as were written down in the 13th century, as the Sachsenspiegel.

l. 1123. der Ring, an old Germanic custom for the assembly; fei, where werde would be expected.

l. 1124. pflanze auf, *set up;* two bare swords were set point down in the earth beside the speaker's chair; der Gewalt, *of authority.*

l. 1127. dreie, the declension of zwei, drei and vier, common in early N.H.G., is now rare or poetical; zwei and drei have dative and genitive endings, while vier has no genitive; when used without a following noun all the numbers up to and including zwölf may form the nominative and accusative in e.

l. 1128. geben, *furnish;* der Gemeinde may be either genitive or dative.

Page 59. — l. 1131. die flehenden, the point is not exactly clear; the gathering was called with equal urgency from the three cantons; it is true that Unterwalden is the only one in which there are two leaders (Baumgarten and Melchthal) in outlawry. But cp. line 678.

l. 1133. das Schwert, i.e. the presidency; one might expect die Schwerter, as two are used.

l. 1134. bei den Römerzügen, *in the processions to Rome* to secure the coronation of the emperor.

l. 1136. As indicated by the general title of nationality, Schweizer, which is merely another form of Schwyzer.

l. 1139. After nehmt sc. fie.

l. 1140. The line will not scan without accenting Ulrich on the ultimate, which is unusual.

l. 1144. Was = Warum.

l. 1145. des Tages, *of the assembly.*

l. 1146. Hände, sense and usage call for Hand (see SD. below: die rechyte Hand).

Page 60. — line 1150. Though in a poetical way, Reding is following custom in calling on some one to state the object of the meeting.

l. 1152. zusammenführte, more commonly zusammengeführt hat.

l. 1156. As we know (see Introd. xli) there was a league formed on this same spot in 1291, which was preceded by one in 1145–50. Before Väter sc. der.

l. 1158. Ob for obgleich.

l. 1160. eines Stammes, i.e. the Swedish; legend identified Schwyz and Swetia.

l. 1162. in den Liedern. The legends of an origin in the north are referred to by Müller, Schiller's authority, who quotes from one song of uncertain age now printed in Rochholz's Eidgenössische Liederchronik; cp. l. 1189.

l. 1165. am alten sc. Bund, which would mean in this connection only the original union of a common origin, not that in 1291.

l. 1167. hinten im Land nach Mitternacht, *up in the land toward the north.* In fact the German tribes did enter south Germany from the north.

Page 61. — line 1170. je der zehnte, ever the tenth = *every tenth.*

l. 1172. Before zogen aus sc. es to introduce the sentence.

l. 1176. So far as this may be supposed to be the real migration it is exaggerated; real migrations go slowly.

l. 1178. die Muotta (pr. Mûot-ta), entering the Vierwaldstättersee near Brunnen; see map.

l. 1179. Switzerland was occupied by Keltic tribes before the Germans came; for nicht read keine.

l. 1184. sich, dative of advantage; gewahrten, *perceived,* an unusual word.

l. 1189. The old song (so called Westfriesenlied) quoted by Müller has „Sie hatten manchen schweren Tag, eh' ihnen das Land einen Nutzen gab ; Reut' hauen war ihr Geigenbogen."

l. 1190. weitverschlungnen, *far reaching, intertwined;* auszuroden, cp. ausgereutet, l. 728.

l. 1191. Gnügen (= Genüge) that, for genügte.

l. 1193. zum schwarzen Berg = the Brünig; Weißland = Hasli or Haslithal ; the latter begins with the pass of the former.

l. 1194. wo, not in Weissland, but beyond it in Wallis (French) and in Tessin (Italian); hinter ewigem Eiseswall interprets wo. The people of Haslithal speak German.

Page 62. — line 1201. sich is reciprocal, not reflexive.

l. 1202. Es is an expletive; giebt sich zu erkennen, *will show itself.*

l. 1205. Völker, *tribes, cantons.*

l. 1208. der Saffen, (from sitzen), *serfs;* viel = viele, to favor the meter; die fremde Pflichten tragen, *who are bound to the service of others*.

l. **1211**. For the accuracy of this see Chronology, p. lvi.

l. **1214**. Schutz und Schirm, an alliterative couplet such as German is rich in; the two words are close synonyms, tr. *shield and shelter*.

l. **1215**. Kaiser Friedrichs Brief, such a charter was given to Schwyz at Faenza (see note to l. 911), Müller says to all the Wald-stätte.

l. **1217**. Read Es muß ein Oberhaupt sein ; es giebt expresses generalities, but realities rather than abstract propositions, therefore sein here, not geben; yet cp. "Faust" I, 3483, Es muß auch solche Käuze geben. The latter is speaking as of a fact in nature.

l. **1218**. Wo = bei dem ; Recht schöpfen, *derive* (lit. draw, dip, as from a source) *justice;* cp. Recht schaffen, to secure justice (for an-other).

l. **1221**. Die Ehre = diese Ehre.

l. **1222**. The imperial title in the limited sense did not express this claim, though it was implied in the official style of the empire, „Heiliges Römisches Reich Deutscher Nation.“

Page 63. — line **1224**. edeln, the contraction of edelem results more commonly in edlem ; gelobt, past participle of geloben, with haben (l. 1219).

l. **1227**. Was drüber ist, *anything beyond that.*

l. **1228**. Heribann, *call to arms*, lit. army-order (from the Latinized form heribannus; the more common form is Heerbann).

l. **1230**. The Römerzüge referred to l. 1134.

l. **1234**. Blutbann, jurisdiction over blood-shed; der höchste B., *jurisdiction in capital crimes.*

l. **1235**. dazu, i.e. to exercise this; bestellt for bestallt.

l. **1236**. Note that Der is not relative.

l. **1237**. Blutschuld, *capital crime.*

l. **1238**. unter offnem Himmel, so always in primitive German courts of law.

l. **1241**. einer = irgend einer.

l. **1245**. bog, *perverted;* zu Gunst der Pfaffen, more commonly den Pfaffen zu Gunsten. See Chronology, p. lvi.

l. **1247**. Einsiedeln, see note to l. 343; such a dispute had actually been carried on through a period of 200 years. uns, dative of possession.

l. 1249. herfürzog, archaic for hervorzog, the unseparated use seemingly due to the government of denn (l. 1246) which was formerly regarded as a subordinate connective; the meter would have permitted the modern order: Der Abt zog einen alten Brief hervor.

Page 64. — line 1250. herrenlose, i.e. according to the Brief, *charter*.

l. 1260. erschaffen, lit. *created*, a strong figure to express the effect of their labor in making the land tillable.

l. 1263. zu einem, more commonly in einen.

ll. 1264-65. The dragon here referred to, the same as in most dragon-legends, is explained literally in ll. 1266-67.

l. 1269. geleitet, lit. directed, tr. *built*.

l. 1271. der fremde Herrenknecht, *this foreign prince's vassal*, i.e. Gessler or Landenberg, as also in l. 1258.

l. 1276. After nirgends sc. sonst.

l. 1277. greift, *reaches*.

l. 1278. getrosten Mutes, adverbial genitive, *with courageous confidence*.

Page 65. — line 1287. vor = für, not yet strictly distinguished in use in the 18th century.

l. 1296. The rude interruptions show that some of the men have misunderstood Rösselmann's motives in ll. 1290-95, which are to temper and test them and bring them out.

Page 66. — line 1300. abtrotzen, governs dative of person (uns) and accusative of thing (the demonstrative element in Was).

l. 1303. sei gestoßen, for werde gestoßen, the use of sein for werden in cases that seem to be true passives is most common in the imperative.

l. 1304. Wer for der ; when the subordinate clause with wer comes first, (as in 1307) it is very common to express the unnecessary der in the following principal clause, but the present case is unusual, cp. ll. 330 to 331, 703, 1146; an connects Ergebung and Österreich.

l. 1310. Though idealized, parliamentary usage is fairly well observed; only here, after Melchthal's 'second,' the vote is given without waiting for the Ammann to put the motion. For instance, the Ammann waits (SD.) for appeals or negatives before announcing the result.

Page 67. — line 1317. wohl gar goes with nicht, *perhaps;* was wir erdulden is logical subject to ist.

l. **1322.** Commonly: **Gott hilft nur dann, wenn der Mensch nicht mehr helfen kann.** There is a profound difference between this and the English, God helps those that help themselves.

l. **1324.** **Rheinfeld,** on the Rhine in Aargau.

l. **1325.** See Introd. xlii; where it will be seen that Schiller uses the account of an embassy for another purpose from that given in Tschudi, and combines with it part of an account of Duke Johann; l. 1326 gives the true object of the embassy.

l. **1335.** **wohl sonst einmal,** *some other time probably.*

l. **1337.** **Herzog Hansen,** Johannes Parricida of the List of Persons, and Act V.

l. **1339.** **Wart und Tegerfeld,** cp. l. 2961.

l. **1343.** **hinterhält,** rare, for **vorenthält.**

l. **1344.** **Mütterliches,** *maternal inheritance ;* not **Erbe** understood, as in that case **Mütterliches** would not be capitalized, yet practically the same in meaning.

Page 68. — line **1345.** **habe,** although no verb introduces the quotation, the subjunctive shows clearly the indirect discourse; begin the line with *saying;* **habe seine Jahre voll,** *was of age.*

l. **1347.** **Was ward ihm zum Bescheid,** *what answer did he receive?*

l. **1348.** **Das sei,** this is the direct discourse, hence imperative.

l. **1357.** Cp. Matthew 22, 21.

l. **1361.** **Die Herrn** (correctly **Grafen**) **von Rappersweil,** a family with estates on Lake Zurich; it became extinct in 1284.

l. **1362.** **zinsen,** *to pay rent;* **steuern,** *to pay taxes.*

l. **1363.** **der großen Frau zu Zürch,** the abbess of the cloister at Zurich.

l. **1364.** **Ihr gebt,** indicative for imperative like English, *You will give.*

Page 69. — line **1365.** After **als** sc. **die.**

l. **1369.** **Es,** expletive; **sehe,** subjunctive imperative.

l. **1372.** **in unsern Schranken,** i.e. within the bounds of our rights, tr. *within bounds.*

l. **1373.** *Perhaps he will be politic enough to control his wrath.*

l **1374.** **sich,** dative, *for itself,* or leave untranslated; **Volk** is the subject.

l. **1380.** **sich rüstet,** *is equipped.*

l. 1382. Uns (also in 1384), dative of possession with £and, or may be read as dative of advantage: *two strong castles tower against us.*

l. 1385. muß, singular as though with the idea of one obstacle, or it may be an extreme case of co-ordinate singulars, cp. note to l. 503; fein, note the effect, i.e the subject must already have passed into the condition indicated by the past participle.

Page 70. — line 1390. The effect of the declined adjective as thus placed in apposition may be represented by: *Zeal too, however good, may betray.*

l. 1394. Das darf uns Uri bieten ! with a threatening tone, which means, Das darf uns Uri nicht bieten.

l. 1397. The modern realism of this parliamentary quarrel is something rare in Schiller; weifen = zurechtweifen. vor der £andsgemeinde, Reding probably means the regular public meeting of the people.

l. 1398. Daß . . . ftört, tr. *for disturbing.*

l. 1400. feft des Ḥerrn, *Christmas.*

l. 1401. Saffen (lit. settlers), *inhabitants*, not, as in l. 1208, serfs.

l. 1403. zeḥen, older uncontracted form of zeḥn.

l. 1405. Die, demonstrative.

Page 71. — line 1408. Zunächft, *near by ;* ḥält = ḥält fich, *will wait.*

l. 1410. Ermächtiget, for bemächtiget.

l. 1414. See Introd. li.

l. 1416. die fchwanke £eiter, *a rope ladder.*

l. 1418. aller, genitive plural; after daß sc. es.

l. 1424. der Waffen Ernft, *the reality of arms.*

l. 1428. On second reading it will appear strange that the question of postponement has been settled without reference to Gessler, who has also a stronghold, at Altorf, and is here spoken of as the most dangerous; Stand, for Widerftand.

l. 1429. furchtbar is adverb with umgeben, but tr. *He has a fearful retinue of troopers.*

Page 72. — line 1432. gefährlich iḥn zu fchonen, seems to be almost paving the way for Tell's act.

l. 1433. Wo's ḥalsgefährlich ift, *where risk of life is involved.*

l. 1437. (e)s, *the issue*, or omit entirely.

l. 1439. nächtlich . . . tagen, it is not likely that Schiller intended this curious conjunction of words.

l. **1443.** This remark must apply rather to the concealment of those going home than to the meeting-place which was on an exposed eastern slope.

SD. ſtiller Sammlung, tr. inverted, *solemn silence.*

l. **1444.** zuerſt . . . von, does not fit the following clause, tr. von, *before.*

ll. **1448-89.** This couplet was a favorite motto during the Franco-Prussian War; einzig, *single,* not einig as often printed.

SD. drei Fingern, perhaps as symbol of the trinity, though this was not requisite in oaths.

Page 73. — line **1455.** Genoßſame, rare for Genoſſenſchaft.

l. **1463.** das Ganze, tr. *for the benefit of all* or *for the supreme occasion.*

l. **1465.** See note to l. 1304.

SD. über den Eisgebirgen, the mountains in the southwest corner of the Canton of Glarus, which attain a height of 11,000 feet.

ACT III.   SCENE 1.

Page 74. — line **1471.** der Weih, lit. the hawk, here poetic for *the eagle.*

l. **1473.** frei, not adjective to Schütze, but *unrestrained,* adverb.

l. **1474.** das Weite, lit. the distance, tr. with l. 1475, *all within the reach of his arrow.*

l. **1477.** Was is relative referring to Das ; freucht, fleugt, older and dialect forms for kriecht and fliegt ; da is untranslatable, it adds perhaps a little of generality to Was, making it == whatever.

l. **1478.** Der Strang . . . mir, dative of possession; mach', *mend.*

l. **1480.** zeitig, for frühzeitig.

l. **1481.** Was == Wer ; general statements are thus made universal in German by the use of the neuter pronoun.

Page 75. — line **1482.** wollte, lit. might God will, not as in English with *I* as subject, yet tr. *Would God.* lernten, subjunctive dependent on wollte, *might learn.*

l. **1483.** ſollen, not should, but *shall* (in Tell's intent).

l. **1484.** ſich friſch ſchlagen, *vigorously make his way.* zu Schutz und Trutz gerüſtet, *equipped for both defence and attack.*

l. **1485.** keiner, *neither.* ſeine Ruh' . . . finden, *be content.*

l. 1486. auch, *either.*

l. 1487. Natur, the omission of the definite article here is very un-usual.

l. 1488. ein flüchtig Ziel, *a fleeting goal.*

l. 1489. erſt, *only;* recht, *aright,* or *thoroughly.*

l. 1490. erbeute, *win,* or *earn;* Schiller has also in the last two lines of „Wallenſteins Lager" :

> Und ſetzt Ihr nicht das Leben ein
> Nie wird Euch das Leben gewonnen ſein ;

and Goethe, in „Fauſt," Part II, Act V :

> Nur der verdient ſich Freiheit wie das Leben,
> Der täglich ſie erobern muß.

l. 1492. ſich . . . härmt, *worries.*

l. 1494. Wagefahrten, *daring doings,* lit. trips; cp. ll. 2638, 2874.

l. 1499. den Fehlſprung thun, *making a slip in springing,* lit. mis-leap.

l. 1500. Cp. l. 649; Rückſpringend goes with Gemſe.

l. 1501. Windlawine, *wind-avalanche;* in Scheuchzer Schiller found very careful, though unscientific accounts of the various sorts of avalanche, this one so-called partly because it was started by a wind upon the soft freshly-fallen snow, partly because it aroused a great wind in its passage.

l. 1502. Firn = Firneis, see note to l. 38.

l. 1504. Gruft, *crevasse.*

Page 76. — line 1508. halsgefährlich, see note to l. 1433.

l. 1509. friſch, *alertly;* Sinnen, *senses,* so almost always in plural.

l. 1510. die, tr. *his own.*

l. 1511. ringt ſich, *will get.* Fahr = Gefahr.

l. 1514. erſpart, *saves* = dispenses with.

l. 1516. auch, *now,* at beginning.

l. 1517. Wie kommſt du darauf sc. zu denken. Es ſpinnt ſich etwas, *Something is plotting.*

l. 1518. ward getagt, (es, subject, understood), *there was a meeting.*

Page 77. — line 1535. The negative which seems to us superfluous is paralleled by the use of *ne* in French; tr. Verhüt', *grant,* or omit negative, translating *forbid.*

Page 78. — line 1539. **Ehni,** Swiss diminutive of **Ahn,** *grand-father,* i.e. the boy's grandfather, Walther Fürst.

l. 1540. One need not wonder at the knowledge of circumstances in Altorf, since Bürglen is less than two miles away.

l. 1541. **laß ihn erst fort sein,** *wait till he is gone.*

l. 1545. **Die,** the first has the effect of a compound relative, and the second **die** is the repeated demonstrative, translate **eben die,** *these very ones;* cp. note to l. 1304.

l. 1546. **an sie kommen,** *get at them* (to harm).

l. 1549. **Da,** resumes the preceding phrase, lit. then, but tr. *that.* **Gründe,** *regions.*

l. 1550. **Schächenthal,** the valley of the Schächen, the stream on which Bürglen is situated, see map. **menschenleer,** *unfrequented.*

l. 1552. **nicht auszuweichen war,** *there was no turning out,* cp. **Was ist zu thun?** *What can be done.*

Page 79. — line 1555. **gegen mich daher,** *along toward me.*

l. 1558. **Herre,** regular old form of the word, as seen in its weak declension.

l. 1560. Cp. ll. 565-66.

l. 1561. **stattlichen Gewehr,** i.e. his cross-bow, the adjective due to the hunter's pride in his weapon.

l. 1562. **da,** omit, or tr. *then.*

l. 1563-64. **Ich sah es kommen daß,** *I saw that he was about to,* etc.

l. 1566. **Bescheidentlich,** for the 't,' cp. note to l. 26.

l. 1574. **Bleib'** . . . **dort weg,** commonly **von dort weg.**

Page 80. — line 1581. **Wälty,** pet form for **Walther.**

l. 1582. **Ich bringe** . . . **mit,** *I'll bring along.*

ACT III. SCENE 2.

SD. **Staubbäche,** brooks which are dashed into spray as they fall; cp. l. 3255.

Page 81. — line 1586-89. Note the rhyme, in accord with the lyric spirit of the scene.

l. 1593. Two parts of the predicate are rarely put first, and here only because of their close relation.

l. 1599. **in die Reih'** . . . **stellen,** *put myself on a par with.*

l. 1600. **euch umwerben** == **um euch werben.**

l. 1603. wirð, cp. note to l. 58; if the personal pronoun is not repeated, the verb does not agree in person.

l. 1607. als euch, *but you.*

l. 1611. naturvergeßnen, lit. who has forgotten the voice of nature,
tr. *unnatural.*

Page 82. — line 1621. Es is expletive.

l. 1630. nicht belongs with an understood Will ich denn.

l. 1636. fie, i.e. the Austrians.

Page 83. — line 1638. ðen | Verachtet fehen, *to see him despised.*

l. 1642. einem, lit. one, tr. *the same.*

ll. 1649-50. alles läßt, etc., read, Eure Liebe läßt mich alles fein
und werden, *your love will enable me to be and become anything.* After
Seið sc. ðas.

l. 1653. Steht zu, *Stand by,* more commonly haltet euch zu.

Page 84. — line 1664. mit ðem großem Erb, i.e. the other
Habsburg estates.

l. 1665. Ländergier = Länderfucht.

l. 1670. Hin, to be read with ziehn, or with Dort, l. 1671.

l. 1671. mein (= meiner), object of harren. Ketten, limited by
Verhaßter Ehe, subject of harren.

l. 1675. Sehnen in ðas Weite, *longing for* (lit. into) *the far away.*

l. 1676. als, *but.*

l. 1684. Note the rhyme in the following lines.

Page 85. — line 1685. Weiten, *the distant fields.*

l. 1687. Die, an article with Mauer, not relative.

l. 1688. allein, limits zum Himmel offen, not Thal.

l. 1689. offen und gelichtet, *open unobstructed to the light of.*

l. 1690. Note the very significant change of pronoun in address.

l. 1692. bethört, past participle (sc. hat).

l. 1695. Freuðefpuren, *reminders of joy.*

l. 1696. mir leben, *live for me.*

l. 1699. fehlte, subjunctive for conditional, for hätte gefehlt. Erðen,
a relic of the old weak singular of this word.

l. 1700. ðie fel'ge Jnfel, *the Island of the Blessed,* according to the
old and widespread legend.

l. 1702. heimifch wohnt, *is native,* or *is at home.*

l. 1703. fich hingefunden, *found its way.*

l. 1706. Note the almost stanza-like form of the next ten lines.

l. 1709. wie ein König wirkt, tr. *like a king ruling.* Reichen, the plural is accounted for only by the exigency of rhyme.

Page 86. — line 1711. weiblich reizend, the effect of such combinations cannot be given in English, lit. womanly charming; the idea is: charming because womanly.

l. 1719-20. dem stolzen Ritter . . . Dem Landbedrücker, seems to mean Gessler, though from the contrast in Hier it might mean any Austrian noble.

ACT III. SCENE 3.

SD. Bannberg, the mountain slope back of Altorf, to the northeast. The details about it, ll. 1771-85, are found in Scheuchzer and Fäsi.

Page 87. — line 1732. sich . . . heran begeben, *come hither.*

l. 1734. doch, *why*, (exclamatory) at beginning.

l. 1736. Popanz, contraction of Popelhaus, *bugbear*, or perhaps from Bohemian bobak, with the same meaning.

l. 1738. Uns zum Verdrieße (archaic for Verdrusse) *to vex us.*

l. 1739. Was, universal compound relative (cp. note to l. 1481), *all who.*

l. 1741. The construction to be expected here is: Als den Rücken beugen.

l. 1742. After Platz sc. gehen.

l. 1744. fang thun, *make a catch.*

l. 1748. Hochwürdigen, *the Host*, i.e. the large wafer in the Eucharist used in processions and for display carried in the monstrance; it is a mistake to represent the priest as having this under the circumstances; he would have a small plain box, the ciborium. But it makes no difference.

l. 1749. Glöcklein, the bell used to call attention at the elevation of the Host.

l. 1751. Monstranz, the ornamental, generally spire-shaped casket in which the Host is displayed.

Page 88. — line 1760. Inversion in an exclamatory sentence is common if accompanied, as here, by doch after the subject, and often even later.

l. 1763. Mag, *let.* da, this word is often used after a relative pronoun as an indefinite particle, but cannot be rendered.

l. 1766. Wollt's = wollte es.

l. 1767. ſchlechter ſtehn um, *be worse with.*

l. 1768. Volk der Weiber = Weibervolk, *women.*

l. 1770. ſticht, *pricks, impels.*

SD. die vordere Szene, *the front of the stage.*

Page 89. — line 1772. Die Bäume bluten, a common popular belief.

l. 1775. Gebannt, in two senses: *charmed,* and literally, protected by law. The penalty quoted is popularly applied to murderers. ſchädige, wachſe, subjunctives of indirect discourse.

l. 1776. Dem, dative of possession; ſeine is a redundant possessive, but very common colloquially. heraus, separable particle; read at end.

l. 1778. Hörner, *peaks,* very common in names of Alpine summits, as Schreckhorn, Matterhorn.

l. 1780. Gletſcher, really the Firnfelder (see note to l. 38) and not *glaciers,* though in Tirol the word is thus used. des Nachts, the –s of the noun is a relic of an old so-called consonantal declension of the word, the des is due to false analogy.

l. 1781. Schlaglawinen, *heavy avalanches,* of névé, or firn-ice; cp. note to l. 1501.

l. 1785. Landwehr, *defence,* lit. militia.

l. 1786. ſind, would also be es giebt, save to avoid repetition; cp. note to l. 1217.

l. 1789. There has been some unprofitable disputing as to whether this land is France or Germany; following the Rhine we come to either, and the 'fair, long fields of grain' and the allusion (l. 1806) to the salt monopoly rather suggest France, but it makes no difference.

Page 90. — line 1798. Himmel, *climate.*

l. 1799. The ſie is emphasized to take the place of the customary die (before genießen).

l. 1803. in = in'n (in den).

l. 1804. Herrn, *ruler.* Gefieder, for Geflügel = Hochflug; cp. l. 900.

l. 1806. das Salz, referring to the monopoly of the salt product maintained by many rulers.

Page 91. — line 1811. es wird mir eng, *I feel oppressed,* as though in imagination he were already there. weiten, *wide.*

l. 1812. Da = darum.

Page 92. — line 1823. SD. Ju die Szene, *into the wings.*

l. 1829. geſchieht, *is being done.*

l. 1834. hätt' gethan, subjunctive of indirect discourse, depending on Du behaupteſt, or the like, understood, or subjunctive of surprise, depending on meinen or some such word understood. Das lügſt du, you lie in that, tr. *That's a lie.*

Page 93. — line 1839. was unſers Amtes (sc. iſt), what is of our office, tr. *our business.*

l. 1840. ſchreiende Gewalt, *violence that cries to heaven.*

l. 1843. einen Rücken an den andern, *backing from the others,* i.e. the other members of the league.

Page 94. — line 1854. was wird das werden, more commonly draus werden.

l. 1859. Geſtrenger, a merely formal adjective, tr. *My lord.*

l. 1860. wohlbeſtellt, cp. note to l. 1235, *duly appointed.*

Page 95. — line 1861. über (commonly bei) friſcher That, *in the very act.*

l. 1872. der Tell, i.e. the Heedless, or Simpleton, see Introd. xlvii.

l. 1873. begegnen, unusual for vorkommen or geſchehen.

l. 1875. jedem, *any.*

l. 1877. dir, dative of interest.

l. 1879. mehr for mehrere.

Page 96. — line 1889. fehlſt, archaic for verfehlſt.

l. 1893. Zu Sinn, for in den Sinn.

l. 1895. The future indicative as in English is a strong form of imperative; so also is the present, as in l. 1899.

Page 97. — line 1903. beſonnen, cp. l. 1872.

ll. 1908-9. Ironical.

l. 1912. Kurzweils, *jesting* (more commonly feminine), object of gewohnt, which takes also the accusative.

l. 1916. Er rühmte ſich, reference to ll. 1876–77 shows that this is a mistake ; compare the story of Toko, Introd. xli.

l. 1917. ihrer hundert, lit. a hundred of them, omit ihrer in translation.

l. 1920. Es gilt, *it is needed,* or *it is very important;* cp. l. 2415.

Page 98. — line 1925. Verwirkt, past participle.

l. 1927. ungekränkt, with older meaning *unharmed.* in ſeine Hütte, accusative, since the idea is ' to go to.'

l. 1933. funſtgeübt, same as geübt.

l. 1942. Dem 's, dative of possession with Herz. 's = das. in die Hand tritt, tr. *affect his hand.*

l. 1944. vor = für, *instead of.* laſſet . . . ergehen, *show.*

l. 1948. hinſtehen, South German dialect for ſich hinſtellen ; cp. ll. 2247 and 2838.

Page 99. — line 1950. fehlen auf, *miss,* (lit. upon) *and hit.*

l. 1952. iſt, ſein expresses the facts of absolute existence, as well as the miscellaneous and accidental facts of existence; es giebt serves between the two extremes to state the general facts of nature and life; cp. l 1217 and note, and l. 1786.

l. 1957. 's, i.e. ſtill halten.

l. 1964. glaubt dir's nicht, *doesn't believe it of you.*

l. 1965. Dem Wütrich zum Verdruſſe, *to spite the tyrant;* cp. l. 1738.

Page 100. — line 1970. mit friſcher That, *promptly.*

l. 1972. vergebens, *for nothing* (ironical).

l. 1975. Dies ſtolze Recht, i.e. of bearing arms.

l. 1977. wer = der welcher.

l. 1980. Gaſſe, *path,* so of any open way with side walls.

Page 101. — line 1987. ja, *Why,* at beginning. alles, *anything.*

l. 1988. wie = wie auch).

l. 1989. Doubtless an allusion to the rescue of Baumgarten.

l. 1990. Cp. Luke 23, 35.

l. 1991. Es muß sc. ſein.

l. 1998. Ich darf's, *I have a right to,* with reference to his position as differing from that of the òthers.

Page 102. — line 2003. ſtill geſchwiegen, *said nothing.*

l. 2005. The sense is: Though my eyes were open, I refused to see.

l. 2020. in beſter Meinung, *with* (in spite of) *the best of intentions.*

l. 2028. Antwort, *satisfaction.*

l. 2030. die, *these.*

SD. (after l. 2036) ſtand = hat geſtanden.

l. 2034. Kommt zu euch, *Be yourself again.*

Page 104. — line 2039. noch in den ſpätſten Zeiten, *down to the remotest future.*

l. 2045. daß interprets dazu.

Page 105. — line 2049. ſtecfteſt ... 3u bir, *hid away*, or *about you.*

l. 2054. wirb bebeutet ħaben, future of conjecture, *I am sure it meant.*

l. 2055. friſch unb fröħlich, *promptly and cheerfully.*

l. 2058. The government of ſichern in l. 2056 is the usual one, here we should expect verſichert.

l. 2060. burchſchoß for burchſchöß' (= ħätte burchſchoſſen), the indicative here conceives the condition and the conclusion as real.

l. 2062. Eurer, for Euer, genitive object of geſeħlt.

Page 106. — line 2071. ſich verfünbigt (sc. ħat), *has been manifested.*

l. 2073. According to l. 2170 Gessler had an official boat on the lake.

l. 2076. See note to l. 1215.

l. 2083. Den, *this one*, i.e. Tell.

l. 2086. vorbei, *all over.*

Page 107. — line 2093. es erbarmt mich, uncommon for eß tħut mir leib.

l. 2096. ſag' = ſoll ... ſagen.

ACT IV. SCENE 1.

Page 108. — SD. ſchließen ben Proſpekt, limit the view, i.e. occupy the back of the stage. The lake is to be conceived as in the background to the right, so that the personages stand sideways or with backs half turned to the audience. Kunz von Gersau is a personage introduced after the play was nearly finished. The fisherman and boy here seem to be Ruodi and Jenni of Act I, Scene 1; they are so named in one MS, and the boy is called Jenni in the text at the end of the scene. But it troubles Düntzer greatly to find them on the wrong side of the lake. This, however, is not referred to as their home, and they could cross the lake freely.

l. 2098. mit 2lugen, uncommon for mit eignen 2lugen.

l. 2102. für bie ,freiħeit gelten, uncommon for bie ,freiħeit gelten.

l. 2106. For im 2ln3ug iſt, unb ber two MSS read „gelvaltig ſich erħoben."

l. 2114. Reding was 2ltlanbammann in Schwyz, Attinghausen in Uri.

Page 109. — line 2115. liege, after a present tense the verb is more frequently indicative.

ll. **2124-6.** Der Mund refers to Attinghausen; der Arm is of course Tell's; das sehnde Auge ... geblendet, at first suggest Melchthal's father, but he is of too little consequence to be mentioned here. Lines 839, 893 and 2005 suggest Rudenz.

l. **2128.** sömmlich, dialect for angenehm.

l. **2129.** Cp. King Lear, II, 3, the speech, " Blow winds and crack your cheeks," which clearly suggested this.

l. **2133.** werdet Herr, we expect Herren.

l. **2135.** Der großen Wüste, dative; cp. l. 1262.

l. **2137.** Abgrund, the lake at this point is said to be 600 feet deep.

Page 110. — line 2144. Eisestürme, unusual for Eis-Türme.

l. **2147.** Klüfte, i.e. *the sides of the chasms.*

l. **2148.** Sündflut, *flood* (lit. universal flood, not sin-flood, as popular etymology makes it seem).

l. **2152.** gebetet werde, tr. *prayers may be offered.*

l. **2154.** Wiege, '*cradle of the deep.*'

l. **2158.** Busen, *bay.* gewährte, subjunctive; cp. French in same case, relative after negative, *might furnish.*

l. **2159.** handlos, without ' Handhabe,' *inaccessible.*

Page 111. — line 2164. Wasserkluft, *watery gorge*; while the whole of the Urner See might be termed a gorge, a reference to the map will show a constriction at the Axenberg.

l. **2167.** er, the antecedent is Sturm. sich, dative of advantage.

l. **2170.** Herrenschiff, *official boat;* see note to l. 2073.

l. **2171.** Dach, *canopy.*

l. **2177.** geben nicht auf, for geben nicht Acht auf, or geben nichts auf.

l. **2180.** *Do not seek to stay the judge's arm.*

l. **2183 ff.** The readiness with which the boatman's religious philosophy is adapted to his new understanding of the situation is startling. Indeed, altogether this boatman talks little like a boatman.

l. **2185.** mitsamt, strengthened form of samt ; dem Steuermann, certainly meaning Tell; but does the boatman anticipate ll. 2247ff?

Page 112. — line 2187. Buggisgrat, a sharp ridge projecting from the Axenberg.

l. **2188.** Teufelsmünster, a steep ridge on the west side of the lake.

l. 2189. The speakers themselves are probably on the northwest slope of the Axenberg, some distance above the water, otherwise they could not see what they describe.

l. 2190. Ḥackmeſſer, another projecting ridge of the Axenberg.

l. 2191. gebrochen (sc. worden ſind), uncommon for Schiffbruch ge- litten.

l. 2193. Fluh, *rocky wall* or slope.

l. 2194. gähſtotzig, *precipitously* (Swiss dialect gäh = jäh, ſtotzig = ſchüſſig).

l. 2196. einer = irgend einer.

SD. Several minutes must elapse between the last speech and Tell's appearance.

l. 2200. wie or zu ſein is redundant.

Page 113. — line 2207. Dort = dorther.

l. 2210. For Seid read Wie ſeid ihr.

l. 2214. ſahen, archaic for ſangen.

Page 114. — line 2219. aufgegebner, *despairing*.

l. 2225. For source of this speech see Introd. I.

l. 2226. am, more commonly im, hintern Granſen, *stern*.

l. 2227. gelangt sc. ſind.

l. 2228. kleinen Aren, really a portion of the Axenberg.

l. 2230. Gählings for Zählings ; cp. note to l. 2194. herfürbrach = hervorbrach).

l. 2232. meinten, unusual for erwarteten.

l. 2238. des Fahrens, for der Fahrt.

Page 115. — line 2239. berichtet. *posted*.

l. 2241. After Wie sc. wäre es.

l. 2246. hiedannen, *out of this.*

l. 2248. redlich, *vigorously*, not with usual meaning of ' honestly.'

l. 2251. ſich aufthät', *might present itself.*

l. 2256. abzureichen, unusual for erreichen.

l. 2257. handlich, dialect, meaning *vigorously*. zuzugehn, unusual for zuzugreifen ; the use of the word seems to be due to a misunder- standing on Schiller's part of ' zugind' (= should pull, imperfect subjunctive, 3rd person plural of ziehen) in his source. See Introd. p. l.

Page 116. — line 2272. kaum etc., *scarcely do I trust my eyes.*

l. 2280. denkt's, for gedenkt's.

l. 2282. Arth, or Art, at the upper end of Lake Zug, see map.

l. 2283. Steinen, and l. 2285, Lowerz, on opposite sides of Lake Lowerz, see map.

Page 117. — line 2288. man nannt' euch mir, in the present text no name is given to the Fischer, but this phrase corresponds with the MSS (see note to SD. at beginning of this act) which name him Ruodi; of course Tell could not thus address a nameless personage.

l. 2290. thut die Lieb' mir an, more commonly: thut es mir zu Liebe.

l. 2296. Sie sollen wacker sein, *Bid them be courageous.*

l. 2298. ein weitres, *something further.*

l. 2299. im Gemüt, for im Sinn.

l. 2302. was er auch unternommen, *whatever he has undertaken.*

Page 118. — line 2304. die Feder, placed there as a test to see whether life was extinct.

l. 2313. Wälty, pet form of Walther. er lebt mir, not 'for me'; rather an ethical dative, *he lives and I have him.* Similarly l. 2314, *Have I thee unharmed.*

Page 120. — line 2334. noch, *in addition.* kränkt, *depreciate*, or belittle (the original meaning of the word is 'to restrict,' or narrow).

SD. mit einem großen Blick, *with a look of reproach.*

l. 2336. du, emphasized in contrast with herself.

l. 2339 ff. The reader may well wonder whence Hedwig has her knowledge of the occurrences at Altorf, since Fürst and her boy have not yet seen her; see Introd. xxxii.

l. 2352. *We need him, ah! and he needs us.*

l. 2355. Wenn er erkrankte! *What if he should become ill!*

l. 2357. Alpenrose, *Alpine primrose*, or soldanel, a shy flower that blooms only on heights close to the snow.

Page 121. — line 2360. Balsamstrom der Lüfte, *the healing breezes.*

l. 2362. Hauch der Grüfte, *atmosphere* (lit. breath) *of the dungeon* (lit. pits).

l. 2369. rettete, conditional.

l. 2374. After gesendet sc. worden, passive impersonal.

l. 2375. sein Herz gefunden, *come to himself, repented.*

Page 122. — line 2380. also, for so.

l. 2382. ist = bedeutet ; er, i.e. der Schmerz. verließ, for hat verlassen.

Page 123. — line **2400**. Cp. l. 2374, *Action will be taken.*

l. **2410**. ift, present for future.

l. **2413**. die Edeln, the lords of Attinghausen and Sillinen (see l. 685) are the only native nobles that are mentioned.

Page 124. — line **2414**. harren (usually with auf) = erwarten. wenn es gilt, *when the time comes.*

l. **2416**. sich solcher That verwogen, *ventured upon* such a *deed* (past participle of verwegen, or ·wägen; in M.H.G. the past participle was verwegen, which is preserved as adjective (see l. **27**); the verb, now rare, has gone over into the class with biegen).

l. **2419**. unferer, with final –er due to false analogy with meiner, in which the final –er is in turn due to analogy with the adjective declension; unfer is more common.

l. **2420**. zu Grabe steigen, *go down to our graves* (steigen may mean to go either up or down depending on the adverb of direction).

l. **2421**. Es lebt, impersonal, *There will be life.*

l. **2422**. *The glorious possession* (to wit freedom) *be preserved for mankind.* Menschheit may be genitive, in which case tr. *the glory of humanity be sustained.*

ll. **2423-24**. The figure is certainly awkward; tr. grünen, *spring.* The boy is used as a representative of the new generation.

l. **2427**. sich um sein Aug' ergießt, *suffuses his eyes.*

l. **2431**. seinen Bürgereid, *their* (lit. its, agreeing with Adel) *oath as citizens.*

l. **2432**. Üchtland, in the middle ages name of a district about the city of Freiburg, which to distinguish it from Freiburg im Breisgau, is still called Freiburg im Üchtland. The historical allusions to the beginnings of Swiss liberty are mostly based on Müller, and have more or less warrant. Thurgau, the northeast canton of Switzerland, formerly extending as far as Zurich.

ll. **2433-34**. Bern and Freiburg were made fortified places about 100 years before the formation of the Rütli League, see chronology, p. lvi.

l. **2435**. Zurich had a regular system of armed guilds in 1336, but it is no violent supposition that these had done military service earlier.

l. **2437**. an ihren ew'gen Wällen, not necessarily those of Zurich alone, but of all the cities named.

Page 125. — line **2439**. Harnischen, one would expect Harnisch.

l. **2440**. harmlos, *peaceable.*

l. **2441.** Impersonal passive, tr. *they fight to the death.*

l. **2442.** Allusion to the defence of passes at Zug and Morgarten. blutige Entſcheidung, *the arbitrament of blood.*

ll. **2443-44.** Allusion to the heroic death of Winkelried at Sempach (1386).

l. **2449.** Hochwachten, *beacon-towers*, also beacon-fires, here the former.

l. **2450.** der Bund zum Bunde, more naturally Bund zu Bunde.

SD. entſeelt, tr. as adjective before Hände. mit Zeichen … Schmerzens, tr. *signs of grief, some silent, some violent.*

SD. (after l. **2452**) hin, lit. thither, tr. *to the corpse.*

l. **2454.** The castle was called: Schloß Rudenz auf Attinghauſen.

Page 126. — line **2459.** Da, *while.*

l. **2467.** In, *upon*, or *by.*

l. **2476.** ſchuldig blieb, *left undone.*

l. **2478.** die eurige (to Stauffacher).

l. **2481.** wiederkehrend, *repentant.*

Page 127. — line **2482.** nichts geachtet, for als nichts geachtet = verachtet.

l. **2483.** *What are we to expect of you?*

l. **2484.** denket = gedenket.

l. **2489.** Stand, *class, rank.*

l. **2492.** *Subjects* (to itself) *and makes it fruitful.*

l. **2499.** 's ſchon vergleichen, *settle it all right*, i.e. the contention over precedence.

Page 128. — line **2507.** gleichwie, strengthened form of wie.

l. **2512.** ward ſchon, *has become.*

l. **2516.** The presumption in Rudenz's attitude shocks a democratic spirit, but royalty to-day is capable of just such arrogance. His patronizing patriotism loses still more of its halo when it appears that he is prompted by his own loss.

Page 129. line **2528.** verwogen, see note to line 2416.

l. **2532.** Wütende = Wütrich.

l. **2533.** ſich erfühnen, same meaning and construction as ſich verwegen, see note to l. 2416; frevelnd, tr. as adjective before Gewalt, *criminal.*

l. **2534.** Before Jhr sc. um.

ll. **2543-44.** *Only out from beneath the ruins of the tyrants' power* *can she be dug forth;* the idea is: She can be rescued only by over-throwing the tyrants.

l. 2546. **Ob wir vielleicht ... dringen,** *if perchance, we may pene-trate.*

l. 2548. **fparen,** for **auffchieben.**

Page 130. — line 2551. i.e. releases them from their agreement to postpone.

l. 2555. **Botenfegel,** rather unusual figure for **Eilboot,** or **Eilfchiff.**

l. 2558. **ftürzt,** the unusual order is justified only by the meter. **Wetters Strahl,** for **Wetterſtrahl.**

ACT IV.   SCENE 3.

SD. **hohle Gaſſe,** *sunken road,* or hollow way.   Gessler, having come along the shore of Lake Zug (see map), proceeds from Immensee through this cut to his castle near Küssnacht.   The highest point of the cut is in the background; the road comes down toward the front of the stage.   See illustration.

l. 2563. **Hollunderftrauch** = **Holunder-** or **Holberſtrauch.**

l. 2567. **deine Uhr ift abgelaufen,** lit. your clock is run down, but Schiller had probably an hour-glass in mind, hence tr. *your hour is come.*

Page 131. — line 2571. See note to l. 285.

l. 2573. **Die Milch der frommen Denkart mir,** *the milk of my kindly disposition,* which was perhaps suggested by "the milk of human kindness" (Macbeth I, 5).

l. 2574. **Zum Ungeheuren,** the usual government with **gewöhnt** would be **Ans Ungeheure.**

l. 2583. **ohnmächtig,** less common for **vergebens.**

l. 2592. **Was du,** not an interrupted sentence, but abbreviated, sc. **dir erlaubt haft.**

l. 2593. After **ſtrenges,** repeat **Recht.**

l. 2594. Common usage does not employ the **der** before **Luſt.**

l. 2595. **Dich ... zu erfrechen,** *to venture upon;* cp. ll. 2416, 2533, and notes.

l. 2597. This apostrophe to a single arrow presumes that Tell was allowed to put his second arrow (cp. l. 2050) into his doublet again. On the other hand ll. 2225 and 2264 indicate that he escaped with his quiver.   It is a slight discrepancy, due to the haste with which the work was composed.

Page 132. — **line 2600.** frommen, *kindly;* undurchdringlich, more appropriate to the arrow, while to a request one is „taub."

l. 2602. Vertraute, here past participle of the verb, *trusted.*

l. 2605. Nur jetzt noch, *only this once more.*

l. 2607. jetzo, archaic for jetzt.

l. 2609. Auf dieser Bank, as though the verb were sitzen ; common usage would require here **diese Bank.**

l. 2611. treibt sich, *goes.*

l. 2614. leicht geschürzte, *lightgirded,* see note to l. 285.

l. 2616. Spielmann, *minstrel.*

l. 2617. Säumer, *freighter;* cp. Saumroß.

l. 2618. ferne, tr. as adjective with Länder. der Menschen Länder, lands of foreign men; cp. Latin gentium, tr. *foreign lands.*

l. 2619. *Every road leads everywhere,* or *All roads meet.*

l. 2624. er bracht' euch etwas, *without bringing you something,* cp. note to l. 1043.

l. 2625. War's, *whether it was.*

l. 2626. Ammonshorn, *ammonite.*

l. 2627. Wie es (for sie) *such as.*

Page 133. — **line 2631.** lieben Kinder, the weak form here is inconsistent with l. 2622, yet all the MSS and the first edition have it; usage in this construction was formerly **divided.**

l. 2635. Läßt sich's, the inversion in exclamatory sentences is usually followed by doch, but for meter's sake often omitted.

l. 2638. zu Fels, found strong only in such phrases, and rarely; now regularly weak.

l. 2640. Scheuchzer relates seriously how the hunter in such circumstances cuts his heel or the ball of his foot, in order to keep himself from slipping as he undertakes a daring leap.

l. 2641. Grattier, *red chamois,* the smaller variety that frequents the summit (Grat).

l. 2646. geschossen in das Schwarze, *hit the bull's eye.*

l. 2649. Den Meisterschuß thun, *make my mastershot,* as though all before were but apprentice-work.

SD. Flurschütz, *field-warden,* a common officer to guard against pilfering, and damage by stray animals.

l. 2651. Klostermei'r, *rent-collector.* Mörlischachen, a small estate of the monastery of Einsiedeln, on Lake Lucerne, see map.

l. 2652. den Brautlauf, *bridal-trip*, but a very different sort from what we know; it is the formal trip made to the home of the betrothed to take her to the scene of the wedding. The word takes us back to semi-savage times when a man actually chased and ran down his bride, or later, when the suitor won his bride by defeating her or a rival in a race; after the savage reality was abolished the form was retained in sport.

l. 2653. Senten, *shepherd-huts* and often also appurtenances, the meadows or the herds.

Page 134. — line 2654. Jmisee, for Jmmensee, see map.

l. 2655. wird hoch geschwelgt, impersonal, *there will be high revelry.*

l. 2656. 's, a strong case of expletive.

l. 2659. Nehmt mit, *accept.*

l. 2662. that is: the two meet.

l. 2663. allerwegen, for allewege.

l. 2664. Unglücks, partitive genitive. Ruffi, *landslide* (Swiss); gegangen, tr. *happened.*

l. 2665. Glarner Land, the canton of Glarus, east of Schwyz. Seite, *slope.*

l. 2666. Glärnisch, a mountain southwest of the town of Glarus.

l. 2669. Da sprach ich, *I just now spoke with a man.* Baden, in Aargau, on the Limmatt northwest of Zurich.

l. 2673. für, archaic for vor.

Page 135. —line 2676. Man deutet's auf, *it is interpreted as meaning.*

l. 2682. After kann sc. auch.

l. 2688. Die Wasser, *the streams.*

l. 2690. der Strom, *the flood.*

Page 136. — line 2691. an ihm, more commonly bei or von ; the accusative is the government after Bitte, or Gesuch an . . .

l. 2695. fahre, for gehe, cp. l. 17.

l. 2702. Mein Lebtag, for Meine Lebtage, (*all*) *the days of my life.*

Page 137. — line 2704. verfünden, more commonly melden.

l. 2706. Jn Grund, for Jn 'n Grund.

l. 2707. Dem (= diesem) Volk (contemptuously), *this crew,* i.e. Gessler and his followers. With bei sc. kommen, *get at, harm.*

l. 2710. wie, *how.*

l. 2712. ihm, i.e. dem Volk. ſanft thun, *pet.*

l. 2715. bring'... an, *present.*

l. 2720. Mir, ' not to me,' but ethical dative, tr. *That I might see them* etc.

l. 2723. drauffſtoßen mit dem Aug', *that their eyes might fall upon it.*

Page 138. — line 2726. Die, demonstrative.

l. 2727. *Things of vast import are being planned and executed.* Logically Werden should precede Werk.

l. 2730. uns, speaking as a representative of the house.

l. 2731. So oder ſo, *one way or another.*

l. 2734. Zu = In den.

l. 2738. Wildheuer, *wildgrass* gleaner, his occupation is explained in what follows. Rigiberg, east of Lucerne, see map.

l. 2739. überm Abgrund weg, *from over the abyss.* freie, *unclaimed.*

l. 2744. *Whatever serious offence he may have committed.*

Page 139. — line 2746. Euch ſoll Recht werden, *You shall have justice.*

l. 2750. in den ſechſten Mond, *going on six months.*

l. 2752. mir Gewalt anthun, *force me.*

l. 2755. So, *as* (i.e. in case).

SD. greift in, *takes hold of.*

l. 2762. nichts nach... fragen, *pay no heed to.*

Page 140. — line 2769. Trateſt du doch längſt, *Why, you have long been treading.*

l. 2772. After Beſſeres sc. zu thun.

l. 2774. Man reiße, *Someone drag,* etc.

l. 2778. In this line as well as in l. 2784 Gessler presumes upon his position rather too much.

l. 2780. Before ſoll sc. ſein.

l. 2781. es (after doch), i.e. the situation.

SD. fährt mit der Hand, *puts his hand.*

Page 141. — SD. dem Rudolf Harras, everywhere else the article is put between name and epithet ; it seems here to be an error for Rudolf dem Harras.

Page 142. — line 2802. Raſt, not the usual meaning: to be furious, but : *to be crazy.*

SD. (after l. 2808) fühlloſen, for gefühlloſen.

l. 2810. die Augen ſind gebrochen, see note to l. 865.

Page 143. — line 2816. geſchlagen, *stricken.*

l. 2817. Wagt es, ironical threat = *Do not dare it!*

l. 2818. hat ein Ende, *is at an end.*

l. 2830. vertrauen, rare for trauen ; Treu', is dative.

SD. Barmherzige Brüder, Brothers of Charity, an order founded in the 16th century. Their introduction here is a harmless anachronism. In Europe the garb is black, in America brown.

l. 2832. liegt, *is down.* die Raben, allusion to the garb of the Brothers, who had weaknesses enough to expose them to the ill-will of some of the people.

Page 144. — line 2834. Es iſt, for Es wird.

ll. 2835-36. Es here is not expletive, scarcely impersonal; it represents fate, or practically the same idea as der Tod. But for confusion with Er in l. 2838 we should perhaps have had Er here.

l. 2838. vor ſeinen Richter, as though the verb were ſich ſtellen ; cp. l. 1948, hinſtehen.

ACT V.   SCENE 1.

Page 145. — line 2845. Das Joch, cp. l. 371. wollte, *promised to.*

Page 146. — line 2855. Was = warum. It is curious that the first news, so far as we know, of the death of Gessler should be announced thus incidentally and received with absolute indifference.

l. 2857. Iſt's nicht genug an dieſen, *Are not these*, etc., *enough?*

Page 147. — line 2864. im Lauf, for im Gang.

l. 2874. mannlich, usually männlich ; mannlich kühner, cp. note to l. 1711.

l. 2876. das Schloß, i.e. Sarnen.

l. 2879. Diethelm, Geßler's Bub', on a stray sheet Schiller had begun a scene in which two servants appeared: Diethelm and Rössling.

Page 148. — line 2889. geliebt, read bedacht ; the idea is, zu ſehr geliebt um es zu wagen.

l. 2890. Bertha, is the object of Ehrte.

l. 2894. ſelbander, archaic for zuſammen (=ander = zweiter, cp. ſelbzwanzigſter, I and nineteen others).

Page 149. — line 2902. Über den, accusative indicating a verb of motion understood.

l. 2905. Nad), this position of the separable participle is rare and poetical.

l. 2910. Urpsede, more correctly Urfesde (the spelling here is due to mediæval Latin urpheda), *a solemn oath*, usually an oath to keep the peace. \

l. 2913. This seems like a pointed reflection on Tell's deed, which Schiller can not have intended; cp. note to l. 2855.

l. 2915. fpät, tr. *years hence.*

l. 2918. This line is intelligible only on comparison of the Dalberg and Mannheim MSS, which have in Act III, Scene 3, unter der Stange instead of unter der Linde. Accordingly it seems that the original plan was to have Walther at the apple-shooting stand against the pole instead of under the linden, and that after the change Schiller forgot to strike out this line.

Page 150. — line 2922. The hat, and the wearing of the hat seems to have been a symbol of freedom from very early times. The student may collect evidence of this for himself.

l. 2929. Cp. note to l. 2855. Here too the death of Gessler is assumed as generally known.

l. 2932. With the comma at the end of the line it is to be read as a condition, with l. 2933 as conclusion; but the dod) tempts to read this as an independent exclamatory sentence, in which case the line should end with a semicolon, as the later Cotta texts have it.

Page 151. — line 2943. Albrecht was murdered May 1st, 1308.

l. 2946. Brud, or Brugg, on the Aar near the junction of the Limmatt. glaubenwert = glaubwürdig.

l. 2948. Johannes Müller, Schiller takes this method of paying a compliment to the Swiss historian (see Introd. xx, xxiv).

Page 152. — line 2953. Datermords, like the English parricide, used of the murder of any relative of the elder generation.

l. 2954. väterliche Erbe, cp. l. 1344; according to Tschudi there were estates from both parents; no reason appears for the variation.

l. 2955. Mahnenden, *claimant.*

l. 2956. darum zu kürzen, *to deprive of it.*

l. 2958. Wie dem auch fei (es, understood, is subject, dem is dative of das), *However that may be.*

ll. 2960-61. The names as well as the details are from Tschudi, see Introd. liii; but for meter there would be a von before Palm.

l. 2965. Stein, the castle overlooking the town of Baden; it was destroyed in 1415.

l. 2966. Gen, for gegen. Rheinfeld, see note to l. 1324.

l. 2967. Leopold, Albrecht's third son, who was defeated at Morgarten.

l. 2974. The old Roman Vindonissa, modern Windisch.

l. 2976. Habsburg (contraction of Habichtsburg), about two miles southwest of Brugg, the original estate whence the Austrian royal family takes its name.

Page 153. — line 2982. See Introd. liii.

l. 2988. frühes, *premature*, rather than early, Albrecht being 58 years old, and in the tenth of his reign.·

l. 2992. Stand, a vague word, *estate* (one of the three governing classes in the empire: nobility, clergy, cities), *rank, class;* practically the line means: *everybody is on his guard.*

l. 2995. des Bannes Fluch, *the imperial ban of outlawry,* not the papal ban of excommunication.

l. 2997. Agnes, for the following details see Introd. liii.

l. 3003. Zeugungen, unusual in this sense, for Geschlechter.

Page 154. — line 3009. um, expresses here result, not purpose.

l. 3012. Sich (dative) selbst ist sie, *It is its own,* etc.

l. 3021. The crown passed to the house of Luxemburg, but not for long.

l. 3022. Wahlfreiheit, *right of election;* the right was in full force, hence behaupten = *exercise.*

l. 3023. was = etwas, i.e. about the probable succession; in fact, Henry VII was not chosen until November, 1308.

Page 155. — line 3029. The line is addressed to the messenger.

l. 3033. Elsbeth, wife of Albrecht.

l. 3041. versieht sich zu, *expects of.*

Page 156. — line 3045. Vorschub thun, commonly Vorschub leisten.

l. 3052. Wessen rühmen wir uns, *What is there to speak of.*

l. 3054. As we have seen, this is hyperbole.

l. 3055. The alliterative phrase here is a primitive Germanic legal formula.

l. 3059. diesem allen, *all this;* diesen allen would seem more natural.

l. 3062. rührte . . . an, subjunctive conditional, for hätte angerührt.

l. 3064. fonnte ... fein, note the form, and the force of the indicative: *It was possible for him to be.*

l. 3067. gemehrt, *advanced*, unusual for geförbert.

Page 157. — line 3073. will, this auxiliary with an impersonal subject is difficult to render; '*can't be made to*' *be our duty.*

l. 3074. will, colloquial English, 'wants to,' *must.*

l. 3076. entrichten, usually with object, as Steuer, tr. *We are under no farther obligation to him.*

l. 3079. So, *at the same time.*

l. 3088. alles, *everybody.*

Page 158. — line 3092. Ging hart ... vorbei, *just missed,* the expression would be more suitable if Haupte stood in place of Leben.

SD. (after l. 3103) zerftörten, for verftörten.

Page 159. — line 3109. The line begins with an anapest and requires particular stress on ift in order to scan.

l. 3112. Wie auch, *However much.*

l. 3120. wohnt, *belongs.*

l. 3124. fchnürt mir das Innre zu, *oppresses my heart;* cp. Faust, l. 3493.

Page 160. — line 3129. für, archaic for vor.

l. 3134. lebe nur der Freude, *give yourself up to joy.*

Page 161. — line 3138. There is not even a legend behind this: the relic is nowhere preserved.

l. 3147. Even this fugitive, who dares scarcely speak to anyone, knows of Tell's deed; cp. note to l. 2855.

Page 162. — line 3158. wäret, subjunctive of conjecture, *Is it possible you are.*

l. 3163. We are left to conjecture how Tell knows of this; does Schiller here and in 2855 attribute to his characters the information given to the spectators?

l. 3167. Euch leuchtet, *shines for you.*

Page 163. — line 3179. das Letzte, *the worst.*

l. 3183. Nichts teil' ich mit dir, *I have nothing in common with you.*

l. 3187. Straße, more commonly in poetry Bahn or Weg.

Page 164. — line 3194. Des armen Mannes, genitive by apposition with the mein in meiner ; tr. of me, a poor man, or *of a poor man like me.*

l. 3197. fonnte, see note to l. 3064.

l. 3202. gleiches Alters, cp. ll. 3243 and 3269.

l. 3212. See Introd. liii; *excluded from friends and exposed to enemies.*

Page 165. — line 3213. offne, usually offnen, only one MS has the weak form.

l. 3216. Mein eignes Schrecknis, *a terror to myself.*

l. 3222. ein Mensch der Sünde, *a sinful man*, as all men are according to theological phrase.

l. 3229. entdeckt, *if discovered.*

Page 166. — line 3237. Was, *whatever.* After an sc. als.

l. 3242. dem Strom entgegen, *up stream.*

l. 3244. Cp l. 2969.

l. 3245. viele Kreuze, one writer reckons thirty.

Page 167. — line 3253. Windeswehen, *avalanches* of light new-fallen snow.

l. 3254. Joch, *ridge.*

l. 3255. stäubet, *is wrapped in mist;* cp. Staubbach in SD. at beginning of Act III, Scene 2, and note. This particular bridge is supposed to be the 'Teufelsbrücke' on the Reuss. See illustration.

l. 3258. Felſenthor, the Urner, or Urſener Loch, opening into the Urſenerthal, above Andermatt.

l. 3264. auf deines Reiches Boden, zieht . . . ein, for zieht einher, *wanders along on*, etc., but perhaps Schiller meant the entrance upon the imperial soil of Italy.

l. 3266. die ew'gen Seen, Scheuchzer speaks of seven such lakes.

l. 3269. ein andrer Strom, the Ticino.

l. 3270. euch das gelobte (sc. Land), *for you the Promised Land.*

Page 168. — SD. (After l. 3280.) bedeutet ihn, *gives him a sign.*-

ACT V. SCENE 2.

SD. Steg, *foot-bridge.* gezogen, with kommen, *come marching.*

APPENDIX.

BIBLIOGRAPHICAL NOTES.

LITERARY TREATMENTS OF THE TELL STORY ASIDE FROM THAT OF SCHILLER.

Ein schön Lied vom Ursprung der Eidgenossenschaft und dem ersten Eidgenossen, Wilhelm Tell genannt, auch von dem Bund etc. Probable date of composition 1477, manuscript of 1501, earliest print 1623.

A stanza from the above:

> Der Landvogt sprach zu Wilhelm Thell:
> " Nun lug, dass dir dein Kunst nit fäl',
> Und merk' mein Red' gar eben:
> Triffstu in nit mit dem ersten Schutz,
> Fürwar, es bringt dir keinen Nutz
> Und kostet dich dein Leben."
> (Cp. Tell, lines 1887-89).

Ein schönes Spiel, — von Wilhelm Tellen ihrem Landmann und ersten Eidgenossen. Probable date of composition 1511, date of oldest print, 1579.

Some lines from the above:

> " Wär' ich vernünftig, witzig und schnell,
> So wär' ich nicht genannt der Tell."
> (Cp. Tell, line 1872).

> " Ich will dich lan verschliessen
> In einen Thurm, da musst du büssen;
> Dich soll b'scheinen weder Sonn' noch Mon,
> Er muss gen Kissnacht auf das Schloss! "
> (Cp. Tell, ll. 2065-8).

> " Ein Pfeil daselbst ich in ihn schoss,
> Dass er todt abfiel von dem Ross."

Ein hübsch und lustig Spil, vorziten gehalten zuo Uri in dem loblichen Ort der Eidgenossenschaft, von dem frommen und ersten Eidgenossen Wilhelm Tellen, irem Landmann. Jetzt nüwlich gebessert — und gespilt am nüwen Jarstag — zuo Zürich im Jar 1545, per Jacobum Ruef (or Ruoſt). This remodeled perhaps from the source of the preceding.

Ein schön new Lied von Wilhelm Tell: durch Hieronimum Muheimb von newem gebessert und gemehret. Date of print, 1633.

Eidgenossisches Contrafeth auf- und abnehmender Jungfrauen Helvetiæ etc. Played at Zug, 1672.

Grisler, ou l'ambition punie. Tragédie en cinq actes; anon. 1762, (by Samuel Henzi).

Guillaume Tell. Tragédie par A. M. Le Mierre. Paris, 1767.

Gesslers Tod, oder das erlegte Raubthier; 1775.

Der alte Heinrich vom Melchthal, oder die ausgetretenen Augen; 1775.

Der Hass der Tyrannei, oder Sarne durch List eingenommen; 1775.

Wilhelm Tell, oder der gefährliche Schuss; 1775.
                    The four preceding by J. J. Bodmer.

Wilhelm Tell. Ein Trauerspiel, von J. L. Zimmermann; Basel, 1777.

Der Schweizerbund, ein Schauspiel; Zürich, 1779.

Hans von Schwaben und Kaiser Albrechts Tod; St. Gallen, 1789.

Wilhelm Tell. Schauspiel. Zürich, 1791.

Der Neujahrstag, oder die Eroberung von Sarnen. Left un-printed.
                    All four preceding by J. L. Ambühl.

Der Dreibund. . Ein vaterländisches Original-Schauspiel; Basel, 1791. By J. B. Petri (appeared anonymously).

Wilhelm Tell, ein Schauspiel in Jamben, Berlin, 1804, (before Schiller's) by Leonhard Wächter (nom de plume Veit Weber).

Wilhelm Tell der Tausendkünstler, etc. Hamburg, 1805. (A satire on Schiller's Tell.)

BIBLIOGRAPHIES.

Grundriss zur Geschichte der deutschen Dichtung. Karl Goedeke; zweite Auflage, Dresden, 1884–97. Bde. I–VI. Incomplete. The standard general bibliography of German literature.

Zeitschrift für deutsches Altertum. Vols. XI–XVI. 1885–1890. Anzeige, P. Strauch.

Jahresberichte für neuere deutsche Litteraturgeschichte. Stuttgart, from 1890 on.

Das Schiller-Buch. C. W. Tannenberg; Wien, 1859. Very complete for biography and Schilleriana as well as for his works. Many illustrations and facsimiles.

Schiller-Bibliothek. P. Trömel; Leipzig, 1865.

Schiller's Dramen; eine Bibliographie. August Hettler; Berlin, 1885. Numbers 468 to 590 relate to "Tell."

Geschichte der Schweizerischen Eidgenossenschaft. T. Dierauer; Gotha, 1887. For history and legend.

SCHILLER BIOGRAPHY.

Schillers Leben, Geistesentwicklung und Werke. K. Hoffmeister; Stuttgart, 1838–42. 5 Bde.

Schillers Leben. Karoline von Wolzogen; 6th edition, Stuttgart, 1884.

Schillers Leben und Werke. E. Palleske; 13th edition, Stuttgart, 1891. The same, translated by Lady Wallace, London.

Schillers Leben. H. Düntzer; Leipzig, 1881.
—— Translated by P. E. Pinkerton, London, 1883.
Schiller dem deutschen Volke dargestellt. J. Wychgram;
Leipzig, 1895. Richly illustrated.
Schiller. Brahm; Berlin, 1889 and 1892.
Schillers Leben und Werke. J. Minor; Berlin, 1890. Vols.
I, II. Not yet complete.
Life of Schiller. Nevison; London, 1887.

EDITIO PRINCEPS.

Wilhelm Tell. Schauspiel von Schiller. Zum Neujahrsgeschenk auf 1805. Tübingen; Cotta, 1804. This the title
of the first edition, the only one printed under Schiller's su-
pervision.

COLLECTED WORKS.

Sämmtliche Werke, edited by C. G. Körner; Stuttgart und
Tübingen, 1812-15. The first complete edition.
Historisch-kritische Ausgabe, edited by Goedeke and others;
Stuttgart, 1867. The standard edition.
Schillers Werke, edited by Boxberger and Maltzahn, published
by Hempel, 1868.
Schillers Werke, edited by Boxberger and Birlinger, in Kürsch-
ners Deutsche Nationallitteratur; Berlin and Stuttgart, 1882.
Schillers Werke, edited by L. Bellermann; Leipzig, 1895-96.
Schillers Werke. Illustriert von den ersten deutschen Künst-
lern. Fifth edition; Stuttgart, 1896.

ANNOTATED EDITIONS.

**Wilhelm Tell. Mit einer geschichtlichen Einleitung und er-
klärenden Anmerkungen.** C. G. Hugendubel; Bern, 1836.
—— Schulausgabe mit Anmerkungen, Denzel; Stuttgart,
1892.

Wilhelm Tell. Mit Einleitung, dem alten Volksschauspiel von Uri, und Erläuterungen. M. Carriere; Leipzig, 1872.

Schillers Wilhelm Tell, erläutert und gewürdigt für die Schule. E. Künen; Mühlheim, 1874.

—— Mit ausführlichen Erläuterungen in katechetischer Form für den Schulgebrauch. C. A. Funke; Paderborn, seventh edition, 1895.

In English.

—— With English notes by M. Meissner; London, 1859.

—— With introduction and notes by C. A. Buchheim; Oxford, 1880 (5th ed.).

—— With introduction and notes by E. Fasnacht; London, 1887.

—— With introduction and notes by K. Breul; Cambridge, 1890.

—— With introduction and notes by R. W. Deering; Boston, 1894.

In French.

—— Accompagné de notes historiques et géographiques de Lebas et Regnier; Paris, 1840.

—— Avec une introduction, une analyse littéraire et des notes, par Th. Fix; new edition; Paris, 1896, Hachette.

COMMENTARIES AND CRITICISMS WITHOUT THE TEXT.

Schiller-Lexicon. Erläuterndes Wörterbuch zu Schillers Dichterwerken. Goldbeck und Rudolph; Berlin, 1869.

Schiller im Urteil seiner Zeitgenossen. Braun; Leipzig, 1882.

Schillers Wilhelm Tell auf seine Quellen zurückgeführt. Joachim Meyer; Nürnberg, 1876 (revised ed.).

Goethes Faust und Schillers Wilhelm Tell. J. G. Rönnefahrt; Leipzig, 1855.

Schillers Wilhelm Tell. Versuch einer methodischen Er-
klärung. J. Becker; Züllichau, 1868.

Schillers Wilhelm Tell, erläutert von H. Düntzer. Leipzig,
1887 (4th ed.).

Wegweiser durch die klassischen Schuldramen. Gaudig;
Leipzig, 1894.

Studien zu Schillers Dramen. Fielitz; Leipzig, 1876.

Schillers Dramen. L. Bellermann; Berlin, 1888.

Dramaturgie des Schauspiels. H. Bulthaupt; Leipzig, 1897.

Schillers Schriften. Kuno Fischer, 2 series, 1891–2. Second
edition.

Schiller als Dramaturg. A. Köster; 1891.

Die Wechselbeziehungen zwischen Schillers Wilhelm Tell und
Shakespeares Julius Cæsar. H. Schneeberger; Münner-
stadt, 1882.

Zu den Quellen des Schillerschen Wilhelm Tell. R. Peppmüller
in Gosches Archiv für Litteraturgeschichte, I, 461 ; 1870.

Homerisches in Schillers Tell, by the same, in above, II, 544 ;
1872.

SCHILLER CORRESPONDENCE.

Briefwechsel mit Körner, edited by Goedeke; Leipzig, 1874.

Briefwechsel mit Goethe. Stuttgart, 1882.

Briefwechsel mit W. von Humboldt. Stuttgart, 1876.

(Translations of the above in the Bohn Library.)

Schillers Briefe. Herausgegeben und mit Anmerkungen ver-
sehen von Fritz Jonas. Kritische Gesamtausgabe ; Stuttgart, 1893.

TRANSLATIONS.

English.

ROBINSON, London, 1825.

R. TALBOT, London, 1829.

T. C. BANFIELD, London, 1831.

W. PETER, Heidelberg, 1839. Many reprints of this.

E. B. LYTTON, London, 1844.

F. LEBAHN, London, 1852.

CHARLES T. BROOKS, Boston, 1847.

THEODORE MARTIN, London, 1848. (Reprinted in the Bohn Library.)

T. BRAUNFELS and A. C. WHITE, London, 1859.

E. S. PEARSON, Dresden, 1885.

J. CARTWRIGHT, London, 1869.

D. C. CAMPBELL, London, 1878.

E. MASSIE, Oxford, 1878.

TARKÁRI, London, 1879.

P. MAXWELL, London 1893.

French.

Traduit par Merle d'Aubigny. Geneva and Paris, 1818.

In Œuvres dramatiques de Schiller (vol. 5), de Barante; Paris, 1821.

In Theatre de Schiller. Marmier; Paris, 1844.

Italian.

Traduzione, del A. Maffei; Milan, 1836.

SOURCES OF MATERIAL IN WILHELM TELL.

Geschichte der Schweizerischen Eidgenossenschaft. J. von Müller; Leipzig, 1786–95.

Chronicon Helveticum. Aegidius Tschudi; Basel and Zürich, 1734.

Briefe über die Schweiz. Meiners ; Stuttgart, 1792.

Naturgeschichte des Schweizerlandes. Scheuchzer ; Zürich, 1746.

Staats- und Erdbeschreibung der ganzen helvetischen Eidgenossenschaft. Fäsi ; Zürich, 1766.

Schilderung der Gebirgsvölker der Schweiz. Ebel ; Tübingen, 1798.

Geschichte der Deutschen. M. I. Schmidt ; Wien, 1785.

Kronika von der löblichen **Eydtgenossenschaft.** P. Etterlin ; edition of 1752, Basel.

Allgemeine Eidgenossenschaftschronik. J. Stumpf, Zürich.

ON THE TELL LEGEND.

Guillaume Tell, fable danoise. U. Freudenberger ; no place of publication given, 1760.

Défense de Guillaume Tell. F. von Balthasar ; 1760.

Essai sur l'origine et le développement des libertés **dans les** Waldstetten. J. J. Hisely ; Lausanne, 1839.

Geschichte der eidgenössischen Bünde. J. E. Kopp ; Leipzig, 1845.

Les origines de la confédération **Suisse :** histoire et légende, A. Rilliet ; Basel, 1868.

Die Sage von der Befreiung der Waldstätte nach ihrer almäligen Ausbildung. W. Vischer ; Leipzig, 1867.

Tell und Gessler in **Sage und Geschichte.** F. L. Rochholz ; Heilbronn, 1877.

Die Anfänge zur schweizerischen Eidgenossenschaft. W. Oechsli ; Zürich, 1891.

Die Tellfrage : ein Versuch ihrer Geschichte **und Lösung.** A. Gisler ; Bern, 1895.

SUBJECTS FOR THEMES AND INVESTIGATION.

Compare and contrast the deed of Tell in killing Gessler with that of John the Parricide in killing emperor Albrecht.

Compare the deeds of Tell and Baumgarten in slaying the bailiffs.

Compare the action of Melchthal toward Landenberg with that of Tell toward Gessler.

Do lines 433–37 show Tell to be selfish and indifferent? What evidence is there anywhere in the play that Tell is acting consciously for the common weal?

What can be said ethically and artistically of Tell's first answer to Gessler, line 2052?

Discuss the possibility of Tell's shooting Gessler at Altorf, Act III, scene 3, or at the Tellplatte when he escapes from the governor's boat, from the point of view of nature and of the drama.

Is Tell's monologue in the Hohle Gasse inconsistent with his character as a man of few words?

Seek the explanation of Tell's line 1576; if not found in the text, comment on the line.

Discuss the arguments for a real Tell

Discuss the arguments against a real Tell.

How old do you judge Walther Tell to be? Collect his actions and speeches and justify your judgment by reference to these.

Examine the speech of Rösselmann, lines 1290–95, and consider in the light of his position and all his other utterances what effect he means it to have.

Group the scenes in which Tell's part is given, noting what relations are there indicated between Tell and the Rütli conspirators.

Group the scenes in which the Rütli conspiracy and its execution are given, noting what influence is exercised upon them
by Tell and his actions.

Group the scenes in which Rudenz and Bertha appear, noting
their relation to the parts of Tell and the Rütli conspirators.

Note the means, the interests and the actions by which these
three groups of persons and events are brought together.

What purpose is served by the introduction of Armgard and
her children in the Hohle Gasse?

Collect the instances in which the scenery furnishes a contrast
with the nature of the action ; in which actions or characters are
contrasted with other actions or characters.

Collect the lines which express general views on the subject
of government, and formulate from these Schiller's standpoint.

Collect the instances of realistic description and behavior.
(Note that realistic does not necessarily mean vivid.)

Collect the passages which seem to be spoken for the information of the audience rather than of the persons to whom they
are addressed.

Discuss the seeming discrepancies in :

Ruodi's presence on the east shore, Act IV, scene 1.

The presence of so many of the representatives of the three
cantons at Altorf, Act III, scene 3.

Walther's presence and Hedwig's appearance at the manor
of Attinghausen, Act IV, scene 2, and her knowledge of
the apple-shooting.

The knowledge of the death of Gessler possessed by all in
Act V, scene 1, and by Parricide, Act V, scene 2.

Discuss the presence of Bertha in prison at Sarnen, reported
by Melchthal, lines 2872–94.

Collect the pithy sayings from the whole play, noting to whom
they are attributed.

Collect the lines having more or less than five feet, considering how far the irregularity serves a purpose.

Collect a hundred lines illustrating other irregularities of meter, as two unaccented syllables together, cases where natural accent conflicts decidedly with regular scansion, etc., considering whether these irregularities seem to be, on the whole, defects.

Collect the rhymed lines, excepting the lyric stanzas, noting where they occur, and their effect.

Collect the unusual compound adjectives in the play.

Collect the archaic and dialect words in the play.

IMPORTANT VARIANTS.

ll. 2075–76 : thus the first edition ; in two manuscripts the line : Jhr wollt ihn außer Lands gefangen führen? precedes these, spoken by Rösselmann, while Gesellen speak 2077–78.

l. 2107 : thus the first edition; two manuscripts have : Der eben jetzt gewaltig sich erhoben.

Act 4, scene 2 : the Aschaffenburg MS has here a brief scene, numbered 2, and the present scene 2 becomes 3. The scene is as follows :

SCENE 2.

Vorzimmer. Hedwig tritt haftig herein. Baumgarten folgt ihr.

Baumgarten, will sie zurückhalten.

O Frau, was sucht ihr hier im Haus des Todes?
Ihr könnt ihn jetzt nicht sehen. Bleibt zurück.

Hedwig

Wer darf mir's wehren? Laßt mich.
Will eindringen.

Baumgarten

Jch ruf' ihn. Wartet hier. Geht.

Hedwig, dringt nach,

Jch kann nicht warten.

SCENE 3.

l. 2441 : thus the first edition ; two MSS have : Der Freiheit
mut'ge Kinder zu befriegen.

ll. 2687–2708 : the Aschaffenburg MS has instead of these
the following :

Rudolf der Harras, ruft oben,

Man fahre aus dem Weg. Mein gnäd'ger Herr
Der Landvogt kommt.

Tell geht ab.

Armgard

Der Landvogt, kommt er?

Stüffi

Sucht ihr was an ihn?

Armgard

Ja, fretlich.

Stüffi

Warum stellt ihr euch denn

In dieser hohlen Gasse ihm in den Weg?

Armgard

Hier weicht er mir nicht aus; er muß mich hören.
Dort kommt er.

Sie geht mit ihren Kindern nach der vordern Szene, Geßler und Rudolph
der Harras zeigen sich auf der Höhe des Weges.

Stüffi

Wo kam der Weidmann hin mit dem ich sprach?

ll. 2722–25 are found only in the Aschaffenburg MS.

l. 3082. Following this the Aschaffenburg MS gives to
Stauffacher the following lines, and the five lines here spoken by
Stauffacher are given to Melchthal.

Oft ist's der Frevel der den Frevel rächt.
Albrecht war selbst der Mörder seines Herrn ;
Damals — man darf es endlich jetzt gestehn —
Da fiel der beßre durch den schlechten Mann,
Und nicht ein fürstlich Grab wollt' er ihm gönnen.
Wir wollen uns nicht mischen in den Streit,
Der droben herrschet in den wilden Höhen,
Doch Segen quillt und warme Fruchtbarkeit
Wenn die Gewitterlüfte sich entladen.

INDEX.

(For names of persons occurring in the Text, see List of Persons, p. lviii. The references below are to the Notes, by lines unless otherwise specified, and to the Introduction by page. Most references to the Notes have corresponding application to the Text).

abtroßen, l. 1300.
adjective, form after personal pronoun, l. 14.
—— termination omitted, ll. 10, 85, 189, 294.
—— weak declension, unusual, l. 2631.
—— in pairs, l. 761.
Adler, symbol of the empire, l. 884.
Aft, use of in Schiller's dramas, p. 173.
Albrecht, emperor, his death in Tschudi, p. lii ff.
alliteration, ll. 1042, 3055.
Alpenrose, l. 2357.
Alpentrift, l. 1001.
also, l. 232.
Altlandammann, ll. 1086, 2114.
Altorf, ll. 770, 1540.
Alzeller, ll. 128, 717.
Alzellen, l. 66.
Ammonshorn, l. 2626.
anstellig, l. 362.
Arth, l. 2282.
article, with generalizing force, l. 57.
—— with proper names, l. 66.

article, ll. 126, 134, 162, etc. SD. after l. 182.
—— equivalent to compound relative, l. 1545.
—— omission of, l. 1487.
as, the second, in comparisons, l. 264.
Attinghäusers, l. 52.
Auftritt, use of in Schiller's dramas, p. 173.
Aufzug, use of in Schiller's dramas, p. 173.
auxiliary verb, omitted, l. 172.
Arenberg, ll. 2164, 2189.
Aren, kleinen, l. 2228.

Baden in Aargau, ll. 409, 2669.
Bann, l. 2996.
Bannberg, SD. before l. 1732.
Bannerherr, l. 336.
Barmherzige Brüder, SD. before l. 2832.
Baurenadel, l. 825.
Baumgarten, account of in Tschudi, p. xliii.
Beginnen, p. 284.
beilegt, l. 176.

Berg, zu Berg fahren, l. 17.
Bern, l. 2433.
Bescheid wissen, l. 414.
—— werden, l. 1347.
besonnen, ll. 227, 1872, 1903.
Bible, influence of, Introd. xxxvi. ll. 315, 1357, 1990.
Bibliographical Notes, p. 237.
Blutbann, l. 1234.
Blutschuld, l. 1237.
Börne, opinion of *Tell*, p. xxxi.
Botenſegel, l. 2555.
Brant, l. 940.
Brantlauf, l. 2652.
Braut von Meſſina, die, plot of, p. xviii.
brav, ll. 165, 1090.
brechend Auge, ll. 865, 2810.
Brief, ll. 1215, 1249.
Bruck } ll. 2946, 2926.
Brugg }
Brünig, l. 1193.
Brunnen, ll. 721, 725, 1178.
Bücher, die alten, l. 1121.
Buggisgrat, l. 2187.
Bünde, ll. 658, 2450.
Bündnis, l. 1156.
Bürgereid, l. 2431.
Burgvogt, l. 77.
Bürglen, ll. 126, 1540.

Chronology, authentic, p. lv.
—— legendary, p. lvi.
—— of *Wilhelm Tell*, p. lvii.

da, after relative pronoun, ll. 1477, 1763.
—— as adverb, and as conjunction, SD. after l. 506.
Dach, l. 2171.
dative, ethical, ll. 450, 2313, 2720.

dative, of possession, with redundant poss. adj., l. 1776.
Demetrius, p. xix.
Denken, cp. with meinen, l. 41.
—— = gedenken, ll. 528, 2484.
doch, colloquial equivalent of, l. 187.
Don Karlos, outline of plot, p. xiii.
Drachen, ll. 1075, 1264.
drei fingern, SD. after l. 1489.
Düntzer, l. 461, SD. before 2098.

Edeln, die, l. 2413.
Ehewirt, l. 238.
Ehni, l. 1539.
Eidgenoſſen, l. 1108.
eigne Leute, l. 1080.
eilig haben, l. 772.
Einſiedeln, ll. 343, 1247, 2651.
Eisestürme, l. 2144.
Engelberg, l. 1002.
enjambement, Introd. xxxvii, ll. 285, 2571, 2614.
Entſcheidung, blutige, l. 2442.
erbeute, l. 1490.
Erden, weak singular, l. 1699.
erfrechen, l. 2595.
erkühnen, l. 2533.
ew'gen Seen, l. 3266.

fahen, l. 2214.
fahr = Gefahr, l. 1511.
falsch, archaic, l. 741.
Fäſi, one of Schiller's sources, notes from, p. liv.
faßnachtsaufzug, l. 390.
Fauſt, references to, SD. after l. 754, ll. 1217, 1490, 3124.
Favenz (Faenza), ll. 911, 1215.

Feder, l. 2304.
Fehlfprung, l. 1499.
Felfenthor, l. 3258.
Feft des Herrn, l. 1400.
Feuerwächter, l. 964.
fiesko, outline of plot, p. xi.
Finftern, for Finfternis, l. 594.
Firn, ll. 38, 596, 1502.
Flanken, l. 386.
fleugt, archaic, l. 1477.
Fluh, l. 2193.
Flurfchütz, SD. after l. 2649.
fodern, archaic for fordern, l. 571.
Föhn, ll. 109, 423.
Frau zu Zürch, l. 1363.
Freiburg, l. 2434.
Freudefpuren, l. 1695.
Freuden, form of, l. 331.
Freytag, Guftav, opinion of *Tell*,
p. xxx.
Fronvogt, SD. before l. 353.
Frondienft, l. 367.
Frühtrunk, l. 754.
für = vor, ll. 1249, 2230, 2673,
3129.
fürder, archaic, l. 384.
future indicative, for imperative,
l. 1895.
future of conjecture, l. 2054.

gähftotzig, l. 2194.
gählings, l. 2230.
gebannt, l. 1775.
geben, impersonal use of, ll. 1217,
1786, 1952.
geben auf, l. 2177.
Gebirge = Forest Cantons, l. 164.
Gebreften, l. 198.
gebrochen, l. 2191.
Gefieder, l. 1804.
gehäffig, l. 487.

Geläut, l. 47.
Gelüften, ll. 85, 548.
genitive, adverbial, ll. 333, 537,
1278, 1780.
—— partitive, l. 2664.
Genoßfame, l. 1455.
gefegnen, l. 97.
Geßler, account of in Tschudi, p.
xlv ff.
Geftrenger, l. 1859.
gewahrten, l. 1184.
gilt, ⎱
gelten ⎰ ll. 563, 1920, 2102, 2414.
Glarus,   ⎫ SD. before l. 959,
Glarner Land ⎬ SD. after ll. 1465,
         ⎭ 2665.
Glärnifch, l. 2666.
gleich, with verb preceding = obgleich, ll. 1118, 1121.
Gletfcher Milch, l. 1004.
—— l. 1780.
Goethe, pp. xiv, xix, xx, xxiv, xxvi,
xxxi, xxxiv, xxxvii.
—— his use of two comparatives,
l. 761.
Gott, use of in asseverations, ll.
507, 714, 1482.
Gotthard, ll. 519, 876.
Grattier, l. 2641.
Granfen, hintern, l. 2226.
Gründe, l. 1549.

Habsburg, House of, ll. 254, 891,
1664.
—— castle, l. 2976.
Hackmeffer, l. 2190.
Haken, mountain, SD. before l. 1,
SD. before l. 959.
Halden, l. 562, Introd. p. xlii.
halsgefährlich, ll. 1432, 1508.
handlich, l. 2257.

Haslithal, ll. 1193-4.
hat, the, account of in Tschudi,
    p. xlv.
Hausgenoß, l. 650.
Hausrecht, l. 82.
Heerweg, l. 347.
Heimsehnen, l. 843.
Herre, archaic, l. 1558.
Herrenbank, l. 806.
Herrenburg, ll. 625, 770.
Herrenknecht, l. 1271.
Herrenleute, l. 294.
Herrenschiff, l. 2170.
Heribann, l. 1228.
hinsteben, l. 1948.
hinterhält, l. 1343.
Hochflug, l. 900.
Hochwachten, l. 2449.
Hochwild, l. 900.
Hochwürdigen, l. 1748.
hohle Gaffe, SD. beginning of Act
    IV, Scene 3.
Höllenrachen, l. 137.
Hollunderstrauch, l. 2563.
Homer, influence of, ll. 209, 241,
    pp. xv, xxxvi.
Horn von Uri, l. 1091.
Hörner, l. 1778.
Hut, ll. 408, 2916, 2922.

Jberg, l. 240.
Jffland, pp. xxiii, xxiv.
Jmmensee, ⎫ SD. beginning of Act
Jmisee, ⎭   IV, Scene 3, l. 2654.
indicative, for imperative, ll. 1364,
    1895.
—— for subjunctive, l. 356.
—— imperfect of, for conditional,
    l. 2060.
indirect discourse, ll. 92, 1345,
    1775, 1834.

inversion, due to expletive es
    understood, l. 171.
—— in exclamatory sentence, ll.
    1760, 2635, 2769, 2932.

ja, colloquial equivalents for, ll. 108,
    1987.
je der = jeder, l. 1170.
Jenni, l. 37.
jetzo, l. 2607.
Joch, ll. 371, 2845, 3254.
Jungfrau von Orleans,
    die, outline of plot, p. xvii.
Jungfrau, die (mountain), l. 628.

Kabale und Liebe, outline of
    plot, p. xi.
Kaiser, ll. 77, 266, 703, 800, 1221,
    1370, 2943.
Kaiser Friedrichs Brief, l. 1215.
Keltic tribes in Switzerland, l.
    1179.
Klosterleute, l. 1078.
Klostermei'r, l. 2651.
kömmlich, l. 2128.
König, der, ll. 130, 787.
Körner, pp. xii, xix, l. 761.
kränkt, l. 2334.
kreucht, archaic, l. 1477.
Kuhreihen, SD. pp. 5, 173.
Knoni, pronunciation of, p. 174.
Küßnacht, SD. beginning of Act
    IV, Scene 3, l. 2655.

Lämmergeier, l. 1000.
Lande, ⎫ l. 431, 655, 742.
Länder, ⎭
Landammann, l. 813. ·
Landbedrücker, l. 1720.
Ländergier, l. 1665.
Länderkette, l. 872.

Landsgemeinde, } ll. 1109, 1397.
Landgemeinde, }
Landsmann, ll. 50, 158.
Landmann, l. 1056.
Landvogt, ll. 72, 131.
Lawinen, l. 1812.
Lehen, l. 229.
Lehen geben, l. 409.
Lieder (Westfriesenlied), ll. 1162, 1189.
Eifel, l. 47.
Lowerz, l. 2285.
Lucerne, Lake, see Vierwald=stättensee.
Lug', l. 46.
lügen, ll. 258, 1384.
lunar rainbow, l. 975.
Luxemburg, l. 3021.

männlich, l. 2874.
Maria Stuart, outline of plot, p. xvii.
meinen, compared with denken and glauben, l. 41.
Meinrad's Zell, l. 519.
Meisterschuß, l. 2649.
Melchthal, l. 560.
—— account of in Tschudi, p. xliii.
Melknapf, SD. p. 174.
Menschen Länder (der), l. 2618.
meter, ll. 26, 66, 294, 995, 1140, 1208, 1249, 2558, 2960, 3109.
Mettenglöcklein, l. 966.
Mitternacht, l. 1167.
Monstranz, l. 1751.
Morgarten, allusion to, ll. 2442, 2967.
Mörlischachen, l. 2651.
Müller, Johannes von, ll. 240, 1162, 2432, pp. xx, xxiv, xxxix, liv.

Mund der Wahrheit, l. 2124.
Muotta, pronunciation of, l. 1178.
Mütterliches, l. 1344.
Mythen, der große, ll. 39, 727.
Mythenstein, SD. p. 173, ll. 39, 725, 727.
Nachts, form of, l. 1760.
naturvergeßnen, l. 1611.
Naue, l. 37.
negative, parallel to French, l. 1535.
noch, translation of, ll. 272, 543.
numerals, cardinal, declension of, l. 1127.

ob = über, ll. 277, 788.
order of sentence, ll. 462, 666, 1249, 1760, 2905.
Östreich, ll. 184, 868.
Österreich, ll. 194, 1304, 1604.

Pair, l. 818.
parliamentary usage, ll. 1150, 1310, 1397, Introd. p. xxxiv.
Parricida, Johannes, criticism of his part, pp. xxv, xxxii.
—— account of in Tschudi, pp. xlvii, lii.
participle, past, with kommen, ll. 65, 220; SD. beginning of Act V, Scene 3.
—— for imperative, l. 353 ff.
—— absolute, ll. 653, 3229.
passive voice, indirect object in, l. 101.
—— with sein, ll. 1123, 1303, 1385, 2834.
Pergamente, l. 244.
Persons, alphabetical list of, p. lviii.
Popanz, l. 1736.

present tense, for imperfect subjunctive in a conclusion, l. 629.
preßte, l. 251.
pronouns, used in address, ll. 161, 1690.
—— omission of correlative, ll. 331, 703, 1146, 1304.

Rappersweil, l. 1361.
Räuber, die, outline of plot, p. ix.
realism in *Tell*, pp. xxxii, xxxiv.
Recht schöpfen, l. 1218.
redlich, ll. 287, 2248.
Reich, ll. 185, 193, 879, 885, 1223, 1365, 3264.
Reichen, l. 1709.
Reihen, l. 54.
Reihe, l. 1599.
relative pronoun, der, die, das, l. 48.
—— followed by personal, l. 58.
—— compound, ll. 383, 1083, 1481, 1545, 1739, 1977.
Reuß, ll. 2969, 3244.
Rheinfeld, ll. 1324, 2966.
rhyme, ll. 1586, 1684, 1706, 1709.
Rigiberg, l. 2738.
Ring, l. 1123.
Römerzügen, l. 1134.
Roßberg, ll. 77, 1385, 1414.
—— capture of in Tschudi, p. li.
Rudenz, criticism of his part, pp. xxv, xxviii, xxxii.
Ruffi, l. 2664.
Ruodi, pronunciation of, p. 174.
Rütli, ll. 727, 729, SD. before 959; SD. after l. 982.
—— scene, the, pp. xxiv, xxvii, xxx.

Sammlung, SD. before l. 1444.

Sarnen, ll. 1060, 1385.
—— capture of in Tschudi, p. li.
Saffen, ll. 1208, 1401.
Säumer, l. 2617.
Schächenthal, l. 1550.
Schatten, l. 764.
schelten, l. 98, government of, l. 825.
Scheuchzer, one of Schiller's authorities, notes from, p. lv, ll. 11, 38, 975, 1501, SD. before l. 1732, ll. 2640, 3266.
Schiller, sketch of his life, p. vii ff.
Schlaglawinen, l. 1781.
Schlegel, A. W., opinion of *Tell*, p. xxix.
Schloß, ll. 1105, 2492.
Schreckhorn, l. 628.
schreiende Gewalt, l. 1840.
Schutz und Schirm, l. 1214.
Schutz und Trutz, l. 1484.
schwant, dialect for ahnt, l. 501.
(Zum) schwarzen Berg, l. 1193.
Schweizer, } l. 1136.
Schwyzer, }
Schwyz, SD. beginning of Act I, Scene I.
Schwert, l. 1133.
sehnde Auge, das, l. 2125.
selbander, l. 2894.
sel'ge Infel, die, l. 1700.
Selisberg, SD. before l. 959, l. 965.
Sempach, allusion to, l. 2443.
Senten, l. 2653.
Shakespeare, influence of, pp. xxii, xxx, xxxvi, ll. 2129, 2573.
Sigrist, l. 1096.
Sillinen, l. 689.
Simons und Judä, l. 146.
singular verb, with compound subject, ll. 503, 1385.
so, ll. 48, 407, 3079.

fonnenſcheuen, l. 1102.
ſpülen, l. 8.
Staël, Madame de, p. xxiii.
Stammholʒ, l. 208.
Stand, ll. 1428, 2489, 2992.
Stange, l. 2918.
Staubbäche, } SD. before l. 1585,
ſtäubet,   } l. 3255.
Stauffacher, account of in Tschudi,
  p. xlv ff.
Steg, l. 25, SD. beginning of Act
  V, Scene 3.
ſtehnden Fußes, l. 333.
Stein des Felſen, l. 670.
Steinen, SD. beginning of Act I,
  Scene 2, l. 2283.
Stein, ʒu Baden, l. 2965.
stichomythy, Introd. p. xxxvi, ll.
  136, 316, 415.
subjunctive, for imperative, ll.
  969, 1114, 1369.
—— indicative for, l. 356.
—— delicate use of, ll. 490, 673,
  2158.
—— of conjecture, l. 3158.
Sündflut, l. 2148.
suppressed negative, with denn
  in subordinate clause, ll. 1043,
  2624.
Surennen, l. 998.
Sweden, legendary home of the
  Swiss, l. 1160.
Sʒene, use of in Schiller's dramas,
  p. 173.

t, unorganic, ll. 26, 31, 101, 1566.
tagen, ll. 751, 1111, 1439, 1518.
Tag, l. 1145.
Tell, Wilhelm, account of in
  Tschudi, p. xlviii ff.
Teufelsbrücke, l. 3255.

Teufelsmünſter, l. 2188.
Thalvogt, l. 38.
Themes, subjects for, p. lviii.
Thurgau, l. 2432.
Ticino, allusion to, l. 3269.
Toko, Danish prototype of Tell, p
  xli.
Treib, l. 721.
treiben, l. 540, es treiben, l. 541.
Trommete, l. 834.
trutʒiglich, l. 235.
Tschudi, pp. xxi, xxii, xxxvi, ll. 97,
  198, 229, 275, 277, 293, 466,
  685, 1325, 2960.
—— extracts from, p. xlii ff.
Twing, l. 360.

Üchtland, l. 2432.
Ungebühr, l. 550.
Ungebührliches, l. 94.
ungefränft, l. 1927.
Unterwalden, ll. 100, 461, 1131.
Uri,   } l. 279.
Urner, }
Urphede, l. 2910.
Urſener Loch, l. 3258.

Variants, list of important, p. 237.
Vatermord, l. 2953.
väterliche Erbe, l. 2954.
verb, agreement of, l. 1603.
Verdrieße, l. 1738.
verwogen, ll. 2416, 2528.
Vierwaldſtättenſee, form of the
  word, p. 173, l. 1178.
vonnöten haben, l. 349.
vor = für, ll. 1287, 1944.

Wächter, l. 43.
Wagefahrten, ll. 1494, 2638, 2874.
Wahlfreiheit, l. 3022.

Walde, for Unterwalden, ll. 493, 545, 717. hinterm Wald, l. 1078.

Wallenstein, outline of plot, p. xvi.

Wälty = Walther, l. 1581.

Wappenschildern, l. 211.

Was, as universal compound relative, ll. 1481, 1739.

Weidgesellen, l. 153.

Weih, l. 1471.

weil, archaic use, l. 341.

Weißland, l. 1193.

Weite, } ll. 1474, 1675.
Weiten, } l. 1685.

Welschland, } ll. 1222, 1230.
welsch, }

werden l. 645.

—— = zu Teil werden, l. 149.

Wetterloch, l. 40.

Wildheuer, l. 2738.

Wilhelm Tell, account of its composition, p. xx ff.

—— notes for, pp. xxii, liv.

—— criticisms of, pp. xxv, xxvi ff.

—— primary merits of, p. xxxiii ff.

—— style and meter in, p. xxxv ff.

—— history and legend in, p. xxxvii ff.

Windeswehen, l. 3253.

Windisch, allusion to, l. 2974.

Windlawine, l. 1501.

Wirtin, ll. 187, 516.

wohl, l. 524; = wohlan, l. 117.

wohlbestellt, l. 1860.

wollen, peculiar shades of, ll. 2845, 3073, 3074.

Wütrich, } ll. 99, 181, 1965.
Wütende, } l. 2532.

zerstört = verstört, SD. after l. 3103.

Zeugungen, l. 3003.

zinsen, l. 1362.

Zucht, l. 204.

Zug, Lake, SD. beginning of Act IV, Scene 3, l. 2282.

zugezählt, l. 52.

Zürich, l. 2435.

Zürch, der großen Frau zu, l. 1363.

zuzugehn, l. 2257.

Zwing, } ll. 360, 370.
Zwinger }

Zwing Uri, account of in Tschudi, pp. xlv, lii.

www.ingramcontent.com/pod-product-compliance
Lightning Source LLC
Chambersburg PA
CBHW020950030726
47496CB00005B/1447